THE OLD CORSAIR

To Gail and Barry.

Best wishes

[signature]

MICHAEL DESTEFANO

The Old Corsair
Copyright © 2023 by Michael DeStefano

ISBN (Softcover): 978-1-66789-715-8
ISBN (eBook): 979-8-35090-940-1

This novel is a work of fiction. Facts, locales, and historical figures were blended with products of the author's imagination to weave an entirely fictional account. Any similarity to actual persons, living or dead, locales or historical events is entirely coincidental.

All rights reserved. No part of this book may be reproduced or transmitted in any form or by any means, electronic or mechanical, including photocopying, recording, or by any information storage and retrieval system, without permission in writing from the copyright owner. This book was printed in the United States of America.

To order additional copies of this book, visit:
Website: www.LopsidedButterflyBooks.net
Twitter: @LopsidedBflyBks
Instagram: @LopsidedBflyBks

Edited by: Susan A. Hughes
www.myindependenteditor.com

Cover design: Joshua Bruce
www.jbookcoverdesign.com

ACKNOWLEDGEMENTS

No fictional account that seeks to bring a sense of reality to the reader can hope to do so without the expertise of various consultants in their specialized fields. For that, I'm indebted to Matthew Jaquith at the Springfield City Library in Massachusetts, the Head of Library & Archives, Margaret Humberston and Archivist, Cliff McCarthy who put me on to the online colonial newspapers, and Robert Moore at the Springfield Museum. I'm also appreciative of the efforts of the historian briefers at the Mystic Seaport in Mystic, Connecticut, the helpful folks at the American Antiquarian Society in Worcester, Massachusetts, and the Newport Naval Station Museum in Rhode Island. I must also offer my immense appreciation to Mr. Johnny Duhan for his permission to use the lyrics to his song, The Voyage. There's no way I could bring Captain Vernon "Cyclops" Tunney to life for you, the reader, without the visual magic of Joshua Bruce. His unique cover art inspired my writing whenever Tunney made his appearance. And last, but not least, my editor, Susan Hughes for helping me paint with words, the story I wished to convey.

Michael DeStefano
March 4, 2023

AUTHOR'S NOTE

Colonial newspapers in the mid to late 18th century employed a font style known as the Caslon ligature. It is a form of printing characterized by the long (s), the connected (ct), and the offset double (ff), just to name a few of the design curiosities that make this font choice a unique reading challenge. I originally intended to use the actual ligatures from the period when the story required it (the reader shall know when, as this font is described by the characters at the appropriate time). However, for reasons you'll understand later, I decided to employ the Caslon font without the difficult ligature style in order to make the story an easier reading experience.

The period newspapers, sourced through America's Historical Newspapers, GeneologyBank, NewsBank, and Readex and referred to in this work (from 1756 to 1817), especially where quotes from certain papers are specifically used, are identified by date of publication as the source papers within the story wherever possible (except the actual source paper for the *Rebecca* article was the July 3, 1788 edition of the *Independent Chronicle*). America's Historical Newspapers and America's Historical Imprints, including the Early American Imprints, Series I: Evans, 1639-1800, by NewsBank and Readex, were the sources of certain factual information regarding the *Crescent* and of the Ben Stoddart, December 24, 1798 letter with its Chart A. It is with profound gratitude that I am indebted to Mr. Quinton Carr, the Director of Publisher Support and the wonderful folks at NewsBank/Readex for their kind permission to use these literary gems from our nation's past.

To the strongest women I know.
My sister, Terrie and my mother,
Donna (née, Murphy).

PROLOGUE

Federal Hall
New York City
October, 1785

"Gentlemen!" the president shouted as he stood up from behind the desk vigorously rapping his gavel. "Gentlemen, please!"

Still ignoring the president's plea for order, the delegate from Massachusetts continued to shout down his South Carolina colleague. "What sort of preposterous nonsense is this? The topic of discussion was how best to address the deficiencies of the Articles, Mr. Pinckney, not for you to go on another self-indulgent tirade!"

"When you are recognized by the president, Mr. Partridge, then shall I take up your outrageous assumption and not before. You do not have a salient interest in our merchant vessels' ability to conduct their affairs in international waters free from harassment, to say nothing of your intolerable rudeness!" shouted the delegate from South Carolina as a growing restlessness took hold of the assembly. Parliamentary decorum dissolved rapidly as disparate conversations began to sprout up all over the room.

Continuing to slam the gavel so hard he nearly cleaved its sound block in two, the President of the Confederation Congress, Richard Henry Lee, was finally able to restore order to the unruly assembly. When the only sound heard was the repetitious pounding of his gavel, he stopped.

In the silence that followed, he glared at the verbal contestants. "Gentlemen, if cooler heads don't prevail I shall adjourn this session. Do I make myself clear?" He surveyed the surprised assembly unaccustomed to such an outburst from so mild-tempered a man. Staring at the delegate from Massachusetts, he yielded the floor. "Very well. The chair once again recognizes the delegate from South Carolina."

Taking his opportunity to put the Massachusetts delegate in his place, Pinckney said, "You sir, were never wronged by our British adversaries, so your opinion carries no weight!" His glaring eyes lingered upon the source of his anger before turning his attention and his speech to the general floor of the assembly. "Having suffered impressments at the hands of our former English brethren, our fellow countrymen are now under siege with no protections whatsoever from this body!" Hinting once again at his adversary, Pinckney tried unsuccessfully to check his emotions. "In deference to the concerns of Mr. Partridge, we must consider strengthening the common defense article of our confederation. In its current form, the requisite deficiencies of that article become clear when put into practice. Without a standing Navy, we have no sufficient safeguard against aggressive foreign nations in the shipping lanes of the Mediterranean. The European answer to the open piracy of Tunis, Tripoli, and Algiers is absolutely unacceptable. Their ultimatums, Mr. President, are outlandish on their face and insulting to the sovereignty of our young nation."

Partridge jumped to his feet and said abruptly, "Mr. Pinckney, Massachusetts is all too aware of the cost borne by our countrymen, sir! The entire crew of our very own *Betsy* didn't even make it past the Rock of Gibraltar! She was only two months out of Boston when she was taken off the African coast. And now comes word that our schooner *Maria*, with the inestimable James Cathcart aboard, was captured off the Cape of St. Vincent! This adversary was not British, Mr. Pinckney!"

Pinckney's tepid reply was swift. "I understand well the cost you bear, sir, and you have my sympathies."

"Do you, sir? Do you really? As we speak, they are doubtless being sold into slavery somewhere in Morocco!"

Now joining the fracas was Dr. Edward Hand. An ardent patriot and general of the Revolution, he served during the siege of Yorktown and crossed the Delaware on that fateful Christmas Eve with George Washington. At war's end, he once again answered his nation's call to service as a representative from Pennsylvania.

As Pinckney and Partridge were exchanging verbal jabs, a messenger delivered a letter to Hand that carried disturbing news of a fresh attack. The venerable politician was usually a calming influence on the junior members of the assembly, but this time, his measured reserve fell prey to his passions. He made a concerted effort to raise his voice over the rancor of their argument. "Gentlemen, I've just received word that our Brigantine, the *Dauphin* out of Philadelphia, was taken and her crew paraded through the streets of Tripoli! What do you suggest we do to address this latest outrage, Mr. Pinckney? Mr. Partridge?"

With that exchange, Lee rapped his gavel one final time. "That's it, gentlemen! I am summarily placing this assembly in recess until tomorrow morning. Perhaps a brief pause will allow our constituent members the requisite time to contemplate a more thoughtful reserve when addressing each other in open assembly."

With the notable exception of Partridge's cursory, rage-infused stare at Pinckney, the members dispersed. They filed out of the room in small groups as they held hushed, individual sidebars. Seeking to know more about this latest revelation, Lee approached Hand for a brief sidebar of his own.

"Doctor Hand, a word with you, please."

"Mr. Lee?"

"You caught me by surprise regarding the *Dauphin*, sir. Would you be so kind as to tell me what happened?"

"Of course," said a more reasonable Hand. "Please forgive my outburst, Mr. Lee. It was uncalled for."

"That's quite all right. However, you do understand why I had to adjourn the session?"

"Oh, I heartily agree. It's the president who has the ultimate responsibility for maintaining the dignity of the assembly. As to your question, sir, I must tell you I only just received a letter from a witness to the event who wishes to address the open assembly."

"Can this witness make himself available for testimony?"

"According to his letter, he is expected to arrive in New York tomorrow morning. We could allow him some time to offer up his account?"

Lee considered the benefits of such testimony. "I believe that would not only be a good idea but should throw a bucket of water on the tempers of both Partridge and Pinckney."

Hand only nodded at Lee's reasonable accommodation.

The clamor of voices diminished when the door opened and the witness entered. The shocking appearance of the young man caused those who laid eyes upon him first to gasp audibly.

He wore the nautical uniform of his merchant vessel when it was attacked. His sailor's bonnet was in his hands as he moved toward the president. The tongue of one shoe was torn out, its buckle missing. His patched white dungarees were ripped in several places with spots of blood spatter that ran from his thigh, along the left side of his light red waistcoat, and up the side of his white shirt sleeve. The blood-stained cravat partially covered the dressed wound on the left side of his neck. An angry gash crested the bridge of his nose as the bruises over his eyes were beginning to heal.

However, the mustard-yellow color of his healing eye sockets was not as distinguishing a feature as his left eye, the dark-hazel iris of which was so large the eggshell white sclera was almost nonexistent. The young man's physical deformity and injuries notwithstanding, he approached the open floor near the president's table with a determined bearing.

He searched the faces of his audience before locking eyes on Lee. "Gentlemen of the Congress, Mr. President." With a hint of trepidation, he continued. "I can only tell you what I know. It was nearly three months ago now, on the thirtieth of July. We were half a day out of Lisbon before our vessel *Dauphin* was set upon by an Algerian squadron. Captain O'Brien did his best to veer us away, but its lead corsair still managed to draw up alongside us and fire. The first mate was lucky. He was killed with their first shot. Their second volley devastated the gunwale, took out our jackstaff, and snapped the foremast in two. Though the quarter deck suffered light damage, the two crew members standing on it at the time were not so lucky. Their injuries were so severe they later died. Shortly after their third volley, they boarded us with an overwhelming compliment of men.

"I managed to get off a shot from my pistol trying to thwart their attack when someone hit me from behind forcing me to the deck just as one of the blackguards leveled his cutlass at my head. The impact I sustained reduced his killing stroke to a glancing blow." The young man reached up and touched the blood-encrusted bandage over his neck as he surveyed the registry of shock on their faces. "When the fight was over, they had sacked the wardroom, placed our surviving crew in chains and dragged us aboard their vessel. During the journey to their homeland, they took turns beating us with leather cudgels. They even accused my friend, Thomas Martinson, of trying to steal food and immediately cut off his right hand."

No one said a word as they tried to digest what the young sailor, Vernon Tunney, had just told them.

Lee scanned the assembly. "Are there any questions for Mr. Tunney?"

It was Hand's Pennsylvania colleague who stood first.

"If I may, how were you able to determine who was attacking you?" asked a skeptical James Wilson.

"We identified the jack as Algerian when the lead vessel came alongside us to bring her weapons to bear," answered Tunney.

"Could you identify that particular vessel if you saw it again?"

"Yes sir. The ship's profile was unique. It was larger than a brig but smaller than a galley. As she bounded away so her sister ship could wrest us from the *Dauphin*, I caught sight of her name. It was the *Dey of Reckoning*."

"And what did they do with you and your crew?"

"They forced us into the hold below and kept us there until their ship made port."

Recognizing the frustration in the young man with Wilson's rapid-fire questions, Hand tried to coax a complete answer from him. "Tell Mr. Wilson and the assembly what you told me."

With a puzzled look reserved for Hand, Tunney readdressed Wilson. "Once the ship docked they lined us up along the pier so they could march us through the streets. The population was incited to hurl insults and rocks at us by their ruler."

In a more direct tone, Wilson asked, "If you were chained to each other, then how was it possible for you to effect your escape?"

The young sailor responded with a cutting edge to his voice. "Our bonds were individual, Mr. Wilson. I was only cuffed at my wrists and ankles." He threw up his arms to reveal the thick bruises around his wrists.

Embarrassed into silence, Wilson retreated into his seat.

Making an effort to secure the answer Wilson was looking for, Lee asked gently, "How did you manage your escape, Mr. Tunney?"

The young man returned his attention to the confederation president.

"I was last in line of my fellow shipmates as they led us through the crowded streets. Just as we rounded a corner, a large rock hit me in the face." Tunney then traced his finger across the bridge of his nose before he continued. "The force of the blow knocked me down."

"Can you recall what happened next?" asked Partridge.

"No, sir. I lost consciousness. I don't know how, but I found myself aboard a Dutch merchant vessel bound for Philadelphia. Once we docked, I dispatched a letter to Dr. Hand informing him of our misadventure and the fate of my shipmates."

"Then, you have no way of knowing what happened to them or the missing crew members from other vessels?" asked Lee.

"No sir," said Tunney reluctantly.

"So you can offer no evidence of impressments of American crews serving aboard foreign ships?" stated Partridge as he tried to get a rise out of Pinckney.

Turning to address the Massachusetts delegate again, Tunney said, "Regrettably, no sir, I cannot."

Silence hung in the air after Tunney's final reply.

"Are there any other questions for Mr. Tunney?" asked Lee. Seeing no other interest in the matter, Lee turned to the young man. "Thank you, Mr. Tunney. You have our sincere admiration for your service and testimony."

"Thank you, Mr. President."

As Tunney turned to leave, he saw his Pennsylvania representative and noticed the older man nod. He returned it knowingly, realizing he was expected to wait for a response outside the hall.

Loud, muffled voices emanated from behind the hall door as incoherent grumblings continued to grow in veracity. This behavior was disappointing to Tunney. He always believed that gentlemen of the political gentry should be models of civil propriety, deportment, and courtesy. He was, therefore, dismayed to discover the animal passions emanating from the other side of that door divulged their true nature.

It took well over an hour before the voices grew quiet. Moments later, the doors flew open. The delegates exited the hall in groups of two or three. When Tunney saw Hand, he was still in conference with Lee. Their low conversation was barely perceptible, but he knew they were discussing his situation. After nodding to one another, the two men moved out of the hall toward Tunney.

Lee extended a welcoming hand. "Your tale stirred a firestorm of debate, Mr. Tunney."

"That was not my intention, sir. I merely wished to bring attention to the plight of my shipmates."

The two politicians simply looked at each other.

"How much open water experience do you have?" Lee asked the young man.

"I come from a seafaring family, sir. Raised on the banks of the Patuxent River, I was ten years old when my widowed father, Alistair, taught me how to pilot his schooner, *Hypatia*. At fourteen, I began serving aboard merchant vessels, first as a deckhand aboard the USS *Alliance* under Captain John Barry. I was aboard as she took part in our little skirmish with Cornwallis at Yorktown. I had signed on with the *Dauphin* a week before she sailed."

"So you plan on signing up with another vessel, do you?"

"At the earliest opportunity, sir," said Tunney with gusto.

The cresting corners of Lee's mouth gave away his approval. "We'll be getting back to you, Mr. Tunney. Where are you staying so that we may reach you?"

"I haven't had time to locate suitable lodgings," he said flatly. "But I can find something if you need me to stay in New York."

"Excellent. Dr. Hand shall secure a room for you at the Independence Inn across the street so we might notify you when we have news."

Tunney acknowledged with a dip of his head.

Vernon Tunney heard virtually nothing from his representative in nearly a month. He spent his days walking the docks near the Battery trying to sign on with a new vessel. Failing that, he ventured back toward the public house just off Broadway from his rooms at the Independence Inn.

The Charter Oak Tavern boasted an impressive crowd that night. A piper sat next to the bar regaling the oblivious diners with an old sea shanty. Competing alongside the distinctive scent coming from the bar's row of bayberry candles was the aroma of steak and potatoes that came from the open kitchen. On each dining table were large, spermaceti candles. They were used in place of the beeswax variety since they offered customers better lighting by which to enjoy their meals, froth-topped tankards of ale, and their charming dinner companions.

Into this den of unsavory characters and ambrosial pipe tobacco walked Tunney. Most of his injuries had healed, but people were still put off by his odd looking left eye. Anyone who addressed him would eventually focus their attention on his unusual facial anomaly. Right eye dominant, he perceived them as looking at his left eye and not him, driving the merchant marine to extreme self-consciousness. And anger.

The young boatswain's mate, late of the vessel *Dauphin*, located a corner table and ordered a pint of brew. He reached for his father's old churchwarden with one hand as he padded at his coat with the other searching for a small pouch that contained the Virginia aromatic he favored. With no tinderbox handy, he set the pipe between his teeth, filled the bowl with flake then grabbed a candle from the table to light it. Tunney puffed away on his pipe while observing the crowd in the dimly lit room.

There were some faces he recognized from the inn, but most of them were strangers. A group of four men were discussing their latest bounty of fish. A pair of men nearest Tunney spoke with outlandish crudeness, mainly about what they would like to do with the comely wench from the bar down the street. But the most vulgar lot was a group led by a boisterous fellow with a thunderous belly laugh. Thankfully, they were located on the furthest side of the tavern.

A waiter arrived with his pint drawing Tunney's attention toward the entrance. Raising the tankard to his lips, he noticed his Pennsylvania representative walk in with an unknown, well-dressed gentleman beside him.

The manner in which this new stranger was dressed demonstrated greater attention to style than those who normally frequented this establishment. His demeanor was completely incongruous with the tavern's present clientele. The newcomer remained quiet as they approached.

"We were hoping to find you here, Mr. Tunney," said Hand.

The younger man's eyes were trained on the stranger as he responded to Hand's statement. "I thought you had forgotten me." Tunney got up and invited them to join him.

"No, Mr. Tunney. Your situation was front and center," Hand responded. "I dare say it took up so much time, the outcome of our congressional elections last month hinged on it."

The waiter stopped and asked, "What can I get you gentlemen?"

"Another round of ales, please," Hand said. When the waiter left to get the drinks, Hand looked from his companion to Tunney and announced, "Consequently, Mr. Lee is no longer the confederation president."

"What happened?" asked Tunney.

"The election resulted in a second round of deliberations, which added more receptive members to your cause, including a new president." With that last statement, Hand gestured toward the well-dressed stranger sitting next to him. There was an uncomfortable pause before Hand reached into his jacket. "After careful consideration, the congress decided to retain your commission."

"I don't understand."

In a practiced and charming voice, the well-dressed stranger said, "Mr. Tunney, we are dispatching the vessel, *Justice*, to investigate these blatant acts of piracy."

Grinning briefly at the newcomer, Hand placed the letter he retrieved from his jacket on the table in front of Tunney and said, "I have influence with her captain, Arthur Ledbetter. If you are amenable, this letter of introduction shall see you to your next assignment."

"I appreciate that, sir."

The waiter dropped off the drinks as the newcomer reached into his pocket to retrieve a sealed letter. Once another passing waiter was out of earshot, the newcomer spoke again.

"This favor on your behalf comes with a price, Mr. Tunney." Then he slid the second, larger letter over to Tunney.

"What's this?"

"This, Mr. Tunney, is our response to your address."

The letter was stamped with the seal of the Confederation Congress. This particular one was addressed to Tunney himself.

"Captain Ledbetter shall receive a companion letter," said the stranger. "Only you two shall be aware of your mission's true object. The captain has orders not to open his letter until you are underway, but you may open yours now."

At their urging, Tunney broke the seal and quickly read what was expected of him. The note was nothing short of a Letter of Marque and Reprisal with a simple directive: Capture the *Dey of Reckoning* and her crew. Bring them to the bay of Portsmouth, New Hampshire.

The letter was signed by the Confederation Congress's new president, John Hancock.

ONE

A stateroom aboard the USS *New York* (LPD-21)
April 3, 2013
01:28 hours

The young woman's head swished across the pillow like the sole audience to a private tennis match. Light perspiration dotted her brow. For the first time since Terrie Murphy entered the Navy, the nightmare returned.

She tried to force it from her thoughts, but her unconscious mind was insistent. She was gazing into a mirror as her sightless reflection stared back at her. The parochial khaki uniform faded, replaced by an elegant formal gown. Sapphire eyes morphed into a set of green ones. The coalescing image was not hers, but that of her older sister, Margaret.

Her star-quality looks held for the briefest of seconds before her countenance altered from grin to grimace. Her healthy pallor deteriorated into a decomposing corpse. A crimson droplet ran from the corner of her dissolving eye. The image raised its right hand to offer a sad wave, but with each side-to-side motion, a fingertip would burst into dust. Joint by joint, each finger followed suit, until the hand itself surrendered its position, separating from the wrist in a most unnatural way. Only flaps of ravaged skin covered and uncovered the remnants of bone with each wave.

That devastating day in April 2004 replayed itself—the day Terrie received the box containing the gruesome evidence of what they did to Margaret. Out of nowhere, three loud bangs jolted her upright in her bunk. Her gaze fell upon the dimly lit mirror, searching for the counterfeit reflection that had disappeared.

Three more loud knocks brought her back to the present. Someone was outside her stateroom. "Yes, who is it?"

"Yeoman Stevens with a message for you, Lieutenant," said a voice through the closed door.

Terrie attempted to compose herself but her cheeks remained flushed, her eyes unable to hide the gruesome sight she witnessed.

The young sailor gasped at the sight of her. "Are you all right, Lieutenant?"

"Fine," she replied, rubbing her eyes. "What is it?"

"I'm sorry, ma'am. This message came in for you from PERS-4."

"Thank you, Yeoman."

He handed Terrie the slip of paper and returned to his duties without another word.

Terrie received several messages during her temporary duty aboard the USS *New York*, but she looked forward to this one: the location of her first permanent assignment. She was to report immediately to Commander Brooks Crabtree, chief of naval intelligence at Portsmouth.

Terrie had to read the notice twice to confirm what it actually said. Her assignment was Portsmouth, but not in Virginia, where her ship would soon be moored.

It was the Portsmouth Navy Yard in Maine.

TWO

Philip gazed at the morning commuter traffic outside his Portsmouth safe house. Checking the time, he made sure to close the blinds before he switched on his tablet.

A few swipes across the screen and the retinal scanner came to life, waiting to authorize his access. The coffee butler over the minifridge announced its readiness to provide his wake-up juice. Philip took a moment to enjoy his coffee before a blue instant message box appeared on the screen with a one-word directive, "Report."

He engaged the written discussion with his contact. "Search parameters negative."

"Was afraid of that. And the renovation project over the target location on Badger?"

"Starts this week."

"Excellent! Confidence is high this location will yield results. Keep me informed. I need to know if something comes of it."

"I'll see to it."

"Call if necessary."

"Are you sure that's wise?"

"IMs becoming a problem. Standard communications now sent through secure email from SV address only. For immediate contact, use secure voice."

"Understood."

"One more thing. Your contact's new team member is on her way. Go over the dossier in your secure email. She's your responsibility."

"Will get to it when we're done here. Anything further?"

"Yes. Encourage your contact to assign her the Badger Island detail. You know how to handle it, don't you?"

"I have an idea."

THREE

Terrie pulled into the visitor parking space next to a chain-link fence with a sign attached to it. The sign read, WARNING: Restricted Area. It is unlawful to enter this area without permission of the Installation Commander. In red letters below this warning, it said, Use of Deadly Force Authorized.

A tall woman wearing pristine service khakis with bronze clusters stood at parade rest near the turnstile inside the fence. She never took her eyes off Terrie as she exited her vehicle and approached the entrance.

"Lieutenant JG Murphy?"

"Yes."

"Do you have your credentials with you?"

Terrie reached into her black clutch bag for her common access card to show the woman. She scrutinized Terrie's card for a second before looking at her. Terrie matched the description perfectly, a petite woman with an athletic build, sapphire blue eyes, and a delicate shade of red hair that hinted at the fiery personality of its owner.

"Very good." After the woman punched some numbers into a keypad, an audible click initiated the turnstile's opening. "If you'll follow me."

They walked the few yards to a door with a cipher lock below the knob. The officer punched the combination and a magnetic seal released the door's locking mechanism.

Once inside, the woman's demeanor relaxed. Slightly. "My name is Lieutenant Commander Molly Bannerman. I'll be your sponsor for the next few days until you get your sea legs. I've been ordered to escort you to the commander's office."

"Thank you."

Making their way to the office, Bannerman asked, "Are you from the Portsmouth area?"

"No."

"Then where do you call home?"

"Claymont, Delaware."

"Have you ever been to New England before?"

"No."

Sensing some resistance on Terrie's part, Bannerman ceased her inquiry. "Here we are. Commander Crabtree will be with you shortly."

"Thank you."

Bannerman turned on her heels and departed down the hall.

The commander's administrative assistant was a dyed-in-the-wool senior chief petty officer with as many hash marks on his sleeve as he had wrinkles on his face. But his craggy expression ran counter to his pleasant disposition. "You must be the new lieutenant junior grade we ordered," he said in grand style. "Senior Chief Raymond Sheffield at your service. But most people just call me Ray. If you need anything around here, I'm the guy you get it from."

Terrie regarded the man, who reminded her of her grandfather. She nodded to him politely but said nothing.

"Right. Do you have a copy of your orders?"

Terrie pulled a piece of paper from the small folio she carried with her and handed it to the senior chief.

"Thank you." He retrieved an in-processing sheet and stapled it to her orders. "Lieutenant Commander Bannerman will escort you around the Yard to complete your in-processing. You'll probably have it done in less than a day, but I'll need the signed form from you by Friday."

"Understood."

Sheffield dismissed her lack of social graces as being unfamiliar with her new surroundings. "The commander is usually here by now. I can't understand what's keeping him."

"I'm not going anywhere."

"So, you can put more than two words together, can't you?"

"Maybe."

The senior chief couldn't read Terrie, and that was just fine with her.

Sheffield had just settled into his paperwork when the quiet of the office was disrupted by a tall strapping, middle-aged man who blustered in.

"Ray, if Captain Derrick calls, notify me immediately," ordered the man wearing service khakis with full commander's insignia. Acknowledging the presence of the new arrival, he aimed an authoritative voice in Terrie's direction. "And you must be Miss Murphy."

She rose to her feet and assumed the position of attention. "Lieutenant Junior Grade Terrie Murphy reporting for duty, sir."

"I apologize for keeping you, but our installation commander, Captain Janine Derrick needed to see me."

His physical presence was intoxicating, with a baritone voice that underscored the point. Normally as infallible as gravity, her intuition was short-circuited by his sensual magnetism.

"Welcome aboard, Miss Murphy. I'm Commander Brooks Crabtree, your new CO."

She simply stared at him.

"Have you been seen to properly? The office tour and all?"

"Not really, sir," she said timidly. "I just arrived myself."

"Well, come on in and I'll give you my spiel."

There. He said it. My spiel as opposed to the spiel. It should have been her first clue to unlocking his personality, but she missed it.

He moved to the table next to his desk to brew up some fresh coffee. "Would you like a cup?"

"No, thank you, sir."

"Suit yourself. Better than the craft stuff at the exchange."

Terrie paid no attention to his self-aggrandizing as his well-formed profile continued to circumvent her perceptive abilities. Her concentration was about to receive a boost when Crabtree finally got down to cases regarding his spiel.

"Have a seat." He blended honey in his coffee before sitting down himself. "First and foremost, are you fixed for a place to stay?"

Terrie occupied her seat as she replied, "I meet with my new landlord this afternoon to sign the lease for my apartment."

"Oh? Where?"

"Portsmouth, sir."

"Do you have your household goods pick up scheduled?"

"Not necessary, sir. It's just me and my personals."

"Well, we still want you to take some time to settle in after your move."

"It's nothing a free weekend can't fix, sir."

"As you wish. We're a small but tight-knit group, Miss Murphy. There are seven of us, including myself. Lieutenant Commander Bannerman and Senior Chief Sheffield are the administration side of things, while you and three others make up the nerve center of our intelligence apparatus. All of you were specifically chosen for your strengths and abilities, and as such, I expect you to function as a team. Our mission is to provide useful intelligence that national command authority may act upon."

An attentive Terrie Murphy took it all in.

"Since we're so self-contained, cohesion and stability are paramount if we're going to be successful, Miss Murphy. Both you and Mr. Jack O'Hara are replacing two former members of the team." Crabtree cast his eyes down a moment before scrolling them back up at Terrie. "You may have noticed a coolness in the lieutenant commander's attitude toward you this morning. Will this be a problem?"

"How did you know that, sir?" Terrie asked, her objectivity returning.

"I know my people, Miss Murphy."

"I obviously assumed the billet of someone she was quite fond of. Naturally, she would resent my intrusion."

"Your assessment is on point, Miss Murphy. Try not to take it personally."

"I don't, sir."

"Good." Crabtree took another sip of his coffee and stood up. "Do you have any questions before I show you the operations center and intro you to the team?"

"No, sir."

"Then let's get going."

They made their way to the end of the corridor. Crabtree reached for the cipher lock, punched in the code, and opened the heavy steel door, initiating a brief buzzing sound. Once inside, he signed the log that kept track of visitors.

The first thing that hit her was the aura produced by the diminished lighting. It made for a calming environment as Terrie noted the layout. Situated above the semi-circle of individual workstations was the senior controller. Multiple flat screens throughout the room monitored the various news outlets. Workstations were compact in size, but with room enough at each to prevent anyone from feeling claustrophobic.

Alerted to Crabtree's presence, Bannerman announced, "Commander on deck."

"As you were. I just want to introduce our new analyst, Lieutenant JG Terrie Murphy. She'll be our resident Middle East Theater expert." Turning to Terrie, he queried, "You are fluent in Arabic, correct?"

"And Pashto, sir."

"You already know Lieutenant Commander Bannerman."

Terrie acknowledged her with an inclined head.

"We met this morning," said Bannerman without making eye contact.

"Aside from being my second, Commander Bannerman is my senior controller, overseeing each area of responsibility and collating all intelligence into a daily SITREP for the upper echelon. She is also a counterintelligence expert and Russian linguist."

Regarding Terrie for the briefest of seconds, Bannerman nodded and allowed herself a slight grin.

Terrie returned it.

"Lieutenant Taro Hattori here monitors the Asian Theater and is fluent in Japanese, Mandarin Chinese, and Korean. His area of expertise is surface defense analysis and counterterrorism."

"Welcome aboard, Miss Murphy."

She acknowledged him silently.

"And here is our air and space defense analyst and electronic warfare guru, Lieutenant Demetrius Theodore."

"Just Theo, Miss Murphy."

Once again, she acknowledged her new team member without a word.

"Theo's area of responsibility is the European Theater, and he can speak German and Swahili."

Terrie noted two remaining workstations and surmised the barren one was hers. Referring to the cluttered one, she said, "Lieutenant O'Hara?"

"That's his station, yes," Crabtree replied. "Jack's currently on leave. He is our strike warfare, combat mission planning, and amphibious defense expert. Aside from being responsible for covering the Central and South American Theater, he can converse in numerous dialects of Spanish."

Terrie nodded.

Not one for shy people, Theo tried to goad the new arrival. "Never mind Pashto, can she speak English?"

Her intense blue eyes directed their gaze toward Theo as she uttered a soft, but stinging, rebuke. "With those who comprehend it, yes."

Smiling as Theo's words were rammed down his throat, Taro said, "Better steer clear of that ship, Theo, or she'll torpedo ya!"

Brushing off the slight, Theo replied, "Not likely."

The intercom at the senior controller's station buzzed. Sheffield routed a call from Captain Derrick to the CO.

While Crabtree took the call, Terrie responded with cutting ease. "The arrogant blindly underestimate their opponent, Mr. Theodore."

Theo's smile evaporated.

Crabtree ended his call with Captain Derrick but heard enough of that last exchange to realize he needed to nip this potential conflict in the bud. "Miss Murphy, walk with me."

Everyone knew what that meant. This was going to be a one-way conversation.

Before exiting the operations center, Crabtree looked to Bannerman. "Commander, I'll be ready for your SITREP in ten minutes."

"Aye aye, sir."

"I apologize for Lieutenant Theodore's remarks, Miss Murphy," said Crabtree as they entered his office.

"Respectfully, sir, I got this."

"You're sure?"

Terrie's rigid stare convinced him she wasn't going to be intimidated.

"As you wish." Crabtree rounded his desk to retrieve a piece of paper with a note scribbled on it. "I normally hand out assignments like this to the next officer in the rotation, but Mr. O'Hara isn't here."

"What assignment, sir?"

"The marina on Badger Island breaks ground on a renovation project in the morning. I need you to make contact with the project foreman, a Mr. R. J. Clendaniel, and let him know you're there to monitor the excavation. If you find anything you deem out of the ordinary, you are to secure it if possible. Safeguard it if necessary. Once they've begun the reconstruction phase, your assignment will be concluded."

"Could you define out of the ordinary, sir?"

"Let's just say anything that doesn't normally belong in the ground."

"Excuse me, sir, but why is the Navy getting involved in the affairs of some private company?"

Crabtree squared his shoulders on Terrie. "How much do you know about Badger Island's early history?"

"Only a little, sir."

"Try me." Crabtree folded his arms and waited for a response.

"Very well." Drawing on her eidetic memory, she made a word-for-word recitation from one of the history books in her personal library. "Named after John Langdon, the man who established its first shipyard, the island's name was changed to honor William Badger, James Hackett's protégé. Under Badger's direction, the island produced over one hundred ships between 1797 and 1830. If memory serves, he's buried there."

"I'm impressed. You've done your homework. What else do you know about it?"

Not sure what Crabtree was angling for, Terrie shook her head.

"The project location happens to be the site of the nation's first intelligence office. Our orders are to assume supervisory control over the excavation and to make sure there are no…relics left behind. Should you find anything unusual, you are to consider it classified, report it, and if possible, retain it as government property."

Effecting her best impression of Bannerman, Terrie responded, "Aye aye, sir."

FOUR

"What the hell's going on, R. J.?" asked Kevin Pederson. In his twenty-five years working construction, the corpulent blue-collar veteran never had to hold up progress at any job site for any reason. Now this.

"Some bureaucrat from the home office legal department called this morning. We're on hold until a subject matter expert from the Pentagon shows up. He's supposed to be from the Navy."

"The Navy?" exclaimed a puzzled Pederson.

"Relax, okay? It's not my decision."

Pederson glared at Clendaniel. "This is bullshit, R. J. Why is the Navy even involved?"

"I don't know yet."

"And how long do we just stand around?"

"He's expected to arrive at eight o'clock. Perhaps then we'll find out what this is all about."

Pederson looked at his watch. It was five minutes to the hour. Raising his head, he noticed a light gray, late-model Chevy with white government plates approaching the work site.

"Looks like we don't have long to wait," said someone behind Pederson.

They were surprised when a childlike person in a Navy uniform emerged from the vehicle and began making a beeline for Clendaniel, who stood in the center of the group. As the officer got closer, it was clear that he was a she. Noticeable tufts of red hair flanked the officer's cover.

"You can't possibly be the one we're waiting for," chuckled Pederson dismissively.

Altering her approach toward Pederson, the officer stopped directly in front of the heavyset man. "R. J. Clendaniel?"

Pederson tossed a thumb toward the foreman. "He's R. J."

"Then no one should be talking to you, should they?"

The man whose early morning shadow enveloped the officer was stunned into silence.

Clendaniel referred to the paper in his hand and read the name. "Lieutenant Murphy?"

"We should talk in your office."

"This way."

Terrie followed the project foreman into his trailer, ignoring everyone else. She waited for the door to close before she spoke. "Did your company brief you about why I'm here?"

"Not entirely."

Crossing her arms, she asked, "What did they tell you?"

"I only received word of your arrival this morning. They were not very forthcoming on detail."

His disingenuous manner didn't fool Terrie. "Then this meeting is premature."

As she turned to leave, Clendaniel was forced to capitulate. "Lieutenant Murphy!"

She looked back at the foreman.

"Okay, the home office told us you were to be given oversight over the excavation phase of the project."

"What else did they tell you?" she asked, her hand still on the door knob.

"That if we find anything, you were to evaluate and clear it before we're allowed to proceed."

"Anything else?"

"I was also directed to act as your liaison while you're here."

"That's correct. I suspect you'll be making that order abundantly clear to your people."

"Sure, whatever you say."

Turning to face the foreman, she folded her arms again and said, "I'll make this simple for you. I don't want to be here any more than you want me here, so let's make the best of it, shall we?"

The foreman nodded.

"Since the building you're tearing down is not my concern, I only need to be here when you actually break ground. When do you estimate you'll get to that point?"

"Barring any complications, we should be ready for you by midday tomorrow."

"That's fine. However, you're cautioned to ensure they don't go any further until my arrival. Is that understood?"

Clendaniel agreed.

Terrie savored the satisfaction of knowing shocked eyes were still burning their laser attention on her as she departed the trailer.

The warmth of the morning sun had dissipated the predawn fog when Terrie drove up to Clendaniel's trailer office. Yellow caution tape and temporary fencing marked the boundary of the construction zone. It was made up of US 1 and the Memorial Bridge on the west side, the parking lot adjacent to Island Avenue to the north, a service road to the east, and ended thirty-five feet from the shoreline to the south.

The crew wasn't quite finished removing the remnants of the old building when Terrie arrived. Most of the location was cleared of rubble, with the exception of the old building's foundation, which jutted out of the ground like a three-dimensional footprint. When the last of the debris was removed, the workers were left with nothing to do. Unless Terrie was present to observe, they couldn't even dig up the old parking lot. That didn't sit well with Kevin Pederson.

Seeing Terrie's car pull up, Clendaniel came out of his air-conditioned trailer to meet her. He noticed she was more aptly dressed in her blueberries and steel-toe boots. She removed a folding chair and a standard-size notebook from the back seat of her car as the foreman approached.

"Good morning, Lieutenant."

"Mr. Clendaniel."

"My demolition team chief, Celio Esteban, says he'll be ready for you shortly."

"Thank you." Terrie took in the progress made. Looking around at the dozen or so workers, it was apparent she was missing some safety equipment. "Mr. Clendaniel, you wouldn't happen to have a spare hard hat and safety glasses, would you?"

"I'm sure we can fix you up, Lieutenant." The foreman caught sight of a crew member standing near the supply trailer and called out to him to round up the safety equipment.

Surveying the spot where the old office once stood, Terrie recalled the building's appearance. It didn't look like it needed to be torn down. "Why destroy a serviceable building?"

"Progress, Lieutenant. A smaller marina office will be built closer to the pier. This outdated office will soon become a luxury two-story condo."

"I see. Do you have a copy of the blueprints?"

"I have one in the trailer if you need it."

"Could you get it for me please?" Terrie set up her chair in the most advantageous location from which to observe the excavation, took her seat, and waited.

Clendaniel scowled before he disappeared into the trailer to get Terrie what she requested.

Witnessing this display of surrender, an exasperated Kevin Pederson yelled down from the rig he was inspecting to voice his indignation. "Hey, R. J.! Do we have Her Highness's permission to get started or what?"

Terrie ignored the insult.

When the foreman gave her the blueprint, she unrolled it and got to work, doing her best to transfer a respectable miniature of its detail onto the graph paper in her notebook. Taking great pains to make an accurate map, Terrie was quite aware that the time she was taking to recreate the site in her notes was getting on both men's nerves.

"Hey, lady, what's the goddamn holdup?" Pederson yelled.

Terrie remained focused on her sketch. "Deal with that right now, Mr. Clendaniel. Or I will."

While Terrie put the finishing touches on her artwork, she could hear an out-of-control Pederson from a distance, screaming obscenities at Clendaniel. Having completed her task, she approached the men in mid-conference.

Clendaniel held up a hand to quiet the angry Pederson. "Is there something I can do for you, Lieutenant?"

Timing her glance at Pederson to match her emphasis, Terrie replied, "You may inform your crew that they have *my permission* to proceed with the excavation."

Terrie resumed her seat with a distinct air of satisfaction that was not lost on Pederson.

"I'm taking this up with the steward, R. J.," he threatened.

"Fine, but right now, you got your wish. I suggest you get to it."

A red-faced Pederson mumbled something under his breath as he mounted his backhoe. Somehow, the expression of indignation on his face only served to make him look ridiculous.

Shaking his head at the surreal nature of the situation, Clendaniel got on the radio and gave his crew their marching orders. He moved toward Terrie to observe the excavation for himself, figuring this was a good time to try establishing a rapport with the obstinate officer. "How long did it take you to get here from Washington, Lieutenant?"

She responded without meeting his gaze. "I didn't."

"Oh. Then where are you stationed, if you don't mind my asking?"

Interrupting her careful study of the details in her reconstructed miniature, she used her eyes to do the talking. They darted quickly toward nearby Jamaica Island before she continued examining her map.

"Portsmouth Navy Yard, eh? You couldn't have been there very long. I don't recall seeing you around before."

"In another week or so you won't have that problem."

"I'm just trying to make conversation, Lieutenant."

"If it's all the same to you, Mr. Clendaniel, I'll just sit here quietly and document my observations."

Clendaniel detected an edge to her Emily Post manner that contained a simple warning: don't push. And after her dressing down of Pederson, he wasn't about to. He just nodded.

Pederson and his crew worked their way around the raised portion of the concrete, going only as deep as required to remove the old foundation. When he tried to remove the last of it near the northwest corner, the backhoe's tines made a loud banging sound as they came down on something immovable.

Terrie happened to glance up when she heard the unusual sound. "What was that?"

The foreman was on his radio immediately. "Kevin, what's the problem over there?"

"Looks like we hit a huge boulder."

"How large?"

"I don't know yet. I'll try digging around it."

"All right. Keep me posted."

Pederson nodded back to the foreman as he brought the bucket around to try another location. Moving to his left, he managed to clear the target depth he'd been using all afternoon. He tried a few feet to the right of the obstruction and was making progress. Inching his way closer to the object, he made contact with it again. Although it was made of stone, it didn't appear to be natural. The sides were hewn, like it was some kind of wall.

The frustrated backhoe operator got on his radio. "R. J., come take a look at this!"

With Terrie in tow, Clendaniel moved to look at the anomaly that was cutting into their tight schedule. They evaluated the furrows Pederson had created on either side of the stone wall. As they cleared away some of the loose dirt around it, they noticed how the top of the exposed rock surface kept its natural form, while the sides were cut by artificial means.

With her orders in mind, Terrie took immediate control. "This is not what you expected to find, is it?" she asked Clendaniel.

"No, it's not." The foreman scratched at his chin.

"Could you have him clear the dirt on either side of this stone to see how far it goes?"

The foreman looked up at Pederson in his backhoe. "Kevin?"

Holding his tongue, Pederson began digging a trench on either side of the wall. The narrow wall's length progressed toward the shoreline at a ten-degree angle away from the northwest corner of the old marina. Pederson continued to expose the wall until it reached the opposite side of the removed foundation, but the stone wall continued beyond their boundary. The wall was little more than a foot wide, but it was strong, with three-inch-diameter holes drilled through the top of the wall at regular intervals.

Nothing in Terrie's orders prepared her for a situation like this, but she suggested a course of action to the foreman. "Since the top of this wall was discovered at the limit of your original target depth, you may want to consider digging another foot down around the area of the old foundation."

Clendaniel smirked. "We have to take the excavation deeper in order to satisfy the new foundation's code requirements anyway, so that shouldn't be a problem."

"Very good. And to prevent further damage to what might lie beneath the surface, please instruct your crew to proceed with the remaining excavation manually."

"Are you crazy?" he asked, astounded. "This is a construction zone, not an archeological dig!"

"It is now," she told the foreman. Terrie considered her orders, what they'd just discovered, and the time of day. "Tell you what. You contact your superiors to verify my authority in this matter, and we'll pick this up in the morning."

With that, Terrie returned to her seat, made some quick annotations in her notes, packed up, and left.

Knowing they weren't allowed to continue their work unless she was present, Clendaniel called it a day.

⚓

As agreed, Terrie was to call Crabtree and state, "I'd like to confirm my appointment." He would then respond with, "I have you down for…" and specify the time she should report.

This prearranged call meant she had something to report or to bring into the office. It was five o'clock in the afternoon on the second day of her assignment when Crabtree received the first such call.

Twenty minutes later, she was in his office back at the Yard for debriefing.

FIVE

Crabtree poured his last viable cup of coffee from the carafe as he waited in his office. He was stirring the honey and creamer into his mug when he heard someone enter. Expecting Terrie, he addressed her without confirming her identity. "Not a very glamorous first assignment, I grant you."

"Not exactly what I signed up for, sir."

"True, but due to the delicate nature of this assignment, the Navy had to assume operational control."

"Pardon me, sir, but wouldn't a qualified archeologist be better equipped to handle this?"

"Under normal circumstances, I would agree with you." He turned his attention toward Terrie and offered her a chair as he sat down himself. "The circumstances are not normal. This assignment must be handled with discretion."

"Naturally, sir. That would be the logical assumption since our office is involved."

He detected a hint of insolence but was unable to camouflage his amusement for this young firebrand. "I expect a certain level of candidness from my subordinates, Miss Murphy. So long as you couch it appropriately in the company of others, I'm fine with how you express yours."

"Thank you, sir."

"Besides, in view of your early success, I'm hardly in a position to debate you. How long do you think it will take them?"

Terrie squinted her eyes and looked up as though she were viewing her map. "The site is 9,000 square feet, but the actual excavation area is about half that." She directed her attention back to the commander. "That's not a large area to cover."

"They're not going any further?"

"No, sir. According to the plans, the excavation takes in the office building and the parking lot and that's it."

"I see," he said, taking a sip from his mug. "Now to business. You have something to report?"

Terrie took out her notes and pointed to a specific place on her drawing. "They found this odd stone wall in the upper left corner here."

Crabtree craned his neck to see what she was referring to. "What's so odd about it?"

"From the location, you would think it's a foundation, but according to Mr. Clendaniel, the dimensions don't support that conclusion."

"What does he think it is?"

"He didn't say, sir."

Crabtree scrutinized the layout she'd recreated. "Interesting. Did they expect to find it?"

"No, sir. They seemed surprised when they did."

"What's your assessment of it?"

"It's strange, sir."

"In what way?"

"It looks like a natural stone wall, but it's too thin to support any real weight. It has regularly spaced holes on top with no discernible purpose. To better determine what this object may have been used for, I recommend we have them uncover all of it, even if it means going beyond the construction zone."

"Good thinking, Miss Murphy." The CO moved a finger across his pursed lips as he thought. "Since we want to limit such exposure to only authorized personnel, you should inform Mr. Clendaniel to reduce his crew to no more than necessary. Five should suffice, I think."

"Sir, no doubt I will encounter resistance to this suggestion. As it is, they're already pitching a fit that I directed them not to use heavy equipment, just in case they hit something fragile or valuable."

He snapped his head to look at Terrie. "You what?"

"I directed him politely," she replied with a mischievous grin.

His lips curled up in amusement. "No doubt you did."

"Sir, if I may suggest. This renovation is already public knowledge. It's bad enough we got involved. If we start cutting personnel for no apparent reason, this may engender greater public scrutiny. Isn't that something we wish to avoid?"

"Very well. What is it you propose?"

"Now that the excavation is reduced to shovels, we'll need all of their manpower to expedite the mission. I believe any other unexpected changes will draw unwanted curiosity."

"So, you don't want to cut any personnel?"

"I didn't necessarily say that."

Crabtree couldn't contain his smile. "How do you plan on handling the press?"

"With an appropriate balance of artifice and intrepidity, sir."

Terrie's commanding officer stood up and extended a congratulatory hand. "Well done, Miss Murphy. Call in when there's anything else to report."

"Aye aye, sir."

⚓

Her curious meeting with Crabtree over, Terrie returned home long enough to change into her Navy PT gear, and she was on the road. Heading south on Route 1B, she did her best to shut out the tribulations of her day so she could enjoy the coastal beauty and colonial appeal of New Hampshire. The lonely causeways that linked Shapleigh, Goat, and New Castle Islands with the mainland, the colorful buildings that dotted the landscape, and the neighborly people she would pass by all added to the intimate charm of Portsmouth.

She continued her trek on 1A toward South Street to complete her daily constitutional. By the time she reached Prescott Park, residential buildings along her path had started to illuminate and solar sensors instructed the streetlights to turn on.

Terrie slowed down the last ten yards before she got to her apartment. She leaned against the wall to stretch her legs as she glimpsed the Memorial Bridge and Badger Island beyond it. From this vantage point, she noticed how well lit the construction site was. Terrie enjoyed taking in what her new neighborhood had to offer, but the vision of the lighted site redirected her thoughts toward her unusual discovery. Perhaps a shower would rinse the day from her mind.

The cascade of hot water across her face was soothing, but it was no use. The day's events replayed in her head just the same: the unusual assignment that appeared to have nothing to do with the Navy; the less-than-enthusiastic foreman and his cantankerous heavy equipment operator; and the strange wall that, until today, was not known to exist.

Terrie wondered why Clendaniel, who should have had the most up-to-date site maps, wasn't aware of this wall. She thought the company would need to know exactly what they would run into in order to estimate the total cost of the job for their customer. If she could only speak with Margaret about it.

Her older sister always managed to direct the right questions Terrie's way to lead her to the proper conclusions. Thinking of Margaret like this could trigger another nightmare. Prior to departing the USS *New York*, she hadn't experienced one of those terrible dreams for almost five years. She forced herself not to dwell on her sister as she dried herself off and put on the light-gray tie-belt shorts and oversized Eagles jersey she favored.

Terrie poured herself a glass of wine and turned on the radio. The gentle flavor of the semi-dry refreshment was a welcome diversion, although the station's musical selections left her wanting.

Her 12-string guitar rested in the corner of the room. Terrie stared at the instrument, taking a few more sips from her glass before setting it down. She approached her stringed muse and took it up by its neck. A polished performer, Terrie's technique was warm and soothing. She liked playing popular music, though she used her own style to express it. She set the instrument's strap around her shoulder and began to play some ballad from the seventies as she moved to the open balcony. After a statement of the theme, she improvised several variations.

Staring down at the construction site, she was about to complete the coda of the melody when she suddenly stopped playing. She set the guitar down and retrieved her notebook to examine the planned elevation for the new condo.

Like its predecessor, the new foundation's angle was more closely aligned with US 1 and Memorial Bridge than the shoreline. She thought it strange that the gradient of the slope toward the shoreline was more perpendicular to the newly discovered stone wall than the foundation of the old marina.

This was indeed a puzzle and, without all of the respective pieces, an unsolvable one.

SIX

A man none of the crew had ever laid eyes on before came out of the trailer, followed by R. J. Clendaniel. The man was dressed in a light gray suit, his eyes hidden behind mirrored glasses. The crew watched him shake hands with their foreman before he got into his black escalade and drove away.

"Now what?" asked a disgusted but curious Kevin Pederson.

"That was a legal representative from the home office. We are ordered to conform to any orders Lieutenant Murphy issues us, regardless of how outlandish they may seem."

Pederson blurted out, "That does it, R. J.! I'm done!" He looked at the union steward. "Celio, you can't tell me you're going along with this?"

Celio shrugged. "The national office isn't even calling the shots on this one, Kevin. Our local has no choice but to comply with the government's orders."

"This whole thing is insane!" screamed Pederson.

"Look, if we want to stay here on a paying basis, we do what we're told," said Clendaniel firmly.

"Is that so?"

Terrie's car rolled up on the cordon. Silence descended upon the group as they watched her step out and head toward the foreman.

"Mr. Clendaniel, may I address your men?"

"This ought to be good," Pederson stammered.

Given little choice in the matter, the foreman extended his hand toward the assemblage. Terrie took an assertive stance, scanned the looks of puzzlement on their faces, and launched into her address. "Gentlemen, there's been a slight change in plan."

Pederson started to say something, but Celio grabbed his arm and silenced him.

"The priority now is to excavate around the stone wall we found yesterday. Once the surface blacktop is removed, I'm authorized to suspend the use of heavy equipment until further notice. I'm also authorized to extend the site to ensure the complete excavation of that wall."

"Excuse me, lady, but you have no authority to alter our contract!" Pederson yelled.

"The contract you *were* operating under is now held in abeyance. This construction zone is now designated an archeological dig until such time as I determine otherwise. As the government now has jurisdiction, I've been granted the authority to act as I see fit. You will be authorized to work here only at my discretion and direction. Or does that present a problem for you?"

"The problem is yours, lady, because no one here will listen to you."

"Thank you, Mr. Pederson. You just made one decision easy. Since you are reluctant to follow my lead, you're free to leave."

Pederson looked around at the others for support but found none. Seeing no one else willing to stand up to her, an exasperated Pederson gathered up his gear.

Before he departed, he whispered to Clendaniel, "This isn't over."

Terrie patiently waited for the disgruntled heavy equipment operator to go. She allowed the chilling effect of her words to sink in. "Despite Mr. Pederson's dramatic exit, gentlemen, I have no desire to assume control over your jobsite. So, the sooner I get my job done, the sooner I'm out of your hair. Does that satisfy everyone?"

Her words were only mildly reassuring.

"You know the priority. If it means going beyond your original contract, so be it. If it does happen to run into the highway or private property, I need to know immediately."

"In that case, we'll need our heavy equipment," Celio demanded.

"Let me worry about that," she said. With no further challenges to her authority, Terrie gestured to the foreman. "Mr. Clendaniel?"

"I realize you have your job to do, but would it be possible for you to allow us to complete our original excavation of the main office?"

Terrie's eyebrows shot up as an unspoken question.

"It would not only keep us on schedule, but would expose more area you intended to investigate in the first place. Am I right?"

Terrie considered her abrasive attitude since Pederson set her off on that first day. As he was no longer part of the equation, she considered Clendaniel's request. Tilting her head in a curious fashion, she relented. "So long as you maintain the target depth we discussed yesterday, I have no objection."

Terrie's unexpected compromise allowed their anxiety to ratchet down a few notches. With the meeting over, the foreman turned to his crew. "Okay, guys, let's get to it!"

Starting from the side of the foundation nearest the new stone wall, a line of crew members systematically began digging their way from the bridge-side boundary of the old foundation. They cleared the requisite five feet of depth as they went but found nothing. The more progress they made, the less attention they paid to their objective: locating whatever mystical objects this intruder was looking for. This failed to please Terrie, who was observing them with a meticulous eye.

Taking a second to stretch his back after using a shovel for the past two hours, Chris Iarossi glanced at his watch and noticed he had worked straight through his break. Leaning over toward the union steward, he hissed, "It's almost lunchtime. Is she going to keep us working through our lunch hour too?"

Celio may have caved on what was supposed to be accomplished in the construction zone, but he was a fearsome antagonist when it came to upholding union rules and worker's rights on the job. As lunchtime approached, he wasn't shy about enforcing those limitations with management.

Doing his best to rein in his temper, he approached Terrie. "Lieutenant, you may have control over what we do during work hours but not during our breaks or lunch."

Hearing the unfamiliar voice, Terrie briefly looked over her shoulder at Celio. "I never said I did."

Breaching her impregnable exterior, Celio softened his next question. "Then you have no objection to our breaking for lunch?"

Terrie simply extended her arm and unfolded her hand in a giving gesture.

"I'll take that as a yes." He leveled his eyes on Clendaniel for confirmation.

The crew dispersed precisely at noon for their chow break. Terrie took the hint and grabbed a satchel from her car. Opening the bag, she removed a bottle of water and a single-serving container of arugula and spinach salad. Coating her salad with a light sprinkling of slivered almonds, Romano cheese, and sesame dressing, she made short work of her meal with the nimble use of her wooden chopsticks.

After taking in the last morsel, she went over her graph of the excavation to make sure it was in accord with the morning's work. At the rate of 300 square feet an hour, they were better than halfway through the marina's exposed foundation but had found nothing. It was during this short period of isolation that she began to second-guess her decision to accede to Clendaniel's request. Then she heard his familiar voice.

"Lieutenant?"

"Yes?"

"Am I bothering you?"

"Not yet."

"I'd like to discuss something with you."

"The topic?"

He gritted his teeth, knowing full well the response he'd receive, but he said it anyway. "Kevin Pederson."

With complete disinterest, she replied, "He turned down the sheets on his own bed of nails, Mr. Clendaniel. Topic closed."

The foreman's patience with her adversarial responses reached its limit. "Your tongue, like your pencil, sketches a very vivid image, Lieutenant."

"And yours seems given to poetry, Mr. Clendaniel. Perhaps you should consider changing vocations."

"Pardon me for asking, Lieutenant, but what qualifies you for this job? Are you some sort of military archeologist or something?"

"Not exactly."

"Then exactly what is it that you're looking for?"

"What I am looking for, Mr. Clendaniel, requires the appropriate level of security clearance and a valid need to know. You have neither," she replied, with a sharp edge to her delivery.

He smiled for the first time since they'd met. "That's the nicest thing you've said to me, Lieutenant. And in such a pleasant voice too."

Terrie yielded a tertiary glance in his direction and, for the briefest of moments, she smiled. It lasted for a millisecond, but she did it nonetheless.

He smirked as the lieutenant's icy disposition seemed to thaw.

Unable to stifle a grin, she shook her head in disbelief. Attempting to regain her composure, she changed the subject.

"Mr. Clendaniel, I don't believe your earlier suggestion is bearing fruit."

"Excuse me?"

"We're making no progress on that stone wall. And we've found little else."

"What if we split the crew and attacked the remaining foundation from opposite sides? We'll know immediately if there's anything of interest to you on that far end."

Believing the day to be a wash anyway, she gave in to the foreman's proposal. When the crew came back from lunch, Clendaniel shared his plan and had them execute it.

They were barely three feet into the afternoon dig on the parking lot side of the foundation when Devon Taylor shouted back, "Hey, I think I got something here!"

"What is it?" asked Clendaniel as he and Terrie went in to investigate.

"I don't know." Devon cleared away some of the loose dirt to expose more of the object. "It looks like a two-by-four."

Terrie regarded the flat surface of the distressed piece of wood. She surveyed the exposed area with her hands on her hips, pondering what the stone wall and this odd piece of wood had in common. It was probably nothing.

"Mr. Clendaniel, could you have Mr. Taylor expose the rest of this?"

Just as Devon began to dig again, Chris Iarossi shouted, "Over here!"

Chris was leading the effort on the east side of the dig. He'd been manually generating the evenly spaced furrows on either side of the removed foundation when his shovel got snagged on something.

"Whatcha got?" asked the foreman.

"I'm not sure," Chris said.

His shovel got stuck on a thin piece of cord. As he pulled it up, they noticed a leather pouch attached to it.

"Do you have gloves?" Terrie asked.

"Just these leather ones," offered Chris.

Donning a glove and reaching for the item, Terrie worked the artifact away from its blanket of dirt. It was a well-worn leather pouch weighing only a few pounds. Revealing whatever was inside would have to wait for a more discreet location. Terrie wasted no time documenting the discovery and securing the pouch inside the yellow gym bag she had in the trunk of her car.

It wasn't long before Devon found something else. But this time Terrie was on top of it, observing from her perch above them. Climbing down into the hole with surprising dexterity, she asked, "May I, Mr. Taylor?"

Devon yielded his position. "Go right ahead."

Terrie studied the new find, a hollowed-out piece of wood nearly double the width of the two-by-four that crossed beneath it at a 90-degree angle. The wider piece of straight wood had a groove purposefully carved down its center. In logging the measurements on her draft, she noticed how the grooved wooden plank seemed to run parallel to the stone wall they'd found yesterday.

"Mr. Clendaniel, I'd like them to concentrate their efforts right here."

The more they uncovered, the more directive Terrie became, tugging at Clendaniel's last nerve. Aggravated but given no choice, he instructed his crew to comply. "Celio, get some extra trowels and bristle brushes from the supply trailer, will ya?"

"I'll see what's there."

Matching Terrie's hard look, Clendaniel said to the union steward, "Go out and buy them if necessary."

Terrie softened her gaze. "Thank you."

Surrounding the latest find, Clendaniel's crew worked diligently and with great care to remove the debris from its center outward. Chris found a broom in the trailer and used it to sweep all the loose dirt and gravel until Celio returned with the right size trowels and brushes.

They furrowed around the outline of the two-by-four he first located. But in clearing a channel along the length of the wider board, Devon noted an identical two-by-four in the same relative position about a foot away. Following the grooved board, he estimated another foot from the second board and found a third. Then a fourth. Then a fifth.

Between the fifth and sixth two-by-four, Devon exposed a wad of tangled, disintegrated rope, which covered a different piece of dark wood.

From just above him, Terrie kept close watch. Before Devon could move the rope or the unusual piece of wood, Terrie documented the find on her graph.

"Could you hand me one of those brushes?" she asked Celio, who hurried to comply.

Terrie brushed the loose dirt aside to reveal as much of the object as she could. It was relatively smooth with a slight curve to it. She gently worked the bristles over the tightly packed earth but was unable to remove enough dirt to budge it from its resting place.

"Could I—"

"Here you go, Lieutenant," Celio said as he handed her the trowel he knew she needed.

"Thanks," she said, clearly distracted. Using both tools did the trick. She managed to loosen enough dirt to achieve a palpable grip on the frozen relic. Shaking the object freed it from its earthly prison.

The curved object was made of wood, lacquered on one side and splintered on the other, as though it was broken off something larger. The decayed rope that covered it had the consistency of rotten burlap.

Terrie measured the dimensions and location of the boards, the curved wood chip and rope, the distance between them and the wider, central board. She carefully examined the orientation of each board to the stone wall. As she did so, a picture began to emerge.

What they were uncovering looked like the decomposed skeletal remains of a huge vertebrate animal that had died on its back. The chipped piece of wood and rope were the organs lodged within its ribs.

As she was making that correlation, Chris Iarossi cleared out more of the dirt near the service road side of the dig when he came across a second stone wall. It was not only an exact match to the first but ran parallel to it. One end of it continued toward the parking lot and the other toward the service road and into private property.

By the time Terrie was able to annotate all of her observations, it was coming up on five o'clock. Time to call in to report her findings.

SEVEN

Ray fielded the call in his fluid, administrative manner. "Intel, Senior Chief Sheffield speaking. This is an unsecure line. How may I help you?…Yes, I have you down for five forty-five…You're welcome." He hung up the phone and pressed the intercom. "Commander?"

"Yes, Ray?"

"That was Lieutenant Murphy, sir. She'll be arriving in about half an hour."

"Very good, Ray. Could you get Captain Derrick on the line before you call it a day?"

"Yes, sir." Less than a minute later, he was back on the intercom. "I have your call, sir."

"Thank you." Though not in his superior's line of sight, Crabtree felt the need to stand when he heard her voice. "Crabtree here, Captain. Yes, ma'am…Yes, ma'am…Yes, ma'am, I will… Thank you, Captain." The commander slowly placed the receiver on its cradle and lowered himself into the chair.

What the captain wanted was not going to sit well with Terrie. Crabtree's subordinate was to be kept ignorant of the reason for her assignment. Captain Derrick left him little choice. Those were her orders.

As he processed what the captain just told him, he poured the honey into his coffee.

Terrie arrived to an empty intelligence office, with the notable exception of Crabtree. This time she juggled her notebook, purse, and the yellow gym bag as she made her way into his office. "We had a productive day, sir."

"From the obvious weight of that bag you're carrying, I'd say so."

She placed everything on the conference table and stepped aside to allow him to inspect it.

"Let's see what we have here." He gently retrieved the thick strand of dark-brown cordage for inspection.

"The rope looks to be made of burlap," Terrie said.

"If it's burlap, it wasn't made here in New England."

"Why not?"

He didn't answer.

Setting down the rough coil that irritated his hands, he pulled out the semicircular wood chip. The curved surface of the smooth side measured ten inches. The opposing side was nothing but splintered shards, portions of which were starting to petrify.

"What do you think it might have been?" he asked.

"Given the history of the island and the shape of the find, I'd say it was part of a jib, a mast or a bowsprit."

"I would agree. How old would you estimate it was?"

Terrie took out her notebook with the graph paper drawing for a reference and laid it across the table. "Since it was found at the same elevation as these wood two-by-fours, I'd say at least as old as they are." She watched his face to gauge his reaction. He showed no interest at all in what the drawing represented.

"It was when they began digging on the east side of the old foundation that they found this." Terrie handed Crabtree the decaying, dirty laundry bag of a pouch.

The considerable weight surprised him. Inside the bag was an object encased in some kind of packing material. The commander's eyes widened when he removed the last vestige of material. It was a thick metal alloy with properties unfamiliar to Crabtree. The object appeared freshly made, with a high steel sheen and rosy crimson color and shaped into a curved equilateral triangle.

Terrie watched Crabtree as he rotated the object in his hands, then something caught their attention. "What's that?" asked Terrie.

"Nothing."

"I thought I saw something written on the edge of it."

"It's just dirt." He quickly shoved the object back into the pouch.

Her CO wasn't as fast as he thought. Before he could secure the triangle into its hiding place, she managed to be at the optimum angle to read the single word that was made into its edge.

Neptune.

Terrie's third-floor apartment still held much of the day's unseasonably high temperatures. She propped open the windows to provide a much-needed cross ventilation to remove the stale air.

She barely had time to slip out of her uniform and shower before the weight of exhaustion finally caught up with her. After overexerting herself all day, the only thing she could think about was scrubbing the aches out of her muscles. When she was done, she was in no shape for her run. She used the last of her waning physical strength to toss on a nightshirt and drop her head into the sofa pillow. A week's worth of intellectual brinkmanship between herself, Clendaniel, and Crabtree had tapped her cerebral vitality to the limit.

It was bad enough she had to deal with a discordant array of personalities all week. But to be used as a simple tool to extract information, only to be denied the opportunity to perform the analysis on what she discovered? She was being kept out of the loop on purpose, and she didn't know why.

Commander Crabtree's indifference to the strange items discovered where an intelligence office should have been was telling and she recognized the deception for what it was. The thought crossed her mind the same instant a line from The Art of War popped into her head.

"All warfare is based on deception."

Was she at war with her new employer? At war with her own government? Terrie dismissed the idea quickly as her fatigued body surrendered to unconsciousness.

The overcast sky eclipsed the last vestiges of daylight. A plethora of disjointed sounds began to pierce the evening calm. A solitary loon's mournful wail echoed across the bay. The melancholy air horn of a distant US Coast Guard tug belched out its haunting notice of passage as it made its way out to sea. Young lovers strolled past Prescott Park, as the reverberation of their vocal tête-à-tête bounced harmlessly off her apartment building. All these disparate sources of aural stimuli managed to make their way through the window Terrie had set ajar, yet she heard nary a sound. She lay there sleeping for the next several hours, her body motionless at first, unaware of the passage of time. But her recurring nightmare, the one she hoped would never return, reared its ugly head once more.

Flashes of faint memories forced themselves from her subconscious as Terrie's closed eyelids sprang to life. Under them, her sapphire orbs rapidly increased their ricochet within their sockets, like a pair of billiard balls bouncing off opposing cushions. Beads of sweat emerged from her pores. A light moan emanated from her vocal cords each time she tossed her head from one side of the pillow to the other trying to obliterate the images her mind's eye conjured up.

The faint memories began to grow sharper, more detailed, and frightening. They finally crystallized into what was left of her sister Margaret's bloodied and broken body. Then Terrie awoke… screaming.

EIGHT

R. J. Clendaniel came out of his air-conditioned trailer shaking his head. He still couldn't fathom how the Navy's unwelcomed interruption hadn't set their project back by a single day. So far.

Relieved yet wanting to make some progress before the heat index became unbearable, he prodded Terrie. "Are we ready, Lieutenant?"

A paragon of concentration, Terrie stood at the edge of the pit, staring at the exposed artifacts. The stone wall was intact with few worn or missing areas, while the artificial ribcage and spinal column were severely deteriorated, damaged, or missing entire sections. What were they? What was their function?

Reviewing her diagram, she examined the location as a whole. "Of course," she whispered to herself. The island was a shipyard in the 1700s. The artificial ribcage appeared to be stocks for a vessel and its corresponding spinal column the spot where the keel was laid. But the thin nature of the wall precluded the possibility of it being a dry dock. So what could it have been?

"Lieutenant?" Clendaniel barked.

She blinked her eyes and answered, "Sorry, you can proceed."

Now that he achieved what he wanted, it was time to live up to his side of the bargain. Devon Taylor led the effort to unearth what remained of the stocks and the stone wall, but the climbing temperature aggravated their effort.

Terrie barely ventured a word the entire morning. Even as they located a 90-degree corner of the wall under the existing parking lot, twenty feet from the northwest corner of the office foundation, she kept her composure.

Terrie looked on as they located the opposite corner of the wall, nearly thirty feet due north of the eastern border of the dig. She observed the proceedings with her arms folded as the last of the stocks and keel beam were unearthed.

Clendaniel was conferring with Celio, Chris, and Devon on the best approach to use for the remainder of the excavation, when he happened to glance over at Terrie. There was a subtle change about her he couldn't quite put a finger on. Wrapping up their conference, the foreman walked over to Terrie to fill her in and to get her assent on their plan. "Lieutenant?"

Terrie had moved her attention beyond the excavation, past the narrow strip of water toward Prescott Park. Her vision wasn't focused on anything in particular. Not the man sitting on the stone bench near the line of parked cars. Not the jogger taking an afternoon jaunt. Not the vehicles as they passed by. Not even her apartment building. The foreman's unexpected use of her surname snapped her out of her reverie.

"Lieutenant Murphy?"

"Yes?"

"Is there anything wrong?"

"Why do you ask?"

"You seem preoccupied. More than normal, I mean."

Clendaniel may be just a blue-collar supervisor, but she sensed in him something genuine in his ability to read people. He picked up on Terrie's change in attitude that always seemed to follow her nightmares about Margaret. To dissuade his further attempts, she deflected his query with one of her own. "So, you know what's normal for me?"

"Is a stranger's concern that alien to you, Lieutenant?"

Turning to evaluate him, she noted how deftly he employed the use of a question as a reply. A full-brimmed hard hat managed to conceal his thick brown hair, accented with streaks of gray, and ashen-blue eyes set deep in his chiseled face. The tall man owned a sculpted physic, filling out his distressed blue jeans in lean fashion. His safety vest covered a button-down, blue-checked shirt with cuffs rolled up to mid-forearm. His viridian-tinged head gear disguised an intelligence that was slowly beginning to grow on the young woman. But Clendaniel's lack of accent and midcoast demeanor was out of place for a New England native. "A stranger to me or to this area?"

The foreman shook his head with a grin. "What gave me away?"

"Clendaniel isn't exactly a New England pedigree. The name is more native to the Delmarva Peninsula."

"Glen Burnie, actually."

"Thought so," she said before going back to her notes.

"Moved to Portsmouth when I was eleven. I don't remember much about living in Maryland. But how did you... ."

She only smiled.

Clendaniel couldn't help himself as a chuckle rose in his throat. He seemed to relish his protracted discussion with the enigmatic young woman. Judging from her pleasant expression, Terrie appeared to be taking some satisfaction in their playful banter as well.

Remnants of the stone wall, the stocks, and keel beam were completely uncovered, but there was no evidence of the intelligence office Crabtree said she'd find. The afternoon progressed to the end of the workday without further incident, except one.

Rolling up to the yellow caution tape was a tricked-out step van with the WGME News logo plastered all over its side. A man got out of the driver's side and went to the rear of the vehicle to retrieve his shoulder-mounted camera. Exiting the passenger side was a perky young woman, professionally dressed and coiffed. She examined her fingernails to make sure she didn't break them closing the van's door. It was the only real emotion she showed during her visit.

Clendaniel took note of the new arrival and walked up to the reporter with an extended hand. "R. J. Clendaniel, foreman. Is there something I can do for you?"

"Jamie Swanson, WGME News 13." The camera began to roll.

"One of your reporters was here last week."

Her lips contorted into a smirk as she went straight into her interview. "I understand that, but that's not why I'm here. We are following up on a tip and wanted to ask you a few questions." Her gaze moved to Terrie in a not-so-subtle manner.

"Concerning?"

Demonstrating a complete lack of delicacy, Swanson blurted out what she wanted to know. "Could you confirm that a naval officer acting as a site supervisor fired one of your union employees?"

Clendaniel smiled at the neophyte journalist. "Where do you get your information?"

"Can you confirm it?"

"Who was supposedly fired, Miss Swanson?"

"I am not at liberty to reveal my sources. I'm sure you can appreciate that."

"Then I can't help you."

"Is it true, Mr. Clendaniel?"

"I have a project to finish. Now, if you'll excuse me?" He turned away, but Swanson was persistent.

"Mr. Clendaniel, is the Navy really supervising this project? And if so, why?"

Before turning away, he responded, "You might want to ask the Navy that question, Miss Swanson."

Swanson looked over at Terrie scribbling away on her notes. "Is that her?"

He stopped to look where Swanson's attention was focused; on Terrie. "Is that who?"

"Lieutenant Murphy?"

"Why don't you ask her?"

Swanson slapped a hand on her hip. "Is there a reason why you're reluctant to discuss this matter, Mr. Clendaniel?"

"It's difficult to discuss the matter intelligently when you're being cagy yourself, Miss Swanson. Now, are you going to tell me what this is all about, or are you going to leave?"

"Fair enough," she said softly as a tactical retreat. "How about if I ask her?"

He extended his hand toward Terrie. "Be my guest."

Sauntering up to Terrie, Swanson called out to her. "Lieutenant Murphy?"

Terrie continued working on her notes as she responded, "Yes?"

"Jamie Swanson with WGME News 13. I have a few questions for you, if you don't mind."

Terrie folded her notebook and stood up, staring hard into eyes that were only interested in seeking the one scandal that would make their owner famous.

"It's been reported that the Navy has assumed control over this project. Is that why you're here?"

"Are you native to this area, Miss Swanson?"

"Excuse me?"

"Are you from this area?"

"Born and raised."

"Then you must be familiar with the New Hampshire state flag."

"Of course, but I'm here to—"

"Then why would the Navy's involvement come as a surprise, given the nature of the island's proud history?"

"But aren't you the one who fir—"

"The USS *Raleigh*, a US Naval vessel, was built on this island in 1776 by James Hackett, on the orders of the Continental Congress. Therefore, if there's a chance this site has archeological value, the Navy should be required to investigate the matter. Wouldn't you agree?"

"Is that the reason you fi—"

Firmly slamming the door on any further discussion of Pederson's alleged firing, Terrie pressed her point. "Let me set your mind at ease, Miss Swanson. It is with the full authority granted by the Antiquities Act of 1906, and further enhanced by the Archaeological Resources Protection Act of 1979, that Mr. Clendaniel's company is acting in cooperation with the United States Navy on this excavation. As this cooperation is mandated under federal law, I don't see how this should come as such a surprise to a seasoned reporter."

"Well," she began timidly, "since you put it that way… ."

"If you need further clarification, may I suggest you contact the construction company manager or Navy Public Affairs office in Washington. They would be in a much better position to answer any questions you may have, Miss Swanson."

Swanson wasn't going to get Terrie to spill the beans without giving up Pederson as the tipster. Disappointed, she jotted down some notes, thanked Terrie, and left.

Watching the rookie reporter pack up her equipment and depart, Clendaniel shook his head and approached Terrie. "Hmm, I suppose that's what Kevin meant when he said this wasn't over."

"I suppose."

"And how would you have answered that reporter's question about Kevin?"

"He left on his own accord."

"But that's not how he sees it."

"That's on him now, isn't it?"

"Reporters, like disgruntled employees, have long memories, Lieutenant."

"Accusations aren't proof, Mr. Clendaniel."

"That may be, but accusations become the proof when splashed across enough headlines."

"And people wonder why no one trusts the alleged media any longer."

Clendaniel couldn't help but chuckle.

Needing to rework the areas where the pencil marks were smudged, Terrie used a clean eraser to reduce the imperfections to an immaculate starting point before recreating them.

He craned his neck to peek at Terrie's reproduction. He was impressed with her high degree of detail. Her unerring pencil labeled everything.

"You're quite an artist, Lieutenant."

"Thank you."

As the afternoon sun heralded the arrival of five o'clock, the crew began to wrap up their tasks for the day. Chris and Devon's men gathered up their shovels and cleaned up their areas before they left for the weekend. Surveying the work done by his crew, Clendaniel turned to Terrie. "They look to be about done, wouldn't you say, Lieutenant?"

"When they complete the required five-foot depth of the entire area, then perhaps I'd be inclined to agree."

Even with the mutual understanding that started to develop between the two, a residue of mistrust adorned her nonverbal cues, but he let it go. "Till Monday then, Lieutenant?"

"See you Monday."

The foreman locked his trailer, got into his Silverado, and drove away.

Distracted by her conversation with Clendaniel, she thought she may have missed something. To quell her insecurity, she brought her chair and notebook back to the car and made one last inspection of the area before she left for the weekend.

Convinced there was absolutely nothing to find outside the wall, she crawled down the inner diameter to begin her search. Starting at the southwest end of the wall, she walked the entire distance, scanning everything she wasn't able to see from her perch atop the dig. Terrie surveyed the ground ahead of her. She discarded nothing that might disclose the location of Crabtree's mythical office.

She made it beyond the northwest corner of the wall but found nothing. When she rounded its northeast corner, something out of place drew her attention. An area of flat, discolored ground, approximately ten feet from the corner of the wall, protruded out from under one of the last remaining stocks. Brushing some of the loose soil from the flat area until she located its edges, she managed to find enough purchase to extract the item from its resting place.

Terrie's skin tingled when she grasped the magnitude of the find. It was a ship's log for a vessel whose name she instantly recognized. A name synonymous with Navy lore. She'd read about this vessel and the curious circumstances of her disappearance along with that of her captain, Arthur Ledbetter. A vessel called the *Justice*, presumed lost in 1788.

Learning from her last mistake, Terrie decided not to call this one in. She had the weekend, and she was going to make use of it before she dared to turn this artifact in to her boss.

NINE

Several seagulls descended upon the man as he took his seat on one of the stone benches near the parking area between Memorial Bridge and Prescott Park. He regarded the not-so-inconspicuous sign warning against the feeding of wild birds and other animals. Once it became apparent that this stranger wasn't going to give them any handouts, all of the herring gulls flew away. Only a lone ringbill was brave enough to get close to the man in the light-gray suit, his eyes hidden under mirrored glasses. But fowl on the prowl for a quick snack was not why he sat there.

The man's interest focused on the island just across the water from him. He scanned the peaceful park, taking in the crisp, salt-infused air carried on the light afternoon breeze. The drone of a pleasure boat entered his left ear as it approached, passed, and then receded into silence on his right.

Looking back at the construction site in the distance, he spied the news van and observed the action as it transpired. He looked at his watch and timed the TV reporter's visit. With marked amazement, he noted that the uniformed woman took less than ten minutes to dispatch the nosy reporter's curiosity.

Impressive, he thought.

After he observed the van's departure, he took out a notebook from his suit pocket and scribbled something inside. Returning it to its hiding place, he stood up, placed his hands in his pockets, and looked around. Philip's gaze fell on the construction site one more time. A reptilian smile separated his jaw from his face as he turned around to get into his vehicle.

His black Escalade didn't have time to warm up before he put it in gear and drove away.

TEN

Terrie placed the yellow gym bag on the table by the door. She slipped into a civilian PT outfit for a change of pace and headed out the door for some well-earned exercise and time alone to think.

She hadn't reached the first causeway before something she told the reporter finally dawned on her: the historic shipyard of James Hackett was located on the west side of the island, not under the old marina. If this was so, why would she find ship's stocks situated some distance away from the old shipyard? It made no sense. But that wasn't all.

The dimensions of the stone wall and its odd orientation to the marina in relation to the shoreline prompted a new line of thought. Why would someone construct such a wall? It was certainly large enough to encompass the kind of ships they were building at the time, but it wasn't thick enough for a dry dock. Parallel but offset from the stocks, the stone wall didn't appear to serve a useful purpose.

The second point she couldn't dismiss was how the long sides of the wall followed the keel beam toward the bay—a logical direction if one were going to launch a vessel.

But the most perplexing part of this assignment was not finding an intelligence office. Had there been one, she would have discovered administrative artifacts instead. If she was supposed to find something else, why was she lied to about what she was actually looking for?

Terrie finished her physical exercise and continued her mental one for the rest of the evening. Normally sparking her analytical juices, her improvisations on the guitar didn't work this time. She returned the instrument to its stand and walked out onto the balcony, taking in the construction area now hidden behind an opaque blanket of fog.

In the midst of her contemplations, the obnoxious percolation of a rumbling motorcycle grew louder in her ears. It made its way closer until the offending machine and its rider came into full view. To her dismay, rather than continuing down the street, he swung his two-wheel steed into one of the apartment building's assigned parking spaces. The rider throttled the engine twice more for good measure before dismounting the metal beast. He loosened the chinstrap, unzipped his black leather jacket, and removed his fingerless biker gloves as he approached the building.

Please don't be the one who lives in the empty apartment across the hall, she thought. A minute later, the elevator activated. *Great. He can't even take the stairs.*

Terrie retreated into her apartment sanctuary, grabbed her tablet off the end table, and took up residence on the sofa. Opening the device, she logged on to access her email. Skimming down the list of new messages, she smiled when she saw a familiar name. Her Aunt Barbara's timing was always impeccable. As she clicked on the message, Terrie's cell came to life. "Hello?"

"Hey, girl. Don't you ever call or write anymore?" her aunt chided.

"Sorry, I've been distracted."

"By what?"

"This new job isn't what I thought it would be."

"That's surprising, given the research you accomplished before you chose to dive into it."

"Yeah" was all Terrie could manage. Margaret's lifeless eyes flashed in Terrie's mind for a split second, cutting off the rest of her intended sentence.

"I still have your books. Do you intend to pick them up sometime this year?"

"I will. How about next weekend?"

A raucous electronic guitar riff accompanied by hard-driving drums seemed to come from nowhere, as her new neighbor boldly declared his musical preference. *Nice. I have a headbanger living next door.* Terrie put a palm over her ear to block the sound.

"Are you all right? You sound distracted."

"I'm fine. Just trying to adjust to a new location and a job I really haven't started yet."

Aunt Barbara wasn't fooled. "I can tell something's wrong. What is it?"

"I'll have to fill you in when I get a better grasp on it myself."

Terrie's perceptive aunt was more reliable than a polygraph. She had the kind of intuition that bordered on precognition. Terrie believed she inherited her strength of will and determination more from her aunt than her mother. While her mom remained a housewife to her dying day, her Aunt Barbara was a self-made woman.

Barbara Forester graduated summa cum laude from Stanford University and embarked on a successful career offering companies a dynamic approach to physical and cyber security. Her products became sought-after commodities and consequently made her a wealthy woman. Her sense of independence so richly reflected in her niece that she identified more with Terrie than her own children.

"Okay, if you say so. Do you want anything special for dinner when you come down?" Barbara asked.

"Not really."

"Suit yourself. When you're sure of your plans, call me."

"Will do. Love you."

"Love you too."

For a split second, Terrie's train of thought had derailed. What she'd been doing when her aunt called slipped her mind until she spotted the tablet on the arm of the sofa. Moving a finger across the pad to get her email to come up, she skimmed the remaining messages. She deleted the junk before logging out and was about to close her browser when she saw a byline story from WGME about the dig on Badger Island. She ignored the embedded video, preferring instead to read the article.

> **Construction Site at Badger Island Declared Archeological Dig**
>
> PORTSMOUTH, N.H. (WGME) – What started out as a run-of-the-mill renovation project on Badger Island turned into a major archeological find. The new condominium project that broke ground earlier this week is now on hold pending evaluation from an unusual source: the US Navy.
>
> Project foreman R. J. Clendaniel did not comment on why his company agreed to allow the Navy to oversee their efforts, but their presence at the site was declared "routine" by the Navy's representative, Lieutenant Terrie Murphy.
>
> "Since the USS *Raleigh* was built here and the ship is on New Hampshire's state flag, it shouldn't be a surprise that the Navy would send someone to observe and, where appropriate, preserve that history," said Murphy.
>
> Federal law would seem to back up Murphy's assertion.

Swanson's watered down coverage amused Terrie. Even though Swanson did her best to cover the Pederson firing from an agenda-driven perspective, the fledgling reporter's story was remarkably fair.

As she was rereading the article's last sentence, the headbanger music gave way to a dull rhythmic thumping. Apparently, the iron-horse desperado had a taste for club music. More attuned to the balladeers of the seventies, this ear-splitting noise was not on Terrie's personal Top 100.

She'd had enough and decided to address the problem at its source. She knocked on the door of the apartment but received no response. Fed up, she pounded on it with the heel of her hand. The door flew open, and a toned, unremarkable-looking young man in his midtwenties stood before her. He had a firmly muscled frame, sandy brown hair, and pale-green eyes.

The two neighbors held each other's gaze for a long second before he broke the silence. "Yeah? What do you want?"

"The ability to think inside my own apartment would be a good start."

"Come again?"

"Could you bring down the volume of that music to one on the Richter scale? Please?"

"Nobody ever complained before."

"Then consider this your first one."

Incensed, the young man slammed the door in her face. She waited, but the volume only increased.

Terrie nodded. *Okay, if that's the way you want to play.*

She disappeared into her apartment, rummaged through a drawer, and returned to her would-be antagonist with a little gift in hand. She pounded on the door until it he answered it.

"What?" he yelled as he yanked the door open.

"Here, try these!" She threw a set of used airline headphones in his face and turned to head back to her apartment.

Stunned, he yelled, "Hey, lady!" He went after her, but made the mistake of seizing her by the shoulder.

Terrie reached up and grabbed the young man's thumb. She twisted around, rotating his hand backward in an unnatural position, forcing him to his knees.

"I would advise you never to attempt anything like that again," she hissed.

"Yeah, whatever. Let go of me!"

With a confident smirk, she added, "Touch me like that again and I won't stop at just one turn of that thumb, got it?" Tossing his hand back in his face, she let loose her captive and disappeared into her apartment.

The young man gingerly got up from the hallway floor, cradled his sore hand, and retreated into his apartment. Seconds later, the thumping ceased.

⚓

The last remnant of twilight had given way to evening by the time she sat down to eat. She grilled the seasoned pieces of chicken breast and placed them on the bed of salad she prepared earlier. Still perturbed over her unsavory encounter, she tried to concentrate on the flavor and aroma of the meal instead. The dry chardonnay was the perfect complement to the moist texture of the chicken. Terrie finished her dinner as she considered how successful she was conveying her personal noise threshold to her new friend and the resulting consequences that would ensue should he choose to exceed them again.

Despite this amusing thought, she knew the remainder of the evening was a bust. Terrie's ability to concentrate on her reading suffered most this time of the day. In the proper state of mind, she could dissect raw data and assemble it into a logical hypothesis. One that could stand up to the most rigid scrutiny.

With all the day's distractions, she decided the secrets of that battered journal in the yellow gym bag would have to wait until morning to be explored.

ELEVEN

Saturday morning's sunlight pierced through a slight opening in the curtains of Terrie's corner apartment. Its bright rays slowly moved across the room to her face, providing a silent, but persuasive, inducement to rise from her slumber. She was not in the habit of sleeping anywhere except her bed, but she found herself on the sofa.

Terrie raked her fingers through her short hair, trying to wake up. She could accomplish nothing without her first cup of tea and toasted English muffins with a thin layer of raspberry preserves. She quickly downed them, an annoying habit she picked up at the academy, where trainees were given a mere twenty minutes for each meal. She learned to eat during the allotted time or go hungry. For a horrifying second, she thought how nauseating it would be to devour her food like that in front of a prospective suitor. But then again, it had been so long since she'd been on a date that she'd forgotten what it felt like.

With the last morsel of raspberry-covered muffin clenched between her teeth, she threw open the curtains and let in the full might of the sun's warmth. The gym bag, now bathed in that light, was the next item to receive her attention. It held earlier clues Terrie wished she still had at her disposal. Clues that were currently in Crabtree's hands.

She wasn't enterprising enough to examine them ahead of time and was kicking herself for it now. Determined never to make that mistake again, she grabbed the bag from the table and retrieved yesterday's discovery from its hiding place to commit its contents to memory.

Terrie sat down in her easy chair with a hot cup of berry-flavor green tea in one hand and the old log in the other. Taking a quick sip of her tea, she examined the book's exterior. A case-bound, dark leather tome and typical for a ship's log of the day, it was a thick volume nearly filled with entries. The preponderance of the writing was in a graceful, flowing hand. The cursive letters were formed by a pen that was gently pulled from the right in a standard forward-slash direction. But toward the end, she noticed how the handwriting was distinctly sharp, heavy and pushed from the left. Its harsh letters leaned in the direction of a backslash. Clearly there were two authors—one graceful and right-handed, one gauche and left-handed.

The discolored pages could not disguise the legibility of the entries, which were, in most cases, no longer than a quick sentence or two. The authors were like Terrie, not given to flights of lengthy allegory.

She returned to the title page, which identified the log as belonging to a ship and a captain she had read so much about.

American Merchant Ship Justice
Capt. A. Ledbetter
1780 — 1789

She recalled the vessel as described in her reading: a square-rigged, three-masted carrier modified with a formidable mix of nine-pound cannons and four-pound swivel guns mounted on each corner of the ship. She recalled the proud history of the *Justice* and her gallant, but modest, captain. But the most striking thing she recalled was that both the ship and her captain mysteriously disappeared.

Arthur Ledbetter became a merchant marine at age sixteen and served under General Edward Hand during the revolution. Ledbetter piloted the craft that carried Hand across the Delaware in 1776. His final commission came from the Confederation Congress in 1785 and the last reported sighting of Ledbetter and the *Justice* was near Cadiz in April of 1788, by a Dutch East India Company vessel.

Terrie hoped the answer to the ship's fate was contained in the log she now held in her hands. She leafed through the pages to get an idea of the complexity of the entries. The log began in January of 1780, but abruptly ended in June of 1788, with the remaining pages left blank. Something must have gone terribly wrong if the entries stopped before they were expected to. Her cursory evaluation done, Terrie warmed up her tea and started a detailed examination of the entries.

Ledbetter documented day trips between Maryland's eastern shore and Annapolis. They were reminiscent of a coaster, the smaller vessels used to shuttle cargo between the islands or the colonies. The captain even commented on how schooners with shallow hulls would have been better suited for this kind of duty. It was all quite routine.

As the *Justice* was more like a galleon with a hull deeper than most, she could withstand the pounding of the open ocean. With greater firepower than most merchant vessels of her class, the *Justice* took on whatever contract she was paid to accomplish, and by the end of 1783, it appeared she was making it as far as the Mediterranean.

Terrie flipped through the early pages of one-liners until she came across an in-depth entry detailing a strange commission the captain received. One that didn't involve cargo, but escort duty.

Writing in his log on June 1, 1781, Captain Ledbetter stated that he was to provide safe passage for a special envoy to the *Congress*, under the command of Captain George Geddes. He was to rendezvous with the *Congress* near the waters of the West Indies.

On his return, the *Justice* ran afoul of a corsair raising the Jolly Roger. Ledbetter ordered his ship to engage the vessel and the ensuing contest raged for over an hour. Unable to endure the relentless firepower of the *Justice*, the rogue ship attempted to escape. One final barrage from the long nines decided the issue in favor of Ledbetter and the *Justice*.

It was the longest entry of the right-handed captain for many pages. With most of the entries becoming more blasé, Terrie thumbed through the pages until she came across another lengthy entry written by the first captain.

> 12th December, 1785
> Received a sealed commission from the Confederation Congress by special courier this morning. We are to arrive at the port of New York by the 28th instant and await the arrival of our handpicked first mate. As this person is unfamiliar to me, I cannot say I'm looking forward to this new mission with any enthusiasm. ~ L

Intrigued, Terrie searched for an explanation why the Congress would handpick this first mate. Ledbetter never addressed it.

Neither did the left-handed captain. A captain who, for every entry save one, affixed his initial in the manner of his predecessor. Despite the jarring difference in writing style and prose, this new captain's brevity was yet another nod to the man he succeeded.

The last log entry was June 21, 1788, the very day this new captain sailed into Portsmouth. Reading that last entry, something hit Terrie as strange: this new captain never made any references to the *Justice*. She reread all the left-handed entries to be sure. She found an obscure reference to something, but it wasn't the *Justice*. Named the DOR, it didn't sound like the name of a vessel. After this particular entry, the captain penned his complete surname. He called himself, Tunney.

Terrie couldn't believe it. The log entries left her with more questions than answers. Questions like why this Tunney never relayed how he inherited this log; what fate befell Ledbetter and his ship; and how the *Justice's* log came to be buried on Badger Island. Did Tunney have something to do with their disappearance? No answers were forthcoming in the log.

With a degree of frustration, she remembered the lost opportunity in the other artifacts she'd handed over to Crabtree. If only she still had them to examine.

The day receded into late afternoon. With little else to go on, she decided to take in a run to consider all the artifacts discovered so far: a piece of broken bowsprit, rigging rope, the log to a missing ship, a thin stone wall with circular holes on top, ship stocks with no evidence that a keel was ever laid, and all discovered over the location of an alleged intelligence office.

Since there was no evidence to prove the existence of such an office, she wondered why her CO would waste Navy resources on so hapless an errand. There had to be a reason why the government was interested in this plot of land.

Rounding Route 1B with Prescott Park in her sights, she thought the upcoming Memorial Day weekend would be better suited for her trip to Delaware. Two days travel time and one day to visit. Perfect. Making her way into her apartment, she thought she'd better call her aunt, just in case she had plans for that particular weekend.

Barbara must have read the caller ID. "Well, two times in one week. I hope this becomes a new trend for you."

"It's not normal of me, I know."

"What's going on? New boyfriend I hope?"

"No, not a boyfriend," Terrie said, not wishing to start an argument.

"Something about work, then?"

"You could say that."

"Thought so."

"I may not be able to stop by next weekend."

Hearing something strange in her niece's voice, Barbara played a hunch. "Then you did meet someone."

Terrie thought about Sheffield and Clendaniel, the only two people who engaged her in friendly conversation, and how she repaid their kindness—with distance. Sheffield was more like a grandfather than a beau. Clendaniel, the likelier of the two, was still too old for her taste.

Barbara took Terrie's silence as an admission. "Tell me about him, or is it a state secret?"

"He's nowhere close to a boyfriend, but he was a Marylander originally."

"A promising start. I was beginning to wonder if anything Marg—" The wound would always be fresh and painful, so Barbara shut down that line of thought. "I'm sorry, Terrie." After another uncomfortable pause, she continued. "Do you see him often?"

"Every day last week."

"Then I gather this relationship is not work related?"

"It's not a relationship, and it *is* work related."

"No need to get snippy. Is he a descent sort?"

"He's more like a father figure."

"A father figure wouldn't keep you from picking up your books next weekend."

"And what's a father figure supposed to be to me now?"

"Sorry, Terrie, but you really need to get past the life's-not-fair stage. Life isn't fair. It's not required to be."

The oft quoted aphorism and her aunt's tone while saying it softened Terrie's response. "I know."

"You must focus on the future, not the past. The way you're talking about this man sounds like you need him in your life somehow."

Barbara's affirmation was met with silence.

"In any event, you do need to get out and forge some friendships."

As Terrie gave her aunt's suggestion a passing thought, an idea popped into her head. Something she could query Clendaniel about. Something even her aunt might know.

Terrie remembered the first time she went to her Aunt Barbara's house as a young girl. Like most homes in the area, it was common to have a nautical themed exterior. Terrie always thought her aunt took it to the extreme, with all manner of cross-stitches and models of full-rigged ships all over the house. Aunt Barbara had an affinity for tall ships. One image that settled clearly in her mind was the full-rigged vessel centered above the fireplace surrounded by books. It was an accurate replica of the USS *Constellation*, one of six ships ordered built in 1794 for the fledgling United States.

"Hey, do you still have that old textbook on the carrier ships of the Chesapeake?" Terrie asked.

"Not sure if I know exactly where it is right now, but I can look."

"Can you recall anything from it?"

"Possibly. Like what, for instance?"

"Does the name Ledbetter mean anything to you?"

Barbara paused before she responded. "Wasn't he the captain of the first privateer vessel engaged by the federal government at the end of the Revolutionary War?"

"Yeah, that's him."

"It seems I recall that they retained his ship because it was so well-armed."

"That's the book I'll need, if you can find it."

"Didn't he disappear in the late 1780s off the coast of Africa?" There was no confirmation from Terrie one way or the other, so Barbara left it there.

"I'll see you in a few weeks. Love you."

"Okay," her aunt offered in a noncommittal way, "Love you, too."

Terrie stopped to reflect on how abruptly she ended the conversation with her aunt. She was rude and she knew it. She must remember to apologize to her next time.

Grabbing the log from the sofa, she attempted to put it back into the gym bag when a sharp object pricked at her finger. Pulling out her hand, she found and removed an offending splinter. Uncertain what might have caused it, Terrie turned the bag upside down and gave it a good shake. A sliver of wood bounced onto the table, a twisted piece of twine caught on its sharp, uneven surface.

Terrie couldn't believe her good luck. She now had evidence the Newport lab could identify. But what would the analysis of these objects tell her?

In light of Crabtree's secretive nature, she was keen to find out.

TWELVE

Clendaniel glanced at his watch for the third time in fifteen minutes. Ever a stickler for punctuality, his expectations for keeping to the schedule bordered on choleric. His temporary partner in crime was late, an inauspicious beginning to his week.

The foreman eased into his comfort level once a project was underway, especially when the crew settled into a productive rhythm. But productivity on this project was hampered from the beginning. And his temporary co-foreman's absence only added to his growing irritability.

Celio emerged from the trailer with two Styrofoam cups of coffee and handed one to Clendaniel. "What's the story, R. J.?"

Clendaniel gave his watch another peek. "Waiting."

"For what?"

"Our government overseer, who else?"

"I knew that already, but that can't be why you're pacing like an expectant father."

"Something appears to be amiss with our intrepid lieutenant."

"What makes you say that?"

Before he could respond, Terrie's vehicle pulled into the restaurant parking lot across the street. She grabbed her yellow bag out of the trunk and strolled over to where the two men were standing.

"Running a little behind today, Lieutenant?"

"Unlike you, Mr. Clendaniel, I'm on duty 24-7. I don't have the luxury of clocking in or punching out."

"Then I'll rephrase. You were on time all last week, so naturally I assumed something happened to you."

Ignoring the two men, Terrie made a quick survey of the site to evaluate how much time she would need to accomplish her task. Satisfied there was little left for her to do, she turned her attention to the foreman. "Can we talk in your office?"

"Sure."

She glanced at Celio. "Privately?"

Clendaniel turned to Celio. "Have the crew get started on clearing the northeast corner. I'll be with you in a moment."

Celio's contorted expression underscored the contempt he reserved for his unwelcome boss.

The foreman's patience wearing thinner by the moment, he escorted Terrie into the trailer to get this impromptu conference over with. "Okay, Lieutenant, why all the mystery?"

"I've been given new instructions and want you to confer with your home office."

"You never worried about them before, so why do you care now?"

"Just do it. I'll be outside."

"I thought we'd gotten past the antagonism stage."

Terrie answered with a deadpan stare.

"As you wish."

She removed a digital camera from her bag and departed the trailer to accomplish her task.

Celio, Chris Iarossi, and Devon Taylor watched as she climbed into the dig site and began snapping pictures as though it were a crime scene.

After spending an inordinate amount of time shooting the wall and the stocks from every possible angle, she stood back and surveyed the site. She spotted the exposed portion of a high-reach basket from behind Clendaniel's trailer.

"Mr. Esteban, could you take me up in that? I want to shoot the entire area."

Celio grabbed an extra safety harness for Terrie. "You'll have to put this on before we can take you up." After he demonstrated how to don the harness, Terrie strapped it on and climbed into the basket with Celio. "Where do you want it?" he asked.

"Let's start over there," she suggested, pointing toward the bridge side of the excavation. Celio obediently complied with Terrie's direction, moving the high-reach four times to make sure she captured the site from various angles. Clendaniel emerged from his trailer as Terrie snapped her last few shots.

Celio lowered the bucket to let Terrie out. She packed away her camera and approached Clendaniel. "It looks like they'll finish up soon, am I right?"

"If they keep going like they are, very likely this afternoon."

"Did you contact your home office?"

"Yes."

"Do you have any questions?"

"Just one."

Terrie cocked her head in response.

"Why the sudden lack of interest in removing the larger finds?" he queried with genuine curiosity.

"What makes you think that?"

"You only removed the smaller items, not the larger ones. A true archeologist would have stopped all progress on the jobsite for a find such as that, but you didn't. In fact, your reaction to my question only adds to my suspicion that you're not the military archeologist I gave you credit for. Why is that?"

"Expediency, Mr. Clendaniel. It's enough to know they are there and to catalogue them accordingly. We only need to document their location for the record."

"What about the new condo? I don't think the owner would be too pleased if they had to tear it down just to get at something you already knew was there."

"I'm only authorized to tell you that won't happen."

Skeptical, Clendaniel just shook his head.

"As they're nearly done, I should be out of your hair by this afternoon. Will that satisfy you?"

The foreman responded with a silent nod and went about his business.

Terrie jotted down some last-minute notes over her map before she folded the notebook and stood up. For the remainder of the morning, she positioned herself at the edge of the dig with her hands clasped behind her back. Her stern face stared across the water at nothing in particular.

A few minutes before noon and curious that she hadn't moved in over an hour, a concerned Clendaniel approached Terrie. "What's the matter, Lieutenant?"

Her voice was icy when she uttered, "Nothing."

"You sure you're all right?"

She ignored his query and turned to pack up her gear.

Ever the fixer, Clendaniel wasn't about to part from his week-long co-foreman under these terms. "You know," he began, "We should be wrapped up with your part of the project this afternoon?"

Terrie stopped her packing long enough to look at him. "In that case, we should do a final walk-around after lunch to make sure all is in order before I leave."

"That's a great idea," he said, "In fact, why don't you join me?"

The question took her by complete surprise. "For lunch? I really don't—"

"Oh, come now, Lieutenant. If this is your last time with us, what've you got to lose?"

She raised an eyebrow. "All right."

"Seafood or pizza?"

"Your choice."

"The place across the way there serves a tasty pie."

"Fine."

"What do you want on it?"

"Does it matter?"

"I prefer their pepperoni and garlic myself."

"Sounds good." With the rapid back and forth between her and Clendaniel just now, she began to hear Aunt Barbara's voice resonate in her head about opening up to new people. As they made their way to the restaurant, she gave in to her aunt's concerns and initiated a purely social conversation. "You married, Mr. Clendaniel?"

"You're asking me a personal question, Lieutenant?"

"Enjoy it while it lasts."

He had to smile at that. "Twice, but it didn't take in either instance. The first time was for three months, and the second ended after fourteen. You?"

"No."

"Engaged then."

"No."

"You have to have a boyfriend."

"My father died a month after I was born. He was the only male connection in my life, Mr. Clendaniel."

"Then I don't get it. Where do you get your extraordinary inner strength?"

Terrie didn't answer.

They entered the restaurant, found a table, and ordered. Sitting opposite from one another, Terrie couldn't ignore Clendaniel any longer.

"You strike me as a doting father, Mr. Clendaniel. Do you have children?"

"One. She was the reason for the first marriage, but her mom took her and left. I haven't seen them since." He cupped his hands around his glass of water. "She would be about your age now."

Terrie gave him a smile.

"I'd rather like to think she turned out like you, Lieutenant."

"Why would you want her to be like me?"

"You have so much going for you and at such a young age. All I can tell you is, if you were my daughter, I'd be very proud."

Terrie started to feel comfortable enough to probe further. "May I make a personal observation?"

"Shoot."

"I see how your men look up to you. You're the crew patriarch. You take care of and defend them." She dropped her gaze and smiled. "Even Mr. Pederson."

"He comes back after you leave, you know."

"I really don't care." That's all it took to lighten the mood. The two shared a hearty laugh.

"Lieutenant," he began, but quickly changed his demeanor and address. "Terrie?"

Hearing her name spoken by a male voice with such genuine tenderness, she actually blushed as she looked at him. "Yes?"

"I just wanted to say, in spite of everything, I'm going to miss seeing you here every day."

"It's a small town, Mr. Clendaniel. Anything's possible."

Devon Taylor's crew cleared out the last of the earth from around the northwest corner of the dig. Chris Iarossi's team worked to remove what little equipment and debris remained. Satisfied with the completed excavation, Celio turned to find Clendaniel. He ran into Terrie instead.

"I believe you'll find him in the trailer, Mr. Esteban."

"Well, we're done, if you care to inspect it."

"I would, thank you." With gym bag and camera in hand, Terrie descended the ladder into the thinly walled sarcophagus containing its exposed wooden skeleton. She methodically scrutinized the entire excavation. The area's consistency of dirt, rock, and color were all indications that there was nothing man-made left to discover.

She climbed out of the hole, brushed the dirt off her utility pants, and looked up to see the foreman standing before her.

"What do you think, Lieutenant?"

"I think my unwelcome intrusion has come to an end, Mr. Clendaniel."

"Unexpected, yes. But unwelcome?"

Terrie raised an eyebrow.

All R. J. Clendaniel could do was nod with a smile.

She returned it, excusing herself to make her obligatory phone call. Sheffield informed Terrie her appointment was for five that afternoon.

Terrie was fifteen minutes early to Crabtree's office, waiting to detail her final report on Badger Island.

The senior chief with the friendly disposition looked up from his work to see her. "Well, Lieutenant, how goes your assignment?"

"I don't know."

"Too difficult a question?"

"I haven't really started yet, have I?"

A smirk appeared on the old man's face. "Can't wait to occupy your duties here, is that it?"

"Nailed it in one, Senior Chief."

Sheffield bristled at the use of his rank and got up to file the stack of reports residing in his outbox.

"I take it the commander isn't in?"

"He should be arriving shortly. He had a quick meeting with Captain Derrick."

"Does he have these unscheduled meetings often?"

"Who said anything about them being unscheduled?"

"Since he made this appointment, it stands to reason he wouldn't purposefully schedule a conflicting one with the captain, now does it?"

"I'm not sure what's been going on lately, but I can assure you these odd meetings are atypical of the commander."

"I'll get over it," Terrie responded.

From behind her, Terrie heard Bannerman's alto voice chime in. "Ray, I have that SITREP the commander was looking for."

"Thank you, Commander. He hasn't returned from his meeting with the captain."

"I'll wait." Taking a seat, she took notice of Terrie. "Miss Murphy."

"Commander."

"Will we see you at standup tomorrow?"

"I wasn't aware my attendance was required."

"If you've finished with your detail it is."

"Of course, Commander."

Bannerman sported a veiled smile as acknowledgment.

Sheffield couldn't help but observe the tension between them. Before he could turn his attention to his next task, Crabtree called to inform Sheffield he was on his way.

Minutes after Sheffield hung up, Brooks Crabtree thundered into the room. "Commander, I'll be with you in ten. Ray, make sure my travel orders are ready for pick up first thing tomorrow. Miss Murphy, you're with me."

"What ord—"

"Check your email, Ray."

"Aye aye, sir."

Terrie followed him into his office, leaving a puzzled Molly Bannerman to evaluate what had just happened. Terrie watched her CO round his desk while she waited for him to give her permission to either stand at ease or take a seat. He opted for the latter.

"I don't have much time, so give me the *Reader's Digest* version," Crabtree stated in a directive tone while rifling through his desk for something.

"The Badger Island mission is complete, sir."

He froze. "Say again?"

"The excavation is complete, sir. My findings are detailed in this summary."

Still not moving, he stared at her as if she were speaking in Farsi.

"With the exception of the wall and the stocks we left behind, I recovered all there was to recover from the site. There was no office, secret or otherwise. Sir."

"That's disappointing," he said, resuming his frantic actions in gathering the documents he needed for his trip.

Terrie thrust the gym bag onto his desk. "Sir, per your instructions I've taken all the digital photos of the area in the manner you prescribed. And with the exception of one other artifact you may find illuminating, there was nothing else."

"What artifact?"

"A ship's log to a vessel called *Justice*."

Again, she caught the slightest hesitation in his actions, which betrayed his interest—an interest he hadn't expressed since he examined that strange rosy crimson triangle. He was hiding something.

"Was that all, Miss Murphy?"

"Yes, sir, that's all."

"Very well." He shoved the last document into his attaché case before looking at Terrie. "Report here tomorrow morning for duty."

"Aye aye, sir."

As Terrie departed the CO's office, Bannerman entered. She stood watching Crabtree retrieve a garment bag containing his service uniform. Her curiosity still piqued, Crabtree's second wasted no time reporting in. "Yes, sir?"

"Commander, there's something I want you to do for me while I'm out. I'd attend to it myself, but I won't be here."

"I'll try, sir. What is it?"

"It pertains to team harmony."

Bannerman frowned at the prospect.

THIRTEEN

Terrie opened the door to the conference room and found her seat. It was austere, but functional. Like every other office space on the Yard, the Intel Conference Room was small, but spacious enough to accommodate its personnel and maybe a VIP or two.

The nine-by-twelve-foot room housed a rectangular hardwood table surrounded by low-back leather chairs with a single high-back version reserved for the commander. The gold curtain covered a white screen used for briefings. One door situated at the end of a long wall provided the only access to the room.

Terrie sat quietly in her assigned seat. From her vantage point, she could see everyone. The gold curtain and the head chair typically occupied by Commander Crabtree were at the opposite end of the table.

This day was a long time coming. Terrie would finally have the opportunity to direct the full might of her country's intelligence arm against those who deprived her of her sister.

She watched as Sheffield set an updated dossier, the commander's SITREP briefing, and a bottle of water at each analyst's place.

"Good morning, Senior Chief," she said as he approached.

"Ray, please, Lieutenant."

"What's wrong with your proper term of address?"

"I've found it easier on the analysts if I keep my interaction informal. You have to deal with too many formalities as it is."

"Professionalism is not a formality, Senior Chief."

"Right." He scanned the room. "I'm sorry, Lieutenant, but I haven't unpacked your mug yet."

"My mug?"

"The commander gets them for all of his team members."

He ducked into Crabtree's office for a second and returned with the ceramic souvenir. It was a simple, ten-ounce diner-style mug with a Naval Intelligence patch that contained the phrase "In God We Trust…All Others We Monitor." Directly below the patch was Terrie's name and rank. She saw the flaw straightaway.

"I'm not a full lieutenant yet."

"Sorry, Lieutenant. It's not my place to say."

Terrie knew her promotion was forthcoming, but she figured it wasn't until the end of the following month. She spotted a new mug in Jack O'Hara's place as well. "I assume I'm not the only one being promoted today?"

"Mr. O'Hara was going to be frocked last week, but he was on vacation."

Taking her new gift, she filled it with hot water from the dispenser and grabbed a bag of berry-flavored tea from her purse. Dipping the bag several times to obtain its full strength, she looked up to see Bannerman and one of the other analysts enter the room together.

"Good morning, Miss Murphy. Nice to see you again," said Taro.

Terrie responded politely. In acknowledging her fellow analyst, she noticed how imposing a figure Bannerman truly was.

"Ray, Mr. O'Hara will not be joining us again this morning. He's at sick call," said Bannerman.

"Should we reschedule his frocking again?"

"That won't be necessary. We'll do it when he gets back." She regarded the dossier in front of her before acknowledging Terrie's existence. "Miss Murphy."

"Commander." Terrie took her seat to peruse her own black folder. But rather than Intel reports on her AOR, she was given a day's worth of computer-based training to accomplish. *Nice*, she thought, wondering when she would begin the task she joined the Navy to do. "Commander, do we have an NCIS lab on the installation?"

"The Northeast Field Office at Newport, Rhode Island provides whatever forensic support we need. Why do you ask?"

"Just curious."

Silence descended on the room as Bannerman shook her head. Her previous team included her closest friend, Lieutenant Commander Laurie Montgomery. The two were inseparable at the academy. Outward appearances aside, their personalities were twin-like. They were able to complete each other's thoughts. This symbiosis was the driving force behind the team's synergy. It caught the attention of their former commanding officer, Captain Connie Stimson. The former Intel CO was astonished at how her two junior officers were able to interpret data points and return actionable intelligence. Now retired, Stimson had taken a position as a book writer for the CIA and appointed special liaison to the Joint Chiefs of Staff and the SECDEF.

One of Stimson's last duties as Intel CO was to recommend both Bannerman's and Montgomery's advancement. Promoted out of a job, Montgomery transferred to a forward operating base in the Near East. In order to prep for her task, she left for the Pentagon prior to her reassignment. It was a sudden transfer, leaving Bannerman alone and without her closest friend. The two of them were like Xena and Gabrielle, a mutually beneficial friendship that even geography couldn't erode. She may have kept in contact with Montgomery, but the change in office dynamic was disconcerting to Bannerman, who now had to adjust to this new person who outwardly reminded her of her friend. Perhaps that was what she disliked about Terrie the most.

Theo's deep voice was heard even through the closed door. Judging from the tone of the conversation, Crabtree was with him. When the door opened, Bannerman called the room to attention.

"As you were," Crabtree said, taking his traditional spot at the head of the conference table while Theo found his seat. "Captain Derrick has asked me to be part of a joint intelligence confab at the Pentagon, so I'll be leaving this afternoon." He glanced about the table. "Where's our other promotee this morning?"

"Mr. O'Hara is at sick call, sir," Sheffield volunteered.

"What happened?"

"Apparently he injured his arm."

Visibly rankled, the CO looked directly at Bannerman. "Is there a need for me to revisit our safety briefing from last month?"

"Negative, sir."

He softened his eyes. "Before we get started, I would like to formally welcome our latest addition to the team, Lieutenant Terrie Murphy."

Terrie looked around the room, acknowledging her teammates with the dip of her head.

"I wanted to do this with both of you present, but no matter." Crabtree stood up. "Ray, Commander, if you would care to assist?"

With that, Bannerman took position on Terrie's left as the commander stood on her right. Sheffield stood patiently behind the commander, proffer pillow in hand.

"Attention to orders." The assembled members stood at attention. "Pursuant to RIAC approval and in accordance with PERS-92 directives, you are hereby authorized the wear of the rank of full lieutenant until such time as your actual promotion is official. Congratulations, Lieutenant Murphy."

After a brief display of adulation, the team members took their seats. "I'll be out of the office this week, so Commander Bannerman has the conn until my return. Commander, they're all yours." He nodded to his second and departed the conference room.

Bannerman's meetings tended to take much less time. She was more interested in getting down to business. With the Boston Marathon bombing still fresh on everyone's mind, no one was in the mood for idle banter. Crabtree's second made sure everyone had what they needed and, with no further questions, adjourned the meeting.

Sheffield sidled up to Bannerman before they left the conference room. "Commander, I have to make my distribution run and stop to pick up some office supplies. Is there anything you need while I'm out?"

"No, thank you, Ray."

"I'll be back in an hour or so, Commander."

Bannerman followed the rest of the team as they made their way down the narrow hallway to the Ops Center. She observed her team members as they went about their responsibilities.

Taro got to work reviewing his intelligence summary as he nonchalantly queried Theo about his time off. "I suppose you lived in front of your fifty-inch flat screen watching the Final Four this weekend."

"I told you Michigan would make it to the finals."

"You think so?"

"At least my season isn't over yet." Theo's smug response delivered, he started clacking away on his keyboard. Taro shook his head, smirked and got to work.

Terrie took to her computer-based training. Her back was to Bannerman's control chair and away from the other analysts around the room.

The Ops Center settled into its routine as everyone was engrossed in their work. From time to time, Bannerman would glance at Terrie and think about how Laurie Montgomery had once been seated in that very chair. Now, Montgomery's imposter had assumed her station, and the other newcomer would soon take Bannerman's old position. She brushed aside a flush of anger and returned to her duties. With any luck, this feeling about Terrie would go away in time.

Taro looked up from his station and noticed the local time on the digital clock. It was nearly lunchtime, and Jack still hadn't made it back from sick call. "Hey, Theo."

"Yeah?"

"I'm thinking Thai for lunch."

"Not that hot green shit again?"

"No, the yellow curry this time. It's mild enough."

"I'll try it, but if I burn my mouth again, it's your ass!"

Taro called out to their newest teammate. "Miss Murphy, care to join us?"

"I brought," she responded without turning around.

"Suit yourself." Taro asked Bannerman, but she also brought her own lunch. "Commander, do you know if Jack will be back soon?"

"I'm not sure, Taro. From what I understand, he did a good job of hurting his arm, so he might not make it in today."

Theo's face still buried in his monitor, he asked, "Where are you going for it?"

"The Thai place in Kittery. It tastes better."

Unable to concentrate, Terrie put on her headphones.

"I see Her Highness is too good to socialize with the rest of the team," Theo teased.

Bannerman raised an eyebrow at him, but Theo never saw it. As Terrie never heard the remark, the commander never addressed it.

Terrie finished the last of her modules and removed her headphones. Setting them aside, she heard the familiar buzzing of the security door, heralding the arrival of Taro clutching several plastic bags of delicious-smelling Thai curry. And he wasn't alone. He was engaged in casual conversation with another person whose voice was disturbingly familiar.

She turned in the direction of the voice and instantly recognized her neighbor in the uniformed man before her. It was Jack O'Hara.

FOURTEEN

Accessing his secure email, Philip found the promised message from the SV address. He grabbed a fresh cup of coffee and took a sip as he clicked on it to find out what his latest instructions were. To his disappointment, the message contained only two questions.

Reviewing the first one, he answered it with a single word: "No." His eyes whisked across the screen, taking in the second, to which his response was another single word: "Yes."

Frustrated, he closed his email account, logged out, and shut down the tablet. He was hoping his contact would be more forthright about his next move, besides keeping a watchful eye on the diminutive lieutenant.

He opened the curtain with a sweeping motion of one hand while balancing his coffee in the other. Downing the invigorating liquid, he contemplated the latest queries from Runner's representative.

The first question was, "Did she find them?" The second, "Is your Portsmouth contact going to do as directed?"

FIFTEEN

"You!"

Taro, Theo, and Bannerman followed the newcomer's wild-eyed stare to the newly frocked female lieutenant as she sat at her station.

Breathe, Terrie. Breathe, she thought. The fates seemed to be rewarding her with the wrath of the universe. As all eyes trained on her, Terrie allowed one corner of her mouth to curl up into a distinctive smirk. She crossed her legs and folded her arms in a display of superiority.

Jack's anger erupted when he saw her new rank.

"And a full lieutenant!" Jack O'Hara turned to Bannerman to vent his rage. "Who the hell is this?"

"Miss Murphy is our new analyst."

Noting she occupied the station next to his, he screamed, "I'm not working anywhere near her!"

"Why not?" Bannerman asked.

"This is the bitch who assaulted me!"

Taro and Theo just looked at each other in bewilderment.

Terrie softened her gaze. "A defensive response after you assaulted me. Oh, and my proper term of address is Lieutenant Murphy."

"I didn't assault you."

"According to the UCMJ you did."

"What are you talking about? All I did was touch your shoulder."

"And that action is all that's required to complete the offense."

"Prove it!"

As if reciting directly from the Manual for Courts-Martial, she stated, "Article 128 of the Uniformed Code of Military Justice: '*any person subject to this chapter who attempts or offers to attempt to do bodily harm to another person, whether or not the attempt or offer is consummated, is guilty of assault.*'"

"I only touched you! You're not the one whose arm's in a sling!"

"Your action initiated the confrontation and created a, quote, reasonable apprehension of receiving immediate bodily harm, unquote. Your intent has no bearing on the commission of the offense."

"Who the hell is this walking legal dictionary?" Jack asked no one in particular.

"Your worst nightmare if you keep it up," said Taro, organizing his plate of curry on the small table at the center of the semicircle.

"Jack, watch out for the ice queen," Theo said before he took a whiff of his spicy dish to judge its heat.

"It would be interesting to question your previous conquests, Mr. Theodore," Terrie countered.

"What for? So you can embarrass yourself when you find out they measured their pleasure in triple digits?"

"Only in degrees Kelvin, Mr. Theodore. And at the lowest end of the scale."

"You are addressing a superior officer, Miss Murphy."

Terrie turned toward Theo, eyes focused hard on her intended recipient. "You fired first, Mr. Theodore. It would be impolite not to respond in kind."

"So long as you remember who the senior member is in this scenario, Miss Murphy."

"And you remember the old adage regarding the predictable movement of excrement over a steep incline."

"Excuse me?"

"You have a boss too. You would do well to remember that."

The buzzing at the security door escaped everyone's attention as the commander tried to restore a sense of decorum. "That'll be quite enough. If you gentlemen are going to eat, you'd best do it. Quietly."

Attempting to reengage with Terrie, Jack piped up again. "You injured a commissioned officer…Miss Murphy. Certainly there's a charge for that in the UCMJ, isn't there?"

"Only if the alleged assailant knew the victim was a commissioned officer prior to the assault. And if you're opting for round two, I'd advise against it."

"So would I," said a firm and unfamiliar voice of authority.

Taken by surprise, Bannerman recognized her immediately. "Captain on deck." All rose to their feet.

"As you were," Captain Derrick said. She clasped her hands behind her back, rewarding Bannerman's acknowledgement with a hard look.

"Captain?"

Derrick was cordial but direct. "Introduce me to your new personnel, Commander."

"Yes, ma'am." Bannerman turned to the uniformed young man with an arm in a sling. "This is Lieutenant Jack O'Hara. He joins us from the USS *Bainbridge*."

"Captain," said Jack in a professional manner.

Observing that his right arm was out of commission, Derrick held out her left hand in greeting. "That doesn't look too comfortable, Lieutenant O'Hara."

He glanced at Terrie for a millisecond. "It's my own fault, Captain. Won't happen again."

"Let's hope not. Unfortunate first impressions are not what we strive for, Lieutenant."

Without waiting for the formal introduction, Derrick went right over to Terrie. "And you must be the illustrious Lieutenant Terrie Murphy," she said with her hand out in greeting.

"Captain," Terrie responded, reaching for Derrick's hand.

"I normally have the pleasure of meeting my people before I see their name in the local paper, especially if they're acting as an official Navy spokeswoman from my installation."

"Miss Swanson left me no alternative, Captain."

"You handled yourself quite admirably, Lieutenant Murphy." Derrick's look of clemency held a smirk she used only on rare occasions. Bannerman had seen that particular mannerism from the captain once before and understood its ramifications. Terrie, however, did not.

"Just doing what's expected of me, Captain."

Taro and Theo were shocked at the matter-of-fact delivery of Terrie's responses to the installation commander. Theo's mouth opened a second or two before he closed it.

Derrick evaluated Terrie. The new lieutenant was an enigma, unintimidated by top brass, strangers, or physically larger people. She certainly wasn't afraid of the reporter. "Your performance is exemplary…so far." She left it at that to see if she could get a reaction out of Terrie, but the young woman wouldn't reward her probing.

Turning to Bannerman, Derrick said, "I'd like to see you in the CO's office, Commander."

"Aye aye, ma'am."

In the hallway outside of the Ops Center, Derrick asked in a stern whisper, "What was going on, Commander?"

"I'm sorry?"

"The argument between our new junior officers. Or do you come by your social naivety naturally?"

"It would appear that Miss Murphy was responsible for Mr. O'Hara's injury."

"I see." On the way in, Sheffield stood to recognize the captain's presence. The captain looked at him with deadly intent and said, "See that we're not disturbed. I'll want to see you when we're through."

"Aye aye, ma'am," Sheffield replied.

Derrick waited until they were safely inside Crabtree's office, assumed an authoritative stance behind Crabtree's desk, and began staring down a nervous Lieutenant Commander Molly Bannerman. "Riddle me this, Commander. Did I retain the correct officer when I reassigned Lieutenant Commander Montgomery?"

"Affirmative, ma'am."

"I sincerely hope so. From what I just witnessed, I'm beginning to wonder. It would be unfortunate if I were to reconsider that decision, would it not, Commander?"

"Yes, ma'am."

Derrick stared down Bannerman a moment longer. "A question, Commander?"

"Negative."

"Then please send in Senior Chief Sheffield on your way out."

She acknowledged the captain, executed an about-face, and departed the office.

Derrick walked around Crabtree's office waiting for Sheffield to come in. She heard his arrival while her back was turned. "Ray, we have another package on its way to Hanscom, correct?"

"Affirmative, ma'am."

"It occurs to me that this might be an excellent opportunity for our new junior officers to work on their team building skills. See to it."

"Aye aye, Captain."

SIXTEEN

Terrie procured the package authorization form and the keys to the government Chevy she used last week before meeting her reluctant passenger outside the turnstile. She unlocked the vehicle and assumed the driver's position, ignoring Jack completely. He slid into the passenger seat before Terrie had the chance to leave without him.

Most of the hour-long trip was quiet, until they crossed into Massachusetts. Staring out the side window, Jack attempted to engage his zip-lipped chauffeur. "You don't say much, do you?"

"Nope," Terrie replied without taking her eyes off the road.

"How did the Badger assignment go?"

"It went."

"What were you supposed to do?"

"Why do you care?"

"I knew about the new condo, but not why we were ordered there."

Anticipating his next few questions, Terrie shut him down. "Is it standard procedure for team members to brief each other on their classified assignments?"

Frowning, Jack shook his head and looked away. He spent a few moments trying to figure out how to talk to his new colleague without getting verbally slapped in the face. "Where do you call home?"

"The apartment across from you. Unfortunately."

"You know what I mean. Where do you hail from?"

"Delaware."

"I've never been."

"Lucky us."

"When does your personal war against me end?"

"When you stop talking."

Throwing in the towel for the time being, Jack remained quiet until she parked the car in the reserved GOV spot next to the Hanscom Current Ops facility. The two officers entered the building, presented their credentials, and were then escorted to the main office by a Security Forces master sergeant. Terrie and Jack presented the clerk their IDs and authorization form with Captain Derrick's signature. The clerk verified their identification before disappearing into the room behind her. A moment later, she reemerged with a nondescript legal-sized rectangular box. The only writing on it was a Hanscom address followed by the line, ATTN: Capt Derrick/Cmdr Crabtree.

Terrie and Jack signed the receipt log for the parcel, obtained the master sergeant's signature on their copy of the form, and departed with their package. Following procedure, they couldn't let the box out of their sight until it was safely returned to the Intel Office.

⚓

Seated in his black Escalade, Philip sipped coffee out of his travel mug as he observed Terrie's car enter the Terminal/Operations parking lot. His hazel eyes peered through mirrored Ray Bans as he watched the two Navy officers in service khakis enter the building. He wrote the time of their arrival in a notebook.

Less than fifteen minutes later, he saw the same officers leave the building, get into their car, and drive off. Once he logged the time in his notes, he reached into his coat pocket to retrieve a cell phone. He hit a speed dial number with a DC area code and waited for someone to answer.

Hearing someone pick up, he wasted no time getting to it. "The item is here."

"Runner needs confirmation before he can proceed. Inform your contact we need the report on the item ASAP, but no later than this Thursday."

"Got it."

"Oh, and Philip?"

"Yeah?"

"Give this your full attention." The party on the other end hung up. Apparently, phone etiquette wasn't as important as the information being passed along to either party. Philip was used to this style of abbreviated communication. He also understood the meaning of full attention. This task was his highest priority.

He punched another number on his speed dial. This time, the area code was Portsmouth, its Defense Switched Network prefix, the Navy Yard.

Terrie had already turned north on the highway and was five miles into the trip when Jack's stomach told him he needed to refuel. "Can we stop somewhere for something to eat?"

"You couldn't have brought this up when we were still at Hanscom?"

"Sorry, I'm not stuck on the food at the terminal snack bar."

"Why didn't you eat breakfast before we left?"

He favored Terrie with a sour look.

She shook her head. "What do you want?"

"Doesn't matter. A breakfast burrito, I guess."

Terrie took one of the Woburn exits to get Jack something from a fast food drive-through. In short order, they were back on I-95 headed north. Most of the ride was quiet while Jack ate his late breakfast, allowing Terrie to think. This package may be her first true involvement in providing analysis that not only would help her country, but could lead to finding those responsible for butchering her sister. She knew this particular box may not contain that first clue, but she was hopeful.

Jack burst his way into her solitary thoughts with a wagging tongue. "I'm from Medford, just south of 38 from where you stopped for my breakfast." He waited for a response from Terrie, but got none. Taking advantage of his captive audience, he pressed on. "My parents actually have a home on Badger Road. I'm the only family member who didn't become a fireman. In fact, my uncle was deployed to lower Manhattan to assist the rescue and recovery efforts on 9/11." He remained undaunted by her lack of response to his commentary. "Our family came with the first wave of Irish immigrants in the early 1800s. They were shipbuilders, mostly, but by the late 1800s, my great-great-grandfather, Seamus O'Hara, became a smoke eater, and we followed the firefighting tradition ever since."

Terrie gave no outward sign of acknowledgement or interest.

"Lieutenant?"

"What?"

"Do you think it's possible that we could start over?"

Her aunt's admonition involuntarily came into her head. Advice she refused to take, since it ran counter to her current goals. *Nothing injures the soul greater than holding a grudge.* A grudge against her enemies she would never forgive, but was Jack really the enemy? She entered the conversation with a question of her own. "How would you go about it?"

"Well, forgetting about our first meeting at the apartment would be a good start," he offered.

"Now what could you possibly say to make me forget that?"

"I'm sorry?"

Looking at him for the first time, she said, "Are you asking or telling me?"

He turned to meet her gaze with sincerity in his eyes. "I didn't mean for our relationship to begin on a sour note, Miss Murphy. I never meant to be an ass either. I'm sorry for treating you with such disrespect. You are a professional Navy officer, and you deserve to be treated as such."

She lit upon one word out of his lengthy apology. "Relationship?"

He briefly let a smile grace his lips. "As neighbors and colleagues, of course."

"Of course, Mr. O'Hara." She looked at Jack and nodded, offering a veiled smile herself. "Apology accepted."

Terrie returned her focus to her driving. They continued the remainder of the trip in thoughtful silence.

SEVENTEEN

Following standard protocol for chain of custody, Terrie and Jack remained together and in positive control of the Hanscom parcel from the moment they signed for it until they brought it back to the Intel Office. Sheffield logged it in and returned it to Terrie and Jack's custody.

"The commander wants you to proceed to the Ops Center with it," Sheffield told them.

"Is that standard procedure for packages like this, Senior Chief?" asked Terrie.

"When we are informed of classified parcels for pickup at Hanscom, two authorized members of this office are required to pick it up and bring it directly to me to complete the chain of custody. Then it goes to the Ops Center. The team evaluates its contents to determine who is best qualified to receive it. We don't sit on these, Lieutenant."

"I never suggested you did. I only wanted to know the procedure."

"If there's anything here for you, Lieutenant, you'll know shortly."

After Sheffield's terse explanation, Terrie turned over the vehicle key and departed for Ops with the parcel in her hand and Jack at her side.

"I see you two endured each other's company," Bannerman said with a smirk as the two officers entered.

Terrie and Jack regarded one another for a second. "It was an education," said Terrie.

"Okay, let's see what we've got," said Bannerman, before she called down to Theo. "Care to join us, Theo?"

"Yes, ma'am."

The team gathered around the table in front of the controller station. Bannerman donned a pair of nitrile rubber gloves and produced a pocket knife to cut open the box. She pushed aside a slip of bubble wrap to reveal three evidence pouches.

The first one held five zip drives of varying design and manufacture. The note on the label indicated they were examined forensically for latent prints.

"I'd say these go to you first, Theo, so you can access them."

The commander reached for the next pouch that contained a green, spiral notebook. Many of its pages were dog-eared or torn. Bannerman opened the bag, removed the notebook, and flipped open the cover. The initial page had a single phrase in Arabic:

تنظيم قاعدة الجهاد في بلاد الرافدين

"Miss Murphy, I believe this is your bailiwick." She waited for Terrie to put on her gloves before she surrendered the notebook.

Terrie eagerly flipped through the pages to see what she could make of it. Reading the entries, she determined an Iraqi mole working for the US government wrote the notes while spying on the group formally known as al-Qaeda in Iraq. The Arabic phrase read, "The Organization of Jihad's Base in Mesopotamia."

The last pouch contained miscellaneous papers found in a Somali safe house. "Theo, I think you might be best for this one.

If there's anything Terrie needs to be brought up to speed on, I'll expect you to do so."

"Acknowledged, Commander," said Theo.

"Sorry, Mr. O'Hara. Nothing for you this time."

"That's fine, Commander. I have my current stack of intel and emails to go over anyway."

She smiled at him then went back to her seat at the controller station.

Terrie remained at the table, going over the notebook from its beginning. It detailed the duties, times, and locations of meetings, discussions, and names of prominent al-Qaeda operatives. One name repeated constantly, along with a reference to a new group and its more violent activities. What struck Terrie as odd was a notation that the most senior al-Qaeda leader, Ayman al Zawahiri, strongly disavowed the tactics of a new radicalized group, known only as al-Nusrah. Its leader, the one that laid claim to some of these attacks, called himself, Muhammad al-Jawlani. Under this new banner, al-Qaeda in Iraq appeared to have changed its name.

دولة العراق الإسلامية

Terrie's eyes grew wide as she read the implication that went with its disturbing connotation. She softly said the words to herself. *"Dawlat al-'Irāq al-'Islāmiyyah."*

"What is it, Lieutenant?" asked Bannerman.

"Commander, may I have a word?"

Nodding toward the back of the room, Bannerman hinted for the two of them to move toward the Ops Center entrance. "Yes, what did you find?"

"Al-Qaeda's Zawahiri rebuked the actions of a new faction of al-Qaeda in Iraq. And now, apparently, making a break from al-Qaeda itself, there's a new radical leader named Muhammad al-Jawlani who has officially renamed his organization the Islamic State of Iraq."

"Hmm. Do they pose any genuine threat?"

"According to what's written in the notebook, Jawlani's methods include orthodox adherence to several Quranic ayat that are particularly brutal."

"In English, Miss Murphy."

"The smiting of fingers, toes, and necks. In other words, the accepted practice of mutilating and beheading the kafirun. Sorry, Commander. I mean the nonbelievers."

"What evidence does this notebook contain?"

"It documents some of their verified atrocities in Mosul and Fallujah."

"Very well. Summarize this information for the next SITREP. Good work, Miss Murphy." Bannerman favored her with a brief smile. Terrie acknowledged with the dip of her head and returned the notebook to Bannerman before taking her seat at her station.

Terrie found nothing of consequence in her emails. She glanced over at Jack, who seemed to be having trouble with the hunt-and-peck method on his keyboard. "Would you like a little help?"

"I don't know, can you?"

"Seventy-five words a minute is the worst I can do, but if you don't need my assistance—"

"Okay, okay. Could you finish typing this reply for me?"

"All right, let's see what you have so far." She moved over to Jack's station and leaned over his injured shoulder to get a better look at the Word document he had up on his monitor.

Ignoring the feeling of being closely watched by her disabled colleague, Terrie finished reading what was on the screen and stood up. "That doesn't look too difficult to fix." She grabbed her chair by the arm and wheeled it over next to Jack so she could get comfortable. "Let me do a quick edit here, and then we can take it from the top."

"Thanks."

The rest of the Ops Center was quiet. Theo was absorbed in his task, and Taro was out for the day, so he wasn't there to keep Theo entertained. Bannerman occupied herself with the SITREP, occasionally peering at the analysts to monitor their progress. Terrie finished her review and indicated to Jack that she was ready to continue.

She typed as he recited, and in less than a minute, she was done. "Okay, how's this?"

Jack read the document aloud as Terrie stood by just in case he had any corrections. "Wow, not a single error. Are you always so precise?"

"Contrary to popular opinion, Mr. O'Hara, I am human." She glanced over at Theo, but he was still working to unlock the zip drives. The cipher must have been more complicated this time. Theo's legendary programming genius should have helped him crack the code by now.

"Well, thank you, Miss Murphy," said Jack.

"You're welcome." She moved her chair back to her station to work on her SITREP summary.

Terrie ran the information she'd gleaned from the notebook. Jawlani's al-Nusrah group, or JN as it was referred to in the notebook, operated mostly from Mosul and Fallujah. They did not seem linked to any attacks, kidnappings, or reprisals from Sadr City, where Margaret had disappeared. The radical approach this group seemed eager to use fit the modus operandi of the people who kidnapped Margaret, but she found no evidence it was them.

All the clues to Margaret's disappearance and murder started to float in her mind. They captured her in broad daylight on the outskirts of Sadr City. The package Terrie received with the gruesome evidence of her sister's death contained a Sadr City postmark. But this location was not in JN's realm of control at the time of her disappearance, so Terrie's search had to continue.

She theorized that perhaps those responsible were loosely associated with JN or possibly a lieutenant of Jawlani operating on his own.

As she thought about this, Jack called out to her. "Lieutenant Murphy, do you like Italian?"

"Let's just keep our relationship professional for the time being, shall we?"

Visibly deflated, Jack returned his attention to the monitor.

Terrie was grateful for the quiet.

EIGHTEEN

Terrie mulled over all the information she reviewed at the Ops Center during her afternoon run. Still, she could only come up with the flimsiest of supposition that Jawlani's group was responsible for Margaret's death.

Feeling mentally fatigued, she decided to put her effort into making dinner. Jack's steel steed was in its assigned parking slot, but his Silverado was not. *Good, no loud noises for a while.*

Terrie showered the aches from her muscles before changing into shorts and her favorite Brian Westbrook jersey. The jersey was so long that only her well-toned legs peeked from the bottom. She opened the window and set about making dinner, a soft ballad music station playing in the background. Tossing a quick look out her balcony toward Badger Island, Terrie observed how fast the skeleton of the new condo had gone up. Clendaniel and crew wasted no time pouring the foundation and setting the rebar that reached from the ground like outstretched fingers.

She smiled in spite of herself as she thought about the foreman. Terrie had been there for just over a week, but her exposure to Clendaniel had greatly affected her opinion about older men. Or at least this one older man.

Terrie looked at her cell phone and considered calling him to see how he was doing. No doubt Aunt Barbara would consider Terrie's thought process out of character, but she wished to push her niece to trust and accept others. She gave herself another minute or so to think about the kindhearted foreman as she finished making her shrimp fried rice.

Terrie's culinary expertise was limited to single-serving dishes she preferred to eat. And there was never a reason to cook for more than one person.

Terrie was about to sit down to dinner when she heard Jack's Silverado pull into its space.

Oh great. There goes my peace and quiet. She was pleasantly surprised when her noisy neighbor chose not to raise the roof with his stereo again. *I guess he got the message.*

Terrie had nearly finished her dish when someone knocked at the door.

She opened it to find a James Dean look-alike balancing two short-stemmed goblets and a magnum of rosé in his one good hand.

Jack's eyes focused on Terrie, his mouth dropped open for an instant, taking in her ravishing beauty and skimpy clothing. "Did I catch you at a bad time?"

"No, why do you ask?"

"Well, I hope you're wearing something under that jersey."

Shifting her weight to one leg and hoisting a hand to her hip, she gave him a questioning glance. "I can't wear what I want in my own apartment?"

"By all means, wear whatever you want, though Patriots' colors would look better on you," he said, eyeing her up and down. The oversized jersey was just small enough to provide a hint as to the lovely assets it concealed.

"I'm sorry, did you want something?"

"I really want an opportunity to start over."

"You don't give up, do you?"

"Persistence is one of my more annoying qualities."

"Well, I'll buy that." She let go of the door and let him in, returning to eat her dinner as though he wasn't there. Terrie felt his eyes as he followed her inside. "Have a seat."

He set the peace offering on the table. "The rosé should go well with your fried rice."

"No, thank you. I prefer my strawberry smoothie tonight."

Reaching for a goblet, he asked, "Do you mind?"

"Go ahead."

Jack opened the bottle and poured his drink. Taking a seat opposite Terrie, he sipped from the goblet before setting it on the table. He twirled it by its stem, staring at it intently. "Thank you for your assistance today."

"You're welcome." Terrie went back to scarfing down her meal.

"Why do you work so hard to get people to dislike you?"

"What makes you say that?"

"Your table manners, for one thing."

"Never missed a meal at the academy. Can you say the same?"

"I knew where to stash food."

"Is this what you meant by starting over?"

Jack stammered something unintelligible.

"Yes?"

"You really don't make this any easier."

"Am I supposed to?"

Jack smirked at her and changed the subject. "You know, I should have been on that Badger Island assignment."

"You didn't miss anything," she said, wolfing down the last spoonful.

"Tell me."

She squinted at him. "Okay, what the hell." Terrie moved to the balcony and beckoned Jack over. "Do you see the area bathed in light just to the right of the bridge?"

"Yeah?"

"Commander Crabtree insisted this location was the site of the country's first intelligence office."

"Sounds like a logical reason."

"How well do you know Commander Crabtree?"

"I don't."

"That makes two of us." She folded her arms and looked back across the water to the lighted construction area.

"What are you saying? You don't trust the commander?"

"Let's just say I doubt the commander will earn that trust anytime soon."

"Why? What happened?"

She tried to gauge how much she was willing to share. "I can't go into it at the moment. It's only a feeling. Give it a week or so after he gets back then tell me what you think."

Looking out at the skeleton of rebar, Jack said, "You still haven't told me what you discovered there."

"I'll say this. It wasn't an office."

"Then what was it?"

At first, Terrie didn't answer. Her thoughts turned to the story Jack had told of his family's roots and how they were firmly planted in the rich soil of New England's shipbuilding culture. She hoped their later adaptation to firefighting did not obliterate their knowledge of what went on near Badger Island. Stepping out on a limb, she gave Jack the Military-Archeologist-for-Dummies version of all her Badger Island discoveries.

"Wow! That's an intriguing tale. But are you absolutely sure of the location?"

Terrie retrieved a copy of the sketch she made of the area. Jack examined it closely before venturing an opinion. "I agree, this is an unusual place for ship's stocks, given the shipyard was nowhere near this site." Noticing the thin rectangle labeled *stone wall*, he asked, "Are these dimensions correct?"

"Yes, why?"

"If these dimensions are accurate, this wall couldn't have been a dry dock, so what was it used for?"

"I don't know, you tell me."

He rubbed his chin as he heard the lapping of the water against the shoreline. "Did you have the artifacts examined by forensics at Newport?"

"They should be there now, if Crabtree took them there," She replied with a healthy dose of skepticism.

"What makes you think he didn't?"

Terrie didn't answer the question. After an uncomfortable silence, she asked one of her own. "Did anyone from your family ever work on Badger?"

"The son of the first O'Hara to come here, Ronan O'Hara, apprenticed with William Badger himself," he volunteered. "In fact, our family's multigenerational diary Ronan started tells many stories of his adventures in shipbuilding. I'll have to see if I can get it from my father's house the next time I visit."

"Please do. It might prove helpful."

Jack searched Terrie's eyes for a reason why, but found no trace of an answer. He doubted that Terrie would supply one. He looked off into the distance at a passing pleasure boat as it returned from its excursion at sea. "You certainly hit pay dirt with the package we picked up at Hanscom today."

"Why do you say that?"

"Your fourth-down huddle with Bannerman. I could tell whatever you told her impressed the shit out of her."

"Just called it like I saw it."

"She wasted no time updating her SITREP when you two were done talking, I'll tell ya that."

"Isn't that her job?"

"I've never seen her move that quickly to update a SITREP before."

"Until Mr. Theodore gets past the encryption on those thumb drives, I believe the value of my contribution shall remain in doubt."

"Don't kid yourself. Bannerman strikes me as someone driven by ambition, not a sense of duty."

"Why do you think so?" Terrie asked with genuine curiosity.

"Let's just say I've had that feeling ever since I came here."

"I don't really know any of you yet, though Mr. Theodore enjoys pushing buttons."

"It's part of his charm."

"Well, Mr. Charming will soon find out that I don't have a press-to-test button."

Lifting his injured wing, Jack conceded the point. They stood there silent for a time until Jack spoke again. "Can I make a quick observation?"

"Does it have anything to do with my attire?"

Jack chuckled. "No, it has to do with your intelligence."

"You're not seriously challenging my—"

"No, from the notebook you spent so much time on today."

"Oh," she said in an almost apologetic fashion.

"You seemed to be skimming through it as though you expected to find something in particular."

Terrie just stared out at the lighted construction area.

"What's going on, Miss Murphy? Really?"

"I have no idea, but I'm going to find out."

Jack O'Hara left it there.

⚓

Terrie basked in the quiet after Jack left. She felt better after talking with him but still reserved judgment on their relationship. Was he a loyal companion or an ardent competitor? Terrie's fierce, independent spirit and solitary personality only served to make her relationships tricky at best. She needed time to determine if the designation of consort would ever apply to Jack.

At present, her only loyal companion was her Ibanez acoustic. Its fretboard waited patiently to be danced upon by Terrie's talented fingers, yet she decided against picking it up. Her mind was too cluttered with the day's events to concentrate on her playing.

Feeling the climax of the day at hand, she brushed her teeth, turned out the lights, and went to bed. She hoped the conversation with Jack was enough to preclude the onset of another recurrence of her nightmare. Her unconscious mind shattered that hope.

NINETEEN

The dark gray splotch lightened as it grew, shadows moving within its center. A singular shadow, more pronounced than the others, appeared to take on a distinctive shape. The shape of her sister Margaret, alive, well, and sitting in the living room. She just hung up the phone. A very precocious fourteen-year-old Terrie Murphy sauntered in to catch her crying. This was how her nightmare began…

"What's going on now?" Terrie asked her sister.

"That was Jerry from my church group. He said the news is reporting that a group called al-Qaeda is claiming responsibility for the attack."

"They've been saying that for the past few days. Why are you just now—" Terrie cut her thought short, realizing her sister had turned off the television for the past few days. "I'm sorry."

"Why can't people get beyond their hate for how others choose to worship God?"

"Or not," Terrie added.

Margaret turned to Terrie with a look of pity, rather than anger. "Terrie, hate is born of ignorance. It festers in the minds of those who refuse to challenge their perspective." She cupped Terrie's chin as she looked into her eyes. "I don't expect you to understand, but trust me. Before this war we've embroiled ourselves in is over, you will."

The image faded only to be replaced by another one. A pleasant one to be sure, since Margaret's bright smile took center stage within it…

"Why the long face?" Margaret asked.

"Why do you have to go?" sixteen-year-old Terrie asked.

"Because our church group believes in this mission."

"You mean *you* believe in it."

"Terrie, we can't go through life as spectators. Where's the credibility if we say one thing, yet do another?"

"I know, I know, but why you?"

"I was the most vocal member of our group to oppose our government's policies in Iraq," Margaret replied. "People of conscience must not allow incompetents to speak for us when we know they're wrong."

"The ground war may be over, but it's still dangerous. You won't be safe there."

"God does not give people things he doesn't want them to use, Terrie."

"But don't they consider women second-class citizens?"

"The letter we received the other day gives us hope that we shall triumph where our government failed. 'In the language of the holy writ, there was a time for all things, a time to preach and a time to pray, but those times have passed away. There is a time to fight, and that time has now come!' But my weapon shall be the scriptures," said a cheerful Margaret, channeling her inner Muhlenberg.

This last peaceful image melted away, replaced by another, more malevolent, one…

The ashen mass returned, its edges irregular and undefined. As darkened areas moved within it, pale colors emerged at the subject's center, and a barely recognizable woman stood near a jetway entrance. Terrie couldn't tell who it was until the woman turned to look at her. It was Margaret. She presented her boarding pass to the ticket agent, smiled back at Terrie, and waved. To

Margaret's right was the gate placard with its updated electronic flight information. The digital clock with vivid green numerals read 8:45 p.m.

For an instant, the likeness winked like the shutter of an SLR camera but without the clicking noise. The new vision was slightly altered. The time had changed to 8:12 p.m., but that wasn't what confused Terrie. She was watching Margaret wave. The raised hand was not the same skin tone as the rest of her exposed arm, but a glistening wet crimson. Her fingers appeared to be swollen.

No, not swollen, but lacerated clear to the bone as though cut by a spiral ham slicer. The woman seemed ambivalent to the condition of her mutilated hand as she waved it back and forth, its stacked slivers of skin shifting side to side, oozing red fluid as it did so.

The vision winked again. The time had changed in that instant to 5:33 p.m., its digits now glowing bright red. The appearance of Margaret's imposter had also altered. Instead of the mangled appendage, a shortened stump was swinging back and forth where her right hand should have been. The woman's face still had that carefree smile as she waved, the exposed ends of her radius and ulna encased in ripped, meaty flesh. Terrie also noticed the woman was balancing all her weight on her right foot. She had to, because her left foot was missing, the lower hem of her pant leg a crimson-covered mess hovering over a pool of blood.

Once more, the vision winked. The digits in the clock had changed again, but this time they made no sense. The clock's numerals, dripping what appeared to be red paint, read 47:4 p.m.

Terrie flicked her gaze back to the waving woman but wasn't able to see her at first. With the sickening feeling of irrepressible nausea, she saw it. The woman's head was resting at a crooked angle in the palm of her raised left hand. Its glazed, half-lidded eyes stared blindly, while the right arm's stump kept waving, the ghostly left pant leg flapping around the emptiness that used to be an ankle.

No sooner did the realization of that image crystallize in her head then the most frightening wink of them all occurred. The resulting change was another set of confusing digits. The clock read 2:191 p.m. And in the place of the shattered woman was a black-masked apparition brandishing a short curved sword, a shadowy figure with a raspy, low voice. "Kill them wherever you find them and drive them out from where they drove you out. Such is the reward of the disbelievers."

This time the wink was accompanied by a shrieking sound that pierced the darkness. A scream that scared her completely awake. The scream came from Terrie.

She sprang bolt upright with the look of a caged animal on her face, dimly aware of a pounding at the door. She jumped out of bed and ran to answer it. Still tense and shaking from her nightmare, she opened the door to find a horrified Jack O'Hara staring back at her.

"What happened, Miss Murphy? Are you all right?" Genuine fear reflected in his eyes.

She tried to do her best to dissuade him, but her weak assurance was incompatible with the cold sweat still dripping from her forehead. "I'm…fine, Mr. O'Hara. No need to worry about me."

She tried to close the door, but Jack shoved a foot in front of the kickplate. "Want to try again?"

The intensity of this dream was unlike any she experienced in the past. Getting over this one might require assistance, and she knew it. Detecting no intention to withdraw in Jack's eyes, Terrie's feigned bravado deflated. She moved out of the way and allowed him in.

"I'll put up a pot of coffee," he said, moving into the kitchen. "Where's the coffee maker?"

"I don't drink coffee."

"Okay, tea?"

"There's tea in the drawer to the right of the sink," she said, taking a seat on the sofa.

Jack rifled through the drawer and found three packets of flavored green tea. "Which one do you want?"

"Doesn't matter."

Jack rinsed out the pot he found on the stove and boiled some fresh water for her tea. "You scared the hell outta me, Miss Murphy. That must have been one helluva nightmare." He poured two cups and handed one to Terrie.

She took the cup of hot tea, clutching it as though her life hung in the balance. She stared into the hot liquid as it surrendered its heat. Keeping her head down, she darted a glance at Jack. As she did so, another one of her Aunt Barbara's annoying phrases loudly proclaimed itself: *Get it off your mind by getting it off your chest.* When Terrie had asked her what she meant by it, she told her sometimes the simple act of verbalizing a problem allows for clearer thinking, even when no one is there to hear it.

But this problem has too many moving parts to be solved in such an elementary manner. Even so, her aunt was right; sometimes it's a relief to share the burden with someone else. Could she share this with Jack? *Keep your friends close and your enemies closer.* Was Jack truly the enemy?

Terrie took a couple of deep breaths and asked, "Have you ever been brought back to a specific moment in time by a piece of music, a play, or a movie?"

Jack partook of his tea and nodded.

"When I felt troubled as a kid, I used to light one of those red or green Christmas candles. The scent of holly berry or winter pine filled the room. I'd sit there staring at the flame, either empty-headed or contemplating the universe." She paused her narrative, and Jack gave her a quick eyebrow to coax her along. She looked back at him and said pointedly, "I don't do that anymore."

"Why not?"

"Something happened," she said before going silent again.

In an effort to get the conversation moving, he asked, "So what do you do now?"

"I play my guitar, but even that has lost its power to comfort me of late."

"You run, I've seen you," he offered with a smile. "And your strength of character is undeniable."

She allowed herself a brief smile. "Thanks."

"So, what happened to you? Why the bloodcurdling scream in the dead of night?"

"Interesting turn of phrase, Mr. O'Hara. And so hauntingly appropriate for the occasion."

"Jack, please."

Terrie gave no indication she'd comply with Jack's request. She sipped her tea and began to relay her story. "I was fourteen when 9/11 happened. Everyone was shocked and outraged. Even Margaret."

"Who's Margaret?"

"She's...*was* my older sister."

Jack's eyebrow shot up as her emphasis on the past tense piqued his curiosity.

"She was a statuesque beauty who could light up a room. She had wavy, light-brown hair, sultry green eyes, and a shapely body. She was, for all intents and purposes, my mother, since I never knew my real one. She died shortly after I was born."

"Oh," Jack said, his voice softer than before.

It was a comfortable sound to Terrie, who was beginning to feel more at ease with him. "Unfortunately, she was a late-bloomer, a flower child type with every kind of 'Coexist' bumper sticker plastered all over her Smart car. To her, the world's problems were easily solved, one catchy slogan at a time."

Jack sipped more tea, listening intently to every word while never taking his eyes off her.

Terrie wiped a tear from her cheek before she continued. "Something changed inside her after 9/11. She began shifting her ideas from talk to action. She helped form a church group that spent many hours organizing the community into some sort of self-help program. Whatever the community needed, she would lead their effort, but always with the caveat of their assistance. Margaret never believed in providing people with a 'free lunch,' as she called it. One of her favorite phrases was, 'That which is obtained too cheaply is valued less deeply.'"

Jack smiled in silent recognition before taking another sip of tea.

"It was her new maxim of personal conduct. When 9/11 happened, and the country's principles of freedom were threatened, she vowed to do something about it. She believed that by confronting our mutual religious animosity head-on, a peaceful resolution would be forthcoming." Taking a second to shore up her courage, Terrie added, "She was wrong."

"It sounds like she was on the right track," Jack said, trying to be supportive.

Sun Tsu's quote materialized in Terrie's mind: *If you know neither the enemy nor yourself...*With a valiant effort, she tried to continue, "What never made the news was that groups like Margaret's from all over the country, sent citizen envoys to Iraq and Afghanistan to talk directly with our perceived enemies." Terrie went quiet, her eyes glazed over as welled-up tears began to stream down her face.

Jack reached over and touched Terrie's arm for encouragement.

"I'm all right." Wiping her face, she resumed her story. "Stormin' Norman's clone, General Tommy Franks, had accepted the Baath Party's surrender in Baghdad, ending the ground offensive of the war. Margaret thought it would be safe for her group to set their plan in motion.

"She and five others left for Iraq on the evening of May 27, 2003, right after the Memorial Day weekend. She handed her boarding pass to the ticket agent, had it scanned, and proceeded to the door of the jetway. When she got there, she turned around, smiled that big smile of hers, and waved to me. It was the last time I ever saw her…alive."

There was an uncomfortable pause that seemed to last forever. With an audible swallow, Jack said, "What happened to her, Terrie?"

Her eyes made contact with his, unaccustomed to hearing her first name spoken by her one-time foe. She sipped her cooling tea and continued, "Margaret sent me progress reports at least once a week, along with exposed 110 film cartridges. The photos were grainy, but it was good to see her enjoying the fruits of her labor. Her cell phone service was unable to forward any of her camera's inferior images.

"The last word I received from her was on Christmas Eve, 2003. She sent me a package with some presents and a note. It said something about meeting with a representative of a popular Imam on the outskirts of Sadr City, beyond the border of the so-called Green Zone. Then, nothing. There was no word from any of the other five members, no request for ransom. Nothing."

"What did you do then?" Jack asked.

"I called the State Department for assistance, but when they heard she was outside of the Green Zone, they said she was on her own. Days became weeks. Weeks became months, yet still no word. Then those pictures of the charred bodies of the American contractors hanging from a bridge in Fallujah were splashed across the 24-hour news cycle as though nothing else in the world was going on. I was terrified after that. Knowing what those thugs were doing to innocent people simply going about their jobs, I could only wonder what they would do to Margaret, whose religious fervor carried the best of intentions. But folks like Margaret were looked upon as unbelieving infidels. My waiting became torture.

"At the end of April 2004, the press broke the Abu Ghraib prison scandal. By mid-May, several American citizens were beheaded in retaliation for it. The gruesome brutality of their beheadings was plastered all over the internet for anyone to see. Two days after the first of these victims was made public, I received my own gruesome package."

Jack's face turned to porcelain. "What package?"

Terrie got up and disappeared into her bedroom. She emerged with a carboard box, sat down next to Jack, and gave him an intense look. "Are you sure you want to know? Because once you see these, you'll never be the same again."

All Jack could do was nod.

"All right, but don't say I didn't warn you." Terrie removed the lid and took out a stack of pictures for Jack's inspection. The first one was of Margaret enjoying a night on the town. She was smartly dressed in an evening gown, with her full-bodied hair framing her lovely, smiling face. Her radiant teeth and devastating curves were on full display. She had a Hollywood perfection about her that was vivacious and alive.

Jack looked at Terrie and said, "She's beautiful." Terrie's blank expression never wavered.

Jack flipped to the next photograph, a rough Polaroid obviously taken in less than ideal conditions. But what greeted his sight made his stomach queasy. The photo was overexposed, but he got the gist immediately.

It was the open palm of a woman's right hand. Each finger, including the thumb, was neatly and expertly shredded by a very sharp instrument. The cuts went through to the bone. Skin, muscle, and sinew were indistinguishable masses of ground-up flesh. There were even spots where he was able to see the boney knuckles of her thumb and middle finger. The hand was swollen and bloodied, each finger held in place for the picture. Written in the white rectangle below the photo were maroon-colored squiggles like some form of writing. The first one was the outline of a roof next to a colon followed by a single vertical line and what looked like a mirrored number seven hastily written in an obscure font. To Jack's horror, he could see the wrist's tendon was taut, as though it were actively contracted by its owner. Then a sickly thought coursed through him—she was still alive when they did this to her.

He flipped to the next one and it was far worse. It showed gloved hands holding down the forearm and another gloved hand as it gripped the handle of a medium-sized blade. It was beginning to cut off the mutilated hand. The next Polaroid documented the completed deed.

The hand was physically separated from a distorted wrist with slips of torn flesh, on its end a pulpy blob of mutilated meat. He could see the remnants of scrape marks on the ends of the wrist bones, grisly evidence of the knife's passage across them. On the bottom of the photo, as featured in the remaining photos, was yet another set of maroon-colored squiggly lines separated by a colon.

Jack ignored the pain in his injured arm as he used that hand to cover his mouth.

The next Polaroid demonstrated the use of tin snips to cleave off one of the woman's toes from her left foot. The remaining toes seemed to curl in anticipation of being so forcibly removed. Another Polaroid exhibited the severed five digits lying haphazardly on the concrete floor in a shallow pool of red, viscous fluid.

He flipped to the next Polaroid to find the same gloved hands restraining the left shin as another one wielded the blade that made its initial slice through the soft tissue of the victim's ankle, a fountain of blood spurting from the freshly opened wound. The fuzzy quality of the central subject in the photo suggested the foot exercised its final voluntary motion before its separation. The next Polaroid showed the newly made stump next to the biological waste that was once a beautiful foot.

Jack looked up at Terrie before he advanced to the last couple of pictures. "No," he said, shaking his head.

Though Terrie had seen them many times, the impact of their raw depictions never ceased to disgust her. She looked into Jack's eyes in a most sympathetic way. Sharing so powerful an experience may be wearing on him, but it strengthened Terrie. She encourage him with a soft "Yes."

When Jack moved to the next Polaroid, all the color left his face. His eyes were saucers of nauseous loathing, his mouth hanging open in disbelief.

An assailant stood behind the terrified woman, while two assistants held her by her upper arms. All three were masked and gloved. The assailant used his free hand to hold her head up by the hair, while using the thick blade to slice through her neck. The picture caught the very moment the initial cut was made with the horrifying finality etched on her face. Captured for all time was Margaret Murphy's final seconds of life, appallingly documented in this photo.

The next Polaroid captured the eruption of pumping blood from the headless torso's carotid arteries in what used to be her lovely neck. The eyes of her separated head were no longer wide open, for they could no longer see. The face was a permanent expression of pain, surprise, and revulsion.

Jack's ability to hold it together needed only one more shove in the right direction before he could no longer maintain. All it took was the answer to one vexing question.

"What's this writing?"

Terrie simply handed him a scrap of paper that contained the translation. The writing was a series of Arabic numerals painted on with a small brush. Jack looked at the one showing Margaret's decapitation with the number 47:4. On the one showing sliced fingers was the number 8:12. The amputated hand, foot, and toes, 5:33. And below the picture of her lifeless torso and severed head were 47:4 and 2:191.

He knew he didn't want to ask, but he had no choice. "Do you know what these numbers mean?"

"Yes. They're the individual chapter and verse from the Quran for which each respective act of carnage was carried out."

Looking over all the photographs again, he came to a sickening realization. "They wrote these in her blood, didn't they?"

"Uh-huh."

Jack made it to the sink just in time to avoid staining her living room carpet.

TWENTY

Terrie tried to get back to sleep, but her mind was racing to find a way to tie JN's methods to what happened to Margaret. She theorized the possibility of a splinter group or a rogue cell. What was the significance of the name change to the Islamic State of Iraq? Was the name change a way to force all Sunni adherents into their fold or as a recruiting tool to go after the kafirun? And what did Margaret do that suddenly made her a target?

Cracking open an eyelid to look at the clock, she was dismayed to find it was only 4:30 in the morning. Too late to go back to sleep, she opted for an early morning run to analyze the theories that kept her awake.

Terrie managed to beat the ever-present Senior Chief Sheffield into the office. She headed straight for the Ops Center, turning the lights and flat screens on as she went. The media's top story fixated on its further coverage of the Marathon bombing. She lowered the volume on the monitors before settling in at her station. Aside from a few mundane reports, she sat back and observed the multiple screens, alternately reading the chyrons at the bottom of each broadcast.

A buzzing at the door heralded the arrival of Sheffield and Theo.

"Good morning, Lieutenant. Here pretty early, aren't you?" asked Sheffield.

"I had work."

"Three words today," Theo piped in. "I'll have to write this down in my diary."

"You write?" she shot back. "That's astounding, Mr. Theodore. I'll have to call Guinness."

He was about to say something when Terrie eyed him and threw down the gauntlet. "Choose your next words carefully." Unable to come up with a witty riposte, Theo simply went to work at his station.

Thumbing through the short stack of mail he had with him, Sheffield found a letter from Captain Derrick for Theo. "I believe you were expecting this, Lieutenant?"

Theo opened it, eyes eagerly searching for the one phrase he was expecting to see. The uncertainty in his expression reflected the tone of the captain's note. It ended with an assurance that all was not lost and that the captain was waiting on clarification from the Chief of Naval Operations himself.

Theo thanked Sheffield, folded the note back into its envelope, and returned to duty.

Sheffield walked over to Terrie as he located a five-inch-square manila envelope with AOR Seven written on it. "I believe this is for you."

"What's this?"

"My apologies, Lieutenant. I was preparing the remains of the Hanscom package for disposal when I found this beneath the dunnage."

Terrie took the envelope just as the security door buzzed open again. It was Jack, Taro, and Bannerman.

Jack watched Terrie, trying to gauge her emotional state. In light of the previous evening's events, he half expected her to call in sick. On the way to his station, he leaned over to Terrie and whispered, "Are you all right?"

"Fine," she whispered back, placing all her attention on the envelope Sheffield handed her.

She barely had time to look over the envelope when Taro asked, "Miss Murphy, how was your first couple of days?"

"Uneventful," she replied.

"Miss Murphy," Bannerman spoke up, "you may find CNN's morning broadcast of some interest."

Giving up on the envelope for the time being, Terrie asked, "Why's that?" She moved her gaze to the group of conspirators and saw them all smiling.

"You'll see," the Commander replied.

Sheffield joined the rest of his colleagues in the secret society of smiles.

Terrie caught his sideways smirk. "What?"

"Don't worry, you'll like it," the Senior Chief insisted.

She shook her head and went back to checking out the item Sheffield had just given her. Inside the manila envelope was an unlabeled CD. She wasn't sure what information it contained—audio or data files—but based on its formatting, it wasn't a DVD.

Terrie popped it into her secure stand-alone CD-ROM drive to view the content. There was one folder labeled AOR Seven. Clicking on the folder, she discovered one file, a random alpha-numeric sequence with an .mp3 audio suffix. When she clicked on the file, an audio strip to a sound recording popped up over the Media Player's blue field. She clicked Play to listen. The timed recording ran about six minutes.

She listened intently, but all she heard were the low, muffled voices of two people talking, both male. The poor quality of the recording made it difficult to make out the details. Listening to the recording again, through noise-canceling headphones, a word in Pashto was distinguishable—Ar-rhi, meaning ship. Terrie noticed Jack glancing her way a couple of times to see if she was all right.

Bannerman fielded some routine calls and went back to work on her SITREP.

At the top of the hour, Taro turned up the volume on his monitors to check out the news. No sooner did he do so then breaking news scrolled across the bottom of the screen.

> Breaking News—The president has just included an addendum to executive order 13224, officially naming the al-Qaeda derivative group al-Nusrah a terrorist organization and its leader, Muhammad al-Jawlani, a terrorist. Both the group and its leader are now officially placed on the watch list, according to a State Department spokesperson.

"Congratulations, Miss Murphy," Bannerman said as she led the team in a round of applause. "Your diligence resulted in real-time actions initiated by National Command Authority, the highest compliment one of our team can expect to receive."

Terrie's reaction was tepid, but appreciative. She didn't think her contribution was all that special.

As they repeated the story on other networks, Bannerman's phone rang. The team returned to their work while she took the call. Seconds later, her booming voice said, "Mr. O'Hara, Miss Murphy, Mr. Theodore."

The officers approached the controller station.

"Forensics at the Northeast Field Office in Newport has some findings for us. Miss Murphy, I'll need you to check out a vehicle and proceed to Newport to pick it up. Theo, if you would grab the evidence pouch with the last inaccessible thumb drive and hand it over to Miss Murphy, Newport has the equipment and programs to help access it. Mr. O'Hara, I'd like you to ride shotgun."

Jack hesitated before begrudgingly acknowledging her order.

"What's the problem, Mr. O'Hara?"

"I haven't finished my updates yet, Commander. Besides, I'm sure Theo would like to be present if they're instrumental in getting the thumb drive open."

"The updates will be here when you get back. Your AOR has been quiet lately, so I think we can afford to lose you for a few hours. Based on the content Theo managed to get out of the other drives, I'm thinking the results will favor Miss Murphy's expertise anyway."

"Aye aye, ma'am."

"Besides, Mr. Theodore has another engagement," Bannerman said as she turned to Theo. "That was Captain Derrick on the horn. She needs to see you ASAP."

Theo acknowledged, retrieved the requested thumb drive, and headed to the captain's office as ordered.

Terrie retrieved an overnight duffle and a container of bagged evidence from her SUV and placed the items in the back seat of the government Chevy.

"What's all that?" Jack asked, fumbling to open the passenger-side door with his left hand.

"I always have an overnight bag ready in case I have to stay the night somewhere."

"That's a great idea," he replied, staring at the evidence bags. "And that?"

"Remember I told you about the old rope and the chipped wood I found at the excavation?"

"Is that it?"

"I found these in my gym bag after I handed the larger items to Crabtree."

"May I?"

She retrieved the items for Jack's inspection. "Be my guest." While Jack was engrossed with the evidence, Terrie drove them off the Yard and on their way to Newport.

He regarded the tiny splinter of wood before taking a closer look at the flimsy piece of twine. "This was from that deteriorated rope?"

"Uh-huh."

"It doesn't look like much to go on."

She shook her head. "If you only stayed true to your family's roots."

"I stayed true to a different family tradition."

"Yeah?"

"My brothers and I were fiercely competitive when we were kids, but I was the one who never measured up. They focused on physical conditioning, good grades, and going into the family business. Firefighting. I was the unconventional one in the family, who aimlessly daydreamed away his academic years."

"That still doesn't explain how you ended up here."

"Well, it's kind of stupid, actually," said Jack half jokingly.

"Try me," Terrie responded with a smirk.

"My brothers became firemen. Knowing of my poor grades and independent spirit, they bet me I wouldn't amount to anything. The pigheaded part of me took that bet."

Concentrating on the road as they continued on I-95 crossing into Massachusetts, she asked, "Who won?"

Jack responded with a smile.

TWENTY ONE

As they crested the Jamestown Bridge into Newport, the familiar sight of moored yachts dotting the bay, the Rose Island Lighthouse, and the war college campus flooded Jack with fond memories of his time at Newport. Terrie took the exit's figure-eight pattern to the naval station entrance in stride.

The Officer's Club to the left sported its own miniature marina with an assortment of small to midsize yachts. The rest of the island, where the Navy housed its Officer Candidate School, was an architectural paradox. Among the more up-to-date facilities were buildings as old as the Navy's 1883 possession of the island. Despite the age of these buildings, they were vigorously maintained. Even the dated facility housing the forensics lab managed to disguise its state-of-the-art function.

The button by the first deck's glass door labeled "NCIS" allowed the occupants to know an expected visitor needed to be buzzed in. On the third deck, cameras at the far end of the hallway kept a watchful eye on those who made their way to the security door. Terrie picked up the black handset to inform her contact that they were present.

"You must be Lieutenants O'Hara and Murphy," said a welcoming voice. "May I see your identification?"

Terrie and Jack held up their credentials to the camera.

The heavy security door swung open, and a middle-aged man with a trimmed goatee and aviator glasses appeared. His blue polo shirt had NCIS and his name embossed above the left breast pocket.

"Agent Keegan Dempsey," he said, hand outstretched. "I trust you had no difficulty finding us?"

"No real place to hide on such a small installation," said Terrie.

"Prentiss at the RU says hello," Jack offered.

Dempsey grinned at the familiar name. "Tell Geoff he still owes me for lunch."

"Sure thing."

"Now, if you two would follow me." Dempsey handed the officers their visitor badges and led them down the hallway to his office. The confident agent offered Terrie and Jack a seat as he rounded his desk. Centered on it was a blue folder that contained his report and a few close-up photographs. Dempsey handed Terrie the one-page report that summarized his findings.

Her loud exhale telegraphed her disappointment as she read the document. "That's it?"

"I had a difficult time with the artifacts, but your photographs were quite helpful." Dempsey removed the photos from the envelope and spread them across the table. "Whoever took these knew what they were doing. The attention to scale and detail is exactly what we needed."

Ignoring the compliment, Terrie asked, "Were you able to determine if a ship was ever laid there?"

Dempsey smiled and used a pointer to isolate the section of the picture he wanted them to examine. "If you look closely at this center groove where a keel is normally laid, you'll see two sets of horizontal and perpendicular lines carved into the channeled stock. The older indentations are smoothed over, but you can plainly see how something traversed the channel inland then was raised upward. The clearer ones are more pronounced. The second vertical movement shows how the object was then lowered over the older markings. The last clear horizontal line cut through the older ones, smoothing them out, thus demonstrating the object's final movement."

"How do you know the order of movement so clearly?" Terrie asked.

He pointed to a small area on one of the zoomed-in photographs. "Do you see how the wood fibers in the stocks are broken at these locations?"

Terrie and Jack nodded.

"They indicate movement across the channel in four distinct directions. The fibers are broken in the direction of the object that moved across it. Whatever was in this channel was not laid upon it, but dragged across it. The first movement is into the stocks as the object was brought in. The second, as it was lifted, the third, when lowered, and the clearest marks being the final movement toward the water."

"Are you sure there were four movements?" asked Jack.

"The channel of the stock where the keel would normally be laid should show only evidence of a single set of grooves cut into the stock spine and in only one direction—presumably toward the ocean as it was being launched."

"So, the movements you describe would have been atypical for a new ship's construction?" Terrie stated rather than asked.

"That's correct. A laid keel would not have made these auxiliary marks."

Picturing the complete site in her head, an idea surfaced she hadn't thought of before. "Could this have been a refitted vessel?"

"That's what the evidence suggests."

Scanning the pictures in front of her, Terrie pointed to a panorama of the stone wall. "And what's this?"

"That's the puzzle, Miss Murphy. We tossed it around a bit but couldn't come up with anything definitive. There were several innovative wall designs created in New England at that time, but nothing that resembled this. The shape led us to believe it was a dike of some kind, but since there's no water system to hold back, we dismissed the idea. Next, we considered it to be some kind of foundation for a cover, but with no other evidence to support such a structure we were stumped.

"The wall's presence next to the stocks couldn't be just a coincidence," Jack stated plainly.

"I agree, given their parallel nature to each other," Dempsey replied. "If not for its off-centered orientation to the stocks, it might have been a dry dock."

"Why the evenly spaced circular holes?" asked Jack.

"We're not sure. The wall may have been a base to support some form of scaffolding that surrounded the ship. The holes might have supported the posts, but back then, they used square wooden four-by-fours rather than the cylindrical metal poles used today. Also, if it was designed to support scaffolding, the wall would have been placed much closer to the stocks. This large gap along the left side of the stocks presents a problem."

"Well, there's another problem with your scaffolding theory," she said.

"What's that?"

"I found no scaffolding material at the site."

"The only other alternative would be a base for a makeshift blind to keep the ship from being seen. But why would anyone want to hide a ship on an island known to make them?"

"Why, indeed?" she asked.

Dempsey replied with a hint of regret, "I'm sorry the results were not what you were hoping for."

Terrie took a few moments to evaluate the lackluster conclusions contained in Dempsey's report while Jack reread it with growing angst. Skimming through the findings, he noticed two glaring omissions. Jack looked at Terrie and whispered, "There's no mention of the logbook or that curved piece of metal?" He quickly turned toward Dempsey. "What about the curv—"

Terrie placed a calming hand over his wrist and completed the question for him, but not as originally intended. "What about the curved wood sample and remnant of rope? Your findings here were inconclusive?"

Dempsey scowled. "That's not entirely accurate. Of the types of wood used for sailing ships of the period, pine, oak, and maple were favored. Although the wood sample you provided us was largely petrified, we conducted a surface examination of the wood's cross section and its cylindrical size and shape. We determined the artifact to be coniferous in origin, and its diameter would suggest it was a mast. The wood chip's cross section plainly indicates that it was cut from a pine tree, the material of choice for that part of a ship. Determining which coniferous species it was could not be accomplished without a viable sample from which to conduct a DNA test."

"How do you know it wasn't maple or oak?" asked Terrie.

"The shape of the artifact denotes which part of a sailing vessel it was designed for. The lack of color variation between heartwood and sapwood was the first clue, but the unique signature of the resin canals defined it as some form of pine. If the artifact was made from a hardwood like maple, not only would the color of the sapwood be distinguishable from the heartwood, but the resin canal signature would be completely different. And if it were a live oak, the color variant would be much more pronounced even after the sample had begun to petrify."

"Then it was part of a mast?"

"With that size diameter? It's unlikely to have been anything else."

"What about the rope?"

"Unfortunately, what we received was little more than dust by the time we got it. Cross contamination voided any findings."

Dempsey shook his head. "If only we had uncontaminated evidence to examine."

Terrie and Jack looked at each other. "It just so happens that along with two other pieces of evidence we'd like you to process, I also have a piece of twine from the rope evidence and a sliver of wood from the same sample that isn't petrified."

"Perfect," the agent said, excited at the prospect. "Where are they?"

Terrie produced four small evidence bags from her purse and handed them over to Dempsey. "These are the aforementioned samples we intended to bring you and these two are the twine and wood samples you'll need."

Still transfixed on the first two bags, he asked, "What's this?"

"It's a CD with an audio file on it. I was wondering if you could do anything to enhance its fidelity."

"If the quality of the recording isn't too degraded, I should be able to do something with it. Shouldn't take more than a few hours. And?"

"And this zip drive. We're unable to access it."

"That may take a bit longer, depending on the condition of the drive and the complexity of its encryption. Are the two of you remaining in the area for the day, or should I contact your office when I have my findings?"

"We didn't plan to return to Portsmouth until late this afternoon. I can give you my cell number if you wish to contact us." Terrie wrote down the number on a slip of paper and handed it to the agent.

Dempsey grabbed two business cards from the top drawer and slid them across the desk. "Very well. My number is on the back. If I have anything for you today, I'll be in touch."

"Thank you, Agent Dempsey. I appreciate it." Taking their cue to depart, Terrie waited until they returned to their car before she pulled out her smartphone to call up a map application.

"What are you doing?" Jack asked.

"Since Dempsey said he might be a few hours, I figured we could grab lunch in town."

"There's a food court by the Navy Exchange up the street. Why go downtown?"

"I was thinking someplace closer to our next destination."

Jack looked perplexed.

"The Newport Public Library," she told him.

"What business do we have there?"

"Following up on a hunch."

"So how would nosing around the Newport Public Library help us?"

It was Terrie's turn to respond with a smile.

TWENTY TWO

She pulled into the only open space along the one-way street next to a popular Chinese restaurant Jack frequented often.

Terrie eyed the sign before giving Jack a questioning glance.

"I ate here once a week," he said, along with an endorsement, "Try the hot and sour pork."

"No thanks," she replied with less enthusiasm. "I'll stick with my fried rice."

They found a booth and ordered their meals. Terrie now sat face-to-face with her erstwhile neighbor from hell, now collaborator. She found herself relaxing around Jack, a feeling that didn't come easy to her. His genuine concern after the reprise of that horrendous nightmare raised his stock a few ticks.

Lowering her eyes to her lukewarm glass of water, she said, "I never did thank you for last night."

"What?"

"You didn't have to be so…understanding."

"Don't mention it," he said, intrigued by her softened attitude. "I suppose, living and working so close, we should try to get to know each other better."

"Perhaps," she said, keeping her eyes on the trail of water trickling over the side of the glass. "Mr. O'Hara, do you know why I stopped you in mid-question earlier?"

"I didn't at the time, but I got it now. You want to investigate one or both of the missing items yourself."

She grinned. "Very perceptive."

"But why the local library? The War College Library has a more substantial research database, and we could also take advantage of its classified section if necessary."

"True, but I don't want to draw attention to our activities. I don't know how far Commander Crabtree's reach extends, and I don't want him to know I'm following up on the clues he omitted from official inquiry."

Jack nodded with his jaw half open. "Okay, so how do we proceed?"

"We no longer have access to the logbook of the *Justice*, but it doesn't mean we can't use the clues it held."

"What do you mean?"

"I spent the weekend reading it before I turned it over to Crabtree."

"You what?" he shouted back in surprise.

"The last entry was dated the day the author arrived in Portsmouth, New Hampshire, June 21, 1788."

"So?"

"You don't know the importance of that date?" she asked, as the server brought their meals. Jack's puzzled look didn't go away so she answered her own question. "It was the same day New Hampshire became the ninth state to ratify the US Constitution. A comprehensive database of colonial newspapers isn't likely be part of a War College Library, but it's a perfect addition to a large library in New England."

With a healthy dose of skepticism, he cautioned her. "You do realize what could happen to you if the commander finds out what you're up to?"

"Based on what I've uncovered so far, the commander should be more concerned about what could happen to him."

"Okay, I'm in. What the hell. They can't court-martial both of us."

"They can try," she said sarcastically and began to scarf down her meal.

Jack cringed, using one of the many dominant facial expressions Terrie had mentally catalogued since their first meeting. It was the one she liked the least that he was currently sporting as she shoveled several clumps of fried rice down her throat in rapid succession. She stopped in mid-munch and glared at him, a nonverbal cue that needed no translation.

"I can see why you don't date much," Jack snorted.

"It's a personal faux pas you won't need to concern yourself with." Glancing at her watch, she swallowed the last bit of her meal before she said, "Let's pick up the check and get out of here."

"You don't mind if I finish eating, do you?"

Terrie just smirked at him then nodded. Jack took another ten minutes to finish his lunch.

On their way out, Jack asked, "Where's this library?"

"It's one block over on Spring Street and two more blocks up. With parking at a premium on these one-way streets, I figure we'll get there faster walking. I know I could use some fresh air and the exercise." Terrie led the way with Jack in tow, cradling his sore arm and shaking his head.

⚓

The state-of-the-art brick facility had a welcoming contemporary entrance. A breath of conditioned air hit their faces as they walked in.

Beyond the bookcase of new release fiction was the information desk. The librarian looked to be 100 years old, if he was a day. He owned the clichéd arched back, thinning, long, white locks, and reading glasses that were perched midway on the bridge of his wrinkled, aquiline nose. In a scratchy, British accent, he asked, "Something I can do for you?"

Turning on the charm, Terrie leaned forward as she spoke. "Yes, I was wondering if you could help settle a bet between myself and my associate here."

The crusty old man raised a bushy, white eyebrow. As he regarded the two naval officers, a distinct frown turned his lips into his teeth. His distaste for their uniforms was rivaled only by his disdain for their last names. "There's an Irish pub down the street. Take your friend and your bet and settle it there."

Terrie straightened to her full height, folded her arms, and stared straight at the old man. "Not every service member is obliged to follow the warmonger stereotype, whose only off-duty aspiration involves diminishing 32-ounce curls, mister—" The first initial on his nametag was J, followed by a curious surname for a librarian. She took a chance that she was right. "John Milton?"

"My Christian name *is* John, yes. But who'd've guessed someone of your generation would even know who John Milton was?"

Seizing her opportunity, Terrie sneered before quoting a line from Paradise Lost. "'Why should all mankind, for one man's fault, be condemned if guiltless?'"

"You do know your Milton, don't you, young lady?" He studied Terrie and Jack with a quick stroke of his chin before he yielded to her query. "Very well. What can I do for you?"

"New Hampshire was the crucial ninth state to ratify the Constitution, making the document operative. But my friend here is under the false impression that the newspapers of the day all proclaimed this achievement at the same time. In today's 24-7 news cycle, it's easy to forget it took longer back then to get the word out. I believe it took weeks before all of the states received word of this event. So, I thought the best place to find the answer was in a library with a database containing colonial-era newspapers."

"How do you know we have such a database?"

"Your website."

After another evaluating stare, he came out from behind the information desk and curled a beckoning index finger at the two officers. "This way." Milton escorted them to the research section of the library, a sequestered area of neatly partitioned cubicles with space for research notes and a computer. "Do either of you know how to navigate our database?"

Terrie glanced at the monitor to evaluate its homepage. "No, but if you help us get started, we should be able to manage the rest on our own, thank you."

Milton crouched over the cubicle station to log in and called up their genealogy website. He placed a boney, age-spotted hand over the wireless mouse to click down the successive links to the subheading Historical Newspapers. A map illustrating the state-by-state alphabetical listing of newspapers from 1690 to 1922 appeared. "You can narrow your search by selecting the state, place of publication, and specific paper, or you can scroll down to the advanced-search box. This feature will allow you to search by title, article, keyword, and date range."

"That's very helpful," said Terrie, searching the room as if looking for something. "Is it possible to print our results?"

"Yes, but it will come out on the printer by the information desk."

"Thank you, Mr. Milton. I believe we can take it from here."

Terrie waited for Milton to disappear behind the swinging half door of the information desk before she and Jack took their seats.

"I don't think we'll get very far researching that maroon bit of metal with this database," Jack said.

"Agreed. That's why we're going to start with the date of the logbook's last entry."

"Why?"

"Besides New Hampshire's critical news, it is also the day that Tunney brought something called the DOR into Portsmouth."

"Oh. What's a DOR?"

"With any luck, we'll find the answer to that question reported in one of these papers." Eying his sore arm, she asked, "Can you manage enough to take notes?"

He rolled his eyes as he gingerly slid his arm from its loose restraint. "Can we just get started?"

Terrie allowed herself a brief smile. "First, let's search the following words: Langdon Island, the *Justice*, Ledbetter, and Tunney to see if there's anything on them."

"Why not Badger Island?"

"The island wouldn't be known by that name for years after our target date."

"Got it." Jack mulled over the crux of their fictitious bet. "Since Tunney's accomplishment isn't likely to be thought of as news after so much time, I think our date range should be no more than a month."

"Good idea."

Starting with the *New Hampshire Gazette*, Terrie began to fill in the advanced search criteria, using June 21 to July 21 of 1788 as the target date range. She then used her suggested keywords in rapid succession. In all cases, she came up empty.

"Try the other New Hampshire papers," Jack suggested.

Terrie selected all the New Hampshire papers, using the same date range and keywords, but once again the screen would only display an error message with no results. "Hmm. Let's try another approach."

Keeping the same search criteria for all New Hampshire papers, she changed the keyword to Constitution. The screen filled with blown-up rectangles containing a portion of each individual article with the date of publication, newspaper name, and a brief summary of the article next to it. Unfortunately, the order of relevance was best matches rather than the date. She clicked on the drop box to see two more options—newest items and oldest items. Clicking on the oldest, the screen called up the reorganized articles by their dates of publication.

Disgusted, Jack said, "If we have to go through each individual article, this is going to take forever!"

Terrie clicked on the first article. Doing so took her to just the article, with no other headings. In the left margin, she saw an enlarged sidebar with an outline of the referenced newspaper, its full date, volume, and issue number. Below the title were the four hyperlinked pages that made up the issue, and the particular article they were viewing listed in the exploded view of the first page. Clicking on the link to page one allowed them to see the entire front page of the June 21, 1788, edition of the *New Hampshire Spy* and what appeared to be an op-ed that took up all three columns of the front page. The title of the article struck a chord in Terrie's mind: "Observations on the Constitution proposed by the Federal Convention."

Terrie forced herself to read past the unusual typesetting as she began to detect something familiar about this treatise on the Constitution. She recalled these specific words used in one of her reference books that discussed the Federalist and Anti-federalist arguments.

The essay assumed a pro-federalist stance that was not part of the original eighty-five essays of the Federalist Papers. Though this particular observation was not penned by Madison, Hamilton, or Jay, it did speak with great eloquence and optimism about the document that emerged from what its author called the Federal Convention.

Terrie clicked on the link to page two so she could read the conclusion of the article and found a familiar name and title to the essay: "FABIUS, No. IX." She nodded as her recognition of this "imperfect testimony of his affection" declared itself.

"You do know who Fabius was, don't you?" Terrie asked.

"Can't say that I do. Who was he?"

"He was John Dickinson, Benjamin Franklin's fellow Pennsylvania delegate who couldn't bring himself to vote for independence, yet voiced unswerving allegiance to his young nation once the break was made."

Reading on, they noted a lengthy advertisement for cheese and fish, the extract of a letter from a British citizen living in India to his father in London, and two days of resolution proceedings for the Virginia General Assembly, in convention to consider the proposed constitution. Under the heading of BOSTON, June 18, was a remarkable account of the arrival of Ambassador John Adams and "his lady" from his nine-year absence abroad as Ambassador to Britain. Consumed with the Adams article, Terrie clicked on the next page to continue reading as Jack spotted something else more germane to their mutual investigation.

"Huh. Check this out. According to this Marine List from the Port of Piscataqua, two ships entered the port on June 21, but neither was the *Justice*."

Terrie ignored the ship news Jack referred to, clicking on the last page instead. With the exception of an advertisement concerning a derelict schooner found by a William Gibbs the previous February, no mention of any other ships was noted.

"Let's check out the other nearby state newspapers," Jack suggested.

Terrie selected the remaining New England papers for the same date range and Constitution keyword. The enlarged articles were easier to read, but with over fifty pages, each containing twenty blocks of individual articles to review, the faster way was to pull up the entire four pages of each newspaper. Unfortunately, the digitizing process left many pages either too dark or too small to read.

Consolidating their search to individual four-page issues went faster, but Jack's frustration eventually boiled over. "Trying to read this monitor is giving me a headache." He squeezed the bridge of his nose with his good hand.

"Okay, tell you what. I'll print out the issues a month past our target date for the more promising papers, and we'll go over them at the War College Library reading room while we wait for Dempsey's report."

"Sounds good to me."

Jack checked off each paper in his notes as Terrie printed them in turn. He approached the printer as a suspicious John Milton squinted his disapproving eyes over his reading glasses. After observing what appeared to be half a ream of paper growing in the output tray, Milton questioned the officers.

"Miss, I can understand the length of time it took you to research the solution to your bet but not the need to print out all those copies to prove it."

Terrie inserted the truth inside a lie. "You're quite right, Mr. Milton. The bet's resolution was tertiary to our mission."

"That being?" asked the ancient librarian, craning an eyebrow over a grey orb that brimmed with curiosity.

"Research concerning a vessel that had arrived in Portsmouth on or about the day New Hampshire ratified the Constitution. We were hoping to find any evidence that it was the missing ship, *Justice*."

Milton glanced at the stack of paper and shook his head. "Well, if you'd told me that from the beginning, I could have saved you an hour or two of looking and near half a ream of paper."

Now it was Jack's turn to shake his head in disgust.

"Only the Portsmouth-based papers would have covered local ship movements, so you could have limited the scope of your search to them." Milton's souring disposition reflected his growing contempt.

"News of a captured belligerent vessel as the result of a Congressional Letter of Marque and Reprisal wouldn't garner wider interest in United America?" Terrie retorted, using the colonial-era phrase she read in the papers.

Milton softened his expression but not his question. "We weren't at war with anyone in 1788, young lady, so what imaginary demons do you believe we were fighting?"

"There are demons far worse than your literary namesake's antagonist, Mr. Milton. And some of them are homegrown."

Terrie gathered up their research papers, and Jack repositioned his sore arm inside its cloth sling. They left the librarian alone to ponder that conundrum as they headed for the exit and their car.

Making their way down the street, Terrie glanced at Jack's cradled arm. "Does it still hurt?"

"Truth be told, my thumb and my ego are the only things that are still bruised."

"That was difficult to say, I'll bet."

"How much?" he asked as a grin erupted on his face.

"Let's get to the reading room so we can examine these newspapers first. We can discuss the particulars of a wager later."

"I'll hold you to it."

Terrie and Jack made their way back to the Newport Naval Station and the War College Library. They located a vacant desk near the reading room and organized their cache of newspapers by date of publication. Having already perused the June 21, 1788, issue of the *New Hampshire Spy*, Terrie began to look through the next paper in sequential order, *The Salem Mercury* of June 24, 1788, as Jack worked the papers in reverse order.

The second volume, issue 89, was structured much like the other issues she read from the short-lived Salem paper published by Dabney and Cushing, a four-column format that began with "Foreign Intelligence." This news, by any other name, was monopolized by Germany and Great Britain on the first page. A thin black line separated foreign from domestic "intelligence," as the other states were represented in a regional roundup of stories.

Near the bottom of page three, another line introduced SALEM, June 24 news, and the first subject was another story about the Ninth Pillar. Advertising space completed the remainder of the paper. To Terrie's dismay, only three paragraphs mentioned anything about ships. The first concerned the loss of a three-masted vessel near Bristol, England, on June 20. The other two were ads, one for a schooner up for public auction, and the other was the ship *Rebecca* looking to take on cargo and passengers bound for England.

Moving one of the lamps closer, Jack began with the July 17, 1788, edition of the *New Hampshire Gazette*. Not interested at all in the historic entries, he skimmed through the pages looking for any evidence of ships arriving on or about June 21.

Under the title of NAVAL – OFFICE for the Port of Piscataqua, he noted the arrival of a familiar ship, the *Anna*. He found that same ship mentioned again in a previous edition, July 3, 1788. This time, it arrived and departed on the same day. "Looks like this brig, *Anna*, is making the local circuit. It's the fourth time I've seen it mentioned on the Marine Lists of Piscataqua."

Terrie was still engrossed in her own research. Taking up the June 26 edition of the *New Hampshire Gazette*, she reread the inaugural notice of the raising of the Ninth Pillar. Immediately following the article's ratification coverage, she noticed a reprise of the ad for the ship *Rebecca* in the fourth column of page two. Aside from this advertisement, there was no further mention of arriving ships.

Pulling the next four-page gem from the stack, Terrie happened to see a paper she hadn't had occasion to read earlier at the library. Printed in Worcester, Massachusetts, by Isaiah Thomas, the June 26, 1788, issue of the *Massachusetts Spy* looked pristine enough to have been printed yesterday.

What caught Terrie's eye, aside from the period typesetting use of the letter S, was the paper's motto in the title frame. In bold letters, the phrase read, "The Liberty of the Press is essential to the Security of Freedom." This same sentiment was repeated in three other languages—French, Greek, and Latin—a testament to the well-read nature of the paper's subscribers.

Looking at yet another newspaper, the July 3, 1788, edition of the *Independent Chronicle* from Boston, the only ship news Jack could find were two advertisements, one about a schooner for sale and another regarding a ship bound for London. "This doesn't sound right."

"What is it?" Terrie asked as though annoyed by the interruption.

"This ad. It doesn't make sense. Originally published on June 21, it says a ship called *Rebecca* is supposed to sail in twelve days. But that would make the twelfth day the third of July, the day it was printed in this paper!"

"I saw that same ad in two other papers. Maybe it was a publishing oversight."

"Could be." He turned his attention to the next paper, the *Providence Gazette* and *Country Journal* with its garish title frame. He was bemused by the line between the paper's title and its publication date of June 28, 1788. He read it out loud. "'Open to all parties, but influenced by none.' Hmm. Doesn't sound like any newspaper I know of today."

Concentrating on yet another Ninth Pillar article, this time on page three of the *New Hampshire Recorder*, Terrie said, "More's the pity." She scoured the *Recorder* and the next one in the stack, the *Freeman's Oracle*, for any news of arriving ships, but in both cases she came up empty.

Jack found another article repeating the news of the triumphant return of John Adams but no news of any vessels. Setting the Rhode Island paper aside, he reached for the first *Connecticut Gazette* printed after ratification, June 27, 1788. With only a Fabius IV essay on the first page, a round-up of regional interest stories and another Adams article on the second, his diligence was half-heartedly rewarded on the third, near the bottom of the center column listed under NEW LONDON, June 27. "Here's another Marine List, but it showed no arrivals for June 21, only more launches and all from New London."

"It would appear our friend at the Newport Library was correct about the local nature of Marine Lists," Terrie said with resignation.

Too much sitting during the course of their exhaustive day drained both investigators, as their energies seemed to have all gone for naught. Terrie was about to suggest they call it a day and check out the Newport Naval Station's museum at Founder's Hall when her cell phone vibrated to life.

It was a text from Agent Keegan Dempsey. "It's ready."

TWENTY THREE

It was well past five o'clock when Terrie and Jack made their way down the NCIS hallway. Terrie was about to pick up the handset when the door opened and there stood Dempsey.

"Lieutenant Murphy, Lieutenant O'Hara. We have some news about your artifacts."

"Sounds promising, Agent Dempsey," said Terrie.

"We're still working to access the zip drive, but as for the other items you provided us, I'm not sure you're going to like the results."

"You were able to enhance that six-minute audio, I trust?" Terrie asked.

"That was the easy part. Since the file itself was digital, we were able to make the modifications necessary to bring up recognizable voices. It's not perfect, but the dialogue is distinguishable." As they crossed the threshold into his office, he grabbed the CD labeled AOR Seven from his desk. "Here you are, Lieutenant."

"Thank you. That takes care of the audio, so what's the bad news?"

Dempsey opened the file in the middle of his desk. "The news isn't necessarily bad, just surprising."

Doing his best Milton impression, Jack raised his eyebrow. "That being?"

Terrie regarded her colleague as though he were a petulant child.

Dempsey continued his briefing. "If the artifacts you brought in today came from the objects your office brought me earlier, then the ship these came from was not made here."

"How do you know that?" Jack queried.

"The materials and manufacturing methods used were European, not American."

The two officers looked at each other. They closed in on Dempsey as he referred to the evidence.

"The DNA offers us the best clue to their origin. The condition of the find would suggest these items were intentionally discarded."

Terrie and Jack were mesmerized by the agent's explanation.

"Take, for example, this bit of twine. Its outward characteristics are like jute, hemp, or sisal, which are all similar. Both sisal and jute deteriorate in a manner consistent with your evidence. DNA markers confirmed the twine was made from sisal." Dempsey pointed to the spiraled object in the bag. "You see how it's curved to the left?"

The two officers nodded.

"Up until the early 1800s, rope made in New England for nautical use was made of hemp and twisted to the right. From the mid-1800s, manila was favored over hemp for its durability, flexibility, and cleanliness. Since ropewalk production was originally set up for right twisting, they simply continued the manufacture of manila ropes in that fashion."

Curious, Terrie asked, "Did they ever manufacture rope with a left twist?"

"They experimented with twisting directions, but found twisting hemp to the right made the resulting rope more durable. When scientists analyzed hemp microscopically, they discovered that hemp's unique molecular structure made a right-twist stronger. Maritime rope makers in the colonies found that sisal tended to weaken and disintegrate when exposed to salt water, which is why sisal ropes were never mass-produced here."

"What about the wood chip?" Jack asked.

"That's the better news. Though the piece you provided was small, it did give us enough usable material to allow us to sample its DNA."

"Then you know what it is." Terrie said.

"The analysis came back Nordic Scots pine, which would likewise indicate its place of origin. If the sliver of wood came from the piece of wood you originally supplied, its mast was likely made in Spain or Portugal."

"What would colonial Americans have used to make their masts?"

"Ship masts manufactured on Badger were made of eastern white pine, not Scots pine. Colonial ships also used live oak for their hulls and not cedar as most of the European corsairs used."

Attempting to piece together all the clues, Terrie asked, "So, we have the remnants of a ship whose keel wasn't originally laid here. Based on what you told us earlier, it could have been brought into the stocks, refitted, and then launched, correct?"

"That's a distinct possibility, Lieutenant."

"Then what was the stone wall used for?"

Making direct eye contact with Terrie, Dempsey said, "We do not know."

After an awkward pause, Terrie thanked Dempsey before she and Jack left for Portsmouth.

Keeping her eyes on the road, she asked Jack, "What do you think of Dempsey?"

"Seems decent enough."

"Do you trust him?"

"I guess so. I don't think he was deceptive in his analysis, since he went into such detail. Why, don't you?"

"Let's just say I'm withholding judgment for now."

"You don't seem to trust anyone do you, Miss Murphy."

"Experience, Mr. O'Hara, has taught me not to take anything as a given, until tested by the evidence."

"Fair enough," he conceded. "Is your concern based on the evidence Dempsey omitted from his report or our little excursion to the library?"

Terrie took a moment longer to answer that one. "That's what I've been pondering since we left his office."

Again, Terrie wouldn't volunteer any information. "Well, are you gonna share, or do you plan to solve this one on your own?"

"We're partners now all of a sudden?" she said with more anger than she wanted to impart.

"Hey, I'm on your side, okay? Pull back on the throttle a little bit."

Terrie kept her eyes on the road, allowing the silence to reach deafening proportions. "Sorry," she said reluctantly.

"I may not understand you completely, but I've been around you enough to know something's wrong. And I don't think it has anything to do with your nightmares. Are you all right?"

Maintaining a ghostly expression, Terrie turned briefly to look at Jack. "I'm not all right. Not when lies stand for facts and facts are too easily discarded. Not when everything we've understood to hold dear is turned on its head."

Screwing on another of those faces Terrie disliked, Jack asked, "What are you talking about?"

"I'm talking about the voluntary excision of our national identity by those who wish to undermine it."

"Now you lost me."

"If you'd really read those papers instead of skimming over them, you would have answered your own question."

Frustrated, Jack just stopped talking. Apparently, Terrie had recognized something in those papers that he failed to see. Jack wondered if it had anything to do with the Fabius articles or the passive writing style. Or possibly the meaning of the newspaper quotes concerning a free press brazenly proclaiming their will to stand up against the powerful or influential.

"Come now, Mr. O'Hara. You even hinted at it in the library."

"Is it the comment I made about today's newspapers?"

"Bravo, Mr. O'Hara. There's hope for you after all."

Jack didn't take it as a compliment.

Terrie stopped the car in front of the apartment and waited.

"Why are we here?"

"It won't take two of us to turn in this report, and we both had a very long day," she said.

"I should go with you. Besides, my truck is still at the Yard."

"We can go into work together if you'd like. Unless, of course, you have a hot date tonight."

"Fine." Jack got out of the car, slammed the door, and went into the building without looking back.

I could have handled that better, Terrie thought as she headed across the bridge toward the Navy Yard. The sun hadn't quite set, but it was almost eight o'clock. The only car parked by the security fence of the intelligence office was Sheffield's. *Good. I can turn in the car keys.* Terrie took the stack of newspapers she and Jack had copied and placed them in her car before she ventured through the security gate. She punched in the code to the facility's front door just as it flew open.

"Sorry, Lieutenant, I didn't see you," Sheffield muttered.

"No problem, Senior Chief. What are you doing here so late?"

"Just tying up some administrative loose ends."

"Speaking of loose ends." Terrie held up the car keys.

"I'll take care of those for you, Lieutenant."

"Thanks. I also have the report and the audio CD I wanted to review before I turned them in."

"Would you mind securing them in the classified safe when you're done?"

"Will do, Senior Chief. Good night."

Terrie walked down the hall and disappeared behind the door to the Ops Center. She located the audio disc, popped it into the CD-ROM, and listened carefully. She tried to concentrate on the mundane discussion between what was believed to be two Taliban commanders, but the argument with Jack couldn't be banished from her thoughts. After four minutes of the drab conversation, she couldn't stand anymore and turned it off. She placed the CD in with Dempsey's report and secured it in the safe.

All she wanted to do was get home to place a definitive period on her day. She walked into her quiet apartment, tossed the newspaper copies on the kitchen table, and continued over to the balcony.

The Port of Piscataqua Marine List was about ships that passed this particular vantage point. It was right here that something called the DOR made its way in. If it entered, when did it leave?

What did Jack say? The *Anna* seemed to be running the route, periodically entering and leaving. This hinted to Terrie that whatever entered had to leave at some point. Question was, what entered and when did it leave? A ship that didn't leave for months may have been in dry dock. And if so, where did it dry dock?

Terrie couldn't stop her mind from running in eight different directions. Something needed to get solved, and she wasn't going to sleep until it did.

She poured some hot green tea and turned on the radio to a '70s music station to add a subtle background to her contemplations. She was about to turn off the light over the kitchen table, when the stack of papers called to her. Jack had said something regarding an advertisement that didn't make sense. Terrie decided to go over the papers to see if she could find out why.

Shuffling through the stack, she found the newspaper he'd been looking at, the July 3, 1788, edition of the *Independent Chronicle*. She flipped through the pages until she found the ad toward the bottom of the third column on the fourth page.

For LONDON – THE Ship *Rebecca*, George Folger, Master, will sail in 10 or 12 days. For freight or passage apply to the Master on board said Ship, lying at the Long Wharf, or to Joseph Hinkley, at his Store, south-side of the Market.
Boston, June 21, 1788.

Looking the ad over carefully, she noticed something she hadn't before. What appeared to be age spots or ink blemishes had stained through the second, third, and fourth lines of the advertisement. She wasn't sure if it was part of the original newspaper or a result of the digitizing process, but one thing was certain: the advertisement was an exact duplicate of the ones she found in the other newspapers, right down to the style and positioning of typesetting and ship silhouette.

To be sure, she pulled out the other papers where they found the same ad and compared them.

They were identical.

She couldn't recall if this ad was featured in the first paper they'd reviewed online, so she grabbed the June 21 edition of the *New Hampshire Spy* and began skimming through it. She remembered the schooner found by William Gibbs, but there was no illustration that accompanied that advertisement.

Then it occurred to her.

She'd been so engrossed with the story of Ambassador Adams' return on the second page that she failed to really examine the Marine List Jack had referred to regarding the two vessels that arrived into the Port of Piscataqua on June 21, 1788.

Below the title was the heading, Entered. Jack had merely stated that neither ship was the *Justice*, but he failed to mention the names of the arriving vessels. The first was the Brig *Anna* from the West Indies. The second was a corsair that arrived from Gibraltar.

Her smile grew with the understanding of what the vessel's name meant. She reached for a highlighter in one of the kitchen drawers and marked the ship's name with it.

It was the *Dey of Reckoning*.

TWENTY FOUR

We do not know.

Dempsey's words hung there, taunting her all night and into the next morning. Somehow, they were the key to the whole business of Badger Island. But what did they mean?

We do not know.

Someone knows, she thought, or they would not have been so cryptic about the logbook. Or secretive about that chunk of metal alloy. Or willing to take the time to grind the remaining rope into dust. Could that someone have been Commander Crabtree? These things crossed Terrie's mind as someone knocked at the door.

She got the toaster working on her breakfast before she answered it. "Good morning, Mr. O'Hara. My, what you don't look like," she said in mocking fashion. Jack's uniform looked as though he just pulled it from the dryer and threw it on. The luggage under his dark eyes told Terrie all she needed to know about his previous evening's adventures.

Rubbing his forehead, he whispered, "Good morning."

"I assume from your state of post inebriation you didn't eat? Come on in and have something."

"Thanks." He followed Terrie to the kitchen, where she went back to work on the toast. "What's that?"

"They're called English muffins. You want one with some honey tea?"

"Don't you mean tea, honey?" His tired attempt at humor failed miserably. She gave him the toe-tapping-parent look. "I forgot you only have tea, don't you?"

Returning her attention to their breakfast, she said, "Binge-watching your favorite reality program again, I see."

"How'd ya know that?"

"Your show's volume pierced the walls, Mr. O'Hara. It's a wonder you're not deaf."

"What do you watch?" he asked, scanning the room for a flat screen. "Where's your TV?"

"Don't have one, Mr. O'Hara. Real life is drama enough. I'm forced to watch it at work as it is."

"News is not what I'd call entertainment."

"News? Is that what you call it?"

"What would you think it is?"

"You apparently didn't understand what I was getting at yesterday."

"About the newspaper mottoes?"

"Naturally. Of course, that warning from the very first *New Hampshire Gazette* from 1756 is so perfectly relative today."

Jack's eyebrow shot up. "Where did you read that?"

"You didn't happen to notice the background of the historic newspaper home page Milton pulled up for us? I was able to catch a couple of lines from it as the librarian talked us through its use. They underscored the *Gazette's* publisher, Daniel Fowle's, intent perfectly: *The Printer to the PUBLIC.*"

"So, what was the warning?"

"That the, quote, 'fondness of news can be carried to an extreme' and that 'great care will be taken that no facts of importance shall be published but such as are well attested,' unquote."

"Point being?" said Jack, clearly getting frustrated.

"Printers in colonial America respected their readers' intellect, Mr. O'Hara. They took their readers seriously. Today's media believes the public is too stupid to think for themselves."

"What makes you say that?"

"They accentuate the exception and make it the rule."

"For example?"

"Government statistics tell us that about ninety deaths a day were attributed to motor vehicles last year. If each of those deaths were reported in the twenty-four-hour news cycle in the same dramatic way as shootings, this would be considered epidemic proportions, would it not? Yet we're told we have a gun problem rather than a traffic safety problem."

"That's a cynical attitude."

"In both instances, Mr. O'Hara, if the press accentuated the abhorrent behavior that led to these deaths rather than the means, a much clearer picture of the root cause of the problem would have emerged, and the public would have been better served, not the slanted agenda of the publisher."

Jack shook his head and glanced around at the papers Terrie had lying around the kitchen table. He spotted the top one on the stack, a line highlighted in yellow. "You found something."

"No, you did," she said. "Only it's what you didn't say that caused us to miss it."

Jack read the highlighted phrase. "Day is spelled wrong. And what's a Cors.?"

"Look at the entire phrase again. Nothing jumps out at you?"

Flashing Terrie a sideways smile, he replied, "The DOR we were looking for. And Cors. must be an abbreviation for corsair, so Dey was spelled correctly after all."

"Very good, Mr. O'Hara. Now to find out when or if it ever left the Port of Piscataqua."

"Why would that be important?"

"You gave me the clue when you found that the *Anna* had made several trips to and from Piscataqua as reported in the Marine List. If we can show evidence that it never left port, it would mean the ship that arrived on June 21 was either scuttled or refitted and renamed."

"And the evidence you discovered at the excavation would tend to support the latter."

"I believe so. The question is, why the cover story about a lost intelligence office?"

Jack was trying to come up with a plausible explanation, when Terrie brought over his breakfast. "Thanks."

"You're welcome." She wolfed down her muffin, sipped her tea, and looked back at the skeleton of the new condo being built across the way on Badger. "Mr. O'Hara?"

"Yes?"

"Until we can get a better handle on this, I suggest we keep this investigation to ourselves."

Jack nodded as the weight of what she proposed sank in. "How close to a court-martial do you think we are now?"

"I wouldn't hazard a guess." The wheels of a plan started spinning in her head. "Are you doing anything special over this holiday weekend?"

Washing down a morsel of muffin with his tea, he cleared his throat and said, "Nothing, really. What did you have in mind?"

"I'm heading down to Claymont for Memorial Day to pick up my books. Do you think you could check out the Athenaeum in Portsmouth and see if you could word-search copies of the *New Hampshire Spy* and *Gazette*? Maybe double-check to see if the *Dey of Reckoning* ever left Piscataqua?"

"I can do that."

"Meanwhile, my aunt is a veritable treasure trove of maritime trivia. I'll see if she can shed any light on that period and if she knows anything about the fate of the *Justice* or Ledbetter."

"Or Tunney," he added cynically.

The Ops Center was a hive of activity the Thursday morning before Memorial Day. Theo, uncharacteristically quiet, was slogging away on his keyboard. Taro deposed his email traffic while talking up his fantasy baseball team to Theo, who didn't seem to be paying much attention. Jack sat at his station, trying to get back to his normal rhythm, but his unscheduled detour into Terrie's fascinating research project destroyed his focus. Bannerman had just hung up the phone for the sixth time in ten minutes when her intercom buzzed to life.

"Bannerman," she answered, using the speaker.

"The commander would like to see Mr. O'Hara and Miss Murphy," said Sheffield.

"Thanks, Ray. I'll tell them." Calling down from her station perch, she said, "You heard him, Miss Murphy, Mr. O'Hara. You might also bring the NCIS report with you."

Jack got up as Terrie went to retrieve the report from the safe. Terrie half expected Theo to inject another one of his ill-timed insults, but to her amazement he said nothing.

Once in the hallway, Jack asked, "What do you suppose he wants?"

"Surely it's obvious. He knows I'm aware of what should have been turned into the NCIS."

"Then shouldn't he be asking for just you?"

"You went with me. You also know something is amiss."

Terrie finished her response as they made their way into the office. "Please go right in. He's expecting you."

"Thanks, Ray," Jack said.

Terrie shot Jack a scornful glance before she addressed Sheffield. "Senior chief."

Crabtree's pleasant demeanor was the last thing Terrie expected as they came through the door. Her boss was in classic form, his back to them as he tended to his coffee in a tiresome ritual that was becoming all too familiar.

"Please, take a seat." He finished stirring his coffee before reaching for the two additional mugs he just filled. "Allow me to officially congratulate both of you on your promotions," he said, handing each their mug before retrieving his own.

Coffee was exactly what Jack needed, and he got it the way he preferred it. Black.

Terrie was pleasantly surprised to find the scent of hot green tea. "Thank you, sir."

Instead of rounding his desk to sit in his chair, Crabtree took the seat across from his subordinates. "I'm so glad to see the two of you grasp the concept of teamwork so quickly. I have to confess, after hearing of your initial encounter, I had my doubts. Commander Bannerman must have been convincing."

Jack was going to say something, but Terrie beat him to it. "We understand each other, sir."

"Of course," said a mystified Crabtree, wondering how to evaluate Terrie's remark. Was she being capricious or evasive? He decided to let her questionable bearing pass for the moment. "The intelligence confab at the Pentagon tackled several topics this past week but one of particular interest for both of you."

So much for the obvious, Terrie thought.

"The Director of Naval Intelligence invited us to contribute to a report for Congress on terrorism in this hemisphere."

"Isn't that Mr. O'Hara's area of responsibility, sir?"

Crabtree wasn't in the mood for a confrontation. "The focus of your analysis is to determine the level of Iranian activity being exerted in Central America, Miss Murphy. I need you two together on this. The two of you will evaluate all available intelligence indicators gathered over the past six months in compliance with the Countering Iran in the Western Hemisphere Act. Will that be a problem?"

"No, sir," Jack responded.

Crabtree continued, "Determine the extent of Iran's influence in the countries identified and provide any recommendations you see fit."

"When is the report due, sir?" asked Terrie.

"It must be completed and on the director's desk by next Friday."

"Aye aye, sir," Jack said.

Crabtree stood to cue their exit. "Questions?"

Terrie took her opportunity, since she didn't believe she'd ever have another one. "I'm sure they were disappointed when we didn't find evidence of an intelligence office on Badger, sir."

Crabtree's hesitation was fleeting, but she caught it. "What makes you say that, Miss Murphy?"

"You never asked about the results, sir." She handed Crabtree the file. "You weren't even curious."

A V-shaped vein in Crabtree's forehead became more pronounced as he glared at her. "That will be all, Mr. O'Hara. You have your assignment. Please give us this room."

"Yes, sir." Jack looked at Terrie for a split second before he departed smartly.

Crabtree leaned against the desk and folded his arms. "All right, Miss Murphy. What's on your mind?"

"I presume my ability to speak freely remains in force, sir?"

"Now that we're alone, of course."

"You had to know I was going to wonder why NCIS didn't receive all the evidence when we picked up the report."

The frustrated commander made a concerted effort to keep his emotions in check. "The Newport office is ill-equipped to properly evaluate both the alloy you discovered and the logbook, so I was directed to bring them with me to NCIS headquarters. Why should that be a mystery, Miss Murphy?"

"The mystery is why no one who directed the mission seemed all that interested when we found no evidence of an early intelligence office. It was important enough to interfere with a private company's contract and risk media exposure."

"Miss Murphy, as field analysts, our job is to examine the data in front of us and provide the best recommendations we can to the upper echelon—and that's it."

"Like the assignment you just handed us?"

"Exactly."

"Then our recommendations shall be useless."

"What do you mean?"

"How are we expected to accurately report our recommendations when we are relegated to only *available* intelligence indicators?"

"That's the cross we bear in the intelligence community, Miss Murphy. We don't always have the luxury of knowing all the variables."

"Intelligence, like an algebraic equation, requires all the variables to arrive at a valid solution, sir."

Crabtree dropped his head in surrender. "What do you require to arrive at yours, Miss Murphy?"

"Why the cover story, sir?"

"Like you, I'm only acting on the orders given by higher authority."

"The same higher authority that didn't seem interested in what we did find on Badger, sir? Did you not see the need to question their orders when it was apparent the office they sought didn't exist?"

Crabtree raised his head and an eyebrow. "Careful, Miss Murphy."

"Sir, in my four years of service, I've never felt at odds with any orders handed me."

"Commendable, Miss Murphy, so why are you at odds now?"

"I arrived here a little less than a month ago. I was immediately placed on a detail better suited to an archeologist. My findings did not support the original mission objective. Now, two pieces of evidence from that detail are unavailable, thanks to command's lack of reaction to what was and wasn't found."

He gripped the desk with his palms and asked, "What would you like to know?"

"Did Washington come up with anything on those items, sir?"

"They're examining the alloy to determine its origin, and the historians are going over the logbook to confirm its authenticity. If genuine, it might prove that the *Justice* wasn't lost after all."

"Sir, the discovery of the *Justice's* logbook may offer compelling evidence of its return, but if you read the report, the NCIS findings clearly prove that what laid in those stocks was another vessel entirely, not the *Justice*."

Crabtree opened the file and read the report summary carefully. Flipping over the last page he found the blank CD with AOR Seven written on it. "What's this?"

"Agent Dempsey was able to clean up the audio file I received from the Hanscom package the other day. I secured it with the file when we came back last night."

"Have you had the opportunity to examine it?"

"Not completely, sir."

"Then I suggest you make that your top priority, Miss Murphy. It needs to be transcribed and added to Commander Bannerman's SITREP before she sends it out later this morning."

"I'll get right on it, sir." Terrie didn't turn to leave.

"What is it now, Miss Murphy?"

"Sir, you offered me time to settle in when I first arrived."

"And?"

"If you'll allow me to get an early start on it this afternoon, I should be able to retrieve all my belongings from Delaware this weekend."

"You realize that leaves you only three days to complete the director's assignment before it's due?"

"Losing faith in me already, sir?" she asked with a mischievous smile.

"Take the time you need, but the personal consequences of failure shall be swift and severe, Miss Murphy."

"With all due respect, sir, such consequences are equally fatal to sovereign and serf alike."

"You have your assignment. I suggest you get to it."

"Aye aye, sir."

Terrie loaded the CD into the drive and slipped on her headphones. Closing her eyes, she envisioned the two people talking. The first man was never identified, but he called the second man Ra'id. Their discussion focused on popular Arab superstition, a good-luck talisman called the Hamsa, and the Quran. It wasn't until the last two minutes that they discussed something specific about the previously mentioned ship. Recalling an incident while traveling the Arabian Peninsula near the Red Sea in 1991, the first man remembered seeing something in the Strait of Hormuz. He recalled how the Arab legend told of an ominous harbinger of doom that would appear just prior to the destruction of the vessel that saw it. He described how it moved through the water faster than any ship he'd ever seen, before it disappeared. The man named Ra'id dismissed the idea as a heresy against the Quran.

Terrie got to work translating and transcribing the conversation for her report to Bannerman. Before she removed the CD, she made a duplicate copy.

TWENTY FIVE

Terrie made the trip to Claymont in seven hours despite the Jersey Turnpike's dual highway expansion. Its ongoing construction tried to conspire with holiday traffic to impede her progress, but the trip still went faster than expected. She was not thinking about the drive so much as her new post and its atypical office dynamic.

Her initial meetings with Bannerman and Sheffield managed to come off as phony, though Terrie thought Bannerman's standoffish personality was hiding something she didn't want to share with anyone. And Sheffield's over-familiarity with the officers violated military decorum.

The little interaction she had with Theo and Taro made it clear they were more a team unto themselves, similar to Jack and herself. Her only meeting with Captain Derrick was a salutary experience, despite the office's build-up of her iron personae. The only person she remained suspicious of was her attractive, but eccentric, boss, Commander Brooks Crabtree. Then there was Jack O'Hara. As infuriating as he could get, there was something to his stubborn persistence that interested her. The office's dysfunctional social dynamic was something she thought she'd never get used to.

Lurking behind these feelings was a disturbing anniversary. It was that thought that burst into her head with an unwelcome veracity as she exited the Jersey Turnpike for the Commodore Barry Bridge. As fast as the memory came, she forced it out—the image of Margaret's final wave to Terrie before she entered the jetway to board her flight.

Turning south on 13, she was less than five minutes from her Aunt Barbara's home and an early start to her weekend, one that marked ten years since the last time she'd seen Margaret's sweet, smiling face.

Negotiating the last corner, she spotted her aunt on the porch. Margaret's face briefly appeared before it was replaced by her Aunt Barbara's. She allowed herself a broad smile as she pulled into the driveway.

Terrie rolled up her car window but not before her aunt's voice made it through. "Hey there, stranger. How was the trip?"

"Surprisingly quick, given the traffic," said Terrie as she climbed out of the car and gave her aunt a quick hug.

Holding Terrie by the shoulders, she looked her niece over. "You've lost weight."

"I'm eating."

"How many miles are you running a day?"

Terrie sidestepped the question. "I have to stay in shape. Besides, running clears my head."

"Whatever works. I just put up some water if you'd like some tea."

"Love some." Terrie grabbed her overnight bag and followed her aunt inside the house.

"You can settle in the back bedroom. I just finished painting it last weekend."

Terrie dropped off her bag and came out to the breakfast nook, where her aunt waited with a cup of tea in hand. She settled at the table, closed her eyes, and inhaled deeply, savoring the scent of lemon and honey that steamed from the cup and floated on the breeze from the open kitchen window.

Barbara joined her niece at the table. "Not what you expected your assignment to be?"

Cutting through the fog of her solitary thoughts, Barbara's words jolted her to the present. "No," Terrie whispered.

"You didn't really expect it to be easy, did you?"

"That's not it."

"What is it, then?" Barbara asked before sipping her tea.

Terrie looked sympathetically at her aunt, wishing she could unpack her duty's burden.

Barbara cocked her head back at Terrie. "I realize you can't tell me everything, but I would hope there's someone you can talk to. How about your fellow newbie? Can you confide in him?"

"That's just it. I really don't know." *We do not know* echoed in her head.

"Now you're sounding paranoid."

Not if you've seen the mounting evidence, she thought, but her expression gave her thoughts away.

"Okay, don't tell me," her aunt said with a hint of resignation. "What would you like for dinner?"

"The answers to my many questions."

"I don't think I have any in the fridge, just now."

"I'm sorry. Anything would be fine."

"Bay scallops in butter sauce?"

"Mmm. Sounds tasty." Terrie got up and walked over to the window, glancing across the 495 and over the Delaware River at the Jersey Shore. "Did Uncle Kaelen ever confide in you about his work?"

"Only in a general way. He was never too specific."

"Then an intelligence officer must maintain a certain degree of paranoia."

"Paranoia? No, but certainly a healthy degree of skepticism."

"How do I tell the difference?"

"If you can ask yourself that question, paranoia doesn't enter into it." Continuing to stare at her niece, she asked, "So is there anything I *can* address for you?"

Terrie thought about what questions would be the least problematic. "I'm curious if you can recall any of the ships James Hackett built on Badger."

Barbara considered the question. "That should be simple enough. The first prominent ship built by his shipyard was the USS *Raleigh*, the one on the New Hampshire state seal. Other vessels he constructed included a sloop of war for John Paul Jones called the USS *Ranger*; the *Congress*, one of the original six frigates ordered by President Washington; and two tribute vessels—a ship of the line for France's King Louis XVI called *America*, and a 36-gun frigate for the Dey of Algiers called the *Crescent*."

"Did he repair any vessels?"

"No, but in the mid-1800s, the shipbuilders Fernald and Petigrew refitted numerous ships on the island."

Terrie thought of the age of the artifacts she discovered and how they pointed to a time earlier than the 1800s. If the stocks held a refitted vessel, it must have been something the early federal government wanted to keep secret. "Is it possible the AMS *Justice* might have been one of them?"

"The *Justice* never sailed into Piscataqua. She was an armed, Baltimore-based coaster, whose normal trade routes went from Jamaica to Boston Harbor. She was last seen near Cadiz in 1788, where she and her crew were reported lost at sea." Barbara watched her niece as she slipped into another contemplative state. It was obvious Terrie was thinking about work again. In a deliberate attempt to break that chain, she said, "You need a diversion."

"I haven't had time for diversions lately."

"Sounds like an excuse to justify why you're not taking one. I think a good place for you to start would be that foreman you met. Or perhaps your neighbor-slash-coworker, what's his name?"

Terrie shot her aunt a raised eyebrow. "Not that kind of diversion. I was thinking more along the lines of a good book."

Barbara's eyes brightened up as she snapped her fingers. "I have just the thing." She disappeared into her bedroom for a moment and returned with the book on carriers Terrie had asked for and a short-read paperback. "I think we're singing the same tune here. Along with the textbook, I found this in a curio shop on Rehoboth Avenue."

Terrie glossed over the unfamiliar title and author. "Who's Juli Aruem?"

"Juli is a full-time real estate agent turned freelance writer. Her office is located on Pulaski Highway."

"Fiction or non?"

"It started out as her master's thesis, but she parlayed it into a detailed nonfiction monograph about the privateers of the Chesapeake and Delaware Bays."

"More light reading, eh?"

"I'm not sure what you might glean from it, but I think you'll find it useful…for those questions you're unable to ask me."

Terrie smiled. "Was I that obvious?"

"You've been trying not to tell me something since your posting to New Hampshire. I do believe you found something only a study of our early seafaring history would shed any light on."

Giving her aunt a sideways smirk, Terrie asked, "How do you do it?"

"Do what?"

"Know exactly what I need before I do?"

"Because you're my sister's daughter. And I knew my sister quite well. You have her determination to stand your ground when you're right and defend that position at great personal cost."

Terrie read the short synopsis before skimming through the author's thirty-five pages of research notes. "I see she preferred using source material as close to the event as possible. I like that."

"That's what makes the book so intriguing."

"Sourced books with actual copies of the broadsides, historical firsthand accounts of personal correspondence, newspapers of the period…she seems to have covered it all." Then Terrie read the author's biography. "Hmm. She would be about Margaret's age then?"

"Her office is in Bear. Why don't you call her in the morning to see if you could get in to speak with her?"

"I'll do that," Terrie said with a smile.

Philip woke up early in his Portsmouth safe house. A dispassionate loner, he enjoyed a certain level of confidence in his ability to plan for and adapt to a variety of unforeseen contingencies. Yet this current one vexed him.

All the intelligence he had seen to this point led him to believe that what Runner sought was definitely buried under the marina on Badger Island. With no doubts whatsoever, Philip chose to forgo developing alternatives. It was a costly mistake. He couldn't help thinking that what started out as a simple search-and-recovery mission had ballooned out of his control.

To recover, he diverted the six-minute AOR Seven audio from its intended destination to the new lieutenant, who did so admirable a job with the construction foreman and that nosy reporter. Though he had reservations about using someone so unversed and unpolished, the young lieutenant acquitted herself admirably, in his opinion.

He got the coffee butler going before selecting which disguise he was going to use. Inside his case of cosmetics and assorted eye lenses was an impressive array of personally designed latex facial appliances, the envy of any Hollywood makeup artist. He had a variety of wigs to fit any occasion. His facility for vocal impressions and talent for disguise made Philip unrecognizable.

As he fixed a hazel eye lens into place, he received a message from his Portsmouth contact. He was given two pieces of critical information: they submitted a transcript of the audio with the latest SITREP and the young lieutenant who translated it was on her way to Claymont, Delaware, for the weekend.

Philip placed the second lens and then packed for his trip to his safe house in Wilmington. Once there, he switched vehicles to a locally plated Jetta and drove it to a parking spot a few spaces down and across the street from the house of Barbara Forester.

He set up his listening device in time to record the discussion between Terrie and her aunt. They were talking about some local author and her book.

Philip returned to the safe house to plan his strategy. He created a new disguise, switched safe vehicles, and made sure he was in the parking lot of Juli Aruem's real estate office before it opened in the morning. He planned to be there for Terrie's arrival and to learn what they were going to discuss. With any luck, it would put him back on track to finding what he expected to find on Badger Island.

TWENTY SIX

Terrie walked into the real estate office and approached the reception desk. A woman wearing a company blazer emerged from around the corner to confer with the receptionist.

"Miss Aruem?" Terrie queried the thirty-something woman, whose gaze shifted to Terrie's left.

"I'm Juli Aruem," said a soft-spoken voice next to her. "How may I help you?"

"Terrie Murphy, Miss Aruem. I called your office earlier today. My aunt gave me your book," she said, holding it up to the author.

A light flush underscored her embarrassment. "I thought they all went out of print."

"Thankfully, no. I was fascinated by your chapter on the privateers of the late 1700s. I'm in town for the weekend and wondered if I could ask you a few questions."

"Well, I really don't have time right now."

"It won't take but a few minutes, I promise."

Juli glanced at the clock. "I have a twelve-thirty showing, which gives me an hour. I could do lunch now if you care to join me."

"I'd like that, thank you."

"The family diner at the end of the strip mall isn't bad."

"Sure."

Juli opened the door for Terrie as she asked, "What did you have questions about?"

"In the preview, you said the influence of privateers around Delmarva came to an end in 1788?"

"That's correct. After the conviction of James McAlpine that year, the fledgling federal government began to follow the advice of nautically-minded men like John Barry. He believed in supplanting the 'hired gun' for a more permanent naval force. It's the reason he's considered the father of the country's Old Navy."

Terrie smiled as she remembered all the times she traveled across the Commodore Barry Bridge with Margaret whenever they visited the Jersey Shore. But this was no time for reverie. She needed to keep focused on her reason for meeting Juli. "I'm actually interested in the privateers since then. For instance, did your research uncover any clues to the fate of a ship called the *Justice* or her last captain?"

Juli's head snapped toward Terrie. "Her *last* captain?"

She knows, Terrie thought. The only way Juli could know is if she had access to other sources Terrie was unaware of. She certainly couldn't come right out and say she found the logbook of the *Justice* with a second captain's handwriting, but she could say she heard it somewhere. Believing her aunt provided her with the perfect bluff, she pressed the surprised author. "After the Revolutionary War, armed privateer vessels were hired by the Confederation Congress to protect merchant ships as far as the Mediterranean. Popular midshipmen lore held that the *Justice* had its armament upgraded with nine pounders and swivel guns on Badger Island and that the captain who launched her was called Tunney."

Juli squinted at Terrie. "Where do you come by your information?"

"It's a rumored story around the Naval Academy."

"You're in the Navy?" Juli's question was more like an accusation.

"Yes, ma'am."

"I think we're done here," Aruem said dismissively and turned to leave.

Terrie called out to her, "Please wait. I'm not asking as a government representative. I'm asking as a concerned citizen searching for the truth."

"The truth? The truth isn't very popular these days."

"Don't I know it," Terrie said with a slight grin.

After an uncomfortable silence, Juli asked, "Where are you stationed?"

"I'm at the Navy Yard in Portsmouth, New Hampshire, but I'm visiting my aunt here in Delaware."

"Oh? Where?"

"Up the road in Claymont."

Juli tapped a finger over her lips as if considering whether to engage Terrie further.

Terrie took advantage of Juli's indecision by opening the restaurant door and holding out a welcoming arm. "Shall we?"

"Only if I have leave to stop the inquiry at any time."

"Fair enough."

Juli relented and the two went into the restaurant. "If you're asking about the *Justice* and Captain Tunney then you read enough to know they're not in my book."

"That's right," Terrie bluffed again. "I was wondering if you could tell me more about their fate."

"Hmm. You know, they're not in the book for a disturbing reason."

Terrie raised a curious brow.

"It's why I was rude to you. My publisher told me, in no uncertain terms, not to mention the *Justice* or Tunney in my work. I published the book as-is."

"You apparently know something about them," Terrie coaxed.

"Well, first off, your information is incorrect. The last captain of record for the *Justice* was Arthur Ledbetter."

"What happened to the *Justice*, and how does Tunney fit in?"

"In 1785, Captain Ledbetter received a Letter of Marque authorizing him to seize the Algerian ship allegedly responsible for the capture of Captain Richard O'Brien and his vessel, *Dauphin*. Three years later, both Ledbetter and his ship were lost, the latest victims of an Algerian corsair. Through personal correspondence that made it into the newspapers of the period, I discovered evidence that most of the crew had made it back to Philadelphia, but not Ledbetter. The reports convinced me that he went down with the *Justice* on May 30, 1788."

"And Tunney?"

"He was among those who made it back. Curious to know more about him and why he had to be deleted from my book, I did some digging."

"What did you find?"

"What I found resulted in another manuscript, Miss Murphy. Fortunately, I had the foresight to print the entire work before my computer crashed."

"How did that happen?"

"I do not know."

We do not know. Dempsey's recurring theme gave her an idea. Terrie asked the question she really wanted the answer to. "Tell me about this Tunney."

Juli looked about to see if it was safe to discuss the topic. Spying only an elderly couple enjoying their lunch a few tables away and a middle-aged gentleman reading a newspaper with his back to them, she determined it was safe enough to offer up her narrative. "I can only tell you the beginning of his story in public," she said in a low voice.

"Anything you can tell me now would be greatly appreciated."

"Vernon Tunney was born in 1763, near the banks of the Elk River in Maryland. He lost his mother to dysentery before his first birthday and his father to the Battle of Trenton. Orphaned at thirteen, young Tunney signed on with his first vessel, a Philadelphia-based coaster under the auspices of a Delaware entrepreneur named William West. In the process of making routine trips between Philadelphia and Annapolis, Tunney's natural affinity for merchant service attracted the attention of the Board of Admiralty." A waiter arrived to take their order. When he left, Juli asked, "Where was I?"

"If the Board of Admiralty took notice of him, he must have been mature for his age," Terrie prodded.

"That's right. He was only seventeen when the Board of Admiralty recommended he join Captain John Barry aboard the USS *Alliance*. Barry was ordered to take command of the *Alliance* from Captain Pierre Landais in the wake of the latter's dismissal due to his questionable actions during the Battle of Flamborough Head in 1779.

"Barry's own captain's log attests to how the young sailor distinguished himself during the Battle of Yorktown. Unfortunately, America's Old Navy was disbanded after the Revolutionary War. When the *Alliance* was decommissioned, Tunney returned to coaster duty. He became master of the schooner *Hypatia*, the vessel his father taught him how to pilot."

"How did Tunney manage to find his way onto the *Justice*?"

"American merchant vessels like the *Hypatia* were no longer protected by the British or the French. Without naval protection, they became targets for any ships with predatory designs. It didn't take long for someone to act on them."

"That still doesn't explain how he got aboard the *Justice*."

"A year after the war, the *Betsy* became a prize of Moroccan pirates and her crew condemned as slaves. Tunney was outraged by the news and asked to join Captain O'Brien aboard the merchant vessel *Dauphin* on her maiden trip to the Mediterranean.

"Unfortunately, the *Dauphin* fell victim to the Algerian flagship *Dey of Reckoning*, and for the next twelve years, her captain and crew were enslaved by the Dey of Algiers. Tunney managed to escape and communicate their fate to his representative from Pennsylvania, Edward Hand."

"Captain Ledbetter's General Hand?"

"The same."

"What happened to him after that?"

"It's all in the manuscript."

"Do you still have it?"

"In a secure place, yes."

"I know I've provided you little reason to trust me, but would you consider letting me read it? You would help me immensely."

"I don't know," said Juli pensively. "How would you use it?"

"I won't reference you or your work, if that's what you're concerned about."

"It is. I've been threatened by the likes of the Justice Department over this."

"Really?"

"And that's not all."

Terrie sensed her discomfort. "What did they do to you?"

"Nothing directly to me, per se, but I suspect it was they who crashed my computer."

"Why would you believe that?"

"They must have thought I planned on going forward with publication. On a hunch, I went back to my original sources to see if I could find any of the various magazine articles, texts, and online references I used to write it." Juli's healthy complexion turned deathly pale before she added, "Miss Murphy, they're all gone."

"Even the historical reference books?"

"Right down to the card catalogue entries in the libraries I went to."

Terrie paused to think for a second. "If I can read your manuscript, it could provide me the clues I'll need to solve this."

"Solve what, Miss Murphy?"

"I don't know yet, but if you're willing to help me, and I can locate unclassified references to support your conclusions, you can be sure I'll make hard copies to support the publishing of your manuscript."

A tear glistened in the corner of Juli's eye. "Thank you, Miss Murphy."

"Terrie, please," she said as the waiter placed their plates down in front of them.

Terrie polished off one quarter of her BLT in only two bites.

"You must be hungry."

Terrie was about to scarf down another quarter of her sandwich, but she realized where she was and who she was with. "Sorry, force of habit. You learn to eat fast when you're taught that time spent eating risks readiness."

Juli's jaw dropped.

Terrie added a caveat to qualify her answer. "Animals eat quickly to protect themselves against predators."

A horrified look crossed Juli's face. "Who could be stalking you?"

If you only knew, Terrie thought.

The waiter came by as the two women finished their meal. "Will there be anything else?"

"No, thank you, just the bills would be nice," Juli said.

"Make that one bill," Terrie added.

"I can't allow you to—"

"Yes, you can. Please, you've been so helpful."

The real estate agent and sometime author relented. After Terrie settled the bill, the two women made their way to the front door. As they exited the restaurant, Juli turned to Terrie. "Let me think about your request, Miss Murph…Terrie."

"That's all I ask, Miss Aruem."

"Juli."

Terrie offer her an appreciative nod. "Very well, then, Juli."

They were steps away from the real estate office door when Juli turned. "Well, Terrie, thank you for lunch. You're…an interesting lunch companion."

"I should be thanking you. I learned more from you I'm sure."

Juli leaned closer to Terrie and whispered, "Learn the fate of the *Crescent*, and you shall find Vernon 'Cyclops' Tunney." She shook Terrie's hand and disappeared into her office.

"You can be sure I'll make hard copies to support the publishing of your manuscript," he heard Terrie say, listening through the headset as he watched through binoculars from the safety of his parked vehicle.

That was it. Philip waited another ten minutes to make sure. The women had transitioned to more innocuous topics of conversation, which meant he was reasonably comfortable that he captured everything of value. He must now get back to the safe house to change vehicles and his disguise before heading back to the home of Barbara Forester to resume his surveillance.

He heard enough of their discussion to understand that he needed to keep closer tabs on Terrie's movements from now on. If she's gathering intelligence on what they've managed to successfully erase from existence, he needed to be there to ensure the erasures took.

"What do you think she meant by that, I wonder?" Barbara asked.

Terrie cleared her throat. "I'm not sure. Didn't you mention that the *Crescent* was built on Badger?"

"I did, yes. That particular ship had an interesting beginning. It almost wasn't built."

"How's that?"

"Even before she was named, there was debate as to whether she should be completed as planned."

"Why?"

"The peace that followed the Revolution wasn't what the Founders envisioned. Men like Thomas Jefferson saw any standing military force as a threat to liberty. He would come to change his tune after Britain and France refused to defend American merchant ships. Open piracy became more of a threat in the trade routes of the Mediterranean than any of the Founders anticipated."

Terrie warmed their tea and took a seat to take in the rest of her aunt's recitation.

"After the widespread news of America's independence, merchant vessels became ripe targets for privateers and pirates alike, none worse than the likes of the Barbary States. This deficiency of the nation's first constitution, the Articles of Confederation, caused deep divisions. Vessels like the *Betsy*, the *Maria* and the *Dauphin* would be taken before any serious actions to protect our ships were contemplated."

"What did they do to help prevent these attacks?"

Barbara's face was the epitome of concentration. "Nine treaties between the United States and the Barbary Coast nations were negotiated between 1786 and 1836, of varying complexity and dubious results. The early ones promised to act as European nations did, paying annual tributes. The amounts of money and presents stipulated in these treaties took too long to comply with, according to the Dey of Algiers, so the US Congress approved the gift of a 36-gun frigate. The keel for the unnamed vessel was laid in 1796.

It wasn't until after the vessel's first launch on June 24, 1797, that the ship's designer, Josiah Fox, named her the *Crescent*."

"How long before the Dey received it?"

"The ship launched from Portsmouth, New Hampshire, on January 31, 1798. Captain Timothy Newman, along with several officers and men who were previous 'guests' of the Dey, sailed the ship to Algiers. The distinguished passenger on that trip was Captain Richard O'Brien, the former master of the *Dauphin* and new US Consul to Algiers. Consul O'Brien himself reported that the Dey was quite pleased with his present."

"Whatever became of it?"

"I don't know, but I do know who does. The curator of the J. Welles Henderson Archives and Library, Dr. Roger Dagney, is a good friend of mine. The library is part of the Independence Seaport Museum at the Port of Philadelphia. If it's not too late, we can stop by to see if he can answer that question."

Learn the fate of the Crescent, *and you shall find Vernon "Cyclops" Tunney.*

An impatient Terrie grabbed her keys. "Well, are we going?"

Amused by her niece's determination, Barbara said, "Let me call first to make sure he's there."

Philip's second safe car wasn't as reliable as the first. As adept as he was with disguise, he was inept as a mechanic. All he had to do was replace the clogged air filter with a new one, but he diagnosed and corrected the malfunction too late. Terrie's vehicle was no longer in the driveway when he arrived at Barbara Forester's house.

He could only sit and wait for their return.

TWENTY SEVEN

The trip to Penn's Landing took thirty minutes. Plenty of time for the two women to find Roger Dagney before the museum closed for the day. Gliding their car into one of the open parking spots near the entrance to the museum, Terrie noticed a tall man with closely cropped gray whiskers waiting for them near the circular stairs to the walking bridge. His smile grew wider as they made their way toward him.

"Well, mountains do move, don't they?" he said.

"They do at that," Barbara said as she rushed to embrace her friend. "How long has it been?"

"Three years, nine months, and an odd number of days, but who's counting?"

"So you didn't miss me."

"Not at all," Roger replied as the two shared a laugh. "And who is this lovely creature?"

"I'm the reason we're here," Terrie said.

Barbara's disapproving frown emerged. "This is my niece, Terrie Murphy."

"So you're the person I need to thank for bringing my friend up for a visit, eh?"

"I'm afraid our being here is more scholarly than social," Terrie replied.

He looked at his friend. "Ah, the direct approach. Refreshing."

"My sister's daughter can be socially abrasive at times, but her heart is usually in the right place," she conceded, giving her niece the you-had-better-apologize-right-now look.

Anytime her aunt used the phrase "my sister's daughter," Terrie knew she was in for a lecture afterward. "I'm sorry, Dr. Dagney. I tend to be singled-minded at times."

"And what scholarly business brings you here on such a beautiful Memorial Day weekend?"

"It concerns the *Crescent*, our country's tribute vessel to Algiers," Terrie said.

He glanced at Barbara, who made no effort to hide the I-told-you-so look on her face.

"Let's go inside. We can stroll around the museum while we talk." He escorted them along the sidewalk to the museum's entrance. Holding the door open so they could enter the building, he asked Terrie, "I'm curious, why does the *Crescent* engage your interest?"

"I was hoping you could shed some light on what happened to it."

"If you can tell me what you already know, I might be able to fill in the gaps."

"For that, I'd have to defer to my aunt's encyclopedic knowledge of the subject."

Barbara smiled at her niece before addressing Roger. "Well, according to War Department records of the period, she was a 36-gun frigate designed by Josiah Fox and built by James Hackett on Badger Island. Those same records indicate the vessel was named *Crescent* and delivered to the satisfaction of the Dey of Algiers in April of 1798. Unfortunately, I found no references to what happened to her after that."

Roger scratched at his whiskers and responded, "You're essentially correct. At the time she was delivered to the Dey, the *Crescent* was the most heavily armed vessel in the Algerine fleet, rivaled only by a French corvette with 24 guns. Consequently, she became the Dey's flagship."

Increasingly impatient, Terrie peppered Roger with questions. "Is there a reason the ship has no known history beyond the report of its delivery to the Dey?"

"Embarrassment," Roger answered. "In a series of increasingly hostile actions against American ships, our present to Algiers became a slap in the face to those who authorized it."

"I don't understand?"

"Politically, authorizing the ship as a gift made sense, but it didn't work out so well in practice."

"Were any of these actions by the *Crescent* documented?"

"The first reported incident between the *Crescent* and an American ship occurred when the *Phoenix* was boarded in May of 1800. Though she was allowed to depart unharmed, further incidents became more pernicious." Roger paused his narrative while they made their way past a small tour group.

Terrie prodded, "If the Dey was so pleased with his gift, and the peace treaties were our guarantee of safe passage through the Mediterranean, what caused them to harass our ships?"

"A new Algerian captain, a notoriously malevolent man named Rafik al-Ghazali, took command of the *Crescent*. After the *Phoenix* incident, he believed the *Crescent's* former captain violated his duty as a Muslim. Rafik accused him of failing to comply with the tenants of Sharia law and had the man beheaded. The new captain of the *Crescent* savagely enforced such doctrine, earning him the more fitting name of Rafik the Marauder."

"Really? This Rafik character assumed the name and radical views of Abu Hamid al-Ghazali?"

"You've heard of al-Ghazali, then?"

"His work The Nonsense of Philosophers formed the basis for Islam's dismissal of anything that countered the teachings of the Quran or the Hadith of Muhammad. If Rafik followed the doctrine of al-Ghazali, other attacks must have ensued?"

"They did. In 1802 alone, the *Crescent* destroyed a Swiss vessel, captured the American brig *Richmond*, and a Portuguese frigate of 44 guns. Although heavily armed, the inexperience of the frigate captain showed. The Portuguese vessel only managed a single volley before she surrendered. Rafik gave no quarter when he and his crew boarded the frigate. With blades in both hands, they slaughtered all they saw. It was an absolute bloodbath."

Roger paused as they navigated around the last display in the museum and made their way into his office. He closed the door behind him and offered Barbara and Terrie a seat.

Unsatisfied with Roger's answers, Terrie got to the question she came to the museum to find out. "What happened to the *Crescent*?"

"To make sense of that story, I must tell you another." Roger's eyes darted toward Barbara. She nodded before he continued. "The USS *John Adams* and the USS *Enterprise* engaged a Tripolitan polacre in pitched battle during their blockade of Tripoli in June of 1803. The polacre went down in a large explosion. And though there's debate as to which ship should be credited for its destruction, witnesses insist they saw something else."

That there was something else never made the history books and Terrie knew it. "What do you mean?"

"They reported a disturbance a fair distance away from the engagement. Whatever it was had no sails but moved quickly across the water. It turned toward the action for a minute or two before it turned again to resume its original course. She departed the area at extreme speed. Moments later, a fast-moving line of agitated water raced toward the polacre. The ship blew apart the instant the line made contact with it."

"That sounds like a modern torpedo. But self-propelled torpedoes didn't exist yet."

"That's correct. They wouldn't until the Whitehead torpedo was tested in 1866."

Trying to draw the obvious conclusion, Terrie asked, "Is that how the *Crescent* met her end?"

Roger ignored the question and pressed on with his narrative. "Two years later, word of another American treaty with Algiers reached Rafik, who swore he'd have none of it. When American gunboats were sighted passing Gibraltar, Rafik ordered his squadron to engage them. Neither the American gunboats nor Rafik's squadron were ever heard from again."

Terrie's eyes grew wide. "Sounds like a ghost story."

Embarrassed by Terrie's reaction, her aunt could only shake her head.

Roger continued, "The official account is that the American squadron was lost during a storm before they could reach Malta. Though the storm theory is plausible, tales handed down from Arab folklore contend that Rafik's squadron hunted down and destroyed the American gunships. The fight lasted less than two hours, but its ramifications would reverberate for the next two centuries. The *Crescent's* victory over the American gunboats actually sealed its fate."

"How?" Terrie asked.

"As the last burning American hull slipped beneath the surface, Rafik spotted a strange vessel without sails circling them. He tried to come about, but the other ship was too fast. From directly astern came an intense blast. One of the xebecs had ripped into a fireball of splinters. As Rafik ordered the cannons loaded and ready to fire, his 32-gun corsair suddenly exploded next to him with enough concussive force to knock several sailors off their feet. Before he was able to reposition his ship to compensate, a polacre and another xebec, blew apart. A third xebec decided to make its escape.

"In the distance, Rafik saw the enemy vessel's masts rise up and its sails unfurled. She slowly turned her bow to the *Crescent's* broadside. The vessel grew in size, closing the gap and bringing it within range of Rafik's guns. He ordered his crew to fire everything they had. Every cannonball bounced off its hull, making a metallic sound like an echoing laugh. As the ship got closer, Rafik could see the captain of this weird, crewless ship. He had no hat, but wore a dark frock coat with wide lapels and a short cape. He owned a mane of dark hair sprinkled with ashy flecks that made a seamless transition to his similarly colored beard. The opposing captain was tall, broad-shouldered, and powerfully built, much like his vessel.

"Rafik watched as a self-propelled fang departed the bow of this crimson serpent. His eyes remained glued to the swirling line until it touched the *Crescent* amidships. The resulting explosion vaporized its center, a sliver of the ship's wheel sent wildly through the air, slicing Rafik's throat. His legs lost their power and he slumped against the gunwale, one hand cupped against the onslaught of spurting, hot blood. Looking across the gulf of water and smoke, Rafik observed the opposing captain set an ivory pipe in his teeth and light it.

"The forecastle had disappeared into the sea almost immediately. The stern leaned aft, its gaping hole, the remnants of the main deck, began to take on water. The strange ship drew closer as the *Crescent* spewed out a final gasp of air from its hold. Rafik's vision grew dim. Before he breathed his last, he saw the salt-and-pepper-haired captain salute him with a lift of his pipe to the corner of his eye and then turn around. The mythical vessel retracted its sails and masts and retired at extreme speed. Rafik the Marauder never saw this. His world had dissolved to oblivion long before the last whirlpool faded, signaling the end of American's gift to the Dey of Algiers."

As Terrie made the turn out of the parking lot, her aunt said, "You're some piece of work."

"What?"

"You could've at least made the pretense of not being such a jerk around him."

Staring at the highway, Terrie responded, "What would you have me say? You asked me to apologize. I did."

"Right. That's why you went straight into interrogation mode after your so-called apology."

Terrie took the criticism in silence. That didn't mean there wasn't a truck-load of new information to think about, like Juli Aruem's warning about the *Crescent* and Tunney. For all of Roger Dagney's painstaking detail, there was still something about his narrative that bothered her. She was going to broach the subject with her aunt, but Barbara wasn't in the mood for that conversation.

They made it all the way to Governor Prinze Boulevard before Terrie said anything. "I need to call NCIS headquarters at the Pentagon."

"Why?"

Ignoring that question, Terrie said, "Your friend was meticulous in his description of the *Crescent's* demise but said nothing expressly connecting the *Crescent* to Tunney."

Her aunt's light bulb finally illuminated. "That's right, he didn't."

"I need a good run on the problem. I also believe I should press forward with the remainder of this investigation myself." Terrie turned to look at her aunt before she added, "For your own safety."

Barbara's face flushed with anger for the briefest of seconds, but Terrie was right. Her niece was a young adult acting as a rational naval intelligence officer in the throes of what was likely to be a classified investigation.

TWENTY EIGHT

Terrie completed her run through her aunt's Claymont neighborhood. She stretched out the last block before she got to the end of the driveway. That's when she noticed something she hadn't before; a dark gray Jetta across the street. Its driver was behind the wheel, reading.

As Terrie walked past it, she glanced in that general direction to get a look at the driver. He was an elderly gentleman with a jowly face, graying medium-length hair, and horn-rimmed glasses covering tired-looking green eyes. He looked up from his reading material, nodded tersely at Terrie, and returned to what he was doing.

None of her aunt's neighbors were beyond their midforties. This guy had to be in his seventies. Aside from looking out of place on the street, Terrie also suspected something about him she couldn't quite place. She stared at him a bit longer to commit his profile to memory before going into the house. As she opened the door, she looked back over her shoulder in time to see the man get out of his car and search for something in the back seat. He removed a small bag then returned to his seat and resumed reading.

Hearing her aunt in the living room, Terrie asked, "Do you have any new neighbors?"

"As a matter of fact, an older couple moved into the house across the street."

"Have you met them?"

"When they first moved in. They're recently retired from upstate New York."

She was going to ask another question when her phone buzzed on the kitchen table. She read the name on the screen and answered it. "Yes, Mr. O'Hara, what can I do for you?"

"Well, hello to you too."

"Sorry, it's been one of those days. What's up?"

"You did give me an assignment, you know."

"You want to talk about it now?" Terrie hoped he'd take the hint.

"I just finished up at the Antiquarian Society in Worcester."

"What brought you there?"

"Long story. I'll fill you in when you get back."

"Make any progress?"

"More like progress through elimination."

"Sounds delightful. Was there anything else?"

"Well, yeah. I just wanted—" Jack trailed off nervously.

"Wanted what?"

"Do we really have to do this again?"

Her aunt happened to glance her way. "Sorry," Barbara mouthed to her niece.

Terrie gave her aunt a dismissive wave and a smile. Moving her cell to the other ear, she said teasingly, "Go on. You're doing fine."

"Can't a guy worry about his friend without an ulterior motive?"

"You're worried about me?"

After a verbal hiccup, he said, "If you have another episode like that night, who'll be there for you?"

"I'm not alone, you know."

"That's not what I meant and you know it."

"Oh." Jack's burgeoning confidence was getting to her, so she changed the subject. "So you didn't have any luck at the Athenaeum?"

"No, but they did put me on to the Antiquarian. Have you ever been there?"

"No."

"It boasts the largest collection of early newspapers in the country."

"Does it have actual papers from the period?"

"They said they did, but I was only able to familiarize myself with the place and its procedures before they closed for the day."

"Then you found nothing?"

"I didn't necessarily say that. While their availability of bound copies is smaller than the digital library, there are quite a few volumes to go over."

"Any with relevance to our subject?"

"I should find out tomorrow."

"They're open on Sunday?"

"I used the official investigation card. The curator was generous with her time, since she planned on being there anyway."

"Aren't you the charmer?"

"Give me time," he said with a smile in his voice.

Terrie couldn't help but grin, herself. "You have until I get back Monday afternoon."

"Thanks for the warning."

She couldn't believe she was actually growing fond of him. Angry at herself, she cussed under her breath.

"Getting to you, am I?"

"Oh, shut up!"

"Who are you telling to shut up?" Barbara said. Her impeccable timing could always be relied upon to maximize Terrie's embarrassment.

"Not you!" It was too late. She already saw the smile on her aunt's face. Making her displeasure loud enough for both to hear, Terrie yelled, "I'm going to stop talking to both of you if you two don't behave yourselves!"

The silence on the phone was met with a comical look from her aunt.

"See you Monday afternoon. If you're home."

"I'll be there to help you with your books."

"You…never mind. See you Monday." Terrie ended the call and started flipping through her contact list until she got to the number for NCIS headquarters in Washington. She heard the phone ring twice before someone picked up.

"Special Agent Bergman," a pleasant voice announced.

"Agent Bergman, Lieutenant Terrie Murphy, Portsmouth Navy Yard. I'm following up for my CO, Commander Crabtree. He was wondering if you had any results for us."

"Let me take a look." The receiver's secure voice masked the background noise as Bergman's end of the call went silent. In less than a minute he was back on the line. "As I suspected, Daniels is still working that case. He's not in today, but I can leave a message for him to get back with you."

"I'll relay your message to Commander Crabtree. Thank you."

Terrie hit the red phone icon to end the call. Her plans temporarily thwarted, she looked down the hall at her room. She decided to work on packing her library. After that, all that remained would be to get in the car and leave. She heard her aunt rummaging around in the kitchen. Peering out the living room window, she noticed the Jetta was no longer there. Dismissing her suspicions, she got to work.

She loaded the first few boxes without incident until she got to a set of illustrated reference books. It was a large edition describing the evolution of naval power throughout history. Another one discussed the etymology of nautical superstitions from various countries and cultures. They were about the same size as the books her aunt had saved, so she boxed them together and highlighted the box with an asterisk to open first when she got home. Terrie stretched a piece of packing tape across the lid of the box as her aunt entered.

"You certainly got busy today. It looks like you're already done."

"I have two more boxes to finish up."

"You're not planning to leave tonight are you?"

"No, just want the car packed and ready."

⚓

With the aid of his parabolic dish, Philip heard Barbara say she would take a shower while Terrie was out for her run. He stowed the small but cumbersome devise and waited. Spotting Terrie as she left the house, Philip made his move.

He approached the house like he owned it, key ring in hand. Identifying the mechanism as the kind of cylinder used in most residential homes, he located the correct universal key to gain entry. Again, luck was with him. Confirming the cell on the kitchen table was hers, he made a copy of its SIM card and headed back to the car. He spied Terrie rounding the corner as he situated himself behind the wheel. He waited for her to pass him before he retrieved a clone phone from the back seat and united it with the copied card.

His initial test was more successful than he'd imagined. He listened as Terrie made her call to the Pentagon. She received disappointing news from a familiar agent he knew was working on the case. The disguised Philip smiled. Daniels was a known alias for one of Runner's operatives within NCIS. Secure in the knowledge that Terrie was stopped for the moment, Philip returned to his Wilmington safe house to prepare for his trip to back to Portsmouth.

TWENTY NINE

Terrie pulled into her reserved parking spot and saw Jack's bike and Chevy. *Good, he can help move the boxes out of the car.*

She grabbed the first box and made her way up the stairs. Coming down the hall, she heard Jack's stereo, though it was a fraction of the volume he was used to. Terrie juggled the box to get at her keys. Safely inside her apartment, she placed the box on the table and went back to Jack's apartment to roust him off the couch.

"Just a minute," he yelled. The music ceased, and a few seconds later he stood before her. "Miss Murphy, how was your trip?"

"Productive, Mr. O'Hara. Did you eat?"

"I was about to order a pizza. Care to join me?"

She grimaced, thinking of Clendaniel's garlic and pepperoni version. "No thanks. I was going to ask you over for supper so we could compare notes."

Jack frowned. "You don't think of anything else, do you?"

"You could help me with my books?"

"I already planned on it."

"My little reference library is rather heavy," she warned.

"Not a problem. I can…Wait a minute. Define little."

"Only a small library. Say, fifteen boxes."

Resigning himself to his fate, Jack grinned. "Let me get my shoes on."

"What do you feel like eating?"

"A pizza actually, but I could go for some Mexican."

"I could make some chicken enchiladas."

"Homemade or frozen?"

"I don't do frozen," she huffed.

"Do you do fresh bacon?"

"I can add it if you want."

"If you don't mind."

Jack got his shoes on and the two went downstairs to the parking lot. She opened the hatchback of her Ford Edge, and Jack reached in to pull out a medium-sized box.

As Terrie hoisted up a smaller one, she asked, "How's the arm, any better?"

"My thumb's a bit sore, but the arm's fine."

"Good." She then placed the box on the one he held in his hands. "Too heavy?"

With some effort to shift the weight, Jack replied, "It's fine…now."

"Great! About three more trips ought to do it."

All Jack could manage was a grunt of acceptance. The two worked over the next twenty minutes to liberate the library from her car.

With her hands on her hips, Terrie surveyed the stacks of boxes on the floor. "Could you give me a few minutes to freshen up before I start supper?"

"Sure. I could start going through the boxes and arranging the books on your bookcase if you'd like."

"I'd appreciate it. The boxes are marked and alphabetized. Can you read my writing?"

"No problem." He got straight to work on the first three boxes Terrie wanted opened.

Since the studio apartments were all the same, Jack knew the bedroom offered Terrie the privacy she needed to clean up while he got busy organizing the library.

He moved two asterisked boxes onto the kitchen table and ran the jagged edge of his apartment key across the seam at the top of the first one. Pulling open the flaps, he saw the first book under the Bubble Wrap. It was a well-worn, leather Bible. Flipping open the cover, he noticed it belonged to Terrie's sister, Margaret.

Beneath her sister's revered tome, he found several reference books: a Manual for Courts-Martial, The Military Commander and the Law, The Oxford Companion to the Supreme Court of the United States, Sun Tsu's The Art of War, Frederick Bastiat's The Law, and a copy of The Communist Manifesto.

In the second asterisked box, Jack found another unusual collection—an assortment of religious texts, from the Torah, the Bhagavad Gita, and Buddhist scripture, to both Arab and English copies of the Hadith of Muhammad and the Quran. At the bottom of the second box were books on Asian history and culture.

Turning his attention to the third important box Terrie had indicated, he found Juli Aruem's book on the privateers of the Chesapeake and Delaware Bays, along with the book on the colonial carriers she wanted. Under those were books on naval history, Adam Smith's Wealth of Nations, and an annotated reference copy of America's founding documents.

"A little light reading, Terrie?" he mumbled as he stacked the books on the table.

Jack was startled when Terrie's voice issued from behind him. "Keeping up with the latest mind-numbing TV programs doesn't interest me," she said, breezing past him on the way to the kitchen.

"Legal and religious texts? History?"

"Doing my best to round out my incomplete education, Mr. O'Hara. Even our friend Milton would've been hard-pressed to keep up with the infinite amalgam of reference sources available."

Scratching his stubbled chin, Jack said, "No wonder you don't have friends."

"Contained in those informative publications is drama enough for a lifetime, Mr. O'Hara."

"Well, that explains it."

"What?"

"Why you don't socialize like a normal human being."

"I don't socialize, as you put it, Mr. O'Hara, because I have yet to meet anyone whose company I would enjoy."

Annoyed, he said, "You don't find my company enjoyable?"

At times like these, her sister's encouraging suggestions about relationships were most needed. The one that came to mind this time was humility, a trait that was absent in her daily life. The closest alternative to Margaret was R. J. Clendaniel, and right now she could use his counsel.

"Mr. O'Hara, you, and a short list of others, are the exception to my rule of shutting out the world."

"I wouldn't have guessed you let anyone in, Miss Murphy."

"Didn't you just call me Terrie a second ago?"

"Oh, don't worry. I won't make that mistake again." Terrie reached for his arm when Jack got up to leave.

"Wait. Please."

Jack shoved his hands in his pockets and stared straight at the door. "When we agreed to start over I was hoping it wasn't just me working at it."

"You're right. You've been more open and approachable, while I've been quite the opposite."

The rift in the flow of the conversation was painful, but she didn't have long to wait for a riposte.

"And arrogant."

She smirked. "I deserve that."

"Why do you always have to be right?"

"I don't have to be. It just so happens that I am. It's when I vigorously defend positions proving me correct that people think I'm arrogant."

"That turns people off, ya know," he said, aiming his accusation directly into her eyes.

"So we're just supposed to propagate lies to make people feel better?"

"That's not what I'm saying."

"Then what are you saying?"

"You can't offer an opinion without being offensive?"

"Ah, the eternal paradox. People crave honesty but find it objectionable when confronted by someone like me who refuses to sugarcoat it."

Jack gave her statement some thought. "So long as you attack the position and not the person."

"Most people refuse to make that distinction," she responded. "They either can't or won't tell the difference."

"Such as not finding my company enjoyable? That's not personal at all, is it?"

Terrie lowered her head in submission. "Okay, that could be considered personal."

Giving Terrie's Eagles jersey the once-over, his eyes lingering where it accented her curves, he selected an appropriate, but trite, sports metaphor. "You mean I actually scored a touchdown?"

"More like a field goal." The two mirrored each other's amusement. Yielding the conversation to Jack, Terrie started supper while he got busy with the rest of the library. She gathered the ingredients on the counter as she watched Jack dive into another box of educational treasures. Slicing up the chicken breasts, she asked, "Find anything of interest?"

"Your taste in literature is certainly eclectic. Have you read all these books?"

"Three a week for ten years."

"And you retained all this information?" he asked, skeptical.

"Grab the next book out of the box," she directed.

He reached in and pulled out a book titled, Pseudo-Religion versus Pseudo-Science, and held it up. "How about this?"

"Open it to any page you want, and tell me which sentence from any paragraph you want me to recite."

"Oh, come on. You're kidding."

"Indulge me."

"All right." He flipped through the book, stopping somewhere near the end. "How about page 347, third sentence of the last paragraph?"

Squinting and looking up in the air as though she were reading directly off the page, she said, "'True science is a collaborative, multigenerational, multicultural enterprise that celebrates the contributions of Alhazen in equal measure with that of Aristotle.'" After quoting the line, she went back to chopping up the onion she had just sliced in two.

"How…Never mind," said Jack as he went back to the task at hand.

"Perhaps now you understand my reticence to warm up to people, especially when they realize I memorize most of what I read." She finished prepping the ingredients and asked, "How many enchiladas would you like?"

"Three would be fine, thanks."

"I only have refried beans and rice."

"They'll do. By the way, who was Alhazen? I've never heard of him."

"Nor of al-Khwarizmi, I'll bet?"

Jack's screwed-up expression responded for him.

"Though Aristotle is considered the father of scientific method, it was Alhazen who first used experimentation to prove his theories. And if you know the terms algebra and algorithm, you are acquainted with al-Khwarizmi. Algebra comes from his word for quadratic equations, al-Jabr, and algorithm is the derivative of his name in Latin."

"Where do you—"

"It's all in that book you were holding. Politics is the new pseudo religion, Mr. O'Hara. Its repetitious propaganda has its tentacles in more than just our government. Our educational institutions, schools of journalism, and pop culture are all infected by its rigid hold over public opinion."

"Based on what?" his eyes narrowed in skepticism.

"The facts, as outlined in books like that one, are readily available for public consumption. Unfortunately, facts are overshadowed by an establishment media all too willing to do or say what's necessary to preserve their false narratives. As a nation, we're too dependent on the opinions of the so-called experts. We no longer think for ourselves, Mr. O'Hara. In today's volatile world, that's a dangerous combination."

"To what false narratives are you referring?"

"That despite government and establishment media denials to the contrary, we're still engaged in a war against terror. They also believe we don't know why the current enemy hates us. Radical Islam is our enemy, not the Arab community, and it's been that way long before we were a country. Even a cursory study of the facts in that book demonstrate it."

"But wasn't Islam started on the Arabian Peninsula?"

"Not all Arabs are Muslim, Mr. O'Hara. Likewise, not all Muslims are radical. Take, for instance, their many contributions to Western academia."

Terrie's revelation hit him between the eyes. "Such as?"

"Were you aware that the greatest library in the thirteenth century was not from the West? It was the House of Wisdom in Baghdad."

"No, I wasn't."

"Or that the first degree-awarding university was actually established in Morocco in the ninth century by a Muslim woman?"

"Aren't women considered property by Muslim men?"

"That wasn't popularly espoused until al-Ghazali's writings began to flourish in the late eleventh century. Where al-Farabi demonstrated how science could address questions the adherents to Islam couldn't answer, al-Ghazali condemned anything outside Islamic orthodoxy."

"Then how do we address the radical side of Islam?"

"The ultimate solution to that lies within the Muslim community itself. They are going to have to confront it head-on if Islamic-based terrorism is ever going to go away. They'll have to decide what they truly stand for as the world community judges them by their deeds, not by their beliefs."

"Well, it's obviously not working."

"If Muslims prefer a caliphate, governed by orthodox Islamic tradition along with its legal framework, they must understand that their version of Islam is incompatible within a free American society."

"That's a bit harsh, isn't it? You're sounding xenophobic."

"Am I? Remember the wanton destruction of the Buddhas of Bamiyan in 2001? They stood for hundreds of years, but because they existed in contradiction to the Quran, they were ripe targets for destruction for centuries, until the Taliban finally succeeded in destroying them. That doesn't sound xenophobic to you?"

"You're dodging the question."

"Okay, how about something closer to home. Would you allow the caliphate to employ the same justification to reduce Saint Patrick's Cathedral or Mount Rushmore to a pile of rubble? Or to set a match to the Declaration of Independence, our Constitution, or the Bill of Rights? Not exactly the ringing endorsement of peaceful tolerance espoused in sura 109 ayat 6."

"What's that?"

"The verse in the Quran that states, 'You to your religion, me to mine.'"

Jack didn't have an answer.

Running smack into the brick wall known as Terrie Murphy, Jack did his best to change the subject. He reached into the box and pulled out another historical reference book, Non-Western Inventions. "Hmm. All right then, which non-Western invention discussed in this book was the most important?"

Her eyes searched the cover of the book Jack held before she answered. "Very well, what is it you hold in your hand?"

"A book, naturally."

"And the two most profound inventions that ultimately resulted in books?"

"Papyrus and ink?"

"Paper and moveable type," she pronounced. "And who created these momentous inventions, responsible for the mass production of ideas?"

"The Chinese developed the first process for making paper, but I suppose you're going to sit there and tell me it wasn't Gutenberg who invented moveable type?"

"He didn't."

"Then who?"

"Would it surprise you to learn that China invented moveable type made of ceramic more than 400 years before Gutenberg?"

Shaking his head, he said, "I guess we didn't learn that in school either."

"Which goes to my point. It's one thing to feel a sense of pride in one's country and its history of accomplishments. It's quite another to assign credit for such deeds without the benefit of perspective. Did Gutenberg invent moveable type? No, he didn't. However, he did come up with more durable materials that became the standard in Western printing until the computer age. And it's that accomplishment that should be delineated and celebrated."

"Remind me never to enter into a debate with you."

Terrie chuckled, "Do you honestly need reminding?"

He gave her that disappointing smirk again.

"Besides, you can hold your own when you employ logic."

"Was that a compliment you just threw at me?"

Terrie softened her demeanor but didn't answer him. "Supper's ready. You hungry?"

"Starved," he said, eyeing the plate she put in front of him. He cut one of the enchiladas with his fork and dived right in. "Mmm. That sauce is amazing!"

"Thank you." Terrie took her seat and began to chow down.

"You cook like this all the time?"

"I usually don't have much luck doubling my recipes, but today it worked out."

Jack made short work of his remaining enchiladas, almost as fast as Terrie.

She finished her last bite then asked, "You never said why you were referred to the Antiquarian Society."

"Oh yeah, I meant to tell you about that." Terrie grabbed the plates and brought them to the sink as Jack talked. "Anyway, I went to the Athenaeum after work last Friday. They set me up with a computer, a printer, and logged me into their historic newspaper database. I was there for two hours word-searching *Dey of Reckoning*, DOR, searching the Marine Lists, anything that would indicate our target vessel had left Piscataqua. Nothing. So I concentrated on the *New Hampshire Spy*, since we originally found her arrival in that paper. I looked at every issue from the edition where we first encountered it to the final issue of March 2, 1793. Still nothing."

"What did you find?" Terrie asked as she worked on the dirty dishes in the sink.

Jack went to help dry. "I noticed the Marine Lists of certain newspapers were compromised in some way. They were faded, torn, wrinkled, or otherwise illegible. To determine if the digitizing process was the cause, I asked if they had the original copies. Unfortunately, the only bound copy they had on hand was one containing issues of the *New Hampshire Recorder* from August 21, 1787, to February 24, 1791."

"And?"

"Again, I struck out. I found no references to the *Dey of Reckoning*, captured vessel, DOR—"

"How did you end up in Worcester?" she asked abruptly.

"They recommended I confer with a Dr. Miriam Aponte at the Antiquarian Society. She was responsible for the most extensive study ever completed on early American newspapers, and she orchestrated the preliminary digitizing process for all those papers a few years ago."

"What did she have to say about our discrepancies?"

Jack frowned, "Unfortunately, she no longer works there."

"Did they give you a reason why she left?"

"She opened her own bookstore."

"Where?"

"In Exeter, New Hampshire. They gave me her contact information."

"Good. Were you able to find out anything else?"

"Yeah, the curator said something unusual happened just prior to Dr. Aponte's departure. A nonprofit group had come to preserve some of the Society's rarest books whose bindings were badly deteriorated. Most of the colonial newspaper collections were among them. She showed me several examples, including *The Salem Mercury*, the *Massachusetts Gazette*, and the *New Hampshire Spy*."

Excited at the prospect of a comparison, Terrie asked, "Were you able to read the original copies any better?"

"As a matter of fact, I was."

"Did you compare our online versions to the originals?"

"For the *New Hampshire Spy*, yes."

"Where did the defects originate?"

"In most cases, they were from the originals," he said. Terrie watched Jack's face as he appeared to be considering what to say next. "Come to think of it, I remember the curator commenting that the *New Hampshire Spy* was the first volume taken but the last one returned. The binding was immaculately rendered, so I went directly to the Marine Lists to compare them against what we had. The sources matched the online defects, for the most part."

Terrie's optimism turned to disappointment. "That deserves some explanation."

"One of the papers containing a Marine List was severely torn in a manner that didn't reflect the digital copy we have. When I asked about it, the curator said they used a variety of sources. When I asked about them, she told me the collection for the *New Hampshire Spy* was not extensively published. In fact, only five books still exist today."

"Did she tell you who has them?"

"Yeah. Besides the one they had in Worcester, there are copies at the Library of Congress, the National Archives, and the Newspaper Museum in DC, but the last one is in the hands of a private collector."

"Were all of them rebound by the same nonprofit group?"

"All except the one owned by the private collector."

"Did she say who the private collector was?"

"It was an unconventional name, as I recall."

Terrie observed his face as he appeared to be reliving the conversation with the curator.

Jack suddenly blurted out the answer as though he were reading the ingredients off a cereal box. "Reginald Justinian Clendaniel."

Philip pulled his Jetta into the detached garage of his Wilmington safe house. The concrete driveway looked like one of a dozen along the street, with its long access to the left of the house leading to the two-car garage behind it.

He maintained his geriatric persona while he made his way into the house. After he was inside, he shuffled across the carpet to the front window to close the blinds before he straightened his posture. He felt and heard a distinct pop in the shoulder he dislocated a few years ago.

He reached up to pull off his wig, revealing the bald cap he had on underneath. He yanked it off and slipped a finger under the edge of his facial appliance. It never came off in one piece, but within minutes, the only thing that wasn't him were the pale eye lenses he would soon restore to their hiding place.

He located the briefcase that contained his laptop and retinal scanner. Accessing his secure account, Philip drafted his update to Runner's representative.

> Confidence is high that the items recovered by our Portsmouth contact are genuine. The properties, proportions, and color of the curved, triangular-shaped object are all consistent with target item. The secondary handwriting in the logbook was positively identified as belonging to Tunney.
>
> Recommendation: Allow the lieutenant to progress our investigation. Will ensure she doesn't get too close to the *Neptune's Trident* or the Lost Books.

He sent his draft and was about to respond to his message with a question about Terrie when his cell announced an unknown caller. "Yeah?"

"Do you really think that's such a great idea?" The voice at the other end was devoid of humor.

"Look, it was you who fed me the bad intel on Badger, and it was you who forced her into this situation," Philip snapped.

"If she just found the books or clues as to the location of the *Trident*, she wouldn't be taking an unwelcome interest in our affairs."

"Well, the way she's going about it is helping us. Stopping her now will only pique her curiosity."

Philip waited for a response. Silence was his answer.

"I'll continue to monitor her progress." Philip hung up first. Not a bright idea, given the circumstances.

THIRTY

Terrie blanched. She dried her hands, tossed the dish towel to Jack, and made a beeline for the yellow gym bag in the closet.

"What's wrong?" Jack watched Terrie with amused fascination as she turned the bag inside out, frantically rifling through its pockets. "What are you looking for?"

Engrossed in her task she ignored him. Finding nothing in the bag, she picked up her purse and went through it with similar results.

"Is there something I can help you find?"

She stood with her hands on her hips and an expression Jack never associated with Terrie. Confusion.

"What is it?"

She snapped her fingers and went into the bedroom. She reemerged with a satisfied look on her face and the black clutch she used when she was in uniform. She reached into one of the inside compartments and retrieved a folded piece of paper. She held it up for Jack's inspection.

"What's that?"

"Crabtree handed me this when he assigned me to the Badger Island detail."

"You can recite any line out of a four-hundred-page book from memory, but you can't remember what a simple sticky note said?" he muttered before reading the name R. J. Clendaniel, followed by a date, time, and phone number. "You're kidding. Dr. Pasteur's maxim about a prepared mind is certainly working in your favor today."

For the first time, Terrie looked at Jack with appreciation for his quick-witted allusion to her intelligence. "Thanks." She grabbed her cell and called the number as she made her way to the balcony. A blanket of ominous-looking gray clouds had rolled in, blotting out the sun. She gazed out toward the construction site to see two men in hard hats. From their outlines, she believed she recognized Chris Iarossi and Celio Esteban walking toward a section of the new building. After the fourth ring, the call defaulted to Clendaniel's voicemail.

"Damn! He's never without his cell. His people are there, so where is he?" she grumbled.

"Maybe he's off today. It's still the holiday weekend."

Terrie dismissed the explanation as she tried to call again. When all she could get was his voicemail, she ended the call and threw the phone on the sofa. A light, warm breeze kissed her cheek as she stared out at the new building, watching the two men talking with their hands.

Jack moved in behind Terrie in a conspicuous fashion so he wouldn't be on the receiving end of another martial arts calisthenics lesson. Gauging the minimum safe distance to halt his approach, he asked, "May I make an observation?"

Terrie didn't react.

"You dwell too much on your failures and not enough on your successes." Getting nowhere, he broke the barrier of her personal space. Nearly shoulder to shoulder, Jack imitated her folded-arm stare at the site across the way. "You need a change of perspective." Still no response. "Stewing motionless in the same place won't help. Perhaps what you need is a diversion."

Terrie heard her Aunt Barbara's voice echo the words as he uttered them. The pane of her Johari window that exposed her faults to everyone except herself must have been larger than she thought. *How could he notice what my aunt could see? Could it be he's sensitive to my moods, getting closer to me somehow? I haven't made it easy on him.* Her aunt's voice of reason came blasting through that thought. *Yes, he is trying to get closer to you, idiot. Perhaps you should take a chance and let him.*

Yielding to her aunt's admonition, she broke her silence, if not her posture. "What do you suggest?"

"Since we did the late lunch thing already, what say we take in a movie?"

"Recycled themes from old TV series of the '50s and '60s?"

"Okay, how about a stroll around Fox Run? Or better yet, the beach?"

"On opening summer weekend?" she chided. "Too many people in both places."

"It's summer. How about getting in a few laps at the Pierce Island pool?"

The question goaded her to look at him with mock surprise.

"You're right, too much sun," Jack relented. "What about the indoor pool at the Jarvis Center?"

Terrie couldn't help notice Jack's eyes taking in her shapely curves. "You can't wait to ogle me in a bikini, now can you?"

"What's wrong with that?" His misguided suggestion was met with a cynical face. Shaking his head, he was reduced to one last suggestion. "Okay, fine. How about a quiet evening at the public house down the street? We could shoot pool rather than swim in one. Bikini's optional, of course."

Terrie couldn't help but break into a smile. Jack was slowly creeping into her mind, and in a much warmer fashion than when they first met.

She turned to look at him and gently placed her hand on his shoulder. "Why don't I pop the cork on some chilled wine, whip up some fresh bruschetta topping, and we can just enjoy some light conversation and hors d'oeuvres?" Terrie's face turned white as though she'd seen a ghost. "I haven't simply talked with anyone in years."

"I'll pour the wine," he said softly.

Terrie's eyes opened slowly as her brain did its best to recount the evening's events. A plate of bruschetta and seedless white grapes washed down with a bottle of the distilled variety had been more than sufficient inducement to get their conversation off on the right foot.

Normally insufferable, Jack had been anything but. He'd been patient and understanding company, allowing Terrie to unpack her burden. No doubt her aunt would've criticized her for taking so long to do so.

To spend quality time with someone and not have it shattered by her current reality was exhilarating. She wasn't sure if it was the food, the wine, or the company that contributed to her revitalized mood, but she was grateful for the feeling.

She sat up and shut off the alarm. Her jersey had ridden up on her, exposing her panty-clad bottom. Hopping out of bed, she made her way to the bedroom door that was closed for some reason.

As she reached for the knob, she heard activity in the next room. Her heart leapt as she opened the door.

"Good morning!" Jack said. The English muffins popped out of the toaster, and the water for her tea was already boiling.

Now she remembered tossing a blanket over the unconscious form of Jack O'Hara after he fell asleep on the sofa. Rather than wake him, she just let him crash right where he was.

"How'd you sleep?" she asked as she padded to the kitchen.

"Believe it or not, your couch is comfortable."

"I'll take your word for it." Terrie was well acquainted with the limitations of her sofa. "You're going to work like that?"

"I'll change after breakfast."

She hummed with a mischievous smirk. She took out the toasted muffins, quickly spread jelly over them, and wolfed them down. "A good night's sleep does wonders for the appetite. I suppose I have you to thank for it."

"I accept full responsibility."

"Yes, you will," she said as she disappeared into her bedroom to get ready for work.

"Did you want to go in together this morning?" he called through the closed door. "Since we're on the same project, I'd say it's a fair bet we'll be working together all day."

"If you're ready by the time I am, sure."

Then he heard the sound of her shower. Jack scarfed down his muffin and retreated into his own apartment to get ready.

THIRTY ONE

Everyone was in attendance as Crabtree walked into the conference room. He wore the same "blueberry" working uniform everyone else had on, in accordance with Captain Derrick's directive: Tuesday was Navy Work Utility day.

Bannerman snapped out of her chair as she saw the door open. "Commander on deck."

Crabtree made his way to the head of the table. "As you were. I trust each of you had an enjoyable weekend."

"Taro and I watched the Sox stomp the Phillies from the Monster yesterday," Theo said.

"What was the score?"

"Nine to two," Theo responded, his silent partner, Taro, nodded. Itching to nettle Terrie, he added, "That would be your favorite team, right, Miss Murphy?"

"Certain sports interest me, Mr. Theodore. Baseball isn't one of them."

Seeing his opening, he took it. "Then you must prefer contact sports, like, say—"

"Stow it, Mr. Theodore," Crabtree warned, trying to restore some semblance of decorum.

An unmoved Terrie Murphy stared at the chastised officer. Theo cast a snide look at her as Taro sat quiet, turning a bright shade of pink. Bannerman's stern face informed Theo of her displeasure with his inappropriate jest.

Crabtree assumed his seat and control of his meeting. "Ray, do we have any action memos that require our attention?"

"Negative, sir. Just the SECNAV's report for Thursday."

"Commander Bannerman?"

"NCIS managed to crack Theo's zip drive. It's ready for pick up."

"Outstanding! Taro, you're with Theo this morning on the Newport run. Perhaps Mr. Theodore will use that time to think about how to properly address his fellow officers."

Smarting from his public reprimand, Theo acknowledged the order with a nod.

Crabtree then turned his gaze toward Terrie and Jack. "As for you two, you have the short suspense and a shorter week to get it done, so concentrate on that report. I want it ready to send out by noon Thursday."

Terrie nodded, but Jack's response was a swift, "Aye aye, sir."

"Does anyone have anything for me?" More rhetorical than an actual inquiry, he let the unanswered question hang in the air just the same. "Very well then. Let's get to it." Everyone stood up as Crabtree got up to leave.

Taro and Theo followed Ray to the office to sign out a vehicle for the trip to Newport. Terrie and Jack headed to the Ops Center with Bannerman in tow.

"Where are the reports we're supposed to go over?" Terrie asked Jack.

"Ray brought them to us last week, but I didn't have time to look at them, so I secured them in the safe. I'll get 'em, if you could get us our morning constitutionals?"

"Sure." Terrie warmed up her tea and poured Jack a mug of black coffee. Returning with their liquid rejuvenation, she eyed the stack of intelligence at her station. "That's mine?"

"My pile isn't much smaller."

Under normal circumstances, Terrie was able to hide her exasperation, but spending so much time with Jack O'Hara, she was unable to disguise it from him. His disarming smile was beginning to grow on her.

"Stop that," she chided, "let's get busy." They recaptured their sense of propriety and got to work.

Over the next hour, they poured over their respective mountain of intelligence. Taro and Theo wouldn't be back until the end of the day. The occasional phone call, fielded by Bannerman, and the soft drone of flat screen news were their only distractions.

Jack flipped through another report with a questioning look on his face. "When were US sanctions first applied against Iran?"

Terrie thought for a second. "In 1979 during the Carter Administration. He pressed for sanctions after the Ayatollah Khomeini took fifty-two of our embassy staff and citizens hostage." Reviewing the subsequent history of financial actions against Iran and their lackluster results, Terrie nudged Jack's arm and whispered, "That's it."

"What's it?"

"Follow the money." She typed out a final thought for the paragraph she was working on as she said it.

"What money?"

"This report could write itself if they just connected the financial dots."

"Then you figured it out?"

With Bannerman occupied at her desk, Terrie felt confident to tell him. "For both this report and our investigation."

"How do you mean?"

"There has to be a money trail that leads to the refit of the *Dey of Reckoning*."

Jack stared at his monitor working on his portion of the report while inclining his head in agreement.

"There's documentation showing funds for the original six frigates that included the USS *Constitution*. We can search the records to see if funds ever reached Portsmouth."

Jack looked at Terrie, who was smiling. "Let me guess. You have a book in that library of yours that might answer that question?"

"Perhaps."

As Terrie and Jack finished their conversation, Bannerman received a call from the front office. She got up from her station and approached Terrie. "Miss Murphy, the Commander would like to see you in his office."

"Yes, ma'am," Terrie responded.

"Would you like some assistance?" Bannerman asked.

The sympathetic look in Bannerman's eyes was a pleasant sight. "Thank you, Commander," Terrie said, "We appreciate it."

Sheffield was occupied on the phone when Terrie entered the outer office. Covering the receiver, he said, "Go right in, Lieutenant. He's expecting you."

Terrie spotted Crabtree hovering over his coffee machine like he was defending it from all comers. Assuming he knew she was present, she stood at attention and reported in.

He made a tertiary glance over his shoulder. "Have a seat, Miss Murphy." He went back to stirring the honey in his coffee before moving behind the desk. Placing himself in this position of authority immediately set a disciplinary tone that wasn't lost on Terrie. "I received a call from a Special Agent Daniels from the Pentagon. Would you mind telling me why I received such a call?"

"I thought I'd follow up on the remaining Badger Island evidence while I was in the neighborhood."

"If memory serves, Miss Murphy, I told you not to worry about it. When I give an order, regardless of how it's tendered, I expect it to be carried out. Do I make myself clear?"

"As a bell, sir."

"So, why did you feel the need to ignore that order?"

Unsure if he was part of this deception, she replied, "I like being thorough, sir. They have pieces of a puzzle I found. I could've solved it for you and placed an appropriate period on the entire detail. Or don't you expect that from me?"

"You're right. I expect much from you. I demand your very best, and you continue to give it. But even I must obey orders in this instance."

"Surely that doesn't include blind obedience, does it, sir?"

"Careful you don't tread on insubordinate ground, Lieutenant."

"My apologies, Commander. I was under the impression that I had permission to speak freely when we're alone in your office. I won't make that mistake again," she said with more finality than intended.

A startled Crabtree took an extra millisecond to reclaim his composure. He eyed Terrie to evaluate her words before he offered the slightest capitulation. "Not that you've been privy to them, Lieutenant, but I've said my piece with more than my share of senior officers, to include the CNO. At no time have I ever felt the need to impart a contrary opinion with as much sarcasm as you seem hell-bent to use." Crabtree studied Terrie's reaction, looking for signs of weakness. She held her ground and her bearing. Her eyes expressed complete disinterest. The silent standoff was broken by Terrie.

"Will that be all, sir?"

What he really wanted to say never left his lips. Forced to curb his outrage, he said the only thing decorum would allow him to say. "Dismissed."

Crabtree made it abundantly clear that this avenue of investigation was closed. Fortunately, Terrie had taken the time to read the *Justice* log before it was turned in. With all remaining collections of the *New Hampshire Spy* rebound by this nonprofit, the only person who could possibly own an untainted copy of it now would be R. J. Clendaniel. She had to contact him to see if she could examine it for herself. And she had to do it in person, which meant a meeting. She also knew it was unsafe to set up that meeting from the office.

Terrie waited until she and Jack were at lunch to call Clendaniel. In the afternoon, they worked to put away their conclusions and summarize their SECNAV report. She couldn't wait to go through her library to check on the financial link between Tunney and the *Dey of Reckoning*. It was also a comfort to know Jack would be with her.

The ride home from the office was like her afternoon at work—quiet and productive. Jack understood the value of silence, and Terrie cherished him for that. Crabtree's intoxicating physical stature aside, he failed to move her in any other way, especially after he tried to dress her down this morning.

The initial impression her neighbor and colleague made on her had been less than stellar, though he wasn't that difficult on the eyes. It was his initial behavior that revolted her.

There was nothing about Jack that stirred Terrie's pheromones. But his intelligence, emotional stability, and honesty were burrowing their tentacles into her thoughts. Moment by moment, he was becoming someone of importance to her. Someone she needed around her. The last person she really needed like that was Margaret.

Though Aunt Barbara and, to a lesser extent, Clendaniel, could offer her sage advice, Jack was different. An emotional bond was taking hold of her heart, and she was slowly becoming accustomed to it. Terrie had never felt this way about any man from the inside out. Was it love? Could she say that word and Jack O'Hara in the same sentence?

Completing the U-turn on the Portsmouth side of the bridge, Terrie stopped in front of the apartment to let Jack off. "I'm gonna take a run before we get started. Care to join me?"

He got out of the car and bent down to look at Terrie. "Running's not my thing. I usually hit the gym."

"See you in about an hour?"

"Will do," he replied before heading into the apartment building.

Terrie used the requisite time during her run to prioritize her strategy. She needed to go over her library to track down the funding for a possible refit of the *Dey of Reckoning*. Her volume on the War Department papers would be on that list. She hoped Clendaniel's untouched volume could also shed light on the mystery of the *Dey of Reckoning*, the *Justice*, the *Crescent*, or Tunney. Her next stop would be the Antiquarian, to research the actual newspapers and compare them with the digitized copies they had. Based on what they might find, they could be in a better position to approach Dr. Aponte and find out why she chose to leave Worcester.

And most importantly, she needed Juli Aruem's manuscript to tie it all together.

Learn the fate of the Crescent, *and you shall find Vernon "Cyclops" Tunney.*

With this final thought in her head, Terrie reached the east end of Prescott Park. She stretched out for the remaining distance to her apartment building, taking in the sound of seagulls as they glided overhead. With all of this expended energy thinking about the Badger Island detail, she hadn't worked on her main motivation for being in the Navy—tracking down her sister's killers.

She had to do a better job of maintaining that priority. But as long as the scent was still strong for her unofficial mission, she'd follow it to its conclusion.

Terrie recognized Jack's distinctive, rhythmic knock.

"It's open," she called out from the kitchen.

Jack entered the apartment bearing gifts. "Wasn't sure what we were having, so I brought red and white."

Stirring raw shrimp and sesame oil in a wok, she said, "Shrimp fried rice."

He held up the translucent green bottle. "Then white it is." He brought the bottles over to the table where Terrie had a couple of books and a laptop. "That smells good."

"It's sweet and sticky rice mixed together. I turned on the rice cooker before my run."

"You want a glass now?"

"Absolutely." Terrie finished chopping up the garlic and onions and prepared to fold them into the wok. Referring to the books on the table with a tilt of her head, she said, "You can start looking through those if you want."

"All right." Jack placed Terrie's glass next to her as he moved toward the table with his. "Which one first?"

"Try the top one. It's a collection of War Department papers from 1775 to 1800. If you can't find what we're looking for there, perhaps some online resources will help us."

Jack took a seat and grabbed the first book, which contained letters of correspondence between Congress and Secretaries of War

Henry Knox and James McHenry. It also contained documentation supplied by the shipbuilders of Badger Island, James Hackett and Josiah Fox.

"So what did the boss want to see you about this morning?"

"I made the mistake of calling the Pentagon about the crimson alloy and the logbook he brought with him. I was hoping to get some answers that would help us. Apparently, the commander wasn't happy. He warned me off the investigation."

Jack finally looked at her. "Okay, so why are we still doing this?"

Mixing the rice with the veggies and shrimp, she asked, "Have you ever felt like someone wanted you to gather up the pieces but not solve the puzzle?"

"Not me personally, but I get where you're going." He resumed his search. "Then you suspect something larger is going on?"

"Why not?"

"There's got to be more to your suspicions than that."

Terrie grabbed two plates from the cabinet, scooped out three heaping spatulas of fried rice per plate, and brought them to the table. "I really didn't tell you about my weekend, did I?"

"No, you didn't." He tasted his first spoonful. "You should open a restaurant, Terrie. This is wonderful."

A warm feeling surrounded her at his open use of her first name. "Thank you." Taking her seat, she consumed her dish as though it was her last meal.

Jack, wide-eyed, shook his head as he stared at her. "I have to make it my personal mission to get you to stop doing that."

With a mouthful of rice, she mumbled "What?"

He exhaled a laugh and continued eating without comment on her barbarous dining etiquette.

Terrie swallowed the last of the rice and took a swig from her glass to clear her throat. "See the next book in the stack?"

"Yeah?"

"It's the one I asked my aunt about. Note the author's name."

"Juli Aruem? Never heard of her."

"I met her this weekend."

"Really?"

"I had lunch with her. Contained in that book is a comprehensive description of coaster vessels and their captains operating in the Chesapeake and Delaware Bays from the mid- to late-1700s. There was no mention of Tunney anywhere in that book."

"Then why is her book important?"

"She was warned against mentioning him. When her publisher did so, she got real curious about Tunney. She told me she had enough documentation on him to write another book. So, she did."

"When does she plan to publish that one?"

"She was about to, when a government agent approached her. He told her it was in her best interest to drop it. Alarmed by the confrontation, she went back to verify her original sources. She was dismayed to discover they were all gone."

Surprised, Jack looked at Terrie. "How could her sources simply disappear?"

"Everything she used had vanished. Library texts, old correspondence, period newspaper articles, everything. They also managed to hack into her computer and corrupt her hard drive. Fortunately, she printed a copy before it was hacked."

Finishing his meal, Jack policed up their plates and asked, "What have you gotten us into?"

"Yeah, I know." Terrie took a sip of wine then grabbed the next volume of War Department papers and skimmed through it, looking for something she recalled earlier. "Remember when I said to follow the money?"

"Yeah?"

"I was thinking of a letter written to Congress by the first secretary of the Navy, Benjamin Stoddart, on Christmas Eve of

1798. Accompanying that letter was a chart detailing the strength of the Navy at the time, current and future ships, and an annual budget request for $2.4 million."

"Is the chart in there?"

Terrie kept flipping the pages until she came to it. She turned the book around so Jack could read it for himself.

The chart was laid out in eleven columns. The first five described publicly- and privately-owned vessels and revenue cutters in service, including prize vessels like the late *La Croyable* from the quasi war with France. The other six columns detailed ship tonnage, number of guns, number of men, where the ship was purchased or built, the ship's captain, and annual operating expenses per ship.

The first vessel on the chart was the frigate *United States*. It was 1,576 tons with 44 guns and a crew of 400. It was "built or purchased" in Philadelphia and commanded by John Barry, with an annual operating budget of $125,780.89.

"Interesting, but what am I looking for?" Jack asked.

"Look down the middle of the chart. See the list of galleys identified by the Carolinas and Georgia?"

"Two for the north, two for the south, and four for Georgia. But the *Dey of Reckoning* wasn't a galley."

"No, but if you notice, each of them have the identical 368 tons but no other identifying information."

"They must be the same design, since they grouped the eight of them together in the expenses column. They want $83,974.32."

"Not exactly," she said, pointing to the unnamed column next to the annual expenses. "It says the requested annual expenses for each ship was $9330.48. Multiplied eight times, that's only $74,643.84."

"Then the total is wrong?"

"No, look at this next line. See what it says?"

Jack's lips parted in amazement. In a line below the list of galleys was a lone statement: "One wanting to complete the present establishment." There was no tonnage, no number of guns, no personnel, no place of manufacture or purchase, and no master, but they wanted an extra $9330.48 for it. This amount was lumped into the Annual Expense column along with the other eight galleys.

"Why would the secretary of the Navy request money for an unidentified ship?"

"Interesting question. Until we find something more credible, this is the best lead we have."

THIRTY TWO

Theo and Taro had already left for chow. Terrie helped Jack make the final changes to their report and saved it for transmittal.

Before sending it out, she printed a copy for Bannerman's review. "Commander?"

"Yes, Miss Murphy?"

"Here's the SECNAV report along with our recommendations."

"Already? That's fast work, you two."

"Your assistance yesterday was a big help," Jack offered.

"Not at all, Mr. O'Hara. Miss Murphy, why don't you take this to the commander's office, and while you're there, you can pick up your new package from Ray."

"He has something new for me?"

"Newport cracked Theo's zip drive. The information it contains requires your unique talents."

"Permission to start it in the morning, Commander? I have appointments after lunch today."

"First thing, Lieutenant," Bannerman admonished with a smile.

Jack walked up to Terrie and said, "As to that, lunch is on me. What would you like?"

"How about the pizza joint on Badger?" Terrie suggested.

"Why th—" Then Jack remembered the meeting with R. J. Clendaniel. "Um, okay. I haven't had their pizza in a while."

Terrie asked Bannerman if she wanted anything, but she politely declined. Jack held his tongue until they made their way outside the gate.

When they were safely in the car, he asked, "Are you nuts?"

"What? It's the least we could do, since she helped us with the report. Besides, as Ops must be manned at all times, she couldn't come with us."

"I suppose. And Team Dynamite hasn't come back from lunch yet."

Terrie gave Jack a scowl and queried, "Team Dynamite?"

"You know, Taro-N-Theo? TNT?"

Terrie shook her head as she drove away from the Intel building. The five-minute trip to the restaurant was a quiet one. Terrie parked her SUV in a slot that gave her a commanding view of the new building's skeleton. Scanning the construction site, she spotted the strong build of the foreman heading toward them.

"Terrie Murphy, what a pleasant surprise. How've you been getting on at the naval station?"

Terrie reached out to shake his hand. "Making out okay. I see the condo is up."

"We still have the interior to finish."

"It's looking good so far." Terrie pointed to her uniformed partner. "This is my colleague, Lieutenant Jack O'Hara."

Clendaniel held out a welcoming hand. "Good to know you, Mr. O'Hara."

"Jack, please."

"Would you two like to see the inside? The walls are framed, so you can get an idea of the layout."

"Perhaps another time," Terrie responded. "No need to give Mr. Pederson a coronary."

Clendaniel couldn't contain his amusement. "That would be a reunion I'd like to see."

"Masochist," said Terrie playfully.

The trio entered the restaurant and found an empty table. Clendaniel ordered for them all and paused for the waitress to leave before addressing Terrie. "So, what are you up to these days? Or can you even tell me?"

"We're working with the station historian, conducting research into Pierce Island before the Navy took it over in 1800."

"Have anything to do with why you were here a couple of weeks ago?"

"I doubt it."

Clendaniel grew a mischievous smile. "So much for the direct question."

Jumping into the conversation, Jack added, "Our research took us to Worcester and the Antiquarian Society."

"That's off the beaten path. The Athenaeum in Portsmouth should have all the research materials you need."

"Their digitized copies were difficult to read, so they put us on to the resources in Worcester," Jack said.

"What resources?"

Terrie chimed in before Jack could answer. "Colonial newspaper collections. The *New Hampshire Spy* collection, for one." She looked into Clendaniel's eyes for a reaction. She got one.

"Then today's lunch isn't purely social, is it?" Clendaniel queried.

Aunt Barbara's voice came in loud and clear. *Tact, my dear, will win you your objective.*

Terrie bowed her head and continued the discussion while Jack listened. "Not necessarily. I was thinking about you and our last conversation in this very restaurant."

"Were you?"

"I even told my aunt about you."

"Nothing too terrible, I hope?"

"Don't worry, I fictionalized the good parts to protect the guilty."

"That's a relief." Clendaniel laughed. "Why are you so curious about my collection?"

"Worcester's copies of the *Spy* were just as illegible as the online content. We confirmed all other available copies were just as bad. We understand you may be in possession of the last remaining copy."

"Believe it or not, I found it at an estate sale in Nashua. I took it to the Antiquarian in Worcester to verify its authenticity."

Hoping he might have run across Dr. Aponte, she asked, "When?"

"Shortly after I bought it a year and a half ago. I was surprised to learn it was genuine. The lady who confirmed its authenticity wondered if I'd be interested in selling it."

Terrie was about to ask who the lady was when Jack diverted the subject with a question of his own. "Why the interest in old newspapers?"

"Do you have any hobbies, Jack?"

"I ride my Harley."

"Mine is the history of modern journalism, thus I collect old newspapers. Not just the front pages, mind you, but entire issues. My collection goes as far back as the Civil War and takes up the four walls of my home office."

"Why since the Civil War?"

"It was during Reconstruction that journalism came the closest to genuine, disinterested reporting." He looked over at Terrie before he added, "I could show it to you whenever you have the time."

"That would be helpful," said Terrie.

After the waitress dropped off the drinks, Clendaniel asked, "Do you recall which issues were illegible?"

"Not specifically," Terrie said. Jack's face began to contort into one of his skeptical looks before he caught himself and stopped. Terrie elbowed her colleague, hoping Clendaniel wouldn't notice.

"If you could tell me which ones they were, I might be able to save you a trip."

Not wanting that information broadcast in the open, Terrie played ignorant. "I think it would be best if we saw the entire collection in person."

"As you wish." Clendaniel took out his smartphone and pulled up his calendar. "I'll be tied up here until Monday evening, if you can wait."

"Six o'clock?" asked Terrie.

"I'll text you the address."

The three spent the remainder of the lunch hour engaged in benign conversation over slices of thin-crust, brick-oven pizza, the pride of any restaurant in New England. Jack entertained his companions with a humorous anecdote about the first time he spilled his motorcycle, while Clendaniel took in how Terrie looked at Jack. When she caught him doing so, a silent exchange ensued between them using the mutually understood language of the eyes.

He seems like a fine young man.
Maybe. I don't know yet.
He likes you, Terrie. It shows. Give him a chance.

Her aunt's instincts about Clendaniel were right. Terrie took tremendous steps to wall herself off from her fellow human beings. The thought of feeling the intense agony of losing someone the way she lost Margaret was inconceivable, yet something about Clendaniel told her he would never do anything to harm her. Aunt Barbara knew that, somehow.

Terrie inclined her head, giving the foreman the knowing eyes in silent gratitude.

As Terrie eased her car into an open spot on Regent Street, she looked over at the dome above the brick structure of the Antiquarian Society building.

Jack and Terrie made their way into the building and signed in at the security desk. Terrie processed into the system, as Jack had on his last visit, before they entered the main library's rotunda. He asked the security guard if the curator was in.

"She doesn't usually get here until five o'clock on Wednesdays."

"That's right, you close late on Wednesdays."

"Eight o'clock. If you'd like, I'll tell her you'd like to see her when she comes in."

"Thank you." Jack and Terrie entered through the double glass doors and made their way past the rows of research tables to the main desk.

"Good afternoon, how may I help you?" the attendant said with a smile.

"We'd like to look at your colonial newspaper collections, specifically *The Salem Mercury*, the *New Hampshire Gazette* and *Spy*, and the *Independent Chronicle*."

"I'm sorry, but we only allow one volume out at a time. To speed things up, you can borrow one each, and I can have the rest available for you in turn if you'd like."

"One at a time will be fine, thank you," Terrie said, looking at Jack. "Could we begin with the *New Hampshire Spy*?"

As the attendant went to retrieve the requested book, Jack asked, "Why don't you want me to look at one of the other volumes?"

"We should examine them together. We don't want to miss anything." Jack gave Terrie that hurt look again.

The attendant handed pairs of white gloves to Terrie and Jack. "Please use these. The bindings are relatively new, but the papers inside are original and very delicate. Should you need anything, I'll be at the desk."

They went straight for the June 21, 1788, edition of the paper and confirmed that their online Marine List was the same as the page in the book. They took great pains to read each story and advertisement to make sure they covered all their bases. The amateur sleuths' detailed examination spared no article, ad, or eccentricity. Knowing what they were looking for helped move the process along but not fast enough for Jack.

"This is annoying," Jack whispered to Terrie.

"I don't believe I've heard any genuine researcher describe this activity as glamorous or exciting."

An East Indian man doing research a few tables away glanced toward Jack and Terrie, his irritation visible on his furrowed brow. Jack offered a raised hand in silent apology. The young man grunted his acceptance before returning to his work.

Terrie glanced in the young man's direction and witnessed the exchange, catching his full profile. She initially thought there was something familiar about him, but quickly dismissed her suspicion and chalked it up to an overactive imagination.

"It would be more exciting if we found something," Jack whispered, turning to the second to last issue, dated February 23, 1793. When he did, Terrie spotted something and smiled.

"Like this?" She pointed a white-gloved finger at an ad listed under TUESDAY's POST on the front page.

"It's an advertisement. So what?"

"Look at it again. Note the topography."

"What about it?"

"It's not the same as any ad or story on any page of this paper." Taking a closer look at the small caption that took up approximately two square inches of space, she compared the lettering with other issues and found it unique to this one ad. "See if you can get a magnifying glass from the desk."

"Sure." He retrieved one from the desk and was back in a flash. "What are you looking at?"

"Read this article carefully. What do you see in it that you don't see in any of the other articles?"

Jack read it three times, squinting as he caught something on the last go. "I'll be a son of a bitch."

The Indian man's sensitive ears managed to pick up on the sound of Jack's voice. Annoyed, he reached for some ear buds he had in his coat pocket.

Terrie couldn't see the device the portable headphones were plugged into. Keeping her eye on the young man, Terrie quietly responded to Jack. "Do you see it?"

"The s's are not the lineless f's like in the rest of the paper. The double f's are the same size, and the ct's aren't connected either."

"Those were features of the Caslon ligature, the font favored by colonial printers. They didn't start transitioning away from it until the turn of the nineteenth century."

"So, this paper's been—"

"Shh. That's right, it's been altered. We need a copy of this."

The man could barely contain his disgust. The limit to his patience reached, he gathered his belongings and moved to the other side of the room with his back to the two investigators.

Jack retrieved the copy along with a volume of *The Salem Mercury.*

As she had with the *Independent Chronicle,* Terrie went directly to the issues of the *Mercury* that contained the *Rebecca* advertisement. In all cases, the individual papers matched the online resources perfectly. It was obvious that these different publications had the exact article cleverly inserted into each of them. What she didn't know was why.

Jack looked up at the clock above the circulation desk as he waited for the last copy of evidence showing the *Rebecca* advertisement. It was twelve past five. Directing his glance toward the entrance, he spotted the curator as she entered the building. She smiled when she recognized him.

"Back so soon, Jack?" she said cheerfully.

"Paige, so good to see you."

"Conducting more research?"

"The research actually belongs to her," said Jack referring to Terrie. "Allow me to introduce you to my friend and colleague, Lieutenant Terrie Murphy."

"Welcome to the American Antiquarian Society, Terrie. I'm Paige Turner. Has my staff been taking good care of you?"

"Yes, they have." Terrie kept her skepticism to herself as she processed the forty-something woman's name.

"I know. Ridiculous, isn't it? A person with such an obvious name working in a research library? My parents had a unique sense of humor. My twin sister's name is Lana. As you can see, neither of us looks anything at all like the actress."

"Of course," responded Terrie blandly. "I was actually wondering if we could talk somewhere more discrete."

"We could go to my office."

"If you don't mind."

The curator led the mini entourage through the security door next and to her office. "Have a seat," she said, gesturing toward the two chairs by the small coffee table. "Would you like some water?"

"No, thank you," Terrie said, going right into interrogation mode, "I'd really like to know what happened to Dr. Miriam Aponte. From all accounts, she sounded like someone too indispensable to lose."

"Oh, that she was. She'd been with us for sixteen years."

"What were her duties here?"

"Miriam did an exhaustive study of early publishers like Daniel Fowle, Isaiah Thomas, John Melcher, John Osborne, and Thomas Cushing. She was also at the forefront of the digitizing process for all of our irreplaceable documents, books, periodicals, and historic journals and papers."

"Sounds like she was really into her work," Jack said.

Terrie touched his arm and took over the interview, "Was she happy here?"

"She was, up until eight months before she left."

"What concerned her?"

Turner thought for a second. "It started soon after the new digitizing software was installed. She noticed some irregularities between the original hard copies she had on hand and those that were digitized online under the new system."

"Did she report these irregularities to anyone besides you?"

"She catalogued and reported anomalous differences in at least four of the collections to the software developer and in turn, we informed the Board of Directors for the Antiquarian Society."

"That couldn't have been what caused her to leave," Terrie said, attempting to get a concrete response.

"No, it wasn't," Turner said, lowering her eyes. "A few days later, a group from the National Archives showed up to rebind our most precious volumes. The rebinding project included all the hard copies of the colonial-era newspapers. When Miriam reviewed the rebound copies, she became upset."

"Do you know why?"

"She never told me. A month later, she resigned her position."

"How long ago was that?"

"A little over a year ago. She followed her ambition…moved to Exeter and opened a bookstore."

"Do you know the name of the store?"

"I think she called it Exeter Rare Books."

"Has she stayed in touch?"

"I only talked with her once after that."

"Do you remember the context of that conversation?"

Turner thought for a second before she replied, "Yes. It had something to do with a strange call."

"What call?"

"Not long after she left, a woman called for Miriam. She seemed put out when I told her Miriam left. I let the woman know about the store, but she hung up before I could give her the number. I called Miriam to let her know about the call."

"Did this woman leave her name?"

"She said it, but I was too busy at the time to write it down."

"And you didn't hear from Miriam after you talked with her about this woman?"

"No, but I remember her voice before she hung up. She sounded scared."

"What would have scared her?"

"I don't know."

Terrie got up and signaled Jack to do likewise. "Thank you for your assistance, Miss Turner."

"You're quite welcome."

The curator watched as her guests moved through the metal detector, past the security guard, and out the front double doors. As she turned to go back to her office, the young man with earbuds around his neck approached.

Agitated, he asked in a heavy Indian accent, "Miss, what books were those people looking at earlier?"

"They were colonial-era newspapers," Turner responded. "Would you like to see them?"

"If it's no trouble."

"Which one would you like me to get for you first?"

"The first one they were reading, I think it was the *New Hampshire Spy*."

Paige Turner was back in five minutes with the book Terrie and Jack reviewed. When she was out of sight, the man turned to the exact edition that contained the *Rebecca* article. Then he flipped over to the front page of the February 23, 1793, issue.

What the young man saw made him smile with a grin that nearly separated his jaw from his face. It was how Philip always smiled when he realized his plans were working.

Terrie and Jack stopped off at a rest area on I-290 to grab a bite to eat on their way back to Portsmouth. Jack was thinking about the conversation with Miss Turner when Terrie's voice interrupted his solitary review.

"When we finish work tomorrow, will you come with me?" she asked.

"Where?"

"Exeter. To Dr. Aponte's bookstore. I want to see if she's willing to share with us what the old newspapers actually said in place of those *Rebecca* ads."

"In direct violation of Crabtree's orders?"

"When did he order me to stop looking into a possible cover-up by the National Archives?"

"Oh, you're going to play word games now?"

"The media does it all the time. And they have the gall to call it news."

"Yeah, sure, I'll go along. It's always entertaining to watch a train wreck in progress."

Terrie put the car in gear and drove toward the highway. And home.

THIRTY THREE

The sun had slipped beneath the horizon, painting the clouds in an angry orange hue. Philip rolled his Ford Focus into the driveway of his Portsmouth safe house. He made sure no one observed him exiting the car, as his latest disguise would surely be noticed by his neighbors.

His hands, upper arms, and ears were the most difficult to create, but he managed it flawlessly. He had to admit, the masterpiece of this makeup was the application of the dark beard stubble, his appearance as a foreign exchange student from New Delhi was quite convincing.

Once inside, he got straight to work removing the makeup, hazel eye lenses, and black wig. A quick shower and a meal and he was ready to log into his secure email account to report in and check on any new directives.

His report was simple. The two officers may have detected an anomaly in one of the newspapers, but it could easily be dismissed as such. They found no hard evidence that could lead them where Runner didn't want them to go.

Philip spotted one new message. It was short and to the point. "Call when you get this."

He had nothing to eat since breakfast. After a quick meal, he was ready to deal with Runner's representative. The party on the other end answered on the first ring, an unlucky omen.

"You haven't reported anything lately."

"I had no reason to till now," Philip replied.

"Then you have something?"

"Nothing to worry about. There was a mistake in the planting of the articles, but without copies of the original papers, they're left with nothing but speculation."

"That's good. Another loose end was tied today."

"Then we can cease our surveillance of the lieutenant?"

"I still want her movements watched closely. Have your Portsmouth contact put tracking in place."

"Is that necessary?"

"That comes directly from Runner."

"I'll get on it tonight. Anything else?"

"One more thing. A little housekeeping item."

"What's that?"

"Have your contact retrieve and destroy everything pertaining to the six-minute audio transcript."

"Everything?"

"Make it a priority."

"Why?"

"Just do it! I'll take care of any exposure at the Newport end."

"As you wish." Philip pressed the red phone icon, wondering what Runner's representative meant by another loose end.

Putting that thought aside, he scrolled through his contact numbers to find his agent in Portsmouth. Then he made his call to set up what Runner wanted accomplished.

THIRTY FOUR

"Miss Murphy," Bannerman called out from her station, "I need to see you in the conference room."

Terrie secured her computer and followed the lieutenant commander out of the Ops Center. "What's this about?"

Bannerman said nothing until they were inside the conference room with the door closed. Inviting her to take a seat, she said, "Before you review the DVD that came from Theo's corrupted zip drive, I need you to do something else first."

"What do you need?"

The lieutenant commander knitted her eyebrows with discomfort before issuing the order. "I have to ask you to locate and destroy all physical and electronic traces of the six-minute audio you translated and sent last week. It can't exist."

"Doesn't that violate records management directives?"

"This directive comes straight from command authority."

"In that case, no problem, Commander." Terrie watched her superior as she looked almost defeated. "You don't appear to be yourself, Commander. Is anything wrong?"

Doing her best to appear human, Bannerman softened her expression. In a joking fashion, she replied, "None of your business."

Terrie made her way to the front office to have Sheffield work on his portion of Bannerman's request, but he wasn't in. She went back to the Ops Center to retrieve all hard copies of the report and the official copy of the CD from the safe. She deleted all the files, including emails and backups. All that remained was to get Sheffield to eliminate anything pertaining to that audio in his records. The only proof she had of its existence was the private copy she made for herself.

Terrie approached Bannerman at her station. "Commander, everything is done per your request except what's in the senior chief's records."

"I'll have him take care of it."

Terrie thanked her and went to work on the DVD.

The Ops Center door buzzed. Terrie was hoping it was Sheffield, but Crabtree's unmistakable silhouette appeared instead. Before Bannerman could react, Crabtree told everyone to keep their seats.

The commander waited until he had everyone's attention. "I wanted to pass this news along to you personally. I received a call from the SECNAV's office. They wanted to congratulate our team, especially Mr. O'Hara and Miss Murphy, for their insightful contribution to the SECNAV's report to Congress. Your unique conclusions figured prominently in his report. You both should be proud."

A round of applause ensued—all except Theo.

"Just doing our job," Terrie said.

"Commander Bannerman was a big help too," Jack added.

Crabtree acknowledged his second with an appreciative nod. Switching the subject, he looked toward the other two junior officers. "Taro, I want you to get with SA Prentiss. He's working a developing problem with the NSA's PRISM surveillance program. The issue may have ramifications for us, so I want you to team up with him and provide whatever assistance you can."

"Will do, sir."

"Theo?"

"Yes, sir?"

"The captain asked if you could stop by her office this afternoon."

"Did she say what time, sir?"

"At your convenience."

"Aye, sir."

When Crabtree left Ops and the team members got back to work, Terrie glanced over at Theo. His ability to hold his feelings was practiced, but Terrie could tell something put a chink in his pride.

She originally intended to query him about the DVD after she reviewed it, but she decided to take the opportunity now. "Mr. Theodore?"

His indignant response was "What?"

"I have a few questions about that zip drive, if you have a moment."

All Theo's high-profile tasks seemed to be going to the two newbies. Unable to find a way to stand out, he chose to raise the white flag for now. "What would you like to know?"

"Where did these zip drives come from?"

"The first one came from Fallujah. The other one from outside Sha'ab."

"Do you have any idea when they were made and by whom?"

"They were recorded within the past year by a paid intermediary imbedded with a splinter group of al-Qaeda in Iraq."

"Do we know how to contact the agent who recorded them?"

"I'll look into it and get back with you."

"Thanks." Terrie took out the DVD and started her examination.

Taro straightened up his station before he left for Prentiss's office. Glancing over at Theo, he said, "I'll be doing lunch with Prentiss, if you care to come along."

With disgust, Theo responded, "Sure. I've got nothing better to do than play errand boy for everyone else."

Terrie heard the remark, but let it pass. Concentrating on her task, she loaded the disc and put on her headphones to isolate as much background noise as possible. Though the clip was somewhat pixilated, she was able to distinguish the room's environment and that the videographer was looking down from an elevated location.

The initial image was shaky, supporting the supposition that it was not a planned recording but one of opportunity. The image settled on two subjects, both speaking Arabic. One man was dressed in a long white thawb with a checkered head scarf, the other in a jubba with the prayer cap of an Imam. The adherent was facing the camera, while the cleric had his back to it. The video captured an interrogation, the cleric asking questions and the adherent responding.

Near the end of the clip, she witnessed the cleric move suddenly. A flush of darkness grew over the adherent's chest. At the same time, she heard a loud garbled scream before the adherent dropped out of the frame. Ignoring the video for the moment, she ran through it again to concentrate on the audio.

The two subjects were conversing at normal volume, but hindering Terrie's efforts to listen was an insistent droning noise close to the videographer. The individual who shot the footage must have been next to an operating air conditioner. Though she found it difficult to screen out the sound, she was better able to hear the inquisitor than the respondent. Most of the exchange was hard to make out, but a single word struck her as familiar: wraith.

She ran the DVD three times, trying to screen out as much of the white noise as possible, but it was no use. She needed to get a cleaner copy, and for that she'd need Theo's help.

Terrie's mounting frustration peaked as she tossed her headphones on the desk. Looking over at Theo's empty workstation, she thought, *Great, he's still not back from—*

"Lunch?"

Jack's query startled her. "I'm in the middle of this, and I want to get it done," she answered.

"You want me to bring you something?"

"I'm not hungry."

Taking the hint, he simply asked, "Are we still on for Exeter?"

"Five-thirty from the apartment. Don't be late."

"I'll drive this time, okay?"

Terrie begrudgingly agreed.

THIRTY FIVE

The two investigators found Exeter Rare Books nestled between two historic buildings on the Squamscott River side of Water Street across from city hall. Jack eased his truck into the spot adjacent to the store's entrance. Opening the front door, they heard the clang of a metal bell announce their arrival to the proprietor.

"May I help you?" asked a cheerful voice from behind a row of books on the second-floor balcony.

"Dr. Aponte?" Terrie inquired.

"She's indisposed at the moment" came the cryptic response.

Jack couldn't help himself. "We're doing research for a project, and we were referred to her by the folks at the Antiquarian Society."

"And the subject of this research?" the voice questioned.

"Seagoing merchant traffic in the late 1700s," Jack said.

"I'll be right down."

In less than a minute, a woman in her midthirties with reading glasses suspended around her neck appeared before them. She took a hard look at her new arrivals. "Is it merchant traffic in general you're looking for, or is there a specific area of research you're interested in?"

Terrie shot Jack an I-got-this look and did her best not to smile when he returned it with a childish pout. "We're actually interested in the merchant traffic in and out of the Portsmouth area. We consulted the available resources at the Athenaeum but couldn't find what we were looking for. We were hoping you could help us."

"I'll need to know specifics, like destinations, cargo, passenger manifests, and so on."

"It's nothing of that nature," Jack injected.

Terrie elbowed him, but the woman had taken her place behind the counter and hadn't noticed. Attempting to clarify, Terrie said, "It's more about a time frame, say between 1788 and 1800."

The woman's eyes narrowed at Terrie's request. "Are you looking for a specific captain or vessel?"

"We're trying to locate a ship that entered the Port of Piscataqua but never cleared."

The woman rested her elbow on the stack of old books near the register and brought her hand up to her cheek before letting out a sigh. "And the name of this vessel?"

"The *Dey of Reckoning*." Terrie stared intently into the woman's eyes. Her startled reaction was Terrie's answer.

"Where did you say you found this ship?"

"In a June 1788 edition of the *New Hampshire Spy*."

Quick to respond at the mention of that particular newspaper, the woman said, "We don't have that one, but you're free to check out our local interest section over there." She pointed to the aisle of books near the spiral staircase she descended earlier.

"Any particular titles we should look for?"

"There are a few volumes of maritime history for the Portsmouth area you may find useful."

"Thank you."

"If you need anything further, I'll be upstairs."

Terrie scoured each row for the titles that would get them on the right track. The closest were three early texts about the colonial economy of Portsmouth and a rare book that discussed carrier ship routes and the ships that ran them. On the third row of the last aisle, Terrie found two oversized books containing early issues of the *Worcester Gazette* and the *New Hampshire Recorder*. "Jack, over here."

"What is it?"

"Look at this." She held up the immaculate copies of the two published treasures. "Did you see either of these at the Antiquarian?"

"I saw them, but I wasn't able to review them."

"Both newly bound, no doubt?"

Raising an eyebrow, Jack said, "They both were, but how did you know?"

Terrie's optimism vanished as she opened the book and searched for the target date of June 21, 1788. She scoured each page, looking for Marine lists or articles that may hold the key to the *Dey of Reckoning's* fate. Terrie called up to the clerk. "Do you have any other newspaper collections?"

The woman came back downstairs. "We did. What titles were you looking for?"

Terrie's thoughts jumped to those papers with the duplications of the *Rebecca* ad. "Any newspapers from that time period, like the *New Hampshire Gazette*, *The Salem Mercury*, or the *Independent Chronicle*."

"I'm sorry, but those titles are currently out of print," she replied with a nervous vocal twitch.

"Thank you for your time," Terrie said.

The two investigators quietly walked out of the store. As Jack started the truck, he turned to see Terrie give a hard look at the woman through the shop window. "She's hiding something," Terrie muttered, more to herself than to him.

"What makes you say that?"

"A part-time employee wouldn't just tell us something is out of print off the top of their head. That information is something I'd expect the owner to know."

"What are you saying?"

"I believe we just met Dr. Miriam Aponte."

"Why wouldn't she tell us who she was when we first came in?"

"Why, indeed?"

The woman reached for the keys to lock up for the evening. She found them exactly where she always left them, on a hook below the register counter. Next to the keys were three large, thickly bound, old leather books. On their spines, handwritten in permanent silver ink, were their titles—the *Independent Chronicle*, the *New Hampshire Spy/Gazette*, *The Salem Mercury/Gazette*—and their dates of publication. On top of the three volumes was a copy of an online article she had printed that morning. It was from a Delaware newspaper dated that day. The lead story covered a horrific multi-vehicle accident that left eight people dead.

Miriam recognized the name of one of them.

THIRTY SIX

Commander Crabtree's departure from the conference room signaled the end of the Friday morning meeting. Terrie thumbed through her daily brief, waiting for the room to clear.

Standing by the door, Jack called to her, "You coming?"

Meeting his gaze, she responded, "In a minute. I want to heat up my tea."

"Why didn't you want to carpool in this morning? Did I do something wrong again?"

She lowered her eyes to the contents of the black folder on the table. "No."

Her cryptic, one-word answer didn't sit well with him. It meant he was on the losing end of her internal deliberation. "You're considering everything we've accomplished so far, aren't you?"

She gave him the guilty-as-charged look. "See you in Ops."

"Don't be too long." He closed the door behind him, leaving her alone in the conference room.

Terrie sipped her tea as she finished reading the summary. Skimming over the annotated list, she felt increasingly somber.

1) Wednesday, May 29, 2013: A US drone strike in Pakistan killed a high-level Taliban member. They promised to retaliate against the government for their cooperation with the US.

2) Thursday, May 30, 2013: Sectarian violence in Iraq claimed 33 lives, totaling 500 for the month.
3) Thursday, May 30, 2013: The Syrian National Council declined to attend the UN-endorsed peace negotiations in Geneva next month, citing the ongoing slaughter of Syrian civilians by the Assad regime.

Terrie closed the folder, refilled her mug with hot tea, and headed for Ops. Only the crisis in Iraq offered any hope of finding the clue that would lead to Margaret's killers and to introduce them to justice. She promised to make it happen, despite the numerous hurdles put in front of her. It was a promise she made to herself.

As she signed in she could hear her colleagues in the midst of a hotly contested debate. She quietly assumed her station, trying to ignore Taro's response to Theo's latest question.

"My family can trace their lineage back to a survivor of the Battle of Dannoura in 1185."

"Isn't that from the Tale of the Heike?" asked Theo.

"That's the clan name of the fictional account. The true name of our clan was the Taira."

"If the tale is true, there were no survivors."

"Are you calling me a liar?"

"Let's just say I find it hard to swallow."

"In point of fact, there were a few scattered survivors. According to the stories my grandfather told my parents when they were in Manzanar, we are the direct descendants of General Taira Tomomori."

"Didn't he commit suicide by tying an anchor to his feet and throwing himself into the sea?"

"Legend has it, yes. One of his sons managed to escape to the Ryukyu Island of Ishigaki. His descendants later moved to Kyoto in the early 1400s, during the Ashikaga Shogunate."

Theo just realized the magnitude of what Taro had just told him. "Wait a minute, your family was interned in Manzanar?"

"What's Manzanar?" Jack asked.

Taro answered, "It was an American gulag located in the San Fernando Valley of California. President Franklin Roosevelt directed Japanese Americans on the West Coast into what he euphemistically called 'relocation' camps. We were forced to stay there from 1942 till the end of the war. Roosevelt's most controversial executive order, it remains a blight on his presidency to this day."

"They didn't lock up first-generation German Americans, did they?" Jack queried again.

This time, Theo chimed in. "They certainly did. This only goes to prove how racist our country truly is."

Jack scowled. "Do you always have to view the country through a race-colored lens?"

"Look how we've responded to the radical Islamist threat, by racially profiling all Muslims."

"So now we should treat all 85-year-old white women to the same level of scrutiny at airport checkpoints for the sake of political correctness, is that it?" Jack answered Theo.

Unable to concentrate on her work as the discussion got louder, Bannerman folded her arms and kicked back in her seat to listen to the debate. Terrie did her level best to ignore the hackneyed banter.

"I'm talking about profiling based solely on race," Theo emphasized.

"And I'm talking about profiling in general, to which the race of a suspect is relevant, based on eyewitness accounts," Jack responded. "The racial component is just one characteristic of a suspect profile."

"That's still discrimination."

"Really? If a gang of black teens is videotaped shooting and robbing a convenience store, the cops should ignore the suspects' verifiable ethnicity when putting out a BOLO because to do otherwise is racist?"

Theo's anger got the best of him. "We're not talking about a small group here, Jack, but an entire race of people and a major religious group being stigmatized because terrorists happen to be Middle Eastern and Muslim."

"Then we should just set aside sound investigative techniques because we're afraid of offending someone?"

"That's not what Roosevelt's executive order did," Taro said, trying to get the conversation back on track. "It violated American citizens' due-process rights and all because of race."

Objecting to Taro's distinction, Jack said, "The country didn't swear out a warrant for the planes that bombed Pearl Harbor. We declared war, and, right or wrong, the president exercised his executive powers to protect the nation. And that makes him racist?"

"No, it makes him vulnerable to impeachment," Taro insisted.

"Roosevelt wouldn't have been impeached by a congress who took less than two hours to pass the needed legislation to enforce his executive order. The exercise of law enforcement and the prosecution of a war are two different things," Jack replied.

Taro pressed on with his opinion. "No congressman, senator, or president, is above the law. And taking race completely out of it, ask yourself if the chief executive has the constitutional authority to unilaterally deny due process to our country's citizens."

"He doesn't," Jack responded. "Likewise, he's not allowed to selectively enforce the law, either. With the Constitution under attack by those sworn to defend it, I'd say the only change needed is a return to its original intent."

Theo became roiled. "Does that original intent support the theory that African-Americans are property?"

"Where do you get that nonsense?" Jack asked.

"From the treaty ending the Revolutionary War, signed by Franklin, Adams, and Jay. A sentence in Article Seven of that treaty required King George III to remove his armies without 'carrying away any Negroes or other property of the American inhabitants,'" Theo said. His deliberate mockery of Terrie's citation of the UCMJ was a subtle dig, but he didn't even get a rise out of her.

Continuing the idea, Taro added, "Not only did our second president trample over the Declaration of Independence within the text of that treaty, but our Bill of Rights as well, with the Alien and Sedition Acts. In fact, Roosevelt cited them to justify locking up my family during the war."

Bannerman did her best to put a cap on the rhetorical debate. "In every human epoch, the duplicity of the politician remains timeless." Her entry into the conversation allowed an authoritative pause for reflection, but it didn't last long.

Taro had to toss one more grenade into the foxhole. "Because my trust in politicians is so diminished, I'm less enthusiastic about engaging in their conflicts."

"No sane government actively seeks conflict, but diplomacy backed by force is usually more successful," Jack suggested.

"Force never solved anything. It begets more violence." Then, as an afterthought, Taro added, "I don't believe the use of force is ever justified."

Hearing this, Terrie interrupted her analysis. She spun around in her chair to focus her attention on Taro. "Are you willing to put that affirmation to the test, Mr. Hattori?"

Taro eyed Terrie with a curious expression. "How do you mean?"

"A simple demonstration to prove your theory invalid?"

Taro looked around the room for support, but had none. He glanced back at Terrie. "What do you have in mind?"

"A human being is hardwired for violence, Mr. Hattori. You can't escape it."

"I can, by simply refusing to take part in it." He folded his arms in a display of arrogance.

"Ah, but I can make you, Mr. Hattori."

"Don't bet on it."

"I have no wish to steal your money."

"Prove it, then."

Terrie's eyes were laser-focused on her target. "You know the traits that make up strong emotions, like lust, jealousy, and aggression?"

"Yeah."

"Where do they reside in the triune of the human brain?"

"The R-complex, of course."

"The seat of human instinct, primitive thought, and aggression, would you agree?"

"Naturally."

"And as a man of evidentiary proof, with Creationism being an improbable theory, in your estimation, you would agree that we're descended from the lower forms? Our DNA contains the base pairs from these lower forms?"

"Absolutely."

"Then I submit to you that encoded in our DNA is the very essence of aggression. It resides in every human brain, including yours."

"I'm not arguing that point."

"Then what is your point?"

"In civil society, higher brain functions can overcome instinct."

"Dedicated terrorists move within civil society, Mr. Hattori. It's the ultimate camouflage. They refuse to listen to logic. And they won't stop at mere words. Trust me, evil knows no such restraint."

"Well, I won't use force."

"When threatened, you will retaliate. Your built-in fight-or-flight reflex leaves you no choice." Terrie got out of her chair and began to walk toward Taro with fire in her eyes and determination in each step.

Bannerman's pained expression telegraphed her concern that this was getting out of hand.

"I'm a dedicated terrorist, Mr. Hattori. Try to stop my impending attack."

"Miss Murphy, knock it off," Theo said. She ignored him.

"Terrie, come on. This isn't funny," Jack added.

"No, it's not." She still advanced on Taro. "How do you intend to stop me, Mr. Hattori?"

"Talk—"

"I won't listen."

Uncomfortable with the direction and tone of the conversation, Bannerman jumped in. "Miss Murphy. You can't—"

"Defend yourself," Terrie said, nearly on top of him.

"Miss Murphy!" Bannerman yelled, but it was too late.

In a lighting move, she executed a flawless spinning wheel kick, employing precise control till her foot came within half an inch of Taro's face. Not sure if she was actually going to hit him, he threw up a successful block.

"Miss Murphy, that will be quite enough!" yelled Bannerman. "Report to the commander's office now!"

Terrie regained her composure, keeping her gaze squarely on Taro. "The block itself would be considered use of force, Mr. Hattori. Your intentions aside, the enemy would interpret your actions as force and respond in kind."

Bannerman put a definitive period on the incident. "Miss Murphy, did you hear me?"

"On my way, Commander." Terrie gathered her belongings and left Ops for Crabtree's office.

Terrie tried to report in, but Crabtree silenced her. "Take a seat, Miss Murphy." Terrie's icy demeanor was evident in her eyes, an expression that forced the vein in his forehead to wax prominent. "Would you mind explaining what just happened in the Ops Center?" He folded his arms and waited for an explanation.

"On or off the record, sir?"

"Right now, I want your side of it."

"If you're planning on any disciplinary action, shouldn't my Article 31 rights come into play?"

Crabtree stood up. "Believe me, Lieutenant, if I wanted to bring legal proceedings against you, we wouldn't be talking right now. If the story is true, you're also responsible for the injury to Lieutenant O'Hara."

"That was before we were officially introduced."

"You appear to have significant anger issues, Lieutenant."

"Do I appear angry, sir?"

"Don't fence with me, Lieutenant!"

"The incident with Mr. O'Hara was self-defense, not anger. What happened in the Ops center was a mutually-agreed-upon demonstration."

"How do I know that?"

"Ask them, sir."

"Oh, I intend to, Lieutenant. Meanwhile, I suggest you take the rest of the afternoon to think about how your actions during your short tenure have adversely impacted our team dynamic."

"Then I won't be subject to any disciplinary action, sir?"

"We'll discuss it Monday, Lieutenant. You're dismissed."

Terrie left without another word.

Terrie picked up her bundle of mail from the lockbox without bothering to look at it. A week that began with so much promise had ended in such dire personal consequences, yet she knew she wouldn't have done anything different. Still angered, she threw the bundle on the kitchen table and decided on an early run instead.

When she returned from her run, she felt calmer but still uneasy about her current predicament. The hour-long diversion did little to repress her unsettled thoughts. She freshened up with a shower and changed into her shorts and Eagles jersey. Emerging from her bedroom, her eyes fell on the bundled mail. She removed the rubber band as her cell phone came to life. The name on the screen was Aunt Barbara.

Her aunt's harried voice barged in before she could say hello. "Terrie, I know you're at work, but I had to call you."

"It's all right," she didn't correct her, "What's the matter? You sound upset?"

"It's been on the news for the past couple days."

"What has?"

"There was a terrible accident on the Kirkwood highway. Eight people were killed."

"And that means what to me?"

"Terrie, they just released the names of the victims. Juli Aruem was one of them!"

Terrie was immersed in thought about Juli and her haunting last statement about the *Crescent* when Jack's telltale knock broke her concentration. She let him in and retreated to the balcony without greeting him.

Jack, still in uniform, followed in her wake. "You left in a hurry today," he said. She crossed her arms, continuing to stare at the pleasure craft on the water. "Interesting demonstration you put on in the Ops Center," he continued, "Not sure if you know it, but Taro got the message." Getting no response, he chose to break her silence with a question. "What did the commander have to say?"

"He wasn't amused," Terrie stated.

"That's an understatement. Bannerman was still shaken by it, even as we left for the weekend."

"I'm really not interested."

He tried to cheer her up by changing the subject. "We did okay with the SECNAV report, didn't we? And we made progress tracking down leads regarding the *Dey of Reckoning*."

"That investigation's done."

"Why?"

"I don't want to talk about it right now, okay?"

He headed for the apartment door but stopped. "It may have been a bad week for you, but at least you didn't receive a reprimand for your stunt with Taro. It's not like you killed someone."

"The investigation is over because it hit a brick wall."

"What wall? I thought you said the manuscript from that Delaware author would help our investigation?"

"There will be no manuscript."

"Why not?"

"My aunt called earlier. Juli Aruem was involved in a car accident Wednesday afternoon. She's dead."

Jack's posture deflated. "I'm sorry, Terrie."

"Since we're fresh out of leads, I suppose I'll get back to searching for my sister's killers."

Jack's exposed skin resolved into gooseflesh at her reaction. "Terrie—"

"Leave me alone."

"All right," he responded softly. "I'll be next door if you need me."

Terrie watched the door close behind him. Spying the mail on the table, she dismissed the idea of going over it. The week was replaying fast-forward in her head. Try as she might, the dots were not lining up. She needed that manuscript, and now it slipped through her fingers. The image of Juli Aruem flashed in her mind. The real estate broker and author was a young, vivacious woman, much like her sister.

There was something she missed. Something she spotted or heard on that grainy clip was driving her crazy. She replayed the entire video in her head, trying to nail it down. Then she remembered something besides the word wraith that sounded familiar; it was the voice of the inquisitor himself. She heard it before, on that six-minute audio. But that's not the only place she remembered hearing it. She heard it somewhere else.

Terrie's belly grumbled and thinking on an empty stomach didn't work well for her, so she got started on supper.

Finding corned beef in the freezer but no cabbage, she settled for a baked potato instead. The meal wasn't as satisfying as she'd hoped. Terrie's headache got much worse. She took a hot shower and headed off to bed. Sleep didn't come easy, but it came nonetheless. It was surprisingly peaceful rest. Until her nightmare's savage reality show added a frightening new episode to the season's lineup.

THIRTY SEVEN

Conflicting images faded in and out like an old cinematograph operating in slow motion. The colorless image of Margaret Murphy's exquisite face went from flawless to frightening, one still image at a time.

The first clear picture Terrie could discern was a perfectly coifed, ideally made-up Margaret showing off her pearly whites. Her face stayed that way for the first few moving stills. The frames of stop-motion animation focused on Margaret's expression as her eyes lost their brightness. Her smile diminished, retracting in on itself until she looked indifferent.

Five frames later, her eyes grew concerned, then wide. Eight frames later, her look altered drastically, from surprise and shock to fear and pain, her lips curled into a grossly distorted caricature. A jagged shard of bloody glass burst through her larynx, ripping a portion of her left vocal cord as it emerged. It dragged the delicate membrane with it as the barb-edged triangle tore through her throat. Blood spray radiated its high-velocity spatter outward, covering everything in its path. Severed from its cervical stalk, her head lolled off to one side, exposing her C-3 and C-4 vertebrae. Her mouth moved as though she were trying to speak, but nothing came out. Margaret's skin changed from a healthy pink to an ashen gray speckled with blood. Her eyelids drooped slightly as her life force withdrew from dying pupils.

Of all the dreams she had about her sister, this was by far the most frightening. She never experienced Margaret's death like this before. She couldn't understand why a shard of glass decapitated her when the blade of an Islamic radical was responsible for the gruesome act.

With each new frame, the image of Margaret changed. Terrie's restlessness increased as the eyes, nose, cheekbones, and hair morphed into those of someone else. The woman's lifeless eyes took on an unsettling familiarity. A new face materialized before her. Someone Terrie instantly recognized. It was the lifeless countenance of Juli Aruem.

Eyes still vacant, the violently amputated head moved its jaw in an effort to speak. It managed a strong, gurgling whisper as dark fluid ran from the corner of its mouth, the lips astir over blood-stained teeth to form a single word: "Terrie!"

The peaceful stillness of a Portsmouth apartment complex cradled its slumbering residents, until a bone-chilling scream pierced the tranquility of night.

Terrie bolted out of bed, her eyelids thrust open to extract every ounce of light. Every muscle in her sweat-drenched body was on fire, causing her extremities to spasm. The pain was unbearable.

Dimly aware of a sound beyond the dying echo of her screams, she heard a banging at her apartment door. Someone was yelling her name.

"Terrie, goddamit, open the door!" The pounding continued until she could answer it.

When she threw the door open, she saw a shocked Jack O'Hara staring back at her.

"What happened? Are you all right?"

Mentally absent, she didn't recognize him.

"Terrie! It's me. Jack."

She tried to say something, but it was too late. Her eyes rolled back in her head as she collapsed toward him. Jack managed to catch her in time to prevent her from dropping to the floor.

When she woke, she found herself lying on the couch, uncertain how she got there. Still dazed, Terrie could only make out a dark figure in front of her, snapping his fingers in her face.

"Wha—"

"Terrie, it's Jack."

Slowly coming into focus, two uniformed officers were visible over his shoulder—a man and a woman.

The male officer spoke. "We responded to a 911 call from this address, ma'am. Are you okay?"

Terrie tried to sit up, but slumped back to the sofa, light-headed and weak. Jack grabbed her wrist to assist her. "Terrie?"

"What happened?"

"You woke the building with that scream," Jack responded. "It must have been a doozy this time."

Terrie put on a brave face as she tried to blot out the ghastly memory. Processing the officer's question, she responded, "I'm fine, officers, really." She glanced at Jack and added, "He's my neighbor. I'm in good hands."

"You sure?" asked the female officer, casting a suspicious eye toward Jack.

"Definitely."

"Very well, then. Good night." The officers saw themselves out.

Still holding Terrie's wrist in one hand, Jack softly reached for her cheek with the other, holding her head with a caring touch. "Was it Margaret again?"

Terrie couldn't bring herself to relay what she'd experienced. With the calamitous week she'd endured, she was totally distraught. The authority Terrie wielded over her conscious world melted away. Catching a glimpse of Jack, Terrie's dam of tears burst forth as uncontrollable sobs.

Jack wrapped his arms around Terrie and whispered, "It'll be all right, Terrie. Just let it out."

She mumbled something unintelligible. Jack rocked her back and forth, humming an old Irish folk tune.

Pulling her face away from him, she asked, "What song is that?"

"It's something my brothers and I used to sing."

"You sang in a group?"

"Still do. We're an Irish quartet. In fact, we have a gig at a friend's party in Chelsea tomorrow."

Meeting Jack's gaze, Terrie said, "Sing it. Please?"

He drew Terrie close and began to sing Toora-Loora-Looral.

As Jack's rendition weaved its spell in her ears, it took her back to Margaret's leadership of her church choir. The angelic quality of her mezzo-soprano could easily have made her a fortune in the recording industry, but that wasn't Margaret Murphy's way. She freely shared her natural instrument with the world.

Jack's delivery was calm and inviting. She felt something she hadn't felt in a long time: safe. Not since her sister was alive had she felt so completely at ease with someone. Not even the presence of her Aunt Barbara was so consolatory.

When he finished, he looked at her. "How was that?"

"You have a soothing voice, like my sister."

"Thank you." He got up, still holding on to her. "Are you going to be fine for a second?"

"Sure."

"Do you have any milk?"

"No, why?"

"I'll be right back." Jack disappeared into his apartment and came back with a tray holding a quart-size container of milk, a jar of honey, nutmeg, and a shot glass of brandy.

"What are you doing?"

"You need something to help you sleep, so I'm making you some warm milk."

"You're making a hot toddy?"

"What's wrong with that?"

"Nothing," she said, softly. "It's very sweet of you."

"So, your sister sang?" Jack said as he got to work on her drink.

"She was a natural talent."

"My brothers and I started singing when we were kids. When did your sister start singing?"

"I can't remember a time when she didn't sing."

"Did she ever do it professionally?"

Feeling more herself, Terrie said, "Our family was devoutly religious. When we first moved to Wilmington, Margaret found the most welcoming church imaginable. Once she met the gregarious choir director, Pastor Geno Vitarelli, it was all over. Talk about a voice. His rich signature baritone was the envy of any church in the area."

"Hmm. Sounds like someone I'd like to know."

"When they found out she had a voice strong enough to complement his, they couldn't say no to her."

"She was that good?"

"A handmade musical instrument is only as good as the talent that plays it, but a natural singing voice is unique, with the precious individuality of fingerprints. There may be an infinite number of tenors, but only one Luciano Pavarotti. What a tragedy it would be if his recordings were lost to the world."

Terrie began to drift away again. Jack poured the hot mixture into her mug, substituting a sleep aid for the brandy. "Here you go. This should calm you down enough to get some rest."

Reaching for the mug, Terrie said something she hadn't before. "Thank you, Jack."

"Jack?" he queried in mock disapproval. "Not Mr. O'Hara? You're slipping, Miss Murphy."

"That's what happens when I'm not myself." She took a sip to test its flavor. "Not bad." Deciding the concoction cool enough, she downed the entire mug.

"I guess you liked it."

"It was quite delicious, thank you."

"How could you tell?" he teased. Observing her pink flush of embarrassment, he allowed himself a quick grin. "My oldest brother came up with the recipe. I drink it when I can't sleep."

Terrie set the mug down on the reading table and glanced back at him. "Will you do me a favor?"

"Anything, within reason."

"Would you sing that song to me again?"

Jack sat next to Terrie, clasped her hands in his, and began to sing. "Over in Killarney, many years ago…"

At the beginning of the chorus, she leaned into his chest and closed her eyes. Jack tenderly rocked her in his arms until he finished the song.

Comforted by Jack's warm touch as he held her in his protective grip, Terrie said, "Sing something else."

Thinking what tune would be appropriate, while wishing the lyrics could convey how he truly felt about her, he began to sing a more modern Irish work. "The Voyage" was better suited to an older married couple reflecting on their lives and the children they had together. It was wishful thinking, but Jack liked the melody so much that he sang it anyway.

"I am a sailor, you're my first mate. We signed on together, we coupled our fate…"

As the last note hung in the air, Terrie turned her tear-streaked face toward Jack. Their lips nearly touched as he looked down at her. Surrendering to the moment, she closed the gap between them, yielding to her desire for a deep, loving kiss.

THIRTY EIGHT

Relentless orange embers grew brighter over Terrie's closed eyes. Allowing one to crack open, she caught sight of the digital alarm as it flicked over to the next minute. It was after nine in the morning. Still groggy from her doctored sedative, she couldn't figure out how she made it to bed.

Then she remembered. Jack had given her something to help her sleep. The last thing she recalled was being with Jack on the couch. Apprehensive at the prospect of not being alone in her bed, she rolled over. No one there. *Where the hell is he?*

She opened the bedroom door to find Jack sprawled out on the couch, an unrecognizable throw covering him. He must have retrieved it from his apartment. He must have stayed the night to make sure she was okay. That's when the clarity of what happened the night before sank in.

She'd kissed him.

Cursing herself, she banished the memory from her thoughts and made breakfast. As she waited for the English muffins to achieve their desired tint of brown, Terrie's eyes fell on the mail she left on the kitchen table. She went to pick it up, when she heard a sound from behind her. Jack O'Hara stood next to the sofa, still dressed in the clothes he had on the evening before.

"Well, good morning. How did you sleep?"

As he asked the question, the toaster surrendered two perfectly browned English muffins. Diverted from examining her mail once again, she completed fixing her breakfast. "That wasn't just a hot toddy, was it?"

"Guilty as charged. There was barely enough brandy for flavor, not effect."

"Then how did you—"

"I added an over-the-counter sleep aid to your toddy."

"Why?" she yelled, her temper flaring.

"After you woke up half of Portsmouth last night, I figured you didn't need any more unwanted attention."

There was an uncomfortable truth cleverly seeded within his attempt at humor. She squinted at him to evaluate his motives. "How did I get to bed?"

"You fell asleep on my shoulder while I was singing to you. I picked you up and put you to bed."

Noticing she was still had on her jersey and shorts, Terrie began to calm down. Allowing the slightest trace of a smile to grace her lips, she asked, "Do you want breakfast?"

"You're welcome."

Shaking her head, she switched conversational gears. "When do you have to be in Chelsea?"

"The gig is at five, but we have to be there at two to set up."

"What time do you plan on leaving?"

"I figure around eleven."

She tossed two more muffins in the toaster, handing him the first two. "Butter or raspberry jelly?"

"Jelly's fine."

"I suppose you won't be around this weekend?"

"I'll be back by tomorrow afternoon, why? Miss me already?"

Terrie gave Jack a harder look than she intended. "Listen, the only reason you're not dead is because I didn't find you lying next to me this morning."

An affable smile erupted on his face. "Be mad at me all you want. I wasn't the one who got emotional last night. You kissed me, remember?"

"I'm trying to forget." She slathered her muffins with jelly and scarfed them down. In her haste to set a new world record for consuming her breakfast, she unknowingly left a vestige of jelly on the corner of her lip. She waited for Jack to finish his breakfast before she policed up their dishes. As she reached over for his plate, Jack was looking at her strangely. "What?"

Without a word, he reached up to remove the glistening red blot from her face. He immediately licked it off his finger. "Mmm. Delicious."

"Oh, knock it off," she quipped with mock irritation.

He spotted the oven clock and noticed the time. "It's almost ten. I've got to get ready."

"See you when you get back."

As Jack got up to leave, he had to settle her fears about the previous evening. "Terrie, I realize you weren't in any state of mind to know what you were doing when you kissed me."

Terrie gave Jack an evaluating stare.

"What?"

"I thought guys like you were an extinct species."

Out of the many trademark faces she'd watched him make over their short association, she hadn't seen this one before. It was one of deep meaning and purpose. His voice conveyed as much. "If there's anything real between us, we'll find it. Together." He closed the door behind him.

The dishes taken care of and the room to herself, she could finally address the mail that had been waiting since yesterday to be read. She went through the numerous legal-size envelopes. Bills, bills, and more bills, along with two mail-order catalogues and a menu flyer from the newest pizza joint to open.

As she separated the bills from the circulars, a yellow postal form dropped to the floor. It was a notice of a package too large for her post office box. The form never told her where it came from or who sent it. She had just enough time to pick it up before the post office closed.

The package was a small, nondescript rectangular box. It was postmarked in Camden, New Jersey, and sent by a stranger with an unusual name.

Who the hell is Estel Atrea? Reading the name over again, she realized something wasn't right. The name Estelle wasn't spelled correctly, but the phonetics was familiar. Then she understood—the name was an anagram. Taking the last letter from Estel and placing it at the end of Atrea, the word real jumped out at her. Putting the At after the t in the remainder of Estel, the word became Estate.

Could it be? Suddenly feeling self-conscious about where she was and who might have sent this, Terrie waited to get home before opening the package.

She grabbed a steak knife from the drawer and sliced the clear tape across its seam. Removing a leather satchel, she unfastened its flap. What she found inside reinvigorated her investigation.

It was Juli Aruem's manuscript.

THIRTY NINE

Philip's frustration was mounting. His surveillance of the lieutenant had yielded nothing. She wasn't using any of the devices his sources managed to track.

At work, she used her computer to accomplish her mission, not surf the net. She hadn't used her vehicle outside commuting to and from work. Beyond checking emails on her home laptop, she rarely, if ever, responded or used it for any form of entertainment. No YouTube videos. No music downloads or research of any kind. Outside of a few incidental calls and a text or two, his return on investment in cloning her phone wasn't worth the risk. She hardly used it.

His efforts weren't paying off. He'd have to employ more traditional forms of surveillance, which meant the use of planted listening devices. Obtaining authorization to bug her workstation was out of the question, but her vehicle and apartment were fair game. Getting his Portsmouth contact to take care of her vehicle was the easy part. Her apartment, on the other hand, was another matter. He'd have to attend to it personally.

FORTY

Under the title page was a short cover letter addressed to no one in particular. Reading its contents, Terrie knew it was addressed to her.

> Here's it is, as promised. The complete manuscript, source materials, and bibliography are together in this package. May it help you in your quest.

She skimmed through the manuscript to preview its narrative and wealth of sourced information. Terrie filled a snack bowl with pretzels, heated up her favorite tea, then plopped down on the sofa for a long read.

Introduction

The succeeding pages detail the extraordinary account of the Elk River native whose nautical exploits might have rendered his name world-renowned were it not for the clandestine nature of the service to his country.

Orphaned at 13, he embarked on a career as a merchant marine. A colorful individual, he rubbed shoulders with the titans of early American naval history, yet no one's ever heard of him. When referred to at all, it was never by his own name; Captain to his crew, Cyclops to his enemies, and as his legend grew with his advanced age—living well into his 80s—he was known as the Old Corsair.

He was a monolith of a man, tall and powerfully built with a hard disposition. Salt and pepper beard and locks adorned his craggy, olive-complected face. A lengthy scar crossed the bridge of his brawler's nose, a souvenir from his brush with Barbary pirates. Bushy eyebrows crowned his hazel eyes, of which a deformed left iris obliterated the scalera, leaving him with the nickname, Cyclops. He wore a thickly striped muffler under the huge lapels of his dark frockcoat.

From his earliest days as the skipper of his father's schooner, *Hypatia*, the Old Corsair kept faith with his duty to country, even when the path he chose was not in keeping with official government dictates. The eccentric captain held loyalty above all things. His intense dislike for cowards and traitors was the foundation of a savage temper he often acted upon.

This is the tale of the mysterious maritime figure whose disappearance in 1850 became the stuff of legend, the story of the Old Corsair, a Maryland coaster born into this world as Vernon Cavendish Tunney.

Terrie read page after page of detailed information that backed up and augmented everything she'd been investigating since her Badger Island detail. She downed an occasional handful of pretzels, reading well into the evening, pausing occasionally for a stretch. One section, from a chapter entitled "The Captain," really caught her attention.

Notorious and most sinister of America's "old navy" ship captains, Vernon "Cyclops" Tunney never figured prominently in the annals of nautical stratagem. A pity, since his tactical and strategic savvy managed to elude even today's best efforts to locate him or the vessel he captained to his alleged demise in 1850, the *Neptune's Trident*.

A model sailor in his youth, Tunney's eccentric behavior manifested itself with the 1796 release of his former captain, Richard O'Brien, from his twelve-year captivity with the Dey of Algiers. Two years later, upon hearing that President Adams appointed his former captain US Consul to Algiers, Tunney became apoplectic. He reluctantly accepted the commission offered him by [REDACTED] to oversee the refit of the *Dey of Reckoning*.

Admitting to a peculiar aversion to hats, he begrudgingly wore one as a young sailor. But as captain, he dispensed with the accessory. It was the dark great cloak he always wore, along with his straight, flowing, salt and pepper locks and beard, that set the perfect contrast, distinguishing himself from the rest of his crew. The scarred nose, the shocking appearance of his left eye and his revulsion for disloyalty encouraged the crew to keep their distance from the temperamental captain.

A well-chronicled account of an argument between himself and a junior officer aboard his merchant vessel *Hypatia* detailed his ferocious temper when provoked. He ended the verbal contest with a thundering right hand, stoving the man's jaw to the back of his head.

Tunney's favorite tobacco was Virginia aromatic, properly tamped in the tar-stained bowl of his father's old churchwarden. The story of how he replaced that pipe resides in the mythos of legend. In a published account, a young sailor who witnessed the aftermath of the battle between the *Justice* and *Dey of Reckoning* reported the new captain's heinous actions that would become the Old Corsair's grizzly calling card from then on.

'Mr. Tunney's eyes burned red as he stood over the corpse of the nameless captain. He spotted a bent ivory, eagle-claw meerschaum near the man's lifeless left hand. Mr. Tunney picked it up, sniffed the bowl, and let out a malevolent growl. Stepping on the dead man's neck, he thumped out the unused *tobacco over the bloody skull and filled the pipe's bowl with the Virginian blend he preferred, lit it, and puffed away with a satisfied look on his face. Before the mortally wounded* Justice *could slip beneath the waves, Mr. Tunney ordered me to collect the logbook while the rest of the crew tossed the pirates' bodies off the deck of our newly captured vessel.'*

It's from this story we learn of Tunney's macabre ritual, designed as a fate accompli to any vessel foolhardy enough to run afoul of him and his ship—a tradition he performed all the way up to his final victory at sea in 1847.

In possession of a privateer's commission signed by President Jefferson to enforce the Embargo of 1807, Tunney engaged any ships he considered the enemy. While other privateers were restricted in their targeting to just British ships under Madison's commission of 1812, Tunney honored no such restriction. From his actions during the Barbary Wars to the Battle of San Gabriel in 1847, he refused to capture "prizes." Tunney considered enemy vessels to be fair game for destruction. He concluded each engagement in the same fashion. Tunney would take the eagle-claw meerschaum from his cloak pocket and set it between his teeth. Taking a few puffs to light it, he assumed his place on the forecastle, used the pipe to salute the sinking vessel, then turned away.

On the afternoon of July 16, 1850, a merchant ship captain spotted *Neptune's Trident*, with Tunney at the helm, heading into the path of an oncoming hurricane somewhere near the Delmarva Peninsula. Though she was alleged to have made numerous appearances afterward, Tunney was never seen or heard from again.

Terrie kept reading through the night. Before dawn broke, she finished the manuscript, its resource materials, and several bowls of pretzels. She drifted to sleep where she sat until roused from her slumber by a pounding at the door.

"Just a minute," she yelled, moving slowly, trying to clear the cobwebs.

"Jesus, Terrie! Don't tell me I got you up?"

She ran her fingers through her hair, searching for the clock. "Yeah, what time is it?"

"It's nearly two in the afternoon. What have you been doing?"

Terrie's mischievous smile broke through the exhaustion in her eyes. "You're not going to believe this."

He followed her to the coffee table where he saw a rectangular box next to a ream of paper. "What's that?"

"See for yourself."

Taking up the hand-bound manuscript, Jack began flipping through its pages. His excitement was mixed with confusion. "I don't understand. How did you get this if Juli Aruem died?"

"Note the postmark on the box."

"May 28th?" Jack's question hung there. "She mailed it parcel post, which means it should've come sometime next week."

"I received a generic notice yesterday. Mailing a package priority, she would have to identify herself and the recipient, which meant traceable documentation. Judging from the name she used on the box, I'd say that was something she wished to avoid."

"It must have been a light day for bulk mail."

Terrie watched him with fascination, thinking how she must have looked when she first opened it.

His head wagged in disbelief. "You read this whole thing last night?"

"It isn't very long, perhaps a hundred and seventy pages in all."

"Okay, so what are we dealing with here?"

"Essentially, the biography of our intrepid Captain Tunney. More important, it advances the best theory about what happened to the *Dey of Reckoning*. According to Miss Aruem, shortly after Tunney brought back the captured ship, he retained his commission long enough to evaluate its refit potential. As he did, he discovered several books in the captain's stateroom. Based on Aruem's vague description, they may be related to something I glossed over in one of my library books, but I can't remember the context."

"You? forget? I find that impossible to believe," he said jokingly.

Smirking back at him, Terrie continued her summation. "Hackett's shipyard wasn't equipped to handle the vessel, so she was moved to Herod's Cove, and that's where the *Dey of Reckoning* remained for ten years."

"What did she say Tunney did during that time?"

"He returned to his father's old vessel, the coaster *Hypatia*. Aruem goes into morbid detail as to his duties, assignments, and his profitable relationship with Delaware entrepreneur William West. Throughout this period, Tunney was in correspondence with someone highly placed within the federal government. Apparently, he was powerful enough to retain Tunney's commission. He was unsuccessful at first, until Tunney's former captain, Richard O'Brien, was released and subsequently appointed US Consul to Algiers. What Aruem doesn't make clear is how the refit was accomplished, only that it was done very quickly. When she tried to obtain a FOIA request for further information, she ran into the Justice Department."

Jack stared at Terrie as he slumped into the sofa. "But how—"

Terrie opened the manuscript to somewhere near the middle pages. "Here, read."

His response was a skeptical grin, but he read it just the same. Jack's eyes quickly scrolled across each line as they made their way down the page.

"So?" Terrie asked.

"A classified refit of the *Dey of Reckoning* would tell us why it never left port."

"And guess who brought it into port?"

"You think it was Tunney, based on your recollection of the ship's log of the *Justice*."

Terrie sifted through the pages until she came to another tidbit of information she wanted to share. "Now we have proof," she pronounced.

She pointed to the enlargements of several familiar colonial newspapers from 1788. The first one was the June 24 issue of *The Salem Mercury*. It showed the *Rebecca* article.

"I don't get it. We already have this article. It's the same as our online resources."

"That's because it's the source paper for the *Rebecca* advertisement." She flipped the page over to show two more enlarged areas, one of the June 26 issue of the *New Hampshire Gazette* and the other the July 3 *Independent Chronicle* where the duplicate *Rebecca* advertisements were run. "Now look at these."

The counterfeit articles were replaced by the original story and in the font style of each particular paper.

> PORTSMOUTH, *June 22.* Yesterday, reported to the Hon. John Armstrong, jun, in a letter from Vernon Tunney, Master, late of the *Justice*, the loss of both the ship and her original Master, Arthur Ledbetter. Tunney further brought the welcome news of the capture of the renegade corsair, *Dey of Reckoning*, believed responsible for the loss of both the *Maria* and the *Dauphin*. Sadly, the crews of both ships remain in a state of slavery in Algiers.

"This is an incredible find, Terrie," Jack insisted. He squinted his eyes at something at the end of the first line. "What's *jun*?"

"That's the colonial abbreviation for junior."

"Oh."

"And the revelations don't end there. As you skimmed through the appendix of photographs, did you happen to notice a sample letter in left-handed writing with the signatory T?"

"Yeah, what about it?"

"That's the exact handwriting of the second author from the logbook of the *Justice*."

"Well, without the original log, that assumption will be difficult to prove."

"Remember that curved triangular alloy I found on Badger?"

"Yeah?"

"As Crabtree examined it, I happen to catch the name *Neptune* written into one of its sides." Terrie could see the gears turning on Jack's face as he considered the ramifications of all they'd gone through to-date. "Think of it. A three-pointed object with the name *Neptune* made into it. Does the shape present instant imagery?"

Jack was still puzzled. "A warped triangle?"

"The name of a new vessel. *Neptune's Trident*."

"Never heard of it."

"I wouldn't have guessed you might. Aruem postulates that a refitted *Dey of Reckoning* is now a classified vessel called *Neptune's Trident* and that Tunney not only oversaw this refit but became its new skipper."

"How did she figure that?"

"A small dispatch box was found near the housing project of a Philadelphia suburb. It contained letters in Tunney's hand, first addressed to a Mr. J. in June of 1788. The letters continued through early May of 1800."

"Who was this Mr. J?"

"No return letters to Tunney were found, but the content of these letters gives us the clue. He must have been someone of significant influence within government circles, based on the level of his political discourse with Tunney. What she did know is this—the location in Philadelphia where the dispatch box was found is a well-known area for congressional delegates to have set up temporary lodgings while in Philly."

Trying to stay ahead of all this information, Jack asked, "Wasn't Manhattan the seat of the federal government until the District of Columbia got up and running?"

"Until late in 1790, it was. After that, they met in Philadelphia. The Sixth Congress moved to DC on December 17, 1800."

"How do you know all this?"

Terrie smirked and nodded toward the bookcase. Looking back at the manuscript, she snapped her fingers, her eyes wide open in surprise. "One other thing. Handwritten in the margin of the last page, Juli wrote several sets of numerals: 355.07, 359.009, 272.792, 623.4, and 629.8. Scrawled under them were the letters LOC and USNWC. Below that, she wrote Class'd Lib, NP4162T."

"What do you suppose those numbers mean?"

"You never owned a library card?"

Jack gave Terrie a disapproving scowl.

"Unless I miss my guess, LOC is the Library of Congress, and those numbers are from the Dewey decimal system for books to be found there. Since she told me those references had disappeared, she must have written them in the margin so I could track them down."

"Then I take it the Naval War College Library is our next stop?"

"Once we identify the books that are tied to those numbers, yes."

"And what about that NP number? It sounds like a commercial aircraft identification."

"Can't be. Such identification begins with the single letter N followed by a numerical sequence. However, it may have something to do with the classified section of the library," Terrie surmised. "Meanwhile, we still have that appointment with Mr. Clendaniel tomorrow night. More pressing, I've got to get something to eat."

"How 'bout we go out? You've been cooped up in this apartment all weekend."

"I don't think—"

"I won't take no for an answer."

Terrie looked up at Jack, trying to maintain a straight face. His puppy dog expression forced a smile out of her. She even flashed him her movie-star choppers. She placed the manuscript back in the box and handed it to Jack. "Do me a favor and put this in a safe place in your apartment while I get ready."

"I can do that. So, what do you feel like?"

"A nice sit-down, four-course meal. Any suggestions?"

"I have a few ideas," Jack said, smiling back at her.

A half hour later, they exited the apartment building and headed for the parking lot when Terrie saw a man, dressed in maintenance coveralls, step from behind her SUV. When she spied his company vehicle on the opposite side of the parking lot, her suspicious nature kicked into high gear.

Acknowledging the two tenants, the man touched the brim of his ball cap. As they passed each other, Terrie caught a glimpse of the man's profile. His nose and cheekbones were unremarkable, but the individual characteristics of his skull and jawline were singular. And familiar. She'd seen this man before. But where?

"Let's take your truck."

"You know him?" asked Jack, thumbing over his shoulder at the man walking toward their apartment building.

"Let's just say I find it odd that he came from the far side of the parking lot where my Ford is, and his van is right here in front."

"Are you always this paranoid?"

"I haven't started talking to myself yet."

Terrie hopped in Jack's truck and buckled up, maintaining her gaze on the balcony.

Starting the vehicle, Jack made his dinner suggestion. "There's a new Italian place in Newington I wanted to try."

"For takeout?"

"Why? Because of that guy we just saw?"

"I've seen him around, but I can't place him. At least not yet."

Terrie and Jack returned to the apartment building with their culinary treasures. Gone less than an hour, Jack pulled into the parking lot and noticed the maintenance van was gone. "I see your friend left."

"Yeah."

"What's the matter? You look distracted."

"Something about that guy."

Trying to be optimistic, Jack said, "Don't worry, it'll come to you."

"My memory isn't what it used to be."

"Hey, if I'd been through what you have over the past month, I wouldn't remember my own name."

"Thanks," replied Terrie, appreciative of his compliment. "Perhaps once I eat something I'll figure it out."

"Your place or mine?"

"Why yours?"

"The manuscript's there, remember?"

"I think I'm all read out. Besides, I'm still curious as to what Mr. Clendaniel's treasures hold. His newspaper collection might corroborate Aruem's evidence about the *Rebecca* articles."

Reaching the third floor, Terrie tossed a directional nod at her end of the hallway. Jack yielded to her implied suggestion with fallen shoulders.

FORTY ONE

Berthed in a slip near the north end of Prescott Park, a distressed pleasure boat's interior lights snapped on. The man cowered down to descend into the cabin below to discard his blue-collar disguise. Grabbing a steel briefcase from under the bed, he popped it open to retrieve a jar of makeup remover. He pealed off his nose appliance and massaged the cream onto his hands and face. As he peered into the case, he noted the lack of facial appliances. He'd have to budget time to make more.

Philip changed out of his coveralls and into attire suitable to a captain of this modest yacht. Entering the wheelhouse, he reached into the minifridge for a bottle of sherry and poured himself a glass of the pale, dry libation. He sipped it slowly, his eyes fixed on the balcony of a third-floor apartment that overlooked Badger Island.

The galley's microwave rang its electronic dinner bell. Frozen meals had become a staple recently. He could easily endure several successive nights of these lackluster dinners, so long as his sacrifice was rewarded with the right information.

He monitored the officers' conversation, mainly concerning Jack's gig in Chelsea with his brothers. The tone of Terrie's responses indicated her growing affinity for her neighbor and colleague. Their discussion went on like that for the majority of the evening. The eavesdropper had to turn up the volume on his earpiece whenever the person talking walked away from one of three microphones he'd placed in her apartment.

When Jack got up to leave, he said something that grabbed the listener's attention. He queried about their appointment with R. J. Clendaniel and the substance of that meeting—an unaltered, original collection of the *New Hampshire Spy/Gazette*.

He adjusted the volume and listened closely as they discussed their plan to compare the contents of the book in his possession with the online resources they'd already collected. Then he remembered the text Clendaniel had sent to Terrie, which included his address. He picked up the cloned phone and began to scroll through the texts until he found it.

Smiling that face-splitting smile, Philip knew exactly what he had to do, but he had little time to do it.

FORTY TWO

As she signed into the Ops Center after morning standup, Terrie noticed Taro and Bannerman were already there, turning on the flat screens. They were tuned to the big-three stations, the major cable news outlets, and WGME to capture the local news. Crabtree had said nothing to Terrie at standup, and Bannerman hadn't alluded to last week's incident either. Perhaps the CO considered it a closed subject.

Terrie and Taro assumed their duties as Bannerman finished going over her inbox. Crabtree's second looked around at everyone's station. As Terrie was reading her emails, Bannerman called down to her. "Miss Murphy, have you seen Mr. O'Hara?"

"He left for his annual physical. He should return after lunch. Something I can help you with?"

Bannerman shook her head. "Taro, do you know when Theo will be back from the captain's office?"

"Sorry, Commander."

Biting her lip in thought, she addressed Taro again. "I need you and Jack on the Hanscom run this afternoon. Leave as soon as he gets back."

"Aye aye, Commander."

Bannerman tried to login her terminal for the umpteenth time without success. "Are you two having issues with your terminals, or is it just me?"

"I'm fine here," Terrie said.

"Me, too," echoed Taro.

Frustrated, she called Sheffield. "Ray, I'm having that login problem again. Can you get IT down here ASAP?"

"If it's the same problem as last time, Chamberlain wants you to stop by his office."

"He can't come here to do it?"

"If it's a software problem, he can fix it remotely, but he still needs you to access certain screens."

"How long will that take?"

"I don't know, Commander."

"Tell him I'm on the way." Bannerman turned to Terrie. "You have the conn until I get back, Miss Murphy."

With just the two of them in Ops, it was the perfect time to ask Taro about something she read in Juli's manuscript. In one of Tunney's letters to Mr. J., he questioned the need to review the events of an ancient battle. Before she did, Terrie had to address something first. "Mr. Hattori, I'm sorry about last Friday."

"Water under the bridge, Miss Murphy," Taro replied as if the incident were genuinely forgotten.

"Mr. Hattori, I was doing some research this weekend and ran across something better suited to your expertise."

"That being?"

"Were there any important wars fought near the Korean peninsula in the 1590s?"

"There were two of them. Which one do you mean?"

"Whichever one contributed to naval strategies or tactics."

"That must've been the First Imjin War."

"Why?"

"Korean Admiral Yi Sun Sin invented and deployed his Keobukseon or Turtle ships. They successfully deterred the Japanese invasion under Hideyoshi."

"What made them so successful?"

"Well, their poison-gas delivery system sucked. The gas released from the open mouth of a dragon-shaped figurehead could only be deployed from upwind. But their other offensive capability had tactical and psychological advantage. They used five-inch-thick, metal-tipped projectiles capable of punching holes through the hulls of enemy ships. Defensively, the iron plating over the top of the ship's hull was an impregnable shield against Japanese artillery. It rendered their attacks useless. And the iron spikes jutting out of the iron-plated deck made a formidable deterrent against any boarding party."

As Taro continued, Terrie began to stare at the WGME feed, thinking about Roger Dagney's story of how the *Crescent* met her end. *Metal-tipped projectiles and a top covered in iron spikes over a sheet of iron. That must have been why Mr. J. wanted Tunney to read up on the First Imjin War.* As she tried to tie the disparate threads of information together, Terrie caught a breaking local news story scrolling across the bottom of the WGME screen. She turned up the volume to listen as the news anchor introduced the on-scene reporter.

> "That's right, Tricia. Here's what an Exeter Fire Department spokesman told me a few moments ago. The fire started at a tire dump near the New England Raceway at around two this morning and quickly spread to the nearby Red Pine Estates just off Route 27 in Exeter. Two minor structures within the housing area were destroyed and one home was partially damaged. Exeter police are investigating the blaze."

Taro and Jack had been gone for ten minutes before it was Theo's turn to run the security door through another cycle. But something was wrong. Terrie caught the look of defeat in his eyes.

"What's the matter, Mr. Theodore?"

He turned toward Terrie as though he was going to attack, but stopped. He knew the situation wasn't her fault, and returned his gaze toward the monitor with the Naval Intelligence logo screensaver waving in front of him. "Nothing that concerns you." He placed his fingers on the keyboard to begin work on another report.

"All right. But if you don't mind, I do have something you could help me with."

"What?" His wounded voice was difficult to ignore.

"Remember that corrupted zip drive made into a DVD?"

"What about it?"

"It's heavily pixilated, and the sound quality is terrible. I was hoping you could work your magic on it."

Theo swung his chair around, arm outstretched and hand open in a give-it-to-me fashion.

Terrie walked over to Theo, handed him the disc, and returned to her station without comment. He placed the disc in the drive and waited for the clip to resolve on the screen. Terrie could just make out the sound of voices but not the words. She turned as the clip ended. Then she noticed her troubled colleague's bearing. He paid no attention to the video. He just sat there.

Terrie folded her arms and exaggerated an exhale. She allowed him a minute to tender some sort of reaction. When he failed to do so, she acted on her intuition. "You know, I've heard a lot about the captain's iron-willed reputation around here, but I didn't know she could muzzle the great Lieutenant Theodore."

His pent-up anger boiled over. "Kiss my ass, you sanctimonious bitch!"

Smiling back at him, Terrie responded, "Ah, the B-word. What's next, the F-bomb?"

His lips formed the word, but he didn't say it.

Delivering the fatal blow, she added, "When the last arrow in your quiver is the personal attack, both you and your argument are effectively disarmed."

Relinquishing the contest, he turned his back to Terrie and stared at his monitor.

"Well, I was right. There is a human being in there after all."

"Leave me alone."

"Come, come, Mr. Theodore. You're better than this. If you weren't, you wouldn't be here."

"In ninety days, I won't be," Theo said in a tone that amounted to abject surrender.

"What are you talking about?"

An internal debate raged inside him as he swiveled his chair to look at Terrie. Should he tell her?

"If you can't confide in your most ardent adversary, who can you confide in?" Terrie offered, noticing his moist eyes. Theo's dark irises were usually surrounded by glowing halos of white, accentuating the pride in his soul. Now they appeared old, used, even bloodshot.

Concern washed over her as she got up to sit next to him. She leaned forward placing both hands on his forearms, attempting to replicate Jack's comforting ministrations. "It'll be all right, Mr."—she stopped herself, believing the address too impersonal—"Theo. Just let it out."

He pulled away then rubbed his eyes. "There's nothing to let out."

"Oh, there's something bottled up inside you. The longer it festers, the harder it'll be to overcome."

"What the hell do you know about it, huh? You've never been held down because of who you are," Theo said, turning his face away from her.

"No, and I've never used gender as a crutch to excuse my personal failings either."

He acknowledged the similarities between the two points of view. "Perhaps, but you can never fathom what it means to be an African-American."

"You must thrive on division, since you're hell-bent to play the race card."

His head spun back toward Terrie, his eyes in a burning stare. "Because we're a divided nation, Miss Murphy."

"That's a cop-out, Mr. Theodore. Hyphenated America is what's dividing us, not race. And the hyphen resides at the heart of any obelus."

"An obelus?"

"A division sign. Its core object, the hyphen, is used by self-proclaimed authority to breed perpetual segregation among our citizens."

"But there'll always be race-based communities. You can't escape it."

"How will we ever get past the racial divide if we can't move beyond the hyphen?"

"Personal experience has taught me different," Theo said with a momentary pause. "You have no idea what I've been through."

"I will if you share it with me," Terrie said with genuine empathy.

Theo glanced at the Ops Center door before he felt comfortable enough to begin.

"My grandmother raised six of us in the projects. I was the fourth child. My older sister became a prostitute and died of AIDS when I was ten. Both my older brothers died violently, one of a heroin overdose and the other was murdered."

Shocked by what she heard, Terrie sat back, yielding her complete attention to her storyteller.

"Without parents or older siblings to look up to, the chip on my shoulder grew large. Living in a mixed Black-Hispanic community, I picked up Spanish from neighborhood friends and taught myself Swahili. I read every book I could get my hands on, quickly learning to be the best at anything I did. I was twice voted class president at Charter High and was captain of the varsity football team. I was the first of my family to attend college, graduating as salutatorian from Columbia."

"That's really impressive. Did you receive an athletic scholarship?"

"Actually, my teachers and counselors encouraged me to apply for an academic scholarship. I was accepted."

"Academic?"

Theo responded like the question rubbed him the wrong way. "It wasn't a sport or minority scholarship."

"Sorry," she said softly, trying to calm him down. "What made you decide on the Navy?"

"My younger brother and sister. They had no role models in their life. They were proud of me for graduating college. I liked that feeling of showing them how to climb out of adversity, to challenge themselves to be something greater than they were. After 9/11, the choice was obvious. A military career. I enlisted before applying to become an intelligence officer."

"That took some dedication."

"Well, they wouldn't accept me without a technical degree, so I worked to get one. I've always been driven to succeed, mainly for my younger siblings and to make my family proud." Theo stopped his narration to look down at the ground. In a defeated voice, he said, "Now that won't happen."

"So, you're just going to give up?"

"In this instance, I have no choice."

"What's changed?"

"The 6110.1J requirements governing the physical readiness test."

"I don't understand. If you were able to pass them last year, how come you're worried about them now?"

Theo grabbed the bottom of his left trouser leg and pulled up. What should have been an ankle was a metallic joint. "Because there's a new supplement to the instructions regarding amputees; now you must complete the PRT without changing prosthetics. The rationale being, if you're on the battlefield, you're not likely to ask the enemy for time to change into something suitable to run or swim in."

Terrie's eyes widened in surprise. "Who else knows about this?"

"It's why I've been meeting with the captain lately. She's the only other person who knows."

"What happened?"

"When I was promoted to junior grade, Captain Derrick hand-picked me for a specific classified mission. I successfully completed it and was on my way back when I had an accident."

"What kind of accident?"

"I would've felt better about it if I'd lost my foot to an enemy attack, but I didn't. I lost it through sheer negligence."

Terrie looked at Theo sympathetically, encouraging him to go on.

"I'd just completed my assignment and reported in. I was exhausted. All I wanted to do was get to my cabin for some shut-eye, so I decided to take a shortcut. Making my way across the cargo deck, I darted between two loaded pallets. As they were moving one of them, my foot got caught between the track and the other pallet, destroying my ankle. There was nothing they could do to save it."

"When did this happen?"

"Three years ago. Captain Derrick requested I be assigned to her here so she could look after me, but recent changes in the PRT program forced her hand. I have no choice but to pass the test under the revised rules or I'm out of the Navy."

Terrie absorbed what he told her in thoughtful silence. "When do you take the PRT?"

"I don't have a scheduled date, but I have to take it within the next ninety days."

Terrie rubbed her chin then looked directly at Theo. "Can you meet me at Prescott Park every morning at 4:30?"

"I'm not a morning person."

"You are now, if you want my help."

"You're going to help me? Why?"

"Because I need that DVD cleaned up. In exchange, I'm going to make sure you pass your PRT. Sound like the plan?"

"It's not gonna matter," Theo said, still feeling hopeless. "No amputee has passed it since they changed the rules."

"Listen to me! You're not just some amputee! And you're not leaving the Navy, if I have anything to say about it."

"Why do you even care? Especially after the way I treated you?"

"Because your life story is a lesson on refusing to give up, Theo. The captain sees it, and so do I."

"I think destiny has taken that choice from me, Miss—" He looked into her eyes and whispered, "Terrie."

"You own your destiny, Theo, no one else. A destiny that's not based on government handouts or the color of your skin but the content of that superior character of yours. *Cultivate strict adherence to method and discipline; thus, it's in the power of the consummate leader to control success.* You *are* that consummate leader, Theo!"

"Where the hell do you get this shit?"

"From the Chinese War Master himself." The two officers smiled at each other.

It wouldn't be the last time.

Preparing to leave for the day, Terrie shut down her computer and started to turn off the array of flat screens. She was about to turn off the local news when she caught the update to the Exeter fire that morning. Scrolling across the screen was the address of the only house to incur damage. Alarmed, she pulled up the text message she received from Clendaniel. The damaged house on the news report was the location of this evening's meeting and his home address: 43 Red Pine Circle, near Route 27, Exeter, New Hampshire.

FORTY THREE

Everyone save Sheffield had left by the time Jack and Taro returned. The two officers turned in the Hanscom package and vehicle key to Sheffield who logged in the classified item and secured it in the safe. Knowing he was going to be late for their rendezvous with Clendaniel, Jack pulled out his cell.

"Sorry, Terrie. I just got back. I'll be there as fast as I can."

Terrie's voice sounded flat with disinterest. "Take your time."

"What's the matter?"

"We'll be meeting with Clendaniel tonight, but not at six o'clock and not at his home."

"Why not?"

"Apparently, the fire reported near the New England Raceway this morning was near his development. Ironically, the only home damaged was his, and the room destroyed was his office."

Jack sucked in a breath in surprise. "Is he all right?"

"He is now. By the time the smoke woke him up, the room was already engulfed in flames."

⚓

Terrie and Jack approached Clendaniel as he sat in a booth at the hotel restaurant. The tired foreman stood up to take Terrie's hand.

"Miss Murphy, so good of you to come, but there's really no point now, is there?"

"Your well-being is reason enough, Mr. Clendaniel. How are you holding up?"

"None the worse for wear."

As with Theo earlier, Terrie's display of empathy was genuine. In a sympathetic voice, she began her inquiry. "I realize it's been a long day, but can you stand for some questions? It would really be helpful to us."

"If it gets you to the bottom of this, be my guest."

Terrie placed her hand over his as a nonverbal thank you. "Have the authorities determined how the fire started?"

"They're still looking into it. Until they eliminate the possibility of arson, they won't let me near the house."

"Do they know the extent of the damage?"

"Everything in the office is lost."

"I'm sorry, Mr. Clendaniel."

"It's not your fault," he insisted.

"Was your collection insured?" asked Jack.

"It was, but how do you put a price on one-of-a-kind items like that?"

A waiter interrupted the conversation long enough to drop off their water and take their order. When he left, the three looked at each other quietly.

Terrie broke the silence. "Where did you say you bought that particular collection?"

"Believe it or not, I found it at an estate sale in Nashua. It was an old colonial-style home listed on the registry of historic places, so naturally I was interested."

"What did the collection look like?"

"The original cover was in shocking condition."

"Original cover?"

"Yeah, I had its cover replaced when I took the book over to the Antiquarian Society for evaluation."

"If memory serves, you told us the Athenaeum was closer? Why didn't you take it there?"

"That weekend, I had a company meeting in Auburn, so Worcester was on the way."

"Do you remember who verified its authenticity?"

"The clerk referred me to Miss Aponte. She was the one who recommended it be rebound."

Terrie and Jack looked at each other for a moment before she continued her inquiry, "How long before you got it back?"

"Two weeks, why?"

Not replying to his question, she asked, "What did the original cover look like?"

"It was black leather with writing on the spine. The entire length of the binding was separated from its cover. In fact, the spine's leather was torn approximately two inches from the top. Inside, below a 1793 frontispiece, was an introduction written in 1843 that discussed its content."

"Do you recall the color of the writing on the original spine?"

"Silver, I think. Yes, it was, now that I think about it. And though significantly faded, still legible."

"Did you happen to go through the book before you handed it over to the Antiquarian for rebinding?"

"No, I didn't."

"So, a comparison of the original volume you turned in against what you got back is now impossible?"

"I suppose so."

"Thank you, Mr. Clendaniel. I'd appreciate you getting back with me if there's anything else you can remember that may be relevant."

"I will," he responded as the waitress brought out their food.

Philip received another call from an unknown number, leaving little doubt who was calling. Runner's representative didn't want a paper trail on this new request.

Philip responded with disinterest. "Go ahead."

"Portsmouth picked up another package from Hanscom today."

"I know. What about it?"

The voice on the other end became agitated. "There are five SD cards and a zip drive in that package. Get your contact to make certain no one can safely access the data on any of those cards."

"And the zip drive?"

"It is of no consequence."

"Anything else?"

"Yes, and this comes straight from Runner."

"I'm listening."

"There's an evidence box somewhere in the bowels of the NWC's classified library. The file number is NP4162T. Locate but don't open it. Since you won't be able to remove the box from the library, you'll have to devise a clever way of making it disappear."

"Why are we taking such steps to secure this information only to destroy or hide it?"

"Are you going to comply, or do I have to get someone to replace you?"

"Compliance doesn't present a problem."

"Good!" The man ended the call.

Philip had done many questionable things as a covert agent, but he'd never actively tampered with evidence before. But regardless of how it was couched, he'd perform his duties. Should he fail to do so, grave harm could befall the security of his country. If he was ordered to neutralize a target, he'd do it without hesitation. At least that's what his psych profile said when they recruited him.

The destination number Philip called was a burner phone with a Portsmouth area code, so his contact would answer it night or day. This time, it rang but the person didn't answer. For security reasons, Philip had instructed his contact not to set the voicemail function. Ending the call after seven rings, Philip waited an additional ten minutes before trying again. This time, the person picked up.

"Yeah?"

"Did you comply with my previous request?"

"There're two tracking devices, one on her POV and one on the GOV in case she takes it. Managed to finagle with Bannerman's computer. She thought there was something wrong with it, so I had Chamberlain get me an in-line surveillance device for the lieutenant's SIPRNET connection. You can track what she does on her station's computer."

"And the listening device?"

"Forget it. Couldn't swing the approval from Derrick."

Disappointed, Philip moved on with his new requests. "Can you get into the NWC's classified library?"

"I can, yes."

"I need you to locate file number NP4162T and find a way to make it disappear."

"I can do that remotely, if you'd like."

"Not good enough. The physical item must be removed somehow. I need you to do it in person."

"That'd require authorization from Captain Derrick, and I don't have a valid need to go."

"Never mind. I'll work it myself. One more thing."

"There's always one more thing with you!"

"If you didn't find the craps tables so fascinating, you wouldn't be in this predicament, would you?" Philip heard a snort on the other end. He knew he had him once again. "Now, the five SD cards you picked up from Hanscom today. Make sure that information is made irretrievable." The pause was longer than Philip cared for. Perhaps his pigeon was having second thoughts. "Do I make myself clear?"

"Yeah, I got it. Heading back now."

"I'll be expecting confirmation in an hour."

Hanging up, the contact grabbed his car keys from the kitchen table. During the short trip to the Intelligence Office, he gave serious thought to what he was about to do. The situation was getting out of hand, even for what he thought was the honorable thing to do. For the last time in his short career as a covert government operative, he was going to violate chain-of-custody protocol. At least, that was his intention.

Returning to the office, he retrieved the latest Hanscom package from the classified safe and stared at the evidence pouch with the SD cards. He had the disc bleacher with him, but as he looked at the cards he considered his untenable position. Getting himself into a compromising position as a direct result of his gambling problem was one thing. But this?

The information he was asked to eradicate had cost the lives of twenty-three people in five locations, twelve of them American. Now he was ordered to destroy it? Something didn't feel right about this. He secured the unharmed cards in the safe, drove home, and reported to Philip that the task was done.

The Portsmouth contact felt an overwhelming sense of betrayal to his uniform, his colleagues, and his country. And he wouldn't feel better until he turned himself over to the proper authorities for disciplinary action.

FORTY FOUR

Reaching the end of Marcy Street near her apartment complex, Terrie and Theo walked the last block to her apartment building.

Glancing over at her running partner, Terrie said, "You didn't do too bad."

"I'm still having trouble maintaining the pace on the downhill stretches."

"It'll come, Theo. Give yourself a chance."

"I have to modify my steps on the declines. It's not easy, ya know."

"What's the problem?"

"The ankle has a built-in step assist that acts like the muscles of a natural ankle. Although it pushes me forward in a natural way on inclines and level ground, I have no control over it going downhill."

"You're able to keep the pace on level ground, and that's where the test takes place, so why are you worried?"

"I don't like surprises."

"Neither do I."

"I just want to feel confident I can handle whatever they throw at me."

"You're keeping up with me on the distance. If you want, we can concentrate on the problem area alone."

Approaching the parking lot, Theo unlocked his car with the key fob as Terrie continued on toward her apartment. "Can we do this for a week first? Just to see if I can adjust?" he asked.

"Sure," she responded. "See you at the office."

Bannerman doled out work assignments as Crabtree and Sheffield headed off for a meeting with the Captain. Taro and Theo got busy on their respective assignments as Terrie and Jack headed out to investigate the Exeter fire. Crabtree took the GOV, forcing Terrie to take her vehicle. Catching sight of the Athenaeum, Terrie pulled into the next available 3-hour parking space.

"What are you doing?" asked Jack.

"Just confirming my hypothesis about those numbers in the margin of the manuscript."

"What hypothesis?"

"The general subjects covered under the 300 and 600 series of the Dewey decimal system might have something to do with what we're investigating, but I'm not certain what the 200 series has to do with it."

"You know the general subjects?"

"The 300 and 600 series cover social sciences and technology respectively, topics essential for a perspective refit of a naval vessel. The 200 series deals with religious topics, but I'm not sure what the relevance is."

"What do the subsequent numbers mean?"

"After the decimal point, the numbers further delineate a grading system I'm unfamiliar with, which is why we're stopping in," replied Terrie while they got out of her vehicle.

"Preparing your answers in advance again, I see?"

"You're learning, Jack."

"Calling me Jack now? And in uniform? You're slipping, Terrie."

She acknowledged with the corner of one lip curled up.

The two officers entered the facility and were referred to the curator by the clerk at the information desk. Jack remembered how helpful he was with the online newspapers, so he approached the curator as he finished assisting another customer. "Mr. Finger?"

"Ah, the young man from a few days ago," he said, "How did you make out at the Antiquarian?"

"They were extremely helpful, sir, thank you," Jack replied. "This is my partner, Lieutenant Terrie Murphy, and this time, she has some classification questions I thought you could help us with."

"Very well," Finger said, turning his attention to Terrie. "What would you like to know?"

"We're trying to narrow down the identity of some books," Terrie said, digging in her clutch for the piece of paper, "but I only have their Dewey decimal numbers." Locating the paper with the numbers from Aruem's manuscript, she handed it to him.

"Do you know the titles and who wrote them?" Finger asked.

"Well, that's what we're trying to find out," Jack replied.

"Unfortunately, without the author or title it'll be impossible to locate them."

"It's more a question of the subject matter the numbers represent," Terrie clarified. "Would you be able to isolate that for us?"

"Now that I can do." Finger led Terrie and Jack toward the information desk.

On their way, Terrie asked, "You're also equipped to access the Library of Congress' online newspapers from the current periodical reading room, correct?"

"What specifically are you looking for?"

"I'm tracking down the dates for any of the missing or mutilated issues of the *Independent Chronicle*, *The Salem Mercury/Gazette*, and the *New Hampshire Spy/Gazette*."

"I believe we can accommodate you there as well," he said helpfully. "Give me a few moments."

Finger disappeared behind the large oak partition that served as a barrier between the general public and their main information desk. As he worked, Terrie and Jack loitered about.

"Okay, what good will it do to prove the nonexistence of old newspapers?"

"Jack, remember, several references Juli Aruem used for her manuscript came from alleged missing sources. She read those issues when drafting her work. After she was threatened, they disappeared. I'm hoping to obtain proof that they're missing from the Library of Congress before we confront Dr. Aponte with what we know. Make sense?"

Jack nodded.

The curator returned with some pages and a smile. "Here you go, miss. I hope this will help you in your search."

"Thank you."

Jack followed Terrie out to the car in silence. Needing to be prepared for their meeting with Miriam, Terrie tossed the keys to Jack. "You mind driving?"

"What are you going to do?"

"Go through these sheets he gave us before we confront Dr. Aponte."

She searched the columns divided by year, issue dates, and volume number for each named paper. Correlating issue dates between the papers that were either missing or mutilated to within two days of each other, Terrie identified and linked similar missing or mutilated issues between each paper and wrote them down separately. Next, she wrote down the numbers Juli had placed in the margin to compare them with the legend of Dewey numbers

Mr. Finger had provided her. The smile on Terrie's face was unmistakable.

"What?"

"Well, according to what the curator just provided us, 272 stands for Doctrinal Persecutions in church history. Books with .792 after it concentrate on Christian doctrine."

"What does the reference say about the other numbers?"

"Without boring you with the details, the 355.07 books cover military research and development. 359.009 references the history of the US Navy. Those numbered 623.4 are ordinance and ancient warfare books, and 629.8 cover control engineering and automation."

"And what do these books have to do with Tunney?"

"Think about it. *Dey of Reckoning* was refitted into *Neptune's Trident*. And with the advanced nature of the alloy I found on Badger, I'd say it's plausible the answers we're looking for are contained in the reference books identified by those Dewey decimal numbers."

Jack's countenance hardened as he continued down the highway to their Exeter location. "Tell me why we're doing this again?"

"Since the fire occurred at the home of the foreman who was in charge of the construction project over our alleged first intel office, we're tasked to determine if the fire was a coincidence or directly related to that detail."

"So, it's the official investigation ahead of our own, I take it."

"Since they seem to coincide, does it really matter?"

Jack smiled.

FORTY FIVE

The tiny bell above the door announced their arrival. The same clerk was on duty, attending to a customer. The uniformed pair migrated to the corner of the store, reviewing the section of reference books the woman had suggested to them during their last visit. When the customer departed and the woman stepped from behind the counter, Terrie made her move. "Excuse me, miss?"

"Yes?" Betrayed by her surprise, the woman immediately repositioned herself behind the counter to address her new visitors. "How may I help you?"

"I do wish you hadn't been so cryptic about who you were the last time we met, Dr. Aponte."

Scrutinizing Terrie's nametag, Miriam asked, "What can I do for the Navy, Miss Murphy?"

Peering at the mirrored wall behind Miriam, Terrie could see the woman trying to cover something under the counter. There was a printed sheet of paper with a photo of fire trucks responding to a residential fire. It lay askance across several books the size, shape, and color of the anthologies of journalism she and Jack went through at the Antiquarian. "You could be forthright regarding the books we asked you about the last time."

"I don't know—"

"For instance, you couldn't help but know the fate of one book."

"What book would that be?" Miriam said in a less than cordial manner.

"The one you're doing your best to hide from us right now. The one you saved from certain destruction in the Exeter fire yesterday. The one that cost author Juli Aruem her life."

The surprise of this last revelation turned Miriam's face a bright crimson.

"If you know something, it would be in your best interest to share it. Right now, Dr. Aponte."

"To be frank, I didn't know the importance of that book until I heard about Miss Aruem's accident."

"It wasn't an accident," Terrie bluffed, not knowing for sure herself.

Shock registered on Miriam's face as beads of sweat appeared on her forehead.

"According to the Antiquarian, only five copies of the entire run of the *New Hampshire Spy* and *Gazette* survive. And I'm willing to bet a year's pay that you know the location of the last original copy." Her eyes drifted down as though she could see the volumes through the counter.

Deflated, Miriam admitted, "That doesn't quite ring true."

"What does?"

Miriam noticed a single patron on the second floor. She glanced back at Terrie with terror in her eyes, they nodded to each other, and waited for the customer to leave. She moved quickly to the front door, locked it, and flipped over the closed sign before turning her attention to Terrie. "What do you know of the *Independent Chronicle?*"

"Only what we've been able to glean from the online databases and Miss Aruem's own notes."

"The story begins and ends with that particular paper. That's why I asked."

"What do you mean?" asked Jack, with puzzled look number seven gracing his features. Terrie folded her lips in over her teeth to stifle a grin.

"Tell us, Dr. Aponte. Please?" Terrie asked.

Miriam didn't know who to trust. She couldn't trust anyone in Worcester. And she certainly couldn't trust the nonprofit that had suddenly appeared to rebind the books. But there was something about Terrie that spoke to her sense of justice and propriety, and she yielded to it.

"Juli Aruem came to me almost two years ago." Miriam hesitated, not sure how to continue.

"Go on," Terrie prodded.

"She said she was looking into the history of an old Navy captain who didn't appear to be in the history books. Intrigued, I offered my assistance. When she told me of his exploits, I wondered if any of it was in the papers of the day, so we looked."

"And you found them in your collections of the *Independent Chronicle*, the *New Hampshire Spy* slash *Gazette*, and *The Salem Mercury*, no doubt?"

Miriam's eyes reflected amazement. "And the *Salem Gazette* too. I found quite a few articles, mostly confined to those papers."

"After you assisted Miss Aruem in her research, what drew your attention back to the articles?"

"Ten months after Juli left, I began upgrading our digital system to span the national library system and make it more user-friendly. When I completed the upload, I was reviewing the results of the online data transfer to ensure they were legible, when I discovered some anomalies. I was in the process of investigating the problem when this team showed up."

"What team?" Terrie asked.

"I was off the day they arrived. My assistant, Miss Turner, was told they represented a nonprofit organization sponsored by the National Archives, traveling the country to rebind our more precious tomes. Before I found out what they planned to do, our copy of the *New Hampshire Spy/Gazette* had been taken already. Not sure of their intentions, I gathered up at least one copy of our remaining anthologies before this team could retrieve them for rebinding. I was too late to save our only original copy of the *New Hampshire Spy/Gazette*, but I did manage to save one original copy each of the others, including *The Salem Mercury/Gazette*."

"So, having aided Miss Aruem with her research, you detected certain anomalies in the rebound copies?"

"I did. I was devastated to see the alterations in the papers Juli had used for her research."

"What did you do then?"

"About a month after this group left, a man came to see me with an unusual book in terrible condition. Again, I wasn't in the building when he came in, so I never met the gentleman. He asked if we could confirm its authenticity. One of the other clerks received the book and left it on my desk."

"But you must have known something about him, or you wouldn't be so protective of that article under the counter. Or the book you're purposely hiding under it."

"I don't know what you're talking about," said Miriam dismissively.

"Stop it! You knew exactly who it was, since Miss Turner already told us the location of the only remaining copies. If you didn't know, why would you print a copy of just this article and then use it to hide the subject book we're looking for? A book with more than just five surviving copies." Terrie paused, waiting for a reply. To coax her she added, "Care to try again?"

"There were actually six," Miriam admitted, the walls of her resistance obliterated by Terrie's resilience.

"What happened to the sixth volume, Dr. Aponte?"

"There were always six, Miss Murphy. Miss Turner was mistaken as to the number available at the Library of Congress. They had two, not one."

"Then how is it that the Antiquarian has a copy, if you have Mr. Clendaniel's original?"

"I managed to convince the Library of Congress to provide us with one of theirs, as I told them our copy was destroyed in the rebinding process."

"A deception?"

"A white lie."

"Why?"

"Realizing our rebound book had been changed, I was hoping the Library of Congress' extra copy was unaltered. I was too late."

"And you took this action around the time Mr. Clendaniel brought his book to you?"

"That's correct," a deflated Miriam Aponte confessed. "Having discovered what they'd done to the copy from the Library of Congress, I kept his original, handed Mr. Clendaniel the rebound copy, and resigned." Weary from Terrie's barrage of questions, she stood silent following the tense exchange.

Catching sight of more than one book under the Exeter fire article, Terrie engaged her questioning once more. "You said the story began with the *Independent Chronicle*?"

"I did, yes."

"Would that journal happen to be among the books you have under the counter?"

No longer seeing the need to conceal the books from her guests, she placed them on the counter. The top volume was the anthology for the *New Hampshire Spy/Gazette*. Its binding appeared exactly as described by its owner, R. J. Clendaniel. Spreading the volumes across the counter, she pointed to the one containing the *Chronicle*. "Here it is."

"What year did those articles about Tunney begin?"

"1785."

"From the missing issues of November 10, 1785 and December 22, 1785, correct?"

Astonished, Miriam asked, "How did you—"

Terrie held up copies of Juli's reference notes, and Jack laid the cross-referenced list of missing and mutilated issues of historic papers on the counter. "Come now, Dr. Aponte. We have Juli's manuscript."

"That doesn't prove anything."

"Citing your references, she documented how duplicate advertisements for a ship called *Rebecca* were purposely placed in two other newspapers, presumably to hide the original articles. Articles that mentioned Captain Tunney."

Terrie received no response from Miriam.

"Jack, could you get the copies of our online newspapers from the car, please?"

"Sure thing," he replied, as Terrie continued to press Miriam.

"They were more than just duplicate articles, Dr. Aponte. They were identical, right down to the water-stained creases in the ads, as our online copies of these newspapers suggest."

Unsuccessful at fending off Terrie's onslaught of facts, Miriam thought saying nothing would save her.

"Do you really want me to read off the exact issue, page, column, and adjacent articles to prove it?"

Miriam relented. She opened one of the volumes, its black leather cover deteriorated with maltreatment and age. The edges of its binding were so completely frayed that she wasn't sure the book would hold up to anymore use. Given no choice now, she allowed Terrie to inspect it.

Terrie laid out Aruem's references and the sheets detailing the missing and mutilated copies for comparison. Opening the anthology for the *Independent Chronicle*, Terrie skimmed through the early issues until she came to the November 10, 1785 edition. Jack returned with a folder containing their copied online newspapers and handed it to Terrie. She pulled up the edition with an article on page one, column four, hawking the sale of flaxseed and wines at Samuel Blagge's store. Comparing it with the original, the counterfeit article had a crooked line delineating the story from the one below it. In place of that false ad, the original edition had something else entirely.

> *NEW YORK, October 29.* – On Thursday last, an eyewitness to the loss of the merchant Brig. *Dauphin*, offered up his account to the Congress. Vernon Tunney, boatswain's mate, late of that ship, described the harrowing details of how he, his crew, and his captain, Richard O'Brien, were taken prisoner by the renegade corsair, *Dey of Reckoning*, of the Algerine fleet.

The article backed up Juli's manuscript dissertation exactly. Skipping to the next cited issue of the *Chronicle*, December 22, 1785, she leafed through the stack to the online copy and turned to its page three. According to Terrie's copy, the article from column two addressed a British revenue cutter that was ordered to intercede near Ireland to stop tobacco smugglers. The anthology's original article was faded but remained legible.

> *NEW YORK, December 20.* – The American Merchant Ship *Justice*, Arthur Ledbetter, Master, will sail in the morning on a mission for the Congress. Accompanying Captain Ledbetter will be Vernon Tunney. As our subscribers shall remember, Mr. Tunney's eyewitness account drew much attention, forcing Congress to act to protect our merchant ships from the predations of foreign vessels.

To confirm her suspicions regarding the *Rebecca* advertisement, Terrie flipped open *The Salem Mercury* book to the source paper as well as the illicit copies from the other two anthologies. Not only was the original ad listed under the obituary for a person named Susana Higginson, but in place of the duplicate *Rebecca* ads from Terrie's online copies, a completely different article was present. It was the exact, word-for-word reproduction of the report Terrie found in Juli's manuscript regarding the arrival of the *Dey of Reckoning*, the destruction of the *Justice*, and the loss of Captain Ledbetter.

Skimming down the list of missing and mutilated papers with highlighter in hand, she identified several suspect dates from the three different newspapers that were within a publication day of each other. She handed Jack the list. "Could you pull up these papers for me?"

"Sure thing." He rifled through their printed copies and retrieved the issues Terrie had highlighted.

"I thought so," Terrie said, "Look here." She pointed to the disparity between the online version and the original issue of *The Salem Mercury*. "Look at the online copy of the December 9, 1788 issue, under American Intelligence, subheading New Hampshire. You'll notice a Philadelphia article from November 15, detailing the unfortunate identification of apprehended thieves as sons of several reputable citizens of Montgomery County. Yet, here, in the original issue, was a completely different article. Jack, we show the December 13, 1788 edition of the *New Hampshire Spy* as missing, correct?"

"That's right," he responded.

Terrie nodded as she stared at that particular issue within the anthology, available and intact. There, on its page three, near the bottom of column four under SHIP NEWS, was the word-for-word rendering of the same article printed in the original *Salem Mercury* issue.

> Portsmouth, Oct. *26*. On Friday last, from aboard the captured vessel, *Dey of Reckoning*, several books of profound historic value were discovered in the master's stateroom while the ship was undergoing repairs in Herod's Cove. Jeremiah Simon, the protégé of George Sale, shall arrive in due course to examine the find.

Terrie's brow furrowed. She recognized the name George Sale from her foreign language training. "Unless I miss my guess, the books found aboard the *Dey of Reckoning* were of Middle Eastern origin?"

"What makes you say that?" asked Miriam.

Terrie didn't answer. She was absorbed by the unexpected revelation that George Sale was somehow involved in the mystery. "What's the next set of articles, Jack?"

"The eighth and tenth of November, 1792, the *Chronicle* and the *Spy*, respectively," he replied, removing a single issue from his stack and handing it to Terrie. "Here's the mutilated copy of the *Chronicle*. That issue of the *Spy* is listed as missing."

She turned to page three in their mutilated copy of the *Chronicle*. It was badly torn, irregular holes ripped from several sections. She found what she was looking for in the first column, under the title "Last Evening's Mail." The article was all but illegible, contiguous words blighted away and a third of the page disintegrated. However, the original in Miriam's journal was pristine. Terrie opened the *Spy* anthology to its alleged missing issue, and there it was: November 10, 1792. Skimming through it, Terrie discovered a similarly worded article from that of its *Chronicle* companion, plainly printed below the heading, American Intelligence.

> Portsmouth, Nov 6. – In a letter to Mr. Henry Knox, the Secretary of War, Mr. Jeremiah Simon proffered an astounding claim. After his detailed examination of books, lately

discovered aboard a captured Algerine vessel, he suggests they may be the cursed volumes related to the destruction of three ancient libraries in the Years of our LORD, one-thousand-one-hundred-ninety-three, one-thousand-two-hundred-fifty-eight, and one-thousand four-hundred-fifty-three.

Terrie shook her head as she read the phrase "cursed volumes." The years mentioned—1193, 1258, and 1453—sounded familiar, but she couldn't recall the names of the libraries associated with the years they were destroyed. She thought one of the books in her personal library might hold the answer, but she'd be damned if she could remember which one. "What are the next dates I've highlighted, Jack?"

"1796, the *Independent Chronicle*'s March 7 issue and the *Salem Gazette*'s March 8. The reference says they're both mutilated."

She turned the pages until she got to the originals in their respective anthologies. She skimmed over the four pages of both papers to find a common article that linked them. In column three of the third page of the *Salem* paper and listed under Ship News, she spotted a familiar name.

> PHILADELPHIA, *March 6.* Yesterday, arrived here, the ship *Hypatia*, Vernon Tunney, Master, 75 days from Cadiz, who brings the following Intelligence regarding the recent Treaty with the States of Barbary.
>
> "Having personal knowledge of my former Captain, the reports submitted by him should be regarded with suspicion, so long as he remains under the spell of his captor. His correspondence lately received should be considered the actual voice of the Dey of Algiers and that his true opinion suppressed until such time as he is released from his present circumstances.
>
> Any treaty that is likely to come from Algeria must be greeted with the utmost scrutiny. Mr. O'Brien's compromised position makes his contribution to the American

cause negligible. I detect, within the clauses of his published accounts, the debilitated state of his hobbled diplomacy. While I am not unsympathetic to the plight of my former Captain, I can't help but be convinced that he is far too lenient with regard to the characterization of his captors and their cause. He appears to shamelessly advocate for their position. While I'm anxious for their release, I believe Mr. O has much to answer for."

"Sounds like someone was suffering from what we now call, the Stockholm Syndrome," Terrie surmised.

"It's likely why Tunney became agitated for the remainder of his life," Miriam added.

Terrie keyed in on Miriam's insight into the historic captain, wondering how much she knew about him.

"There's a jump of three years before we get to your next set of highlighted dates," Jack offered.

"What are they?" asked Terrie, her suspicion about Miriam temporarily shoved to the back burner.

"1799. *The Salem Gazette*, April 19, and the *Independent Chronicle*, April 22."

Terrie looked through the *Gazette* first. When she got to page three, something listed under the heading Naval Intelligence didn't look quite right. Inserted between two letter extracts was a four-line blurb. The topography was so miniscule that she couldn't read it readily enough. Turning to its *Independent Chronicle* counterpart, she found the exact blurb on page two, under Domestic News.

> PORTSMOUTH, *April 26*. – On Tuesday last, an opaque structure composed of black canvas was erected around a derelict vessel. No one from Mr. Hackett's nearby shipyard knows why.

Hackett's shipyard? Terrie thought. *Black canvas? That would be light enough for a thin wall of rounded poles to support a blind. SA Dempsey was right; it must have been a blind. But to cover what?*

Jack gave Terrie a gentle nudge. "You okay?"

"Sure, what's next?"

"There's another set of common dates in November 1799, but both papers are missing," Jack stated as he pointed them out to her.

Passing over the next seven months of papers in each anthology, she came to the issues Jack alluded to. Both editions of the *Chronicle* and the *Gazette* were present and accounted for. And the articles were the same.

> PORTSMOUTH, *October 27.* – Yesterday morning an unusual ship was revealed when the canvas that surrounded it was removed. The ship was a three-masted corsair, lightly rigged with gray sails and armed with sixteen cannon and four swivel guns. Its smooth maroon hull was fitted with a strange door below its bowsprit.

Terrie rubbed her chin as she began postulating a theory. "Based on this article, we can assume the refit of *Neptune's Trident* was completed in 1799, but it still doesn't tell us how. Juli suggested that the books found onboard *Dey of Reckoning* had something to do with the refit, but she never went beyond that."

"If those books had anything to do with it, wouldn't there be other stories reporting it?" asked Jack.

Miriam considered his question. "There is one story that may have suggested it." Reaching for the *New Hampshire Spy* journal, she opened it near the end of the book. Turning to the February 23, 1793 edition, she pointed to the Tuesday's Post in column four of the front page.

Terrie read the article, increasingly disturbed with each passing line.

> PORTSMOUTH, *February, 23d* – An experiment conducted near Langdon Island on the 2nd instant has yielded startling results. The newly created alloy is of unquestionable durability and unique visual properties with a hardness that surpasses even a diamond.

Her thoughts went immediately to the pouch containing the item Crabtree had done his best to hide. The characteristics described in this 220-year-old article fit her artifact to a tee. "While it doesn't expressly identify the origin of the experiment, the location and Juli's manuscript suggest it was connected to those 'cursed' books." Terrie stared at nothing while she thought. Snapping out of it, she addressed Miriam again. "Did they publish any more on this subject?"

"The very next issue was its last, Miss Murphy. The owner, John Osborne, ceased publication."

"Do you know why?"

"He printed an announcement indicating his pursuit of other business opportunities as the reason for his decision in this very paper. As to the real reason, who knows?"

Terrie contemplated the "cursed volumes" and Juli's handwritten Dewey classifications. Was there a connection? There was something about the dates those ancient libraries were destroyed that sounded familiar. As she rolled the idea around, the story that Roger Dagney told collided with Juli Aruem's cautionary warning: *Learn the fate of the* Crescent…*sounds like a modern-day torpedo…a strange door below its bowsprit?*

Miriam, watching Terrie tap her lips while she thought, asked, "What is it, Miss Murphy?"

"Just thinking. After the *Crescent* was delivered to the Dey of Algiers, there were a few published reports subsequent to its delivery, mainly about skirmishes between it and American merchant vessels."

"Yes?"

"Juli's referenced accounts imply that her original captain was beheaded, replaced by Rafik the Marauder."

"That's correct, yes."

She organized her online papers highlighting those encounters and handed them over to Miriam. "Could you review these to see if all of the incidents were captured?"

Miriam glanced at articles that reinforced Dagney's story about the *Crescent's* harassment of American ships and how it became an embarrassment to the country. Then, she noticed an anomaly. "There are three stories missing from your collection, Miss Murphy."

"And they are?"

"Two from the *Massachusetts Spy* and—"

"The last one must have been from the *Independent Chronicle*?"

"Again, you're right on top of it, Miss Murphy."

"Do you have them?"

"Not the first two, but I can summarize them for you."

"Would you, please?"

Now, it was Miriam's turn to spout off. "Through Consul O'Brien in June of 1802, the *Spy* reported the Dey of Algiers' increasing anger over the ongoing US blockade of Tripoli. Despite the existence of a treaty preventing such actions, he reported the capture of the American brig *Franklin*, commanded by Captain Andrew Morris of Philadelphia. O'Brien's demands for their immediate release were rebuffed by the Dey because of the blockade."

"What does this article have to do with the *Crescent*?"

"It doesn't. These articles are tied closer to the mysterious red vessel."

"Oh. Please go on."

"A year later, the paper reported how the USS *John Adams* and the USS *Enterprise* successfully engaged several vessels near Tripoli. In a spectacular explosion, an Algerian vessel was obliterated. A witness from the *Enterprise* claimed to have seen an odd-looking red ship appear on the horizon just before the Tripolitan vessel was destroyed."

Terrie tendered her final question. "Is there a published account of the *Crescent's* end?"

"There was one," Miriam began. "An excerpt from a letter. Its author was never identified." She turned to the anthology of the *Salem* papers. On the second page of the August 20, 1805 issue, the following item was listed under Mail Articles.

> BOSTON – An extract from a letter – "It was reported to me by a survivor of the attack near Malta by the fleet of Barbary, that America's present to the Dey of Algiers is now lost. The 36-gun frigate, *Crescent*, met a spectacular end as she was cleaved in two by an extraordinary blast that ripped the vessel to pieces. She went down in less than a minute.

Terrie read the article then turned to Miriam. "I thought you said the story ended with the *Independent Chronicle*?"

"It does, yes," Miriam admitted.

"We know of the story, Dr. Aponte. One that detailed the end of the *Crescent*." The use of Dagney's words triggered the pent-up emotions Miriam tried not to display. "It was published in the *Chronicle*, wasn't it?"

Head drooping, Miriam reached for the old book and turned to the end. There, on the last page of the May 26, 1817 issue, was a narrative, written by the paper's senior publisher and taking up a full column. Its title: "The Odyssey of the *Crescent*: A summary."

The two officers read the account to themselves. Terrie heard the voice of Roger Dagney in her head as she did so. When they finished, Terrie turned to the journal's last issue, number 3768, volume 49, published on Thursday, May 29, 1817. It was the final issue of the *Independent Chronicle* under Adams & Rhodes. On its fourth page, in the same relative location, was a notice that the paper's copartnership was dissolved, owing to the death of its senior member. The notice and subsequent "concluding address" was written by the surviving partner, Ebenezer Rhodes. "The last issue?" Terrie said.

"Yes."

"Wasn't the paper published through 1840?"

"It was. After the May 29 issue, the name was changed to add *Boston Patriot* to its title."

"Then how come this journal is incomplete?"

"This particular volume was the only one I was able to save," Miriam replied, her cheeks flushed in agitation. "They rebound the 'complete' copy that included all the other issues, up to May 23, 1840."

"I'm sorry," said Terrie earnestly. She looked at the confiscated journal whose rightful owner lived only a few miles west of their current location. "I assume you're going to make sure Mr. Clendaniel receives his book?"

A resigned Miriam conceded with a nod.

"Would it be possible for you to copy them for us, so we have evidence to back up Juli's manuscript?"

Eyes darting between the officers, she said. "Give me twenty minutes."

"One last thing," Terrie said, remembering the reference numbers scrawled in the margin of the bibliography. "Did you help Juli find any books that discussed metallurgy, nautical propulsion, nautical ordinance, or automated engineering?"

"No, why?"

With no interest in rewarding Miriam's curiosity, Terrie fired off another question. "Do you know of any published accounts referencing Tunney or his ship after 1805?"

Miriam thought about it. "There was a rumored article in a July 31, 1813 issue of Delaware's *American Watchman* that detailed an attack of the HMS *Stalwart* by its only survivor, but I never found it."

Terrie pressed Miriam harder. "Juli also described Tunney as a vengeful and violent man, but none of the newspaper accounts documented this. Where did she get that impression?"

"He was," Miriam said with an edge even Jack couldn't help notice. "When Juli first pointed out how Tunney captured the *Dey of Reckoning*, I was intrigued. While researching the ship, I found an obscure text that covered America's old navy and the privateers of the day. Tunney was mentioned, but not in a flattering way."

"Where did you find those books?"

"At the Smithsonian. They described the captain as distant and morose and consumed by anger—an anger fed by his white whale, the Muslim radicals of his day and those who made excuses for them in government circles. Tell me, Miss Murphy, what's feeding your white whale?"

Margaret's lifeless eyes materialized in Terrie's imagination. In a sinister vocal quality Terrie responded, "In the midst of your darkest nightmare, you wouldn't want to know."

FORTY SIX

"Thank you, Inspector," said Terrie appreciatively.

"No problem," the fire marshal replied. "Like I said, since the night watchman admitted to missing the receptacle with his cigarette butt, arson's not an issue. We're declaring the fire an accident."

"So even a strong breeze can carry embers a mile or more to set something on fire?" asked Jack.

"It's not uncommon. In fact, it's one of the many dangers most folks aren't aware of. Even controlled burns can become a hazard when people are careless."

"Well, thank you for your time, Inspector," said Jack.

He contained his frustration until they made their way back to the car. "An accident. Well, that ends any speculation that someone was after Clendaniel's book."

Terrie started the car and headed back toward Portsmouth. "I'm not buying it."

"You really think there's something he missed?"

"They assumed that embers from the burning tires were the cause of the residential fire, so they never bothered to investigate further. I still think it could've been arson."

"Well, without evidence to the contrary, we're back to square one. And what about Clendaniel?"

"What about him?"

"Are you going to tell him about his resurrected book?"

Terrie's head jerked toward Jack. "Really? And how do you suggest we explain the discovery of the very book we were interested in just hours after he lost everything else in his office?"

Jack put on another one of his famous faces. "You've got a point there."

"Besides, we called her out on her deception. You heard me. I practically demanded she return it."

As he was about to reply, his pulsating cell phone interrupted him. "O'Hara. Yeah, we're on the way now. Be there in half an hour."

"Who was that?"

"Theo. They're waiting for us at Ops. Apparently, there's some big meeting."

⚓

The team was seated around the conference table as Terrie and Jack came through the door.

"Please, take your seats," Crabtree said.

The two officers quickly located their chairs as their colleagues sat quiet.

"What's going on?" Jack asked.

"Captain Derrick will brief us when she arrives," said Crabtree before departing to receive the captain.

Looking around the table, Jack noted the absence of a single member. "Where's Ray?"

Again, no one said a word. The wait seemed eternal until Bannerman's eyes lighted on the door. "Captain on deck!"

Derrick and Crabtree moved to the head of the conference table. "As you were." Waiting for everyone to take their seats, Derrick assumed her trademark posture, taking in the faces of her audience. "I'll make this brief. Approximately six months ago, a mid-level analyst violated his security clearance and took actions that compromised the NSA's data mining operations. Last month, he contacted members of the media and promised to reveal the full extent of the NSA's capability. Today, it looks like he followed through on that promise. I don't believe I have to stress to anyone the catastrophic damage this will have on our intelligence operations?"

"That, you don't, Captain," said Crabtree.

Derrick darted her eyes at the commander in a nonverbal reprimand.

"Special Agent Prentiss is currently working with a special task force to determine the extent of the damage." She turned to Crabtree. "Detail someone from your team to assist him, Commander."

"Aye aye, Captain." Since Taro was already working with Prentiss, he knew who it would be.

Derrick bowed her head, considering her next words. "On a separate subject, a matter has been brought to my attention that directly impacts your team dynamic. I won't go into specifics. However, effective immediately, Senior Chief Sheffield no longer works in this building. He is assigned to me for the duration of his service." The captain's face hardened as she added, "You are cautioned not to discuss the matter, even among yourselves." Scanning the room, the captain's raised eyebrow fell on Terrie. "Miss Murphy, I'll see you in the commander's office when we're done here."

Terrie acknowledged.

"Does anyone have anything for me?" She waited for questions she knew wouldn't be asked. Without looking at Crabtree, she said, "I'll need your office, Commander. Meanwhile, make that detail priority one."

"Affirmative, Captain."

Everyone stood until Derrick departed. Terrie watched the captain leave the room before looking to Crabtree for further instructions.

"You heard her, Miss Murphy," he said gently.

Terrie headed for the office commandeered by Captain Derrick. She tried to report in, but Derrick waved her over to the couch. "Have a seat, Miss Murphy. Please."

Terrie did as instructed, never removing her gaze from Derrick, who sat in the chair kitty-corner from her.

"What I'm about to tell you is for your ears only."

"Yes, ma'am."

"This morning, Senior Chief Sheffield admitted several things to me…something of interest to your team and something of direct interest to you."

"Me?"

"Someone with the president's ear directed him to assign you, in particular, to retrieve something from Badger Island. When it wasn't found, he was directed again to track your movements to see how far you could get on your own."

"Track me?"

"Your workstation, your POV, and, quite possibly, your apartment are all under surveillance. It's also possible that you've been under government surveillance since your posting here two months ago."

"Why?" was all she managed. Remembering the man she'd seen by her vehicle the other day, Terrie thought back to all the odd occurrences she'd experienced since her arrival. The death of Juli Aruem so close to her meeting with the author. The altered newspapers. The man in the parked car across from Aunt Barbara's house. There'd been something familiar about the profile of that driver's head. The man's smile was almost reptilian, wide and thick with zipperlike teeth, similar to the man she'd seen in the maintenance coveralls near her apartment. But those incidents occurred several states apart.

Ignoring Terrie's question, Derrick continued, "We've removed the surveillance devices Sheffield confessed to planting in the Intel vehicle, your POV, and around your workstation. I'm authorizing you access to the appropriate equipment to find and remove any such devices from your apartment. I'd also suggest checking your personal electronic devices. They may be compromised as well."

"Did he tell you why?"

"As you were the target of his actions, I'll explain it to you. But it doesn't leave this room. Is that clear?"

"Yes, ma'am. I appreciate it."

"Sheffield incurred a significant debt as a result of his addiction to the gaming tables. Discovering this vulnerability, a federal agent used his influence to absolve the extensive debt and then blackmailed the senior chief into doing his bidding. This man, known only as Philip, directed the senior chief to divert several objects you retrieved from the dig to him—most notably, the triangular alloy and the logbook. Sheffield conceded that Philip appeared interested in only those artifacts."

"Was it the compromised data mining that caught him?"

"If it was, Miss Murphy, you'd be reading about his arrest and general court-martial in the *Navy Times* and not his forced retirement. He did say he was instructed to destroy the five SD cards your office recently picked up. I would suggest you get on those to find out why."

Terrie considered what she was told. It all made sense. Bannerman's request to destroy the six-minute audio and all record of it must have come from Sheffield. Likewise, Crabtree's dismissive comment about what was written on the side of the alloy.

"Captain, do you have any idea what the true object of my mission was?"

"I'm afraid not. The senior chief said he was never privy to that information."

"Thank you for being so forthright, ma'am."

The captain shook her head. "I commend you, Lieutenant. You're surprisingly calm for someone who found out they were used like a pawn on a chessboard. If I were in your position, I don't think I'd be as detached."

"Was this office cleared of surveillance devices, Captain?"

"Yes, it was."

"Since you've been so honest with me, let me return the favor."

"What do you mean?"

"Have you ever heard of the *Neptune's Trident*?"

"No, I'm not familiar with it."

For the remainder of the afternoon, Terrie laid down the entire business, from the beginning of her detail with R. J. Clendaniel, until she and Jack left Miriam Aponte not more than two hours earlier. When she finished, the captain stood up and paced the office.

After much thought, the captain volunteered one more tidbit of information. "Mr. Sheffield's conscience bothered him enough that he reported the alleged destruction of the five SD cards to his handler before securing them in the safe undamaged. May I suggest you get Theo on them right away? Newport NCIS won't be able to help you, since SA Dempsey's been transferred."

Remembering Juli's handwritten reference, Terrie pressed her advantage. "Captain, would it be possible for you to authorize Lieutenant O'Hara and I access to the classified section of the Naval War College Library to conduct research?"

"To what end?"

"The author I met in Delaware sent me her manuscript about Tunney. In the margin of her references, she jotted down the Dewey decimal numbers to some missing reference books and identified two locations where those books might be found. The Library of Congress was one location, and the classified library at Newport was the other. She obviously couldn't get access to the latter."

Captain Janine Derrick smiled at Terrie. "You'll have it within the hour. Anything else?"

"She also referenced another number related to the classified section of the library: NP4162T. Do you know what that means?"

"It's the file number the senior chief was asked to locate within the library's classified section and make disappear."

"What?"

"Miss Murphy, we appear to have stumbled across something beyond normal classification protocols. For your safety, and until we know how far all this goes, it would be prudent to keep this between us."

"Do I have permission to share it with my immediate team members? I might need their assistance."

"You realize the more people involved, the greater the risk of discovery?"

"Strength in numbers, Captain."

"Do what you must, Lieutenant. You have my confidence."

"Thank you, Captain," said Terrie. She stood, waiting for permission to leave.

"Before you go, Miss Murphy, I just want to say I appreciate what you're doing for Lieutenant Theodore."

Terrie smiled before she departed the office.

FORTY SEVEN

Armed with Captain Derrick's authorization letter, Terrie and Jack arrived at the War College Library.

Handing Jack a note, she said, "Run these numbers from the manuscript against the available books, and copy down the list of authors and titles. I'll check the card catalogue."

"Right."

She pulled up the online catalogue to see what she might find. Four of the numbers were listed, but there was nothing under 272.792. Jotting down the titles and authors, she noted at least one of each available number was redacted and its Dewey decimal classification relocated within the classified section of the library.

Jack approached Terrie from behind. "I only found seven applicable books. Three under 355.07, two for 359.009, and one each under 623.4 and 629.8. There were no books listed under 272 at all."

"That's interesting. According to the manual catalogue, there are four under 355.07, three for 359.009, and two each under 623.4 and 629.8. All have a single volume redacted and transferred to the classified section, except 272.792."

"Then there's no such book in the library?"

"It would appear not." Terrie secured their research in her planner before the two approached the petty officer manning the information desk so they could gain access to the classified library.

"Do you have your authorization, ma'am?" asked the petty officer.

Terrie opened her planner and handed the petty officer the letter. He logged Terrie and Jack into the facility, made a copy of the letter, and filed it before handing the original back to Terrie. "We close promptly at 16:30, ma'am."

"Thank you."

Despite the age of the building and dated interior architecture, its digital recordkeeping was state-of-the-art. The two officers couldn't avoid leaving digital breadcrumbs Sheffield's handler could track.

The young man escorted Terrie and Jack to the entrance of the classified library, handed them their ID badges for use on the security system, and they were in.

⎈

Using a disguise familiar to the War College Library's personnel, Philip entered the classified section and began to track down the evidence box his handler said was in the basement. Runner must have been pulling his leg. He could find no such number in any of the referenced indexes. He'd have to search for it manually, which was going to take time. He moved seven aisles of storage units without success. On the third row of the eighth aisle, he found a box with the correct file number written on the upper left-hand corner. He was about to remove it, when the buzzer announced the unwelcome arrival of a new researcher.

⎈

As Jack closed the door, a civilian librarian, whose cologne arrived five seconds before he did, approached them. "How may I help you today?"

Terrie handed the librarian the copy of Derrick's letter. He stared at the file number with a puzzled expression. "Not too many calls for this one, but no matter." His devil-may-care attitude suited Terrie just fine. If he was disinterested in their presence, they might get something accomplished. "The reference aisle is right over there, and the historical research property room you'll find at the foot of the stairs. When you're ready, I'll take you down there," said the librarian.

Terrie offered her appreciation, hoping the fragrant man took the hint. Making their way to the rows of reference books, she suggested Jack take the 300 series while she took on the 600. Locating the correct aisle, she skimmed through the appropriate shelf, looking for the redacted book listed under 623.4, but the closest she was able to get were books classified under 621.8 and 623.65. She found a similar gap in numbers while looking for 629.8.

She made her way to the main aisle just as Jack appeared, shaking his head. "What is it?" she asked.

"Couldn't find 355.07 or 359.009. Only classification numbers on either side of them."

"Same here," she replied. "I suppose our only hope will be the file downstairs."

"Yup," said Jack, meeting Terrie's mischievous gaze. "What?"

She only smiled back at him.

"Don't look at me. I'm not gonna track down our perfumed host."

In the course of deciding who'd embark on that quest, a familiar scent reached them before his voice did.

"Did you find what you're looking for?"

"Yes," she replied with deft obfuscation. "We're ready to inspect the file location."

"Very well. If you'll just follow me."

This time, Terrie observed the librarian as he passed in front of her. The shape of the man's skull was memorable, if not the jowls and his corpulent form. Dismissing her observations, she followed the man to the stairwell.

The basement level was a cavern, taking up the building's entire length and width. Rows of steel, climate-controlled property storage units took up the lion's share of the space. Situated on a tracked roller system, tri-handle wheels allowed the librarian to move the massive units with ease. He searched several of them until he found the unit with Terrie's file.

"Here it is." Using a key, he unlocked the door and swung it open. "Let me know when you're finished so I can lock it up for you." Before he went upstairs, he added, "There's a table around the corner for your convenience."

"Thank you," Terrie said.

Jack grabbed the evidence box and brought it to the table. Inside, Terrie spotted a black file folder that covered an old dispatch box.

"What's that?"

"It's a White House cover memorandum."

"Check out the subject line," Jack said.

They both read it with surprise: Neptune Project, referenced to The Office of the President, the Chairman Joint Chiefs of Staff, SECNAVINST, and classified national security information ONLY. Under Executive Summary, it listed Methodology, Classification, and Referral; clearance only through Director of National Intelligence. The date reflected the latest addition to the file—the contents of a dispatch box discovered during a 2004 renovation project in a Philadelphia suburb, along with its subsequent release to the government by the Franklin Institute on October 6, 2011.

Other memos were included in order of their addition, from the very first memorandum regarding the Neptune Project. They outlined a concerted effort to find *Neptune's Trident* all the way back to 1850, when it was assumed Tunney was lost. To their surprise, sightings of *Neptune's Trident* were documented well into the present day, the last one, November 8, 2009, when an ensign reported seeing a three-masted vessel, maroon in color, and firing a salute before retiring at high speed.

Beneath the memos was a box containing several bundled stacks of Colonial era correspondence. Under the twine were pieces of paper with inclusive dates. She grabbed the earliest stack, unknotted the twine, and opened it, careful not to destroy the letters.

To the Honorable Mr. J.

Sir, I have the distinguishing honor to repeat the news reported to the Hon. John Armstrong, jun., of the capture of a prize vessel, the flagship of the fleet of Barbary, the Dey of Reckoning. However, this action was accomplished at great sacrifice, the loss of our gallant Capt. Arthur Ledbetter, and our vessel, Justice. In the matter of this vessel's disposition, I was requested to correspond with you exclusively. She is currently anchored in the Bay of Piscataqua, her hull being inspected and repaired following our engagement. As she remains out of action, I was hoping to be relieved of this commission and assigned to a new vessel. I await your reply with anticipation.

> *Believe me, dear Sir, to be Your most faithful and humble. sert.,*
> *Vernon Tunney*
> *Portsmouth 23rd June 1788*

Terrie's smile grew roots. "This is the definitive proof I was looking for," she whispered to Jack.

"What are you talking about?"

"I read the *Justice* logbook before turning it in. There were two distinct authors, one right-handed, the other left. This is the exact handwriting of the left-handed scrawl from that log."

The letters were of short duration, but a few piqued her interest. She set those aside and captured them on her new smartphone camera.

"What are you doing?" Jack asked in a panic.

"Preserving the evidence to prove Juli's manuscript was on target."

"How do you know?"

"Read the content."

Terrie had Jack read through them in date order. What emerged was the story of how Tunney became involved with the ship he originally brought into the Port of Piscataqua.

Sir,

I understand your concern with regard to our etiquette in correspondence. I shall do as you suggest. Meanwhile, I am pleased to report the damage to DOR is negligible, though the mizzen mast is unsalvageable and must be replaced. Damage to the quarter deck was not as heavy as originally anticipated. A few planks were destroyed, but the beams remain completely intact. Have you given any consideration to my request to be relieved of this commission? I still await your answer.

    Your most faithful and
    humbl. sert.,
    —T

    Portsmouth 29th August 1788

Sir,

I have the unfortunate duty to inform you of Mr. Hackett's displeasure at your suggestion of his assuming possession of the DOR. Mr. Hackett intimated he is not equipped to modify existing ships. I also have some surprising news. While undergoing repairs to the captain's stateroom, we found a compartment tucked away behind some loose wallboards. When we removed them, we discovered several books. They were all written on parchment and in some foreign language. The illustrations they contain are maritime in origin. Due to the nature and complexity of these illustrations, I think it prudent to translate them to determine their importance. How do you wish me to proceed?

Your humbl. sert.,
-T

Portsmouth 25th October 1788

Sir,

With respect to the books, do you truly believe Mr. Sale's apprentice can help with their translation? In my humble opinion, based solely on the illustrations, I fear the importance of these books could easily be neglected if not quickly interpreted and evaluated. As there is little more I can do here, I regret I must

> return to Philadelphia and my duties aboard the *Hypatia* with dispatch.
>
> Your humbl. sert.,
> —T
>
> Portsmouth 23rd November 1788

He found another one, dated Portsmouth, August 9, 1798, which confirmed that a temporary blind was indeed placed around the ship destined to become *Neptune's Trident*. But what shocked Terrie was that the hull coating took just over a month to complete and that the vessel would only require a crew of seven to operate.

While Jack was absorbed with a stack of late-dated letters, he found something telling.

"Terrie, remember when you first suggested we follow the money to track down the refit of the *Dey of Reckoning*?"

"Yeah, what about it?"

"Well, I think I found the smoking gun."

He handed Terrie one of the letters and she read it with disinterest.

> Sir,
>
> With the inspection and successful launch of *Neptune's Trident* on the 2nd instant, I am happy to report the vessel seaworthy and ready

for trials. To maintain her service will require $15,225.71 per annum.

Your humbl. sert.,
—T

Portsmouth 8th November 1798

"All this proves is that he requested funds from his government contact. There's no such sum quoted in Secretary Stoddart's request," said Terrie as she returned the letter to him.

"There is now." Jack handed her the other, more telling, letter. Terrie's eyes widened as she took in its content.

Sir,

Your approved operating budget of $9330.48 per annum leaves us with a considerable shortfall. To make up this deficiency, I shall be forced to obtain the needed funds from my own meager resources.

Your humbl. sert.,
—T

Portsmouth 25th January 1799

Musing over the identity of Tunney's correspondent, Jack asked, "Could Thomas Jefferson be the illusive Mr. J?"

"What makes you think that?"

"Well, in one 1788 issue of the *New Hampshire Spy*, I recall an article written by Jefferson where he advocated for a modest-size naval force."

"While that assumption is tempting, we need concrete evidence to prove it." Coming to the end of the available letters, she asked, "Was that it?"

"There's nothing left in the dispatch box." Looking around the edges of the metal box, he said, "Wait, there's something under this."

Terrie removed the metal box to reveal a faded, old newspaper, folded and sealed in a plastic bag. In the upper margin, a portion of its title, written in all caps, was visible. "What do we have here?"

She carefully opened it to its full length to read the complete title frame, AMERICAN WATCHMAN AND DELAWARE REPUBLICAN; the days of publication, Wednesdays and Saturdays; and the publisher's name and address. This particular paper was number 416, volume V, Saturday, July 31, 1813.

Skimming the four columns of page one, Terrie found the article that doomed this particular edition of the paper to oblivion, thanks to the auspices of the federal government. It was part of a letter from a sailor who'd survived the attack on the HMS *Stalwart*.

> Extract of an intercepted letter from a British sailor hiding in Groton, CT, to a confederate, dated May 29, 1813.
>
> It was my turn at the crow's watch. We were heading north along the enemy coast when I observed quickly developing weather conditions. A sudden downspout of swirling air made a whirlpool of the water ahead of us. Before it blew itself out, a foggy white mist began to coalesce around the

atmospheric anomaly. Just as I tried to notify the master's mate, I saw something.

What appeared to be a corsair emerged from the mist. It was unlike any vessel I'd ever seen. She glistened in the sunlight like steel, yet her color was that of rosy crimson. She revealed her profile, her gray sails puffed out full. The peculiar-looking corsair was smaller, yet she moved faster than we. What happened next, I'm still coming to grips with.

Rather than run us down to engage our vessel, she maintained her distance, turning her bow toward us. It stayed that way, pointed directly at our port side, until she suddenly turned, the starboard side of her hull growing in length.

Then, as God is my witness, I thought her captain was closing reef, since it appeared her sails were shrinking to her deck. No, to my surprise, it was the masts themselves that had folded toward the deck. In short order, I could only discern the outline of a shiny oval sitting upon the water, darker than the bright blue of the sea. The oval began moving through the water at frightening speed as she disappeared into the squall from whence she came.

I was puzzled! Despite the power of the squall's turbulence, our larger vessel should have been able to match her speed, yet she moved through the water like the devil, with unnatural ease.

Bewildered by such an odd occurrence, I called down to the master's mate to report my observation. When I sought the location where the crimson corsair had first appeared, the ill-tempered wind that marked its arrival had subsided, and the strange vessel had vanished without a trace. It was from that direction I witnessed a slim line of churning water begin to grow toward us. It seemed to get wider and faster as it approached, rushing directly for our hull. Just as it made contact with the center of our vessel, a huge explosion of fire and sound engulfed the deck. The master's mate and the crew who surrounded him were consumed in that conflagration. I felt the nest beneath me give way as the mast which supported us snapped at its base, and I and the mast were thrust into the sea.

I drifted on the surface for what seemed like hours before a whaling vessel picked me up. I did not divulge my status, as their ship wasn't flying the Union Jack. They put in to their home port of Groton, Connecticut, which is where I found a safe harbor till I can make my way back to you.

Once the two investigators finished reading the account, Terrie used her smartphone to document the evidence needed. She returned everything to its reserved location and closed the metal door.

Jack observed Terrie as she was trying to work something out. "What is it?"

"I understand the importance of four of the book classifications, but not the fifth."

"The one we can't find?"

"Exactly," she responded. "If the books were that important to the topic at hand, what was the relevance of the book with the 272.792 classification? That one dealt with Christianity, which had nothing to do with Tunney or *Neptune's Trident*."

Jack suggested something Terrie was trying to dismiss. "Perhaps the key to the enterprise was in this final book?"

"If it was, why did Juli identify it as being in this library when it's obviously not here?"

The pieces on Jack's mental chessboard were moving at lightning speed, yet stalemate was all he could come up with. He resigned further attempts.

Terrie noticed the look of annoyance on his face. "Giving up so soon? Come on, out with it, what are you thinking?"

"I've been meaning to retrieve our family diary from my parent's house. I've never read it, but the stories it's supposed to contain reflect the accounts of my relatives from the mid-1800s through the Roaring Twenties."

"And you think this diary could hold clues pertaining to our investigation?"

"I have no idea."

Smirking at him, she asked, "When do you think you can get it?"

"We can stop by my house on the way back to Portsmouth if it's that important to you."

Terrie responded with an act completely out of character for her—she hugged him.

⎈

The fragrant librarian watched silently as the two Navy officers departed. Having monitored their progress during their visit, he was deeply concerned with the pictures the young woman took with her smartphone, a device she technically shouldn't have brought into the room with her. As an intel officer, she was permitted such lapses in security.

He turned the reins over to his assistant for the day, retrieved his personal items from the locker, and left the building for the parking lot. He waited until he was safely in his vehicle before he checked the cloned phone to see what pictures the female lieutenant had captured—pictures even he wasn't privy to, since his own handler didn't want him opening the box.

His frown deepened. None of the documents she recorded had made it to his phone. He hit the speed dial to reach his contact in Portsmouth. The number was disconnected. Someone had caught on to him. There could be no other explanation. The situation required immediate debriefing.

Philip proceeded to his yacht in Portsmouth to send a secure message. A message he knew would not be warmly received.

FORTY EIGHT

Jack kept flipping through the pages of the thick diary. While he searched through the narratives, Terrie was occupied with the return drive to Portsmouth and couldn't contain her impatience. "Well?"

"Hold your horses, will ya? Much of this is hard to read."

"The handwriting or the ink?"

"Both." Becoming more impatient with himself, he yelled, "There's nothing out of the ordinary in this diary!"

"Well, keep at it," she encouraged, still directing her attention to the road.

Jack leafed through the timeworn chronicle with mounting frustration. "So far, the only thing remotely nautical is something about the HMS *Rattler*'s test against her half sister, *Electo*, and a passage about building a propeller-driven torpedo."

"What year?"

"That entry was dated 1861."

"Anything else?"

With dusk closing in and the car's jostling down the uneven section of highway, graying words blended into the darkening pages. "My eyes must be tired. I can't focus anymore."

Terrie pursed her lips but acknowledged his plight and the length of their workday. With a sense of sympathy, she said, "You're right. We're both all in."

The next forty minutes passed quietly, until they arrived at her assigned parking space. Turning off the engine, she looked at Jack, who was staring into space. "I need a nosh before retiring," she said. "Care to join me?"

"Sure," he grumbled, rubbing his eyes.

"You're really out of it, aren't you?"

"Let's get going, or we'll end up sleeping right here tonight."

Terrie grabbed their research and took Jack's arm as the two made their way to the apartment building. Once past the threshold, she agreed to take the elevator with him. Standing close to one of the mirrored walls, her glance came to rest on a slip of paper sticking out of their research containing Juli's decimal numbers. Staring at it, she picked up on something she hadn't noticed before. The 272 number was out of numerical sequence. It also happened to be the missing book. Was there a connection? She began to wonder if the author had placed it there to alert her that this number was different or altered somehow. Glimpsing the numbers through the reflection in the elevator wall, her eyes squinted as though hit by revelation.

The elevator dinged its arrival to their mutual floor. She planted their research in his hands and gently steered her neighbor toward her apartment. Snapping on the lights, she escorted Jack to the sofa, poured his tired form onto it, and took custody of their research. Placing everything on the coffee table, she located the numbered paper, rewrote them in reverse order and smiled.

Catching his second wind, Jack watched with interest as Terrie jotted down something. "What are you doing?"

"I think I've figured out what's up with that missing book."

"Really?"

"The numbers in this sequence are backwards."

"What made you think that?"

"I caught sight of them in the elevator mirror. I should have known," Terrie said, her voice tinged with self-recrimination.

"I don't understand how?"

Preparing a couple of English muffins for an evening snack, she answered him. "Juli Aruem was worried her information would fall into the wrong hands. It's why she used the Estel Atrea anagram, for one thing. I should have thought about it the second I read what she'd written in the margin. Her placement of this particular number should have drawn my attention to it from the beginning."

"Then you know this book's classification?"

"The Athenaeum curator jogged my memory. I furthered my cultural studies on those books. In the correct order, the 297 stands for Islam and Babism. The 272 suffix compares sacred Islamic states with secular ones."

Believing they'd made a misstep, Jack asked, "Don't we have to go back to the library now that we have the correct number?"

"That isn't necessary. None of the library's 297 classifications extend beyond the second decimal place."

"And you know that how?"

"All naval officers had to use the Naval War College library for their assignments, or don't you remember?"

"Never mind," he responded in deflated fashion. "I remember my time there vividly, but I never saw you."

"We both had other priorities." Terrie delivered her subliminal message with biting ease. She gulped her muffin in three bites before she handed Jack his.

Nibbling his muffin, Jack asked, "If the book isn't there, it must be at the Library of Congress?"

"That's one option," Terrie said, scanning the middle shelf of her bookcase. She spotted the particular reference she wanted and got up to retrieve it.

As she thumbed through its pages, Jack asked, "What's that?"

"It's a monograph on the Golden Age of Muslim Science," Terrie said as she searched for the section that described what

Jeremiah Simon revealed in the 1792 paper. "Here it is. Remember the years the libraries were destroyed?"

"1193, 1258, and 1453, right?"

"You were paying attention," she said smugly. "That's extraordinary!"

He reciprocated her insolent expression.

"The reason why I was drawn to that article was the dates." Taking a seat next to him, she showed Jack the referenced page. "As you see, the twelfth-century date represents the destruction of the ancient library at Nalanda by the Ottoman Turks. The thirteenth-century date was the Mongol invasion of the Bayt al-Hiqma in Baghdad, and the last date was actually the second time the library at Constantinople was sacked. The first time was by the knights of the Fourth Crusade who only partially damaged it in 1204. Many books salvaged from that attack were temporarily moved to Nicaea. In 1453, Mehmed II, Sultan of the Ottoman Empire, completed its destruction."

Jack was feeling out of his depth. "Who destroys libraries? That makes no sense."

"The golden age of Arab science and the birth of Islam arose together in the seventh century. This book explains how Islam is responsible for uniting most of the Arab tribes during that time. The religion quickly spread across the Middle East and India, but so too did their intellectual pursuits."

"Sorry, but those topics never came up in any of my public-school classes," Jack said with a sarcastic edge.

"I don't doubt it. Self-proclaimed authority is obsessed with instilling their politically motivated notions rather than teaching genuine history. The growth of Muslim tradition under the Abbasid caliphs worked to advance both the religion and the cause of knowledge. Science and philosophy grew together in the Muslim world as mathematicians, scientists, and philosophers like al-Khwarizmi, al-Farabi, and Alhazen flourished. Even Muslim women, like Fatima al-Fihiri, are memorialized for their contributions to the age, such as her founding of the Moroccan University of Qarawiyyin, which is still in operation today."

"If modern rhetoric is any indication, their golden age didn't last long."

"You're getting ahead of the story," she chided. "Despite such forward thinking, others came along who believed The Recitation to be inviolate and in conflict with the writings produced by Muslim intellectuals. Rising to the top of this philosophical firestorm was Abu Hamid Muhammad al-Ghazali. His disdain for opinions outside Islamic orthodoxy coalesced into his most famous works."

Finishing her thought, Jack added, "Let me guess. Condemning anything that contradicted the word of the Prophet?"

"Full marks." She grinned and pointed to the next paragraph. "According to this, in the twelfth century, al-Jazari challenged this philosophy as backward-thinking. Like his contemporaries, the physicist and engineer produced many books that are influential today."

Challenging that line of thought, Jack asked, "If such enlightened thinking was so prized during that time, how did it lead to the wanton destruction of these libraries?"

"As the Prophet's word under the Hadith became as widely distributed as the Quran, devotees like Bakhtiyar Khilji followed al-Ghazali's example of intolerance. When Khilji discovered the heretical ideas promulgated by alleged Muslims like al-Jazari, he vowed to do something about it. In 1193, Khilji laid siege to the university at Nalanda, sought out the sacrilegious tomes, and destroyed them."

"So the next one, the Bayt al-Hiqma, was a library?"

"Known to westerners as the House of Wisdom, it was another literary jewel of the ancient world. The most inclusive center of world knowledge during the Islamic golden age, it welcomed peoples of all creeds and backgrounds to study there. As one might imagine, this didn't sit well with Muslim purists. They must have cheered when the Mongol horde under Hulagu Khan sacked the place in 1258. It was said, 'the Tigris ran black with ink, then red with blood.'"

"Hulagu Khan wasn't a Muslim," Jack charged. "Undoubtedly, many targeted in the attack were Muslim. But if religious zealotry wasn't his motivation, then what was the reason behind his targeting of that library?"

"The Mongol Empire was motivated by conquest. However, this chapter suggests that from the time of Hulagu Khan, the empire was also obsessed with the ideas of the peoples they conquered, thus the targeting of their libraries. A loyal librarian knew this and rescued thousands of these works before the siege."

"You said that in 1453, Ottoman Turks completed what the Templars failed to do. But if the Turks were religious zealots, what were the Templars' reasons?"

"The knights of the Forth Crusade weren't noble. Beyond their desire to destroy the Byzantine Empire, they also ransacked the property of Byzantine and Muslim residents of Constantinople. Their actions in the library were characterized as 'rummaging through the volumes,' suggesting they sought certain books."

"The 'cursed' books?"

"Possibly. At first, I thought the books were written by al-Jazari, since he would have been at Nalanda during the sacking, but he never wrote anything advanced enough to result in that metal alloy I saw." Terrie folded her arms and continued. "Whatever they were, one thing we can infer from this chapter summary is that the single goal of the attackers was their desire to obtain manuscripts of Muslim origin written in the Nalanda library."

"What did they have to do with the *Trident* or Tunney?"

"Those dots haven't connected yet. If they are the books discovered aboard the *Dey of Reckoning*, it's yet another puzzle. Since they were linked to those destroyed libraries, and George Sale's apprentice was needed to examine them, it's a good bet they were written in Arabic."

"I noticed you didn't answer Dr. Aponte when she asked you who Sale was."

Trying not to sound too condescending, she asked, "You know who he was, right?"

He tossed her a pathetic look. "Naturally. I just forgot right now, is all."

Terrie found it impossible not to giggle. "He was the British linguist who first translated the Quran into English, a copy of which ended up in Thomas Jefferson's library." Skimming through the volume before she replaced it on the shelf, Terrie hit upon something else. "This is interesting. A tale from Arab folklore that detailed alleged sightings of a mythical vessel as far back as the first Barbary War and reported as late as the early '90s. Witness accounts vary, but they all agree that to encounter it spelled doom for the unfortunate ship that came across it. The survivors of such an encounter gave it a name: the red wraith."

"Why mythical?"

"The manner in which the vessel moved, engaged adversaries, and disappeared, was unlike anything they'd ever experienced before."

"Could it have been the *Trident*?"

"Doubtful. Other than its color, there's no consistent description, I'm afraid."

"Then we'll have to research what happened to *Neptune's Trident* after its supposed demise in 1850."

"Agreed."

He exhaled, "I'll get on it in the morning."

Philip grabbed another bottle of liquid courage from the small fridge in his galley. Having opened his secure account to compose a message to Runner's representative, he spent the last twenty minutes writing and deleting what he'd written. Unequal to the task, he picked up the next burner phone in the queue from his safe to make the call. The phone rang but once. "We've got a problem."

"Apparently so. You never called before."

"Our valiant lieutenant not only gained access to the file but copied documents from it."

"Would you mind telling me how?"

"I found it at the same moment she arrived in the library. There was no time for me to relocate it. And she had extraordinary authorization."

"From who?"

"Do I have to spell it out for you? It was a verifiable member of Runner's staff."

"Not possible."

"The individual was one of four credible signatories authorized to grant such access. And you already know who they are."

"You couldn't stall her?"

"She wasn't alone." The line went dead for several seconds. "You there?"

"I'm here. I presume you retrieved those copies?"

"I missed the opportunity."

"Then lean on your contact. He needs to understand he doesn't have a choice."

"Yeah, about that."

"Now what?"

"He's offline." Again, silence at his handler's end. "What instructions?" Philip asked.

"I'll get back with you."

FORTY NINE

Theo sprinted past Terrie for the last mile of their run. The final stretch of his PRT would be at a comparative slope, so he went for broke. Terrie tried to hustle after him, but he was just too fast. Reaching the end of her apartment building, she caught up to him, hands on his hips and trying to catch his breath.

"Well, that was interesting," she complimented him with pride.

"What?"

"You breezed right past me in your final effort to finish."

"You were being generous the entire route."

"I assure you I wasn't."

"Thanks."

"Although I wouldn't count those chickens just yet, I'd say you have a better than average shot at breezing through the test."

"If I do, my coach can claim the credit."

She frowned. "Absolutely not. I can only motivate and encourage you. The credit for your success belongs to you alone, Theo. Never forget that."

"What do you get out of it?"

"I get what I asked you for," she declared. "Clean up that video and we'll call it square, okay?"

"On that score, see me after morning standup."

"Then you have something for me?"

Theo smiled at her.

Jets of hot water blasted Terrie's closed eyes, its wide reach cleansing her face. Rinsing the conditioner out of her hair, she heard a dull thumping. She turned off the shower to get a better grasp on the source of the noise. Someone was at the front door. "Be out in a minute!" she hollered.

"I found something," said the muffled voice emanating through the walls. It was Jack.

She climbed out of the shower, quickly patted the excess water off her body, and put on a paper-thin wrap to answer the door.

"I found wher—" Jack stood paralyzed at the sight of Terrie's well-defined form, a threadbare piece of material away from au naturale.

Placing a hand on her hip, she used the other to draw his gaze back to her eyes. "Found what?"

Regaining himself, Jack continued. "Where Ronan O'Hara discussed the fate of the HMS *Stalwart*."

"Sounds interesting. Why don't you slow down, come in, and take your story from the top?" She moved toward the kitchen to pop a couple of English muffins in the toaster. "You want one?"

"Sure." Jack took a seat at the kitchen table, steeling a glimpse at her when he thought she wasn't looking.

Terrie could feel the caress of his eyes. "Stop gawking at me and get to the story."

Busted, he dropped his gaze and proceeded with his revelations. "I located where Ronan discussed his encounter with a fellow ship-builder and veteran of the War of 1812. The man, on his deathbed, recounted the destruction of the HMS *Stalwart* and the mysterious ship that allegedly destroyed her. The story is similar to that of the account we found in the *American Watchman* yesterday."

"And?" she asked, handing him his jelly-covered muffin.

"Ronan shared this man's interest in the development of the ironclads of the 1850s. While describing the designs of these ships, it reminded him of sighting the silhouette of a maroon corsair prior to 1850, metallic in appearance, and fast as the devil. Ronan related how the man spotted this strange vessel again the month before he died in 1861. Our Arab ghost?"

"Wait a minute. Before you get too rambunctious, are you sure he was talking about the same vessel?"

"It must be. His description of the silhouette as the masts retracted toward the deck was the same."

"Did he discuss anything related to Tunney?"

"No, but Seamus O'Hara recalled a similar story he was told by a friend of his uncle forty-two years later."

"Forty-two years?" Terrie questioned. "Then there's proof the ship, if not her captain, outlasted its alleged demise?"

"It would appear so."

"What in Seamus' story convinces you it's the same vessel?"

"It was around the time of the Spanish American War. He was talking about the new battleship *Oregon* and how it had just completed its famous dash."

"I know that story," Terrie said. Her interest piqued, she sat at the table with her tea. "The *Oregon* traveled from San Francisco to the Jupiter inlet of Florida in only sixty-six days. But what does that have to do with the *Trident*?"

"He also documented two eyewitness accounts," Jack opened the journal to that particular entry. "The first was from an American sailor serving in Commodore Dewey's squadron. The sailor described the outline of a fast-moving corsair, without sails, and how it destroyed three Spanish ships during the Battle of Manila Bay. Two months later, another sailor engaged in the Battle of Santiago near Cuba observed a vessel with the same silhouette retracting her sails before successfully engaging several enemy ships at a high rate of speed."

Terrie's disbelief was unmistakable. "That's impossible. They couldn't be the same ship."

"Why?"

"The distance from Manila to San Francisco is over 6,000 nautical miles. At a top speed of the day of twelve knots, even the *Oregon* took just over two months to get from San Francisco to Florida. So the dates of those sightings have to be wrong."

"How can you disprove such straightforward observations?"

"Logic. The *Oregon* was the fastest surface battleship in the US arsenal at the time. For the *Oregon* to complete her famous dash, she would've had to travel just over 200 miles a day. In order for this corsair to have made it from the Philippines to Cuba in sixty-six days, it would have had to travel an extra hundred miles a day."

"Well, if your figures are correct, and the sightings were of the same vessel, that would mean this mystery ship must have made eighteen knots or better." Jack washed down the last of his breakfast and got up to leave. "Wanna carpool in? I can wait for you if you'd like."

"Sure," Terrie replied. "Give me fifteen minutes."

Jack knew that puzzling look of hers all too well. "What's the matter, Terrie?"

"The government's interest in this ship. We're not looking for a derelict vessel but one that's still out there. Fast, maneuverable, and equipped with modern weaponry and a stealth technology capable of eluding present-day tracking."

Jack's half-cocked smile disappeared.

As the morning meeting broke up, Terrie took her customary time to reheat her tea. She turned around to find Bannerman staring at her.

"Something I can do for you, Commander?"

She attempted to be discreet. "Lieutenant Commander Laurie Montgomery, your predecessor. I never told you about her, did I?"

"No, you didn't."

"I first met Laurie during an academy lecture. I don't recall the subject; it was that boring."

Terrie's get-to-the-point face rose to the surface, and Bannerman picked up on it.

"I've been in regular contact with Laurie since she left for her assignment in Afghanistan. Nothing work-related, just everyday correspondence between friends. We haven't gone more than a few days without writing one another." In a softer tone, she added, "My last three letters went unanswered."

Terrie flipped over a page from her morning summary to jot down a few notes. "Letters? You don't call, text, or use social media?"

"We haven't called each other since she left the States. We thought it best to use snail mail rather than texts or social media."

"When was your last phone conversation?"

"She called me six months ago."

"From where?"

"Her apartment in Alexandria, Virginia."

"Cell or landline?"

"Landline. She suspended the service on both, since she had little use for either at her new duty location."

"Suspended?" Terrie furrowed her brow and asked, "Have you tried them lately to see if they're working?"

"I did, but all I got was a recorded message stating the lines were out of service."

"Do you know her current DSN?"

"That's the first thing I tried when I lost contact. I got ahold of her unit in Kandahar, but all they would say was that she was unavailable at the moment."

"Ordinarily you just exchanged letters?"

"She did send me a couple of postcards."

"Do you have them?"

"They're in Ops."

The two officers went to the Ops Center so Bannerman could retrieve the shoebox containing the letters. She placed it on the desk for Terrie's inspection.

Sifting through the personal-size envelopes, she paid particular attention to the address and date printed in the circle of the fleet post office cancellation stamp. All the letters originated from the same location. Terrie went to open one but stopped herself. "Do you mind?"

"If it helps you find Laurie? No, of course not."

Terrie allowed her hard expression to soften into something resembling compassion. Opening the latest three letters, she examined Laurie's handwriting and searched for any clues to her whereabouts. Satisfied the letters' contents didn't help, she searched the box for the elusive postcards.

There were two, both displaying popular rug motifs native to Afghanistan. The first one apologized for its brevity, owing to the harried activities of the author. Aside from a platitude or two and an inquiry into the commander's health, nothing hinted at potential travel plans. The other was even more perplexing. There was no message, only Bannerman's name and address. Terrie scrutinized the cancellation date—just over two weeks ago.

"Is this the last correspondence she sent you?"

"Yes. As it was blank and she'd sent me nothing else, I began to worry."

"I'd imagine so," said Terrie with sincere empathy. "Was she scheduled to deploy or to be reassigned?"

"She never indicated such."

"She could be on a remote assignment where mailing letters would be impractical."

"It's possible."

Terrie picked up on Bannerman's discomfort. "I don't mean to be indelicate, but have you contacted the medical center at Tripler or mortuary affairs in Delaware?"

"That's why I'm puzzled. Tripler has no record of her, and the mortuary in Dover hasn't received any female dignified transfers since that date. Her unit doesn't list her as missing."

Terrie nodded as she picked up the blank postcard to give it a closer look. Printed above Bannerman's information was a short paragraph in English about the artistry of Afghan rugs. The font size was small, yet legible. She read the paragraph and went to put the postcard back in the box, when she spotted the blue shavings of a pencil eraser. Moving her thumb across the postcard to remove them, it was apparent the lines were permanent. Upon closer inspection, they were the same color as the handwritten address. The first one underscored the letters Ke in the word Kelim, and along the same line at the beginning of a new sentence, an underscore was placed beneath the letters To in the word Today.

To make sure these aberrations were unique to this particular postcard, she compared the two and found her anomaly. To Terrie, this was an obvious attempt at sending a message.

"Would you know why Commander Montgomery underlined these letters?"

Surprised, Bannerman looked over the postcard. "I never noticed that before."

"Does it mean anything to you?"

Bannerman thought for a moment before responding, "No."

Keeping her suspicions to herself, Terrie placed the postcards and letters back into the box. "My workload is light this morning, Commander. I can look into it for you."

"Thank you, Miss Murphy."

"No problem."

⚓

Theo had cued up the video for Terrie's review when she walked over to him. "Hard at work already?" she asked.

"I did this yesterday, while you and Jack were out."

Within earshot of the conversation, Jack hollered across the room, "I heard that!"

Terrie waved a dismissive hand toward Jack. She studied the image on Theo's monitor and asked, "You have something then?"

"I managed to minimize enough of the pixilation to sharpen the picture, but it's as good as it's going to get. Now let's see what we can do about that audio." Clacking away on his keyboard, Theo brought up a virtual mixing board on his first monitor and got to work. "Eliminating the HVAC noise in the background is going to be the tricky part, but I think I can minimize enough of it to bring out the voices."

"Can I see the entire visual?"

"Sure." With the called-up video on his second monitor, he restarted the clip for her inspection.

She still couldn't make out either man's face, but something about the room was disturbingly familiar. As the video reached the last minute, she was able to determine what it was that caused the interrogated subject to scream. The man with his back to her was armed with a blade the size of a Montana Toothpick and swept it across the throat of the other subject. The video ended with blood spraying from a gaping wound in the man's neck. As Terrie looked at the surroundings of the room, she sensed something recognizable about the dark patterns on the floor. It was reminiscent of the spots of blood pooling where her sister was dismembered, but she couldn't be positive. "How long before you finish the audio?"

"If I can't tighten it up by lunchtime, it's because nobody can."

"You're a speed demon, Theo." Terrie smiled and patted him on the shoulder.

"You helped me do that this morning."

They regarded each other warmly and got to work on their respective tasks.

Terrie was floored when Laurie's photo came up on the screen. Bannerman's friend could have been her doppelganger. They were the same height and general build, with a similar hair color and style.

Coordinating with Laurie's unit wasn't helpful. They knew she was safe, but that's all they would volunteer. They wouldn't even discuss her temporary duty status. Checking with PERS-4 on assignment records over the past six months netted her zip. There were no unusual trends spiking in her AOR summaries either. None of her resources shed any light on what would cause Bannerman's friend to just disappear. Searching beyond the six-month threshold, she noticed Laurie had received numerous short-term deployments from December 2011 until she received her permanent reassignment to Kandahar. Having struck out in her search for information, Terrie updated a grateful Bannerman and promised to look into it further if anything new came to light.

With an attentive ear toward Theo as he ran through the audio, an intonation recalled the unsettling voice of the interrogator. Something clicked in her head as she heard it. "Theo, can you run that last line again for me?"

Theo rebooted the video with its cleaned-up sound. She listened carefully to every nuance, phrase, and quirk. There was no doubt. It was the same man recorded on the six-minute audio. The man called Ra'id. She was sure of it, now.

When it was through, Terrie grabbed the CD with the six-minute audio and handed it to Theo. "Can you make a voiceprint of both files for me?"

Theo winked and said, "Why don't you give me a real challenge?" His nimble fingers flew across the keyboard with the dexterity of Franz Liszt. Opening the appropriate program, he deftly made forensic-quality voiceprints of both recordings and handed the CD back to Terrie. "There are some irregularities as a result of the original recordings, but they're close. We need an untainted third recording to be sure. You think it's the same guy?"

"I know it is. Now I have a baseline for comparison should another recording of his voice surface. Thanks, Theo."

"That's just the first surprise."

"Really?" Terrie asked, stunned. "And the second?"

"I'm still going through the latest zip drive, but I found a reference to an FBI field report that outlined a broad-stroked plot from Bin Laden's Islamabad papers."

"What plot?"

"To establish a global caliphate."

"Does it say who's leading it or how they plan to pull it off?"

"I haven't finished going over everything, so the answer may still be here on the drive."

"What about the SD cards?"

"That's the good news! I've decrypted them for you. Except for a single word document named SS Pettibone, they're nothing but photographs."

"Sounds more like a reference to Secretary of State Alison Pettibone than a ship. What's in the document?"

Theo opened the single-page file so Terrie could look for herself.

Dec 6, 2011	Geneva for Bio/WMD conference with the Syrian national council
Feb 24, 2012	Tunis meeting with The Friends of Syria
Apr 19, 2012	Paris ad hoc ministerial meeting on Syria
Jul 6, 2012	Paris for a Friends of Syrian People/Syrian opposition leaders meeting
Jul 7, 2012	Kabul meeting with President Karzai

After committing the dates and their relevance to memory, she thanked Theo and headed back to her station to go through the SD cards. Loading them each in turn, she scrutinized the thumb-size pictures. The photos were generically labeled with a date-time stamp. Public, wide-angle shots established the location. Three of the cards contained information from Sha'ab, Beirut, Kabul, and Tunis, the fourth from Geneva and Paris.

The photographer was likely a mole as evident from the clear resolution in the close-up subjects. Most were labeled with names and positions. Whoever had taken the photos knew what they were doing. But the last card's photos were taken from a place she knew well: Reston, Virginia.

Setting that one aside, she focused her energies on the others to see if any of the subjects pictured were on her radar. One repeated term made numerous appearances on her daily briefs of late: the Muslim Illuminati.

Based in Sha'ab near Sadr City, their earliest literature claimed the group's Illuminati name was appropriated by Christian zealots. Terrie's intel about their preferred method of dispatching the kafirun considered them extreme, even by al-Qaeda standards.

Only one individual had been repeatedly photographed, a nameless subject whose image established his presence at all gatherings. His facial features were covered by a formfitting hood, but his distinctive, contact-cloaked eyes would help Terrie zero in on the man's true identity. He had to be the organizer, setting the agenda for the meetings.

Terrie scrutinized all the photographs on the cards for repeated names, but none of them shared any insight into who this masked person was. Unsure she'd ever penetrate his disguise, she opened the SD card from Reston. The photographs were likewise named and dated but with a different set of players. The names and base of operations for the other five individuals were superimposed under their headshots. Identified were Fuad, Khalil, Jawad, Hashem, and Salman.

The hooded man with the pale-yellow contact lenses was at each meeting documented on the SD cards. She copied all instances of this person onto a desktop file and arranged them in date/time-stamp order. In doing so, the following pics came up:

>20111206_10:53 Sw
>20111206_10:57 Sw
>20120224_21:58 Tu
>20120224_22:07 Tu
>20120224_22:14 Tu
>20120419_17:31 Fr
>20120706_21:16 Fr
>20120707_19:10 Af
>20120707_19:18 Af
>20120909_16:53 VA
>20120909_16:17 VA

Biting her lip as she tried to make sense of what she was looking at, Terrie went back to the Reston SD card to see if she missed anything. Halfway down the list of pics, she found an odd file extension. It wasn't a .jpg, but a video clip. *Hmm, this is different.*

She clicked on the video and a computer-modified voice began a briefing. The voice came from the hooded figure. Despite the effort used to conceal his identity, something about the way he spoke caught her attention. She concentrated on his verbalizations and peculiar quirks as the tone grew directive.

Acting in the capacity of a mufti issuing an official Islamic ruling, the voice addressed a 2009 sighting of the red wraith, its location, and the importance of finding the nautical apparition. There was something onboard that the hooded figure wanted erased from existence. To ensure its destruction, he designated the vessel, its contents, and the unfortunate individual who perpetuates stories of its existence, objects of an official fatwa. Reviewing the video again, she felt Theo's presence behind her.

"What's up, Theo?"

"On a hunch, I checked with a friend at Langley. He learned through an informant that a DC law firm is representing several Muslim 501(c)3s through an influential lobbying group. Their primary lawyer is also a popular Imam. At a clandestine meeting, this Imam floated the idea of securing agents within the upper echelons of Western governments, but where and how, the informant didn't say."

"Did he say who it was?"

"He called him Kedar Ra'id al Husam al Din."

The six-minute audio played in her head again, filling it with the voice of the man called Ra'id. "Hmm. Powerful leader of the sword of faith," Terrie said, translating the name's meaning.

"He further indicated his obsession with locating and destroying something called *Neptune's Trident*, along with the instructions related to its creation."

At the mention of the *Trident*, Terrie grinned from ear to ear. She looked at the file numbers on her desktop again, and that's when everything clicked. She pulled up the document with the secretary of state's itinerary, opened a second window, and pasted the file numbers to the photos she just placed on her desktop. "See, Theo? These pictures' file names are the dates and times they were taken. Now look at the dates and places of the secretary's itineraries. Notice anything?"

"The first two pics were taken minutes apart on the same day as the secretary's Geneva meeting."

"Keep reading," Terrie encouraged.

"Three pics on the same day as her trip to Tunis, and two pics each from her respective trips to Paris and Kabul."

"Which means?"

"Either someone is tailing the US Secretary of State, or someone from her entourage is working with this hooded figure at all these locations."

"Or worse," she added, "a member of her entourage is the hooded figure. The July 6th and 7th pics are from the same two countries as the secretary's visits, yet this same man is present near both of them. Remember your statement about Ra'id wanting to securing agents within the upper echelons of Western governments?"

"You may be on to something, Terrie," Theo agreed.

"Although we'll need more proof, I'd call your work today payment for services rendered."

"Let me pass that PRT first. Then we can consider payment rendered."

Sporting an irrepressible grin, Terrie returned to her work. She was almost through her stack of daily intelligence for Bannerman's SITREP when the Ops Center door buzzed again. It was Taro, with Crabtree on his heels. And Taro was shaking his head as though he couldn't believe he'd brought home a straight A report card.

FIFTY

"Well, don't you look fat, dumb, and happy," said Theo, his head cocked to one side.

Ignoring Theo's banter, Taro signed into his computer and pulled up the program he and Prentiss had been working on all morning.

"Everyone gather 'round," Crabtree ordered.

Taro retrieved the file and said, "You're not going to believe this."

"We might if you tell us," Bannerman said with a barely discernible eye roll.

Taro ignored the jab. "Working to ascertain the level of damage the NSA breach may have caused, we found this." They huddled around Taro to read the information he brought up. "Someone from a remote area outside of Sha'ab sent blind-receipt emails of tactical operations information to an IP address within the White House."

"What?" Jack verbalized the shock the rest of them were thinking.

"It gets worse. Each of these command and control messages were then forwarded to nonsecure, nongovernment IPs in Baghdad, Kandahar, Somalia, Yemen, Chechnya, Nigeria, and Jolo. The evidence suggests this address is the clearinghouse for such messages before they're passed on."

"Do we know the exact office location of the IP address?" asked Crabtree.

"We would need access to the White House's internet architecture," Theo replied.

"Can you get it?" Bannerman asked.

"I'll try," Theo answered.

Bringing the conversation back to the forwarded messages, Terrie said, "Those locations are considered the hotbeds of Islamic Terrorism."

"That's not the worst part," Taro said. "They're beginning to metastasize, exploiting our open borders as a precursor to building sleeper cells right here in the United States."

"Where?" Jack asked.

"Email traffic between that address and Sha'ab discussed the establishment of command and control points in central California, Minnesota, and the DC-metro area. According to one message, the strategic plan called for installing operational cells in all fifty states by the end of 2016."

Jack's eyes grew wide as the scope of their strategic vision became clear.

"Did you detect any other activity?" asked Terrie.

Looking directly at her, Taro added, "Yeah, and you're not going to like it."

Taro scrolled down the report to a list of places Terrie recognized immediately: all of her initial assignments subsequent to graduating language school. She was also shocked to find messages linked to IPs in Hanscom, Newport, Portsmouth, and, most shocking of all, Bear, Delaware. It's where Juli Aruem met her fate. "I'm being cyberstalked?" she asked.

"It looks that way," said Taro.

Terrie allowed the information to circulate in her head. "Taro, you said someone within the White House received blind-receipt copies of these messages?"

"Yeah, that's right."

"Do you know who?"

"The sole name attached to these messages was a weird one. Simulacra Viro."

"Simu-who?" asked Jack.

"It's Latin for wraith," Crabtree blurted out. His team stared at him in amazement. "What? Dead languages are a hobby of mine."

Bannerman and Jack shook their heads while Taro and Theo chuckled. Terrie crinkled her brow in bewilderment and began pacing the narrow semicircular walkway. Tapping a finger over her folded arms, she thought back to the voice on the six-minute audio. She heard Ra'id's last statement that cautioned how discussion of the red wraith was blasphemy against the Quran.

After a minute, she volunteered her thoughts. "According to the intelligence I've been collating, something big is being orchestrated by an elusive Middle Eastern agent. Until now, all we knew about him was that he's Western educated, and his activities suggest plans to ingratiate himself within Western society. He's training his people to infiltrate civic organizations, lobbyist PACs, and the highest level of governments hostile to their cause in order to set his scheme in motion. He means to influence the policy makers of those governments."

"Sounds pretty ambitious for a splinter group," Bannerman mumbled.

"I wouldn't have believed it myself, but Theo's work on the Hanscom packages confirmed it. And if what we've discovered from the SD cards is any indication, this person may be working in the State Department," Terrie suggested.

"The scope of it is so bold, they might not think we'd consider methods to defend against it," Theo added.

"It wasn't until you confirmed his name that the pieces of the puzzle clicked into place. Ra'id is known as the Wraith outside his inner circle."

"The Arab ghost story?" Jack queried, remembering their discussion over her library book.

Terrie just looked at him with a deadpan expression. "So, we have a mole within the walls of 1600 Pennsylvania Avenue."

"Or at the State Department," said Jack. "You know who it is?"

"No," Terrie replied, "but with a limited number of possible suspects, we should be able to narrow it down."

"All right," said Crabtree, taking the lead. "How many people work at the White House with access to the president?"

"There can't be more than fifty people with direct access to him," said Jack.

"There are around fifteen staff positions, fifteen cabinet secretaries, and about thirty-five so-called czars," Taro offered. "We could start there."

"I can get busy comparing their vocal patterns against the suspect voiceprint I just made," Theo said.

"All right, but what about State Department personnel?" asked Jack.

"Narrow your pool of eligible suspects to those with direct White House access," Crabtree suggested before turning to Bannerman. "Summarize what was just discussed and prepare an EYES-ONLY SITREP for the SECNAV. I'll brief the captain."

"Aye aye, sir," Bannerman answered, looking back at Terrie with undisguised appreciation.

Terrie smiled at Bannerman before getting to work on the directory of all confirmed and unconfirmed presidential appointees. She almost finished the list of White House staffers when her cell buzzed in her purse. She took it out to see who was calling. It was Aunt Barbara.

"Excuse me, Commander. I have to take this."

Glancing at their digital clock for EDT, Bannerman said, "Go ahead and take lunch. I've got Ops."

"Thank you, Commander." Terrie signed out and headed to her vehicle. She waited until the engine was running before she hit the speed dial for Aunt Barbara.

Her aunt picked up on the second ring. "I have to call you at work now to get your attention?"

"Sorry, Aunt B, but now is not a good time."

"And when shall I make that appointment?"

"Is it something urgent?"

"Not really. Roger Dagney walked in on an attempted burglary at his office yesterday afternoon."

"What? Is he all right?"

"Roger?" she responded with a chuckle. "He likely scared them off. They tossed his office, but nothing was taken. He brushed it off as a fraternity prank."

"The malfeasants were kids?"

"Careful now, you're not that far removed from a kid yourself."

"Is this the reason you called me at work?" Terrie asked, raising her voice.

"Yes. And no. The malfeasants to which you referred flipped his desk and scattered several books from his library onto the floor."

Something hit Terrie like a ton of bricks. Remembering Dagney's story of how America's gift to the Dey of Algiers was lost, she wondered how Dagney learned of the *Crescent's* demise with such clarity. The answer was obvious. The tomes were in his office library. Someone else must have discovered what Roger knew about the *Crescent*, the *Trident*, and Tunney. "Aunt B, this is very important. Is he absolutely sure no books are missing?"

"I didn't ask him specifics, but he said nothing was taken."

"Could you confirm it for me, please?"

"What meds are you on?"

"None that I'm aware of. I'm absolutely serious about this, so please drop the sarcasm, okay?"

"All right," her aunt relented. "When are you coming down?"

"I'll try to take some time this week. Sound good?"

"You know I look forward to it, but I won't hold my breath."

"Nice" was Terrie's deadpan reply. Hanging up, she thought about her aunt's security background. Terrie exhausted her resources trying to locate Laurie Montgomery, but perhaps her aunt might provide the fresh perspective needed to find Bannerman's friend.

FIFTY ONE

A naval officer in service whites sat in the outer office of the president's senior advisor, Gerri Valenti. The senior advisor was currently occupied with a visitor who kept her past his budgeted time. When the door popped open, a swarthy man in a blue suit exited, calling back toward Valenti. "Please thank the president for me," he said in a heavy Middle Eastern accent.

"I'll pass along your appreciation," she replied.

The man closed the door and he turned to leave. Moving past the seated officer, the two visitors caught each other's gaze. They offered each other nods before the man disappeared into the hallway. Thinking his facial expression was a bit odd, the officer refocused on her briefing as the receptionist called to her.

"Ms. Valenti will see you now."

"Thank you." The officer proceeded into Valenti's office, finding the advisor shorter than expected, in contrast to her numerous television appearances. Professionally dressed and coiffed, the short-haired brunette's dark-rim glasses did nothing to alleviate her ratlike personae.

"What can I do for the SECNAV today, Lieutenant Commander?"

She removed a top secret file from her attaché case and handed it to Valenti. "He wished me to bring you up to speed on a matter that requires plausible deniability for the president."

"Really?"

As the senior advisor flipped it open to examine the photographs and documents inside, the officer began her briefing. "It has to do with the Neptune Project."

"Can't say I'm familiar with that one."

"It was classified in 1850, when a refitted pirate vessel, designated *Neptune's Trident*, disappeared along with her captain, Vernon Tunney."

"Go on."

"We believe the vessel resurfaced from obscurity and that there's a danger of it falling into enemy hands."

"What evidence leads you to that conclusion?"

"Three years ago, a British weather satellite captured video of an unusual water displacement moving away from the Shetland Mainland. Its excessive velocity and signature transposition are alien to any waterborne movement they're familiar with. London approached us for help in identifying the anomaly."

"And?"

"We couldn't make anything of it at the time. However, we recently documented a similar phenomenon fifty nautical miles south-south-west of the Strait of Magellan and again a week later in the Philippine Sea."

"And what does any of this have to do with the Neptune Project?"

"The speed and description of eyewitness accounts in this file suggest it's *Neptune's Trident*. We used a variety of visual spectrums, including thermal imaging, but couldn't identify a heat signature from its power plant. And biologics can't move that fast. The only way to locate it is through its water displacement signature or line of sight. In this case, searching for such an object is nearly impossible."

"Nearly?"

"We'll work on it, ma'am."

"I'd expect no less. Is that all?"

"No, ma'am. I also have the unenviable duty to report that due to the PRISM program debacle, we stumbled on evidence that someone is using a White House IP address to telegraph operational instructions to our enemies."

"Who?" Valenti asked, outraged.

"We don't have that information yet, but we're working to identify him."

"Very well, I'll brief the president. He'll want the answer to that question the moment you find out anything, Commander."

The officer thanked Valenti and departed. Not certain of the suspected operative's identity, she couldn't share his name with the advisor without concrete evidence. It was information she hoped the other two operatives would bring with them. Before she could report back to the SECNAV, she had one more errand to run—a quick stop at the Office of the Director of National Intelligence.

Waiting behind the wheel of his gray Beemer along the White House's secured 17th NW Avenue parking area, the driver observed a man in a blue suit exit the West Wing with a cell to his ear. A second later, a heavily accented voice came over the speaker system. "It's her. She's in with Valenti now."

"Did you get a name?" the driver asked.

"Montgomery. A Navy lieutenant commander."

"The one I followed from the SECNAV's office?"

"Positive ID. She was spotted near your downrange meetings for the past year and a half. What do you want me to do?"

"If her next stop is where I think it is, I won't be making the Reston meeting on time tonight, Fuad. You'll have to take the lead until I get there. You know what to do."

The driver swung his laptop cradle around to open it. He hacked into the White House SIPRNET and accessed the secure Navy portal and its worldwide list of navy dot-mil email addresses. Word-searching the name Montgomery, it listed five lieutenant commanders with the name, two of them women. One of the two women's official photo was an exact match to the officer he followed: Lieutenant Commander Laurie Montgomery; previous posting, Portsmouth Navy Yard, Maine; current posting, classified. After scrutinizing her personal information, including a photocopy of her driver's license, he secured the laptop and waited.

Montgomery made her way out to her tan GOV, drove out of the parking area, and headed west toward the highway. The driver stuck close to her as she crossed the Potomac. She took the northbound off-ramp on the GW Memorial Parkway, the opposite direction from the Pentagon. A twenty-minute ride later, she took the cloverleaf exit to Dolly Madison Boulevard. Skipping past the turn into the CIA headquarters at Langley, Montgomery headed for the National Intelligence Building.

There was no choice now. He made his decision. Visualizing the address on Montgomery's driver's license, he mapped the quickest route to the officer's residence in Alexandria, Virginia. The man behind the Simulacra Viro personae smiled.

FIFTY TWO

"Something isn't right," said Terrie, clearly frustrated.

"What do you mean?" asked Taro.

"We've run the list of anyone who could possibly have access to the president and came up with nothing."

"And no matches to your voiceprint," Theo added.

"Then it has to be somebody one step removed from an appointee," Bannerman suggested.

"It could be a czar we know nothing about." Jack said.

"Doubtful." Theo responded. "They'd still require clearance to access any IP address in the White House, and that would require chief of staff approval."

Taro theorized, "What if the chief of staff didn't approve it, but the president did?"

"It's possible," Jack responded.

Ever skeptical, Terrie shook her head. "I don't think so. We've eliminated all other alternatives. All things being equal, we must assume the target has to be one of the advisors not requiring senate confirmation, but who?"

"There can't be that many unconfirmed advisors," Taro added. "By the latest count there are thirty-plus so-called czars alone."

"That's not many," Jack thought out loud.

Theo piped in. "We've been through the czars, right after the official and 'unofficial' cabinet. Zilch."

"Then we'll have to scrub the list of their deputies to see if any of their underlings might have more power than we suspect," Terrie said.

The Ops Center door buzzed again. It was Crabtree, straight from the captain's office.

"Have you made any progress, Commander?"

"Sorry, sir. No one from the president's cabinet or his staff match the suspect voiceprint."

"That's unfortunate. We'll just have to proceed as ordered." With that statement, Crabtree had everyone's attention. "Captain Derrick briefed the SECNAV on the situation, so you can suspend work on your SITREP update, Commander."

"What's our course of action now, sir?" asked Bannerman.

"A field agent working at the SECNAV's end alerted the president's senior advisor. What he needs from us is someone familiar with the situation to brief the House Intelligence Committee chairman and then the director of national intelligence. He suspects someone at one of these agencies may be compromised, though the committee chairman is a close friend of his. Miss Murphy, Mr. O'Hara, I want you two to handle that. Watch each other's back on this."

"What do you want us to do, sir?" asked Taro.

"Where did you leave off in your investigation?"

"We've compared the White House staff and all the primary cabinet members and advisors against the suspect voiceprint and eliminated them all. We were about to look into their deputies."

"Good. Keep at it," said Crabtree. "Commander, you're with me. The captain has something she needs us to do."

"Yes, sir," Bannerman acknowledged.

"As for you two, gather up copies of whatever evidence you need to make your cases, and head down to Washington immediately."

"Aye, sir," said Jack enthusiastically.

Concerned over the direction of their investigation, Terrie simply nodded.

"We'll proceed as you suggest, Captain," said Crabtree with spring in his response.

"Very well, Commander. I'll expect you two to be ready the moment you hear from Miss Murphy or Mr. O'Hara."

"We'll be ready."

As Crabtree headed out of the office, the captain whispered to Bannerman, "Commander, might I have a word with you?"

"Yes, Captain." She waited with the captain for Crabtree to depart.

"What I'm about to tell you doesn't leave this room."

"Affirmative, ma'am."

"I understand you're searching for your former colleague, Lieutenant Commander Laurie Montgomery?"

"I've not heard from her in several weeks now. I'm worried."

"All the same, I must insist you be patient."

"Ma'am?"

"She's all right, and she's doing her job. That's all I can confirm at the present time."

"How–"

"The questions you're asking and the places you're asking them."

"Do you know where she is?"

"Presently? The only person who knows that is the SECNAV, and he was very adamant that you cease your activities in this regard. We don't wish to blow her cover."

"Understood, ma'am."

Jack knocked then came through Terrie's unlocked apartment door. "Hey, you about ready?"

"All packed. I figured we could stay at my Aunt Barbara's for the night before we hit DC in the morning."

"You're introducing me to family?"

"Not now, all right?"

"Well, I'm flattered."

"I wouldn't read too much into it if I were you."

Amused, Jack chuckled. "We'll see how your aunt feels about it."

"Want something to eat now or wait till we're on the road?"

"How long before we get to your aunt's house?"

"About eight hours."

"We should grab a bite now."

"I have breaded haddock fillets and dinner rolls. I could make sandwiches."

"Haddock burgers?"

"It won't take but a few minutes to cook up."

"I'll give it a whirl."

Terrie grabbed the fillets from the freezer and tossed them in the microwave to defrost. Waiting for the machine to complete its cycle, she appeared to stare at nothing.

"What's the matter?" Jack asked.

"Something's not right."

"Concerning?"

"Simulacra Viro. The dots aren't lining up."

"Dots?" he said in a deadpan voice.

"First off, he's tracking my movements, which means he's the source leading us on the Tunney investigation."

"Sounds plausible, since Ray told us his handler was receiving instructions from someone in the executive branch."

"And there are only so many IPs associated with the White House, correct?"

"Yeah."

"If this person's cyber activity was exclusive to a single address, we should have found him already."

"Sounds right." Jack watched her eyes flick back and forth as though she were speed-reading a printed overview of their day's efforts. "What is it?"

"Our adversary may have figured out how to bypass White House IT security protocols."

"A virtual personal network?"

"Sure, why not? Utilizing a disguised address, he could act from another location while sending out a false cyber trail."

"If true, this person might not be associated with the White House after all. We should get Theo on this before we head to Washington."

Terrie's cell was already in her hand. "Way ahead of you."

A weather warning flashed over the radio, downgrading the first hurricane of the season to a tropical depression. Even so, the waves were giving Philip's moored ship a good thrashing. Unable to maintain steady hands as he tried to increase his supply of facial appliances, he resigned the attempt.

Checking the parking lot, he spotted Terrie's Ford Edge in its reserved space. She was home early for some reason. The cloud cover was sufficient to require indoor lighting. Seeing the shadow of a table lamp across her kitchen cabinets, he knew she was home.

Hampered by discovery, he had to rely on older, yet reliable, methods of eavesdropping.

Philip placed the headphones over his ears and aimed the handheld dish toward her balcony. To his astonishment, the equipment captured their plans to head for Washington. He listened a while longer before deciding he'd gleaned all he was going to get from the two officers. He could now report back to Runner's representative about this latest revelation.

The phone rang only once before his handler picked it up. "What is it this time?"

"Aren't you in a mood."

"I'm late for an appointment. What've you got for me?"

"Thanks to that idiot hiding out in Davos, the lieutenant and her team have discovered messages sent from Runner's location that didn't originate from there. Do you know what that means?"

The man ignored the question. "Do they know who?"

"No."

"How sure are you?"

"The lieutenant said as much, but they're looking to track down the actual IP address."

"Oh," the man said flatly. Then, dead air.

"What do you want me to do about it?"

"Nothing. I've got this. You just stay on her and report back when you have news."

"Like the fact that she and her colleague are on their way to Washington?"

"Why didn't you tell me that earlier?" the man yelled, forcing Philip to pull the phone away from his ear for a second.

"I'm telling you now. What's the problem?"

His query only stoked the fire. "I question you, not the other way around, understood?"

"Ask the right questions next time," Philip said calmly before hanging up.

He followed the officers down the I-95 corridor, expecting them to take the quickest route to Washington. He was surprised to see them exit the turnpike for the Commodore Barry Bridge toward Claymont, Delaware.

FIFTY THREE

Terrie and Jack made it to her aunt's driveway in just under eight hours. Barbara was standing on the porch when they arrived.

As she walked over to them, Jack approached and introduced himself. "Jack O'Hara. So nice to meet you."

"Likewise, I'm sure." Casting a quick glance at Terrie, she added, "Since my niece isn't in the habit of discussing her friends."

Allowing his eyes to snap at Terrie for a moment, he extended his hand and replied, "We certainly have time to remedy that now, don't we?"

Terrie scowled.

Her aunt returned it. "And you were speeding, too, weren't you?"

"Not as far as you know," replied Terrie with mild sarcasm.

"If you left when Jack called me, taking into account the evening commute and your propensity for a lead foot, you shouldn't have arrived for at least another twenty minutes."

"Do you really have to do that?"

"Jack doesn't mind, do you, Jack?"

"Not at all."

"Let's get you two inside and fed. It's late enough as it is. Jack, you can take the bedroom at the far end of the hall."

The television was on, tuned to national news, the volume turned up higher than normal. Terrie thought it was bad enough that she had to watch this crap at work. "You want me to turn off the TV?"

"I just turned it on," her aunt barked. "It's been a few days since I caught up with current events. The luxury of being retired."

Terrie relented. "Whatever. Could I at least turn it down?"

"If you must. What do you want for supper?"

Jack returned from the back bedroom in time to hear the question. "What do you have?"

"I whipped up some fresh meat sauce yesterday," Barbara said with pride. "We could have it with pasta."

"Rigatoni?"

"Be ready in fifteen minutes."

Terrie observed the smooth back-and-forth between Jack and her aunt with a touch of jealousy for how quickly they established a rapport.

Barbara cooked while looking over the counter at the tube. "Jack, do you like your rigatoni al dente?"

"That's fine."

The meteorologist stood in front of the animation. She rambled on about the remnants of the recent hurricane and the regional five-day forecast to come.

"What brings you down so soon?" Barbara asked her niece. "I thought you wouldn't be here until this weekend at the earliest?"

"We have business in Washington."

"That makes sense. You brought Jack along with you, so naturally it's duty related. Anything having to do with your last visit here?"

Offering up another episode of hands-on-the-hip snark, Terrie quipped, "It doesn't always have to be a massive conspiracy, you know. It could be a simple conference."

"Of course." Barbara grinned and returned to her culinary duties.

A pause in the conversation allowed Terrie to change gears. "Aunt B, to erect secure firewalls you must have examined various ways adversaries attempted to breach your security, right?"

"That's how you beat them. To think like them."

"Then you know some inventive ways to communicate a message by not sending one?"

Still attending to her cooking, she asked, "How do you mean?"

"I'm trying to help one of my colleagues locate a friend. I've exhausted every resource I can think of but failed to locate her. With your background in security, I was hoping you might have some suggestions to put me on the right track."

"What clues are you working with?"

"A single discrepancy that's out of character. She sent a blank postcard, except for the addressee's information. If I were trying to send a message without actually saying anything, how would I do it?"

"It depends on the message. If there's nothing written, she might've tried to convey it with the card itself, through its pictures or symbols. Were there any on the card?"

Terrie remembered the underscores in the paragraph. Grabbing her smartphone, Terrie opened her search engine and hunted for the postcard on the web. She could find few examples offered up by the Afghan ministry of tourism, but it was enough to get the general idea. Clicking on a similar photo, she showed it to Barbara.

"The postcard resembled this one, but the subject showed Afghan rugs with a brief paragraph on their history. Four letters, Ke and To, were underscored within a single line."

"Not a single sentence?"

"No."

"Do you remember the paragraph exactly?"

"I do. Ke was underlined in Kelim and the To in Today, which began a new sentence at the end of that line."

"Were there any other combinations of those exact letters within the paragraph?"

"There were several, one with the word To appearing before Keeping in one contiguous line."

"Then the underscored order meant something."

"Agreed, since the correspondent ignored two other permutations of the combination."

"In trying to decipher the message, we usually rely on the answer to three basic questions."

Jack piped up, "Animal, vegetable, or mineral?"

"As the exact presentation of the letters KeTo don't match anything on the periodic table, I think we can infer the answer isn't mineral."

"Person, place, or thing?" Terrie said.

"If you're searching for a person, the clue would likely be their name or their location. Both would be capitalized. Remember, sending a message with limited options, you keep it simple."

"Okay, but that still leaves us with—"

Terrie's thought was interrupted by a breaking news segment. It wasn't the reporter so much as the feed from the video clip she introduced that caught her attention. Something about a policy meeting between the Congressional Democratic caucus and the president's special counsel for Islamic relations. The clip began with the special counsel summarizing the takeaways.

"What's wrong, Terrie?" Barbara asked.

Without responding, she scrolled her contacts, looking for Bannerman's cell number. She got straight to the point after Bannerman picked up. "Commander, do we have any footage of the president's special counsel for Islamic relations available?"

"We might, why?"

"Turn on cable news. The Congressional Democratic caucus policy meeting story." She waited as Bannerman did so. "Do you hear it? It could be a long shot, but I think we've got him."

"It might be him," Bannerman said. "We'll have to get Theo to verify it. Well done. Oh, Miss Murphy, one more thing."

"Yes?"

"I can't get into it over the phone, but you can hold off on the favor I asked of you."

"Then you've resolved that issue?"

"For now, yes."

"So long as you're sure."

"I am. Thank you, Miss Murphy."

As Terrie ended the call, Barbara announced that dinner was ready.

Philip returned to his safe house to obtain a local vehicle and a quick meal before he took position across the street from the home of Barbara Forester. He turned on the listening device to catch their dinner discussion, mainly small talk. Nothing was mentioned about their mission, except that they would be keeping their appointments in the morning. Gleaning all he was going to get, he decided to pack up and return to the safe house in order to prepare for the busy day ahead.

"Well, thank you, Aunt Barbara. That meal was wonderful," Jack offered.

"She's not your aunt!" Terrie yelled.

"Well, I'm adopting him anyway, missy," her aunt rebuked. "Besides, he's every bit the gentleman."

"On that score, I'm inclined to agree." She meant it more than her words conveyed. Just as the mood brightened, Terrie's cell buzzed to life.

"Terrie, it's Theo."

"Bannerman called you in, didn't she?"

"No problem. You're not going to believe this."

"It's Kerlin Tozer, isn't it?"

"You knew?"

"Let's just say someone you worked with is already on the case."

"Who?"

"Lieutenant Commander Montgomery. It would appear she's been tracking Tozer for the past year."

"Well, not only does he match the voiceprint on all the recordings, he's had an interesting career."

"Tell me."

"He's been into everything, including having his private IP address linked to the White House, yet no one's ever really caught on to his shenanigans."

Impatient, she blurted out, "Cute. Cut to the chase. What did you find out?"

"Kerlin Tozer emigrated to the United States from Iran in 1979, just prior to the taking of the American embassy. A person of Swiss-Iranian descent, his strong Caucasian features led many globalist magazines to term him the American Imam. He graduated from Harvard Law School in 1988, and his burgeoning political resume touts many hats that flew under the radar."

"Such as?"

"He first came to prominence as deputy associate counsel to the president in 2009. Demonstrating his value to the administration, he moved up the DHS food chain until he was offered the job of deputy assistant secretary for policy development prior to election season last year."

"I see. His low-profile position kept him from notice while granting him the ability to influence policy," Terrie added.

"And influence it, he did," Theo continued, "As underling to the administration's Sharia czar, he accused the previous administration of perpetrating a war against Islam and Muslims. He branded the conviction of Shukri Abu Bakr for his financial support to Hamas as illegitimate and politically motivated. His direct policy decisions have not only persuaded the media away from using the term jihad as a holy war, but managed to force federal law enforcement agencies to eliminate any attempts to associate Islam with terrorism."

"How far had he taken this infiltration?"

"He expanded a role for himself within the department, essentially becoming the administration's central clearinghouse on all Muslim-related matters, advising law enforcement agencies on what they can and cannot do."

"Do you know of any other methods he used?"

"Employing classified documentation, he drafted a false narrative to the Advisory Council, advocating the position that Islamophobia was widespread. Misusing this documentation, he coerced state governments to accede to Halal food law, encouraged Islamic prayers in state legislatures, and defended the anti-American Muslim Brotherhood during their Arab Spring. He used his position to strong-arm the exclusion of all council members from accessing the state and local intelligence community-of-interest report. Enforcing the false narrative that the US is an Islamic country with an Islamically compliant constitution, he was fast-tracked to the position of senior advisor at the Advisory Council, a title held by only a small number of select members. But the key is, these positions aren't required to have senate confirmation."

"Great job, Theo. I appreciate it."

After hanging up with Terrie, Bannerman called Crabtree.

He picked up on the second ring. "Crabtree."

"Commander, just heard from Miss Murphy. They've identified the target as Kerlin Tozer."

"The president's Islamic relations special counsel?"

"The same."

"Very well, then. Let's get going. We don't have a whole lot of time."

"Be ready in ten minutes."

FIFTY FOUR

Laurie Montgomery pulled her car into its reserved parking slot near her apartment building in Alexandria. She grabbed her purse from the passenger seat, beeped it locked, and headed for the front entrance. Her thoughts were filled with the satisfaction of knowing her most recent assignment would soon draw to a successful conclusion. The man she'd been tracking would be apprehended, largely due to her efforts and those of her former team members. She smiled thinking about it.

Standing at the front door fumbling with her keys, Laurie located the right one. She inserted it into the lock as a gloved hand reached from behind and covered her mouth, pulling her head backward. She tried to scream, but the perpetrator's grip was too tight. A vindictive voice whispered, "Such is the way with the kafirun."

With his free hand, he drew the blade across her creamy throat in a single, powerful thrust. He felt it graze the cervical vertebrae then sink between two of them, essentially decapitating his victim. Only a sliver of sinew and skin from the left side of her neck kept Laurie's head attached to her torso. Blood shot out of the fleshy stump in rhythmic pulses until her heart gave out.

The driver returned to his vehicle to retrieve fresh coveralls and disposed of the disguise that bore the evidence of his attack. The lights of his Beemer winked on as he got behind the wheel and depressed the start button. The echo of the car's engine died in obscurity long before the sound of the first siren making its way toward the scene of Alexandria's latest homicide.

FIFTY FIVE

"I don't like this, Terrie. Are you sure this is how you want to play it?"

"Come on, Jack. You heard Crabtree. If this is the compromised agency, one of us needs to proceed to the next briefing."

"But I'm not as versed in this thing as you are. And besides, it could be dangerous."

"I'll be all right," Terrie said, patting his hand and exiting their vehicle. In her formal whites with slim leather planner in hand, Terrie ascended the left staircase of the Rayburn House office building. Unfamiliar with the layout, she sought the guard near the glass doors. "Excuse me. I have an appointment with Congressman Latham, the House Intelligence Committee chairman. Can you direct me to his office?"

"The congressman's office is down the hallway to your left, past security. Follow it till you get to the first corridor on your right. It's the second office to the left."

"Thank you." After complying with security protocols, Terrie gathered up her things and marched down the hallway. She made her way into the office and waited until the administrator completed her phone conversation.

"Good morning, I'm Terrie Murphy. I have an appointment with Congressman Latham."

"I'm sorry, Miss Murphy, his committee is in session right now. The congressman asked me to direct you to one of the vacant subcommittee rooms. He'll meet you there as soon as he's free."

Terrie thanked her and followed the directions to a door with the subcommittee's name stenciled above it. She entered what she expected to be an empty room.

In the chairman's seat at the center of the curved desk was a forgettable man with unremarkable features. He wore a light gray suit with an ID badge hanging from a lanyard around his neck. The man with the crewcut and mirrored glasses maintained a disciplined countenance. As he looked up toward the clock above the private entrance, Terrie got a partial look at his profile. She'd seen his distinct cranial structure and that same wide smile before. The first time, behind the wheel of the parked car across the street from her Aunt Barbara's house, and again, near her apartment. A man whose smile could dissect his head. Terrie knew this guy wasn't the congressman.

He folded his arms, a hand still hidden under his blazer. "So wonderful to finally meet you in person, Miss Murphy. You certainly led us on a merry chase."

Terrie stared down her adversary with a steely-eyed gaze. "Led who?"

"Come now, Lieutenant. You're not going to claim ignorance, are you?" The man unfolded his arms, his right hand holding a snub-nosed revolver. His left manipulated a thick, cylindrical piece of metal over it and began screwing them together. Completing the task, he took aim in Terrie's direction.

"I don't believe dragging around a corpse in a blood-spattered white uniform is a good career move for you."

"You forget where you are. In this town, people disappear all the time, and none's the wiser for it."

More angry than frightened, her voice got faster and louder. "Spill it! Who the hell are you?"

He maintained his calm demeanor. "Don't be so naïve, Lieutenant."

Terrie folded her arms and waited for an answer.

"If it matters, you can call me Philip."

"That's not what I meant and you damned well know it!" Her impatience showed with a vengeance.

"Very well. I report to the member of Runner's staff who doesn't appear on his official table of organization."

"And what do you truly know about this so-called staff member?"

Philip only returned the thousand-yard stare. It was becoming obvious he wasn't the top dog.

Terrie shook him with a determined smile. "Ah, so you don't know everything, do you?"

"What is it you think you know?"

Terrie tapped her planner. "Apparently more than you do, since he's not what he claims to be."

"And who do you think he is?"

"Not think. Know."

"I still don't hear anything that will keep me from doing what's necessary," he said, thumbing the hammer back with a metallic click.

"Whose voice was on the original six-minute audio I was ordered to delete from existence? An audio recording we still have, by the way."

Philip's eyebrows arched in a nonverbal query.

"Here's a hint. It's the same voice we identified on a recovered video from a zip drive that was also presumed destroyed. That video featured the killing of an interrogated witness by a radical Imam known as the Wraith. We've matched the voiceprints from both recordings to the identity of someone highly placed in DC politics. Someone with whom you are intimately familiar—senior White

House Counsel for Islamic Relations Kerlin Tozer. No doubt, your secretive staff member. Now do we have your attention?"

"Who's we?"

"Do you really think I'd come here alone and without a slam-dunk case against you?"

"Keep talking."

"Still not convinced?" Ignoring the silencer-tipped barrel pointing in her direction, Terrie walked around the conference table as she spoke. "My team is fully aware of how long it will take me to relay this information to the intelligence committee. Mr. Hattori has the PRISM records, and Mr. Theodore has the complete dossier on Tozer documenting his disloyal activities and that he's still looking for something thought buried on Badger Island in order to destroy it. Mr. Theodore connected the dots pertaining to Tozer, his Wraith personae, and his radical ties to terrorist organizations like the Islamic State and its various metastasized offshoots. My entire Portsmouth command structure, from Captain Derrick on down, was individually briefed on the situation before my arrival. Senior Chief Sheffield has admitted to his complicity in working with you, has accepted nonjudicial punishment, and is officially retired. As a security measure, Commanders Crabtree and Bannerman are in a secure location waiting for me to report, along with the originals of every piece of evidence I intend to present to the committee chairman. If I don't respond at the appropriate time, everything we've uncovered becomes public knowledge. You will be the hunted one, not us. It would be in your best interest to cooperate now."

Philip considered his position, the gun still pointing in Terrie's direction.

"Well? If you're going to kill me, get on with it; otherwise, I have a meeting to attend. Or better yet, you can join me."

"What do you propose?"

"Up till now, you've done nothing that could be construed as treasonous. Though you failed to identify the Wraith, if you'd bothered to study Executive Order 13224 for yourself, you'd have found him: Kedar Ra'id al Husam al Din, the leader of the Muslim Illuminati. Beyond his inner circle, he's known by the familiar nom de guerre, the Wraith."

"And you have the documentation to prove all this?"

"We have his travel itinerary with the secretary of state from 2009 to 2012, which matches the times, dates, and locations where Ra'id held meetings, including a video with him talking. Voiceprint analysis proves Tozer is Ra'id. If you elect to cover for him, I don't believe the intelligence committee or Runner would look kindly on it. After all, your pending actions could either carry grave consequences for the country and your boss, the president, or you could be instrumental in saving both from significant embarrassment."

The ashen color emerging on his features confirmed he was genuinely in the dark about Runner's counsel being a spy. However, he had one card left to play. "What about those reference books I know you never gained access to at the classified library at Newport?"

"What makes you think I haven't accessed the secrets those books contained already?" she said.

"Because they don't exist any longer, as far as you know."

"Apparently you missed the copies located at the J. Welles Henderson Archives and Library, because Dr. Dagney removed them before someone trashed his office." Watching Philip turn a bright crimson, she added, "Using those books and that file from the war college's classified library, Tozer expected to find either the 'cursed' volumes or the *Neptune's Trident* on Badger Island, didn't he?"

"Very good, lieutenant. We were going to call the mission a success since we had the alloy and the logbook, but the sample alloy you found couldn't be duplicated without the books that described how it was made. We had no choice but to encourage you to continue your investigation in hopes you would lead us to either the Lost Books or the *Trident*. Our government couldn't allow that ship or the Lost Books to fall into nefarious hands. You're quite a resourceful young woman, Terrie."

She raised an eyebrow. "Are you always on a first-name basis with those you threaten to kill?"

"Kill?" Philip chuckled. "Not today, Lieutenant." He stowed the hammer and relaxed his shoulders as he put the safety back on and removed the silencer. His eyes hinted toward the door. She took the hint.

Before she made her way out, she asked, "You're not coming with me? You'd be more convincing than I."

"Sorry, but thanks to you, I now have another loose end to attend to."

Terrie assumed she knew what it was as she smiled and headed out the door.

There was something about this young firebrand that appealed to his sense of patriotism. Philip couldn't suppress his amusement, though his next move was already weighing heavy on his mind. That thought didn't have time to complete its complicated circuit through his brain before a muffled popping noise, like someone spitting out a sunflower seed, reached his ears.

In that instant, a vice squeezed his lungs, the wind knocked out of him as though he'd forgotten how to breathe. Bringing his hands to his chest, he felt something warm and wet. His last conscious action was pulling his hands away to see his palms painted in a shiny viscous fluid. Oblivion claimed him as his vision darkened, the end credits rolling on his personal series finale.

The administrative assistant's face went white as a sheet when Terrie exited her meeting with the congressman. Two Capitol police officers were waiting for her.

The tall one gave Terrie a stern look. "Lieutenant Terrie Murphy?"

She responded in the affirmative.

"Please turn around with your hands behind your back. You're under arrest."

FIFTY SIX

Jack was listening to the car radio when he saw the commotion. Several Capitol police officers rushed up the stairs, guns drawn. They disappeared into the building for what seemed like an eternity. Minutes later, he saw Terrie being led out of the building in cuffs.

Before he could react, an unmarked black van raced into position, and its side door slid open. The policemen on either side of Terrie directed her into the van. The door shut as it whisked away toward Constitution Avenue.

Jack looked around for his missing phone until he saw it under a newspaper on the passenger seat. He started the car as he called the Ops Center supervisor's number. It auto-transferred to Commander Bannerman.

"Commander, it's Jack. We have a problem."

⚓

The officer who placed the handcuffs on Terrie sat across from her with a look of utter disgust. She studied the watch on his wrist as the windowless van proceeded to its destination.

"We aren't going to either the Capitol or DC police station, are we?"

"Quiet," the police officer growled.

"If we were, we'd be there already. Both are only a few blocks away from the Rayburn, and it's been seventeen minutes since we left. Where are you taking me?"

"Shut up!"

"Because I have a right to remain silent doesn't mean I'm going to. Now, where are you taking me?"

His flushed cheeks telegraphed his irritation. "One more word out of you—"

"And what? You'll shoot me? If you were going to do so, you'd have done it already. You can't be genuine police officers, since you failed to charge me or read me my rights. Who are you?"

The man gave Terrie a resigned look before turning his attention to the front of the van to check on their progress.

"Based on the turns we've made so far, we must have just entered the cloverleaf to Dolly Madison Boulevard."

His surprised expression gave the game away. "You'll find out shortly. Now, shut up!"

Terrie relaxed as much as she could with her hands secured behind her back. She recognized the last turn into the parking lot for the DNI building, but for some reason, the van felt as if it were moving down a slope. They must have entered the secure garage in the basement. This was getting interesting.

Crabtree and Bannerman waited in their GOV for Terrie or Jack's signal. Should they not receive a call from either of them by 10:45, the captain's orders were to address the situation with the president's senior advisor and the Senate Intelligence Committee chairman.

The captain thought it would be a prudent idea to brief both at the same time as to which agency the president should be concerned about, the House Intelligence Committee or his own director of national intelligence.

They sat quietly in the car, waiting on a phone call when the commander's cell rang.

"Crabtree... Yes, sir?... Oh... Yes, Mr. Secretary, she's here with me." He handed his cell to Bannerman and in a gentle voice, said, "It's the SECNAV. For you, Molly." The commander's tender demeanor and the use of her first name could only mean bad news.

"Lieutenant Commander Bannerman." The long seconds elapsed as she took in the news the SECNAV relayed, her eyes swatting back and forth as though reviewing the same sentence over and over as she tried to process what she was being told. The invisible dam burst, releasing a well of tears that streamed down her cheek and on her uniform. "Yes, sir... I understand, sir... We will, sir." Bannerman's gaze never wavered as she lowered the cellphone and thumbed the red icon to close the call.

Crabtree reached out for her hand and clasped it lightly. "I'm sorry, Molly."

Doing her best to maintain her bearing, Bannerman regained control of herself and looked his way, shaking his hand in a gesture of solidarity. "I'm all right, sir. Let's get back on mission."

"You're sure?"

"For Laurie, sir." Her words had barely left her lips when another call came in. This time on her phone. "Bannerman."

"Commander, it's Jack. We have a problem."

She responded with restored bearing. "What is it, Lieutenant?"

"Terrie's been arrested and taken away in a large black van."

"Who was it?"

"I'm not sure. Several officers entered the Rayburn with guns drawn. Minutes later, a different set of officers brought Terrie out as a van rushed to the curb to take her away. I'm in pursuit now."

"All right. Let us know where they take her."

"Affirmative, Commander."

"And Jack, one more thing."

Bannerman's voice faltered as she relayed the painful news about Laurie.

FIFTY SEVEN

"I must apologize for the way you were conducted here, Lieutenant Murphy," said the national intelligence director. "It wasn't my intention to be so melodramatic."

"False imprisonment and kidnapping are charges that carry hefty consequences, Director," Terrie announced.

"Please, have a seat." The director alluded to one of a dozen chairs by the conference table that contained her personal effects. Reaching across his desk to pick up a manila folder, he sat across from Terrie and blurted out, "It's Tozer, isn't it?"

Terrie observed the director to test his reaction. "The evidence does lead us in that direction, yes."

The director looked resigned to whatever plan was the last option. "Lieutenant Murphy, while I laud your efforts and those of your colleagues, I must now ask you and your team to stand down."

"Why?"

"Believe me when I say you don't have the wherewithal to deal with these people."

"Try me."

The director raised an eyebrow, unaware of the tenacity of Terrie Murphy. "All right. They call themselves the Muslim Illuminati, and they are the embodiment of the quintessential archenemy. They hope to destroy everything we hold dear by doing it from the inside and are willing to go to any extreme to make that happen. The scope of their operation is beyond your comprehension."

"And how does Tozer fit in?"

He looked askance at her. "We've been wary of him and his questionable advancement for quite some time. But the recent PRISM fiasco linking Tozer to this group compelled him to escalate his activities, forcing us to do likewise. That's when we used him to bring you on board."

"What led you to suspect Tozer?"

"It was his proximity to Ra'id that first drew our suspicion. He was on nearly all of Secretary of State Pettibone's Middle East trips between 2009 and 2012. On the two trips she took in '09—the first in April to Iraq and Lebanon, and the second in November to the Philippines—Tozer was with her. As the secretary was meeting with local leaders in Baghdad, Ra'id reportedly held a meeting with local Imams in Sha'ab. During this meeting, he learned of a sighting of a red wraith in the early '90s. The next day, as the secretary was in Beirut for a meeting with the Lebanese foreign minister, Ra'id was again spotted with local Imams. When the secretary announced the administration's new disaster relief program with the Philippine foreign minister in Manila, Ra'id was photographed that same day in Quezon, where he learned of another sighting of the red wraith near Jolo."

Terrie listened intently to the director's outline which matched her intelligence to the letter.

"Tozer also accompanied the secretary on her October 2011 trip to Kabul to meet with President Karzai and other civil leaders to discuss the volatile situation in Syria. On that day, Ra'id met with local Imams to debrief them on the Arab Spring six months earlier.

"When the secretary landed in Paris on July 6, 2012, a subject identified as Ra'id was photographed at a meeting with known Muslim radicals. The very next day, Tozer was in Kabul with the secretary's entourage. Miraculously, the image of Ra'id was captured in Kabul at the same time. But it's Tozer's solo trips to Tunisia and Baghdad last year that really caught our attention."

"Explain," Terrie said with more authority than intended.

Letting her attitude slide for the moment, the director answered her. "His meeting in Tunis with local Imams one month before the attack on Benghazi red-flagged Tozer for us, but the executive branch brushed it under the carpet. Not politically convenient during an election year."

"What do you mean?"

"The president was insistent that the Global War on Terror was over, and therefore, a subject no longer to be brought up. It had to be nixed from the news cycle and the public conscience to maintain his chances for reelection."

"I'm not a politician, Director. I'm an intelligence officer. Thanks to numerous incontrovertible sources, I already know why our embassy in Benghazi was targeted."

Folding his arms at this upstart, the director said, "Please enlighten me, Lieutenant."

"Secretary Pettibone's 2011 missions abroad laid the groundwork to support Syrian resistance against the Assad regime. The secretary hoped that, amid the chaos of the Arab Spring, she could meet with resistance leaders in Libya to find a diplomatic solution to the Syrian crisis before the election. Unfortunately, the ongoing revolution in Libya became the springboard for groups like Ansar al-Sharia and the Islamic Maghreb. Early on, these groups surveilled the secretary and discovered our embassy was being used by the CIA to run weapons to Syrian rebels. This became the catalyst for their planned assault on Benghazi. But what I don't understand is how the red wraith fit into all of this?"

Keeping his arms folded, he replied, "During the meetings conducted by Ra'id, rumors trickled in concerning sightings of the red wraith. You know it as the *Neptune's Trident*. Angered by these continued reports, Ra'id demanded a special meeting in Baghdad to deal directly with this threat."

"Al-Ghazali style, no doubt?"

The director dipped his head to acknowledge her contribution.

"Was that the only reason for his trip to Baghdad?" she asked.

"Ra'id went to Sha'ab to lay out his three-pronged plans to destabilize Western governments: infiltrate to undermine from within, establish a global caliphate, and find and destroy the red wraith. At a meeting on September 9th near Reston to solidify his plans, he discovered one of his US-based Imams was compromised."

"Compromised? How?"

"This agent actually witnessed the apparition, but Ra'id never found out who it was. His purpose in these two meetings was to stifle rumors of its invincibility through an official fatwa. To even speak of it in casual conversation meant severe consequences."

"Death or worse?"

"Very likely," the director confirmed. "It is this subject that we and Tozer's group have in common. We both want to find the *Trident*, but for very different reasons."

"Director, despite your best efforts to hide it, the early newspapers of the day have enough information regarding the *Dey of Reckoning*, Captain Tunney, and the demise of the *Crescent* in the public domain to piece together what's happened. You couldn't hide enough of the source documents to cover this up."

"Thanks to your efforts, no."

"What makes finding this vessel such a priority?"

"It's not only the vessel for what it is, but the documents used in its design."

"Books found aboard the *Dey of Reckoning*, right? Referred to as the 'cursed volumes?'"

The director didn't answer this time.

"Who wrote them, Director?" she queried. "You know I'll find out anyway, so why not tell me?"

"His name was Qassim, a Muslim scientist and contemporary of al-Jazari."

Terrie made the connection. "Go on."

"Known by no other name, Qassim was only forty-six when he died. He attended Qarawiyyin University from 1178 to 1183 before transferring to Nalanda. While at Nalanda, Qassim wrote his most influential works, from which only five books had survived the destruction of Nalanda in 1193. An avid disciple of scientific method and experimentation, he followed the teachings of Alhazen and, likewise, studied the works of al-Farabi. Like Aristotle, al-Farabi believed in the superiority of reason over revelation. Qassim later befriended al-Jazari."

"I still don't understand. Why all the secrecy? And what makes this Qassim important enough to kill for?"

"Are you aware of the fate of the ancient libraries that followed Alexandria?"

"According to one unaltered Colonial era newspaper, the destruction of three of them was linked to those 'cursed volumes.' The dates of their destruction matched the demise of the libraries at Nalanda, Baghdad, and Constantinople."

"You're very astute, Lieutenant. Did you ever find out why?"

"No. They didn't appear to be linked."

"What you were assigned to retrieve for us was none other than Qassim's master works, the Lost Books of Nalanda."

"I'm not familiar with those."

"A brilliant man, Qassim adapted two of al-Jazari's inventions for his own use—the reciprocating piston and the crankshaft—to develop the world's first internal combustion engine and the self-propelled torpedo. His five books covered metallurgy, nautical propulsion, weaponry, mechanical automation, and echolocation.

In 1193, a Turkish Muslim laid siege to Nalanda in search of the heretical tomes, destroying the library in the process."

"I know that story, but how does that sacking relate to the other libraries?"

"Qassim had secreted his life's work to the Imperial Library of Constantinople, where they remained safe for eleven years. In 1204, the Knights of the Fourth Crusade caused considerable damage to the library looking for those books, but without success. Though Qassim died trying to protect the five precious tomes, a confederate managed to whisk them away to the Bayt Al Hiqma in Baghdad."

"The House of Wisdom?"

"You know your history."

"That library was destroyed in 1258," Terrie added.

"But not before a loyal librarian had the Lost Books returned to Constantinople. There, they found a safe harbor until 1453, when the Turkish leader, Mehmed II, completed what the Templars failed to do—the total destruction of the library."

"I take it from your subsequent direction of my actions that you know what happened to the them after that?"

"In the swinging pendulum of militant religious brinkmanship, Cardinal Ximenez and the Knights Templar reclaimed the Lost Books during their 1565 Siege of Malta. Since then, their fate remained a mystery until they were rediscovered in the captain's hold of the *Dey of Reckoning* during an inspection of its hull in 1788."

"And now? Do you know where they are?"

"Miss Murphy, the Lost Books of Nalanda have never been recovered. Neither had the *Neptune's Trident*, which was why you were given the Badger Island assignment in the first place. I was informed that we'd find the books, if not the location of the *Trident*. My source was mistaken."

"And that source was Tozer."

"Gold star, Lieutenant."

"So, why place a top secret classification on the destiny of the *Trident*, Captain Tunney's whereabouts, or his ship's actions after 1850?"

The director looked at the manila envelope on the conference table before placing a hand over it. He then turned his gaze to Terrie. "I consider myself a good judge of character and believe you to be an honorable person, Miss Murphy. However, any suspected action of Captain Tunney or his vessel subsequent to 1850 must remain classified, I'm afraid."

"Despite my having evidence of those actions?"

"I admire your candor, young lady." The director shook his head in exasperated fashion. "I want you to consider such evidence as classified and to treat it accordingly. Is that understood?"

She folded her arms and stared at him.

The director appraised his audience, ignoring her attitude again. "Miss Murphy, you've been unwittingly drawn into a situation you have no business in. Let's leave it at that. I'm now ordering you to—"

"To what? To not discuss this with the appropriate congressional oversight committees? Too late."

"Your rash actions are why we have a man at University Hospital, either dead or dying."

"What are you talking about?"

"Philip, the man you were talking to this morning, was gunned down in the Rayburn House office building shortly after you were with him."

"You think I had something to do with it?"

"It was likely Tozer, but it gave us the opportunity to get you out of the building and bring you here before he could target you."

"Me? Why?"

"You were getting too close."

"And what are you doing about him?"

"Nothing at present. We're not in a position to present our case before the DOJ."

"Well, you may be the director, but you still have a boss. We'll take this up with Runner directly."

An evil smile graced his countenance, scaring Terrie for the briefest of seconds. "Miss Murphy, I am Runner."

"But that's the president's code name."

"It was before the election. Due to this situation with Tozer and for ongoing security reasons, he agreed to change it for his second term. I'm using it now. As far as Tozer was concerned, it wasn't changed." The director's intercom buzzed. "Yes, Miss Purdy, what is it?"

"The SECNAV is on line one for you, Director."

"Thank you." Switching lines, he picked up the handset to take the call. "Tom, what can I do for you?"

"Did my emissary, Lieutenant Commander Laurie Montgomery, make it to your office yesterday?"

"She did, yes. And she gave us exactly what we needed."

"Hopefully, it was enough."

"That sounds ominous."

"Then you haven't heard? The Alexandria sheriff's department called early this morning. They found Laurie Montgomery brutally murdered near her apartment."

With the phone still clasped to his ear, he turned to look at Terrie. "This isn't a good time to discuss it. I'll get back with you in twenty minutes." He ended the call and stood up. "Miss Murphy, unfortunately, I have a pressing issue I must see to. I'll have someone take you to your car."

"Not necessary, Director. If I may use my cell?"

"You may."

She called Jack.

Jack's blood pressure threshold reached a new personal record when his cell erupted into Twisted Sister's "We're Not Gonna Take It." It was the perfect ringtone for his irrepressible colleague. "Terrie! What the hell happened?"

"Cool your jets. I'm fine. Where are you?"

"In the parking lot of the DNI building. Want me to come get you?"

"Why, you old bloodhound! Stay there. I'm on the way out."

Jack peered across the building's entrance to find Terrie on her way down the stairs. Running briskly, she made it to the car and opened the door. "Jack, we have to find Laurie. She's the one who knows where we can locate Tozer."

Terrie didn't notice Jack's face until she was situated in her seat and belted up. "What?"

"Laurie was killed in Alexandria this morning. Her apartment's now a crime scene, so I doubt we'll get anywhere near it."

"I'm sorry, Jack," said Terrie, getting an empty feeling in the pit of her stomach.

"I didn't really know her. The person who did was the one who informed me."

"Bannerman." Terrie's emotions rushed to the surface.

"I'm concerned for the commander. They were best friends. She never had the opportunity to say goodbye. What do we do now?"

Terrie thought about the director. And Philip. "Head to the university hospital right now!"

"What's the urgency there?"

I don't have time to explain, but an inpatient there may have the answers we need."

"Who?"

"Sheffield's handler, that guy Philip."

"What?"

"He was waiting for me in the conference room where I was expecting the committee chairman. We talked for a while then I went to the chairman's office. That's when those charming gentlemen whisked me away to see the director of national intelligence. The director told me Philip was shot by Tozer."

"You mean both Philip and Tozer were in the same room with you?"

"Looks that way."

"Then he's completely aware of your conversation with this Philip guy?"

"It's a good bet he knows."

"Is he in any condition to talk?"

"We need to find out. Let's get to the hospital ASAP."

FIFTY EIGHT

With Jack in tow, Terrie walked up to the nurses' station on the recovery floor.

"Excuse me, I'm looking for a gunshot victim who was brought in earlier today. His first name is Philip."

"You don't know his last name?" the on-duty nurse asked.

"I'm on official government business, and he's a material witness. Now answer me. Is he here or not?"

"He's in surgery right now. When he comes out, he'll be in ICU until he's sufficiently recovered."

"Any idea when we'll be able to talk with him?"

"Not until tomorrow morning at the earliest."

Terrie handed her a card. "When he wakes up, I'd appreciate a call immediately. Is there a law enforcement presence around him right now?

"What for?"

"It's a national security matter. For his protection, he'll need to be guarded till he leaves the hospital."

"If I recognized your authority—"

"We're not leaving until that guard is in place."

The nurse glared at Terrie while deciding what to do. She relented and called the DC police.

Jack tapped Terrie's elbow. "We should check in with Crabtree and Bannerman. See what our next moves should be."

Matching the stare of the on-duty nurse while addressing Jack, she replied, "Stay here. Make sure security is in place while I go make the call."

⚓

"Bannerman."

"Commander, it's Lieutenant Murphy. We ended up at the DNI building."

"What happened?"

"I was 'invited' to a one-on-one with the director at his office. I have a little more insight into the overall situation but prefer not to go over it on an open line."

"Understood, Lieutenant. How did your briefing go?"

"The director countermanded the SECNAV's orders. What do you want us to do now?"

Conferring with Crabtree, Bannerman said, "We play the waiting game. Stand by for further instructions as we receive them."

"Aye aye, ma'am."

Terrie rounded the corner and approached Jack, who kept vigil near the nurses' station. "We're on hold for now. We should find a local hotel."

"Now I know why you keep that weekend bag in your car."

"You didn't bring yours?"

"Give me some credit, will ya? It's next to yours in the trunk."

"You're catching on." Terrie punched in the word hotel on her smartphone's map application. A number of them popped up, and she began calling. The hotel nearest the Washington Circle hospital was full and informed Terrie that it would be the same story for most of the hotels in the area due to several business conventions and a political rally over the next week. Completing her third call, she turned to Jack. "Okay, I got us a room at a hotel across the street from the hospital."

"How did you manage that one?"

"I could only get one room, so we'll have to share it."

A pair of police officers approached the nurses' station. The tall one approached the attending nurse and said, "We're looking for a Lieutenant Murphy."

"I'm Terrie Murphy," she called to them. "Thank you for coming so quickly. The subject is currently in surgery."

"What's his name?"

"Philip. We only have a first name," she responded, handing the officer her card. "I'd appreciate a call should anyone express an interest in him."

"Understood."

Security now in place, Terrie and Jack headed for the elevator.

The adjacent elevator dinged its arrival. Several people exited, including a hospital custodian in utility coveralls pushing a maintenance cart. Legitimate credentials were attached to a lanyard around his neck, but the name wasn't his. Neither was the photograph. It belonged to a similar-looking man whose body lay cooling at the bottom of a hospital dumpster.

The entrance to surgery room 3 was obstructed by two armed guards. Unable to get anywhere close to his target, Tozer cussed under his breath. Peering beyond the far end of the hallway, he spotted the maintenance storage room. He moved the cart down the hall and used the dead custodian's keys to enter the room. Pushing the cart inside, he closed the door behind him and grabbed his cell to make a call.

"Yes?"

"Fuad, my position's been compromised. You'll have to assume control of the meeting tonight."

"Understood. You wish me to brief the others?"

"All four principals must hear the plan at the same time. The five of you must be on the same page. We don't want anyone to feel betrayed by finding out about it later."

"Khalil, Jawad, and Salman have confirmed their attendance, but I haven't heard from Hashem yet."

"Very well. May Allah the Merciful bless our errand."

FIFTY NINE

"Come on! What's taking you so long?" Terrie emerged from the bathroom in a formfitting black jumpsuit that shocked Jack. "Where are you going dressed like that?"

"We are grabbing a quick bite for dinner."

"We're not going to the Library of Congress?"

"Why there?"

"We'd be idiots not to search the Library of Congress for that book we couldn't find in the NWC library. It's only a few miles away."

"The book is no longer in the Library of Congress, Philip saw to that. Besides, what if he gets out of surgery while we're there?"

"You've got a point."

Back into her investigation mindset, she remembered something about the Reston SD card. She grabbed her smartphone and began manipulating it furiously.

"Now what are you doing?"

She shushed him while speed-dialing someone. They picked up quickly.

"Yeah?"

"Theo, it's Terrie. I didn't catch you in the middle of anything, did I?"

"Taro and I are watching the game. What's up?"

"Could you go back to the office and pull up a couple of files from the Reston SD card for me?"

"You want me to send them to your secure email?"

"Not exactly. I'd like you to extrapolate the likeliest direction those pictures were taken based on the angle from a building behind the subjects. Can you do that?"

"What building are you talking about?"

"The USGS in Reston. They inadvertently captured it in two photos."

"Give me a couple of hours."

She thanked him and hung up.

"What are you thinking about now?" Jack said.

"Two pics from the Reston SD card were taken at a backyard party near the sight of Ra'id's Reston meeting place."

"And what possible good can that do us now?"

"Multiple subjects were photographed enjoying barbequed pulled pork and champagne, items forbidden by the Hadith. I guess the rules are different for their leadership."

"That goes for just about anyone in positions of power, doesn't it?"

Ignoring his sarcasm, Terrie continued, "My examination of the photographs revealed an unusual building in the background. It had two towers with sides resembling an eight-pointed star. The one to the left had four more floors than the one to the right. The taller tower's top floor was smaller in size and had only four sides. The only building I've seen in Reston with such an odd design was the J. W. Powell Federal Building, home of the US Geological Survey."

"So? Do you intend to go there?"

"Not yet, but if Theo can map out the compass orientation of the building, I might be able to pinpoint the location where the pictures were taken. That building is an hour and ten minutes away."

"Okay, so what do we do in the meantime? Just sit here? You were threatened by this Philip guy, cuffed and unceremoniously yanked off the case by the DNI, and now were sitting ducks for this—"

Terrie grabbed Jack by his face, drew him close, and planted a passionate kiss directly to his lips.

It took him a minute to snap out of it. "Not that I'm complaining, but what was that for?"

"Are you thinking of anything else right now?"

"Not really, no."

"Then it did its job. Now, relax."

"You want me to relax after that?"

"There's a burger joint two blocks up. Hopefully we'll hear something from Theo when we get back."

"Or the hospital," said Jack with unmistakable sarcasm.

SIXTY

Tozer restricted his movements to the areas around the surgical suites matching the custodian's usual rounds, so he could get close to Philip. He expended a discreet amount of time in each of the rooms to keep up appearances. Upon leaving the sixth room, he'd noticed the security officers were gone. He moved his contrived duties to the next agenda item on the schedule, the ICU.

☸

Her fists surrounded the burger as Terrie munched another big section of it.

Jack winced. "I really have to get you to stop that."

"It's how I eat. Get over it," she replied, gobbling up the last oversized piece in one bite.

Palms up in the air, he relented. "All right, already. I give up!"

Terrie softened her eyes and nodded. She reached for her drink when her phone chimed. It was the nurse's station. They were taking Philip to recovery.

☸

Tozer made his way into ICU, searching for a clue to Philip's whereabouts, but the patient's security escorts were nowhere around. Until they showed up, he was relegated to weaving through all the rooms, executing his fabricated custodial duties until he found the object of his mission.

He cleared ten rooms, but still no sign of Philip or the two policemen assigned to him. Frustrated, Tozer maneuvered his cart closer to the ICU nurses' station to catch a glimpse of the patient legend. Scanning the list, he didn't see Philip's name anywhere. If he wasn't in the ICU, they must have taken him directly to an inpatient room.

Terrie and Jack spotted the armed escort in front of Philip's room and made their way over to the nurses' station. She took out her credentials for the attendant's inspection. "He must be doing better than originally anticipated. We thought he'd be in the ICU?"

"His condition was upgraded to good following the surgery, so they just brought him here. He's not awake yet, but he should be soon if you care to wait."

"Thank you," she replied. "Can we wait in the room with him?"

"I don't see why not."

"I appreciate it."

They made their way to the security escorts who, recognizing Terrie and Jack, let them into the room. Terrie saw the undisguised profile of the man she'd met at the Rayburn a few short hours before. His breathing was a bit labored, but he no longer sounded like he was on death's doorstep.

"Philip? If you can hear me, it's Lieutenant Murphy. We officially met this morning."

Still under the lingering influence of general anesthesia, the bedridden man spoke. "A meeting with a relentless woman such as yourself isn't something one would forget."

"What happened?"

"Someone shot me after you left."

"You know who?"

"It had to be Tozer."

"The intelligence director would agree with you."

Philip's eyes met Terrie's. "Then you know where he is?"

"One of our agents was tracking him. She was found dead this morning near her apartment. You wouldn't know anything about that, would you?"

He shook his head. "Sorry."

"Do you know where Tozer could be right now?"

"He alluded to a meeting he had tonight. He didn't say where."

"You know who the attendees might be?"

"He was always having meetings. Never said with whom, but once. He called him Fuad."

"Our source says there are four more and that you know who they are. A collection of lawyer-partners belonging to a nationwide firm with their flagship office here in DC, right?"

Caught in his deception, he relented. "The firm's partners are from California, Florida, Minnesota, and DC. Khalil and his ever-present paralegal, Baraj, are from Washington. Jawad is based in Minnesota, Hashem in California, and Salman in Florida."

Terrie's lips curled up with recognition of each name. They were identified on numerous pictures on the Reston SD card. Fuad was one of the individuals in the foreground of the USGS building pic. "Then you also knew they were senior Imams with the Muslim Illuminati?"

"No, I didn't."

Terrie was about to ask him something else when a commotion occurred outside Philip's room. She heard two muffled noises and a heavy thud, like bodies hitting the floor. She gave Jack a nudge and whispered, "Cover the door."

"On it." He moved to the hinged side of the door and laid in wait.

Terrie moved the curtain around to prevent someone entering from seeing the patient. "Stay quiet," she whispered to Philip.

The door swung open, slow and silent. The first thing Jack saw enter the room was the smoking tip of a silencer. He looked near him for something to use as a club. With nothing handy, he waited until the intruder's arm was through the doorway. Jack used his knotted fists to knock the gun from the man's hand. Surprised, the intruder scrambled for the weapon only to be pounced upon by Jack. The two men wrestled on the ground, trying to get the fumbled weapon. The coverall-clad intruder elbowed Jack hard in the eye, knocking him over. As Jack tried to get up, the intruder kicked him in the head. Eying the unconscious form of Jack O'Hara, the intruder picked up the gun and turned to find Terrie standing before him.

The shock of seeing the woman he thought he'd dispatched earlier was all the delay Terrie needed. She executed a spinning wheel kick, tossing the gun across the room and out of sight behind the curtain. A subsequent kick sent a crushing blow against the man's left cheek, knocking him off balance but not to the ground.

He grabbed something taped to his ankle and held it out toward Terrie. "Not bad, young lady. You have nice moves."

"You'll find I'm full of surprises."

Using graceful steps, they circled each other, hands prepped for action. The intruder swept his blade in the air like a fan dancer. Closing the gap, she hit his armed fist with two opposing strokes, forcing the knife from his grip. A third strike knocked his arm out of the way, allowing her fourth one to cream the right side of his face. The intruder lost his footing but managed to evade her, affording him the opportunity to pick up the knife. Swinging it wildly, he backed her up enough to use his feet.

Terrie was unprepared for his kick. He applied its full thrust to her chest, knocking the wind out of her as she crashed against the bedside table and crumpled in a heap on the floor.

"So much for you two." Tozer grabbed Terrie by the hair, lifting her head to apply the optimum killing thrust. As he raised the blade's edge to her neck, an intense burning hit his shoulder. The blade sailed out of his hand. Defenseless, with no time to see who it was who shot him, Tozer made a hasty escape.

Jack and Terrie lay unconscious on the hospital room floor. Looking down at them, one hand on the wall and the other on the grip of Tozer's gun, Philip shook his head and smiled that smile. The one that nearly separated his jaw from his face.

SIXTY ONE

The harsh bed light revived Terrie with the mother of all headaches. She opened her eyes slowly, trying to focus on the dark shapes surrounding her. "Who…?" she mumbled.

"How are you feeling, Lieutenant?" asked the person closest to her.

"I've…been better. How long—"

"Two days," Crabtree volunteered. "You slept through everything."

"What?" Terrie asked, looking around the room at everyone for an answer. Recalling her last image of Jack, bleeding on the floor, she sat up the best she could. "Jack? Is he—"

"I'm right here, Terrie," he said from the foot of her bed. "I'm in better shape than you are."

Standing near Terrie's left hand, Bannerman smiled, but with the residue of a tear on her cheek. Looking up at her, Terrie asked, "What is it, Commander?"

"Between the intelligence we located inside Laurie's apartment, Taro's work with Prentiss, Theo's code-cracking and mapping skills, and your dogged determination with Jack, the FBI was able to apprehend the Reston Caliphate."

"Theo tracked down their meeting location?" asked Terrie.

"Two days ago," Jack responded, "When I came around and saw that Tozer had escaped, I got ahold of the commander. He coordinated with the White House senior advisor, who put the

FBI in motion. They were taken into custody that night, thanks to you."

"What about Philip?"

A man in Vice Admiral braids spoke. "An operative of mine on loan from the CIA, Miss Murphy. After he saved you and Mr. O'Hara here from a gruesome and untimely death, he pursued Tozer to Union Station. From there, he traced Tozer's movements to Times Square and LaGuardia. Unfortunately, Tozer made it out of the country. As of this morning, he's been reported in Beirut, Homs, and Najaf. We're keeping that information close to the vest for now. If Tozer believes he can move freely, we might find him faster."

"Admiral?"

"Bradley Timmons, Miss Murphy. The new chief of naval intelligence. You and your team flushed out a man the director of national intelligence only suspected was under his very thumb. We're indebted to you."

"Sir?"

"As recently as the last election cycle, we've known of an entity and their obsession with the *Trident* and the artifacts you've recovered. It wasn't until you were put on the case that the director began to suspect Tozer. While we're appreciative for the recovery of the artifacts like the odd-shaped alloy, we have no idea how to recreate it. The SECNAV and I just briefed the director. He'd like you to be our liaison in tracking down *Neptune's Trident* before Tozer or anyone else gets their hands on it or the Lost Books we suspect are still onboard."

"With all due respect, sir, how do you know that?"

"Based in no small part on your own intelligence, we believe those books never left the ship. We want you to find her, Miss Murphy. Will you do that?"

She turned briefly to Crabtree for approval. The commander nodded with a grin. "Do I have to leave Portsmouth, sir?"

"I think we can accommodate your request to remain in Portsmouth for the time being, Miss Murphy. We don't want to break up a winning team, do we?"

"Aye aye, sir."

"Meanwhile, I think we can allow you time to recuperate first, Lieutenant."

The admiral took his leave as Barbara came through the threshold. "Taking the world on by yourself again, young lady?"

Terrie had the do-you-have-to-embarrass-me-like-that look in her eyes. "I wasn't by myself. I had my team with me. Commanders Crabtree and Bannerman, this is my mother's sister." The two officers acknowledged Terrie's relative.

After Barbara reciprocated their social pleasantries, she addressed her bed-ridden niece. "You had to go there didn't you?"

"In Terrie's defense, she just came out of her coma an hour ago," Jack replied.

Barbara folded her arms. Swapping glances at both Jack and Terrie, she noticed the conspiratorial smirks on their faces. "All right, keep your secrets for now. You're in the intel business, after all."

Terrie scanned the faces surrounding her until she got to Bannerman. Reaching for the commander's hand, Terrie whispered, "I'm sorry about Laurie."

"Thank you, Terrie," Bannerman responded.

The women regarded each other silently.

I'm sorry I couldn't find her for you in time.

It wasn't your fault.

Crabtree interrupted. "Miss Murphy, you'll be on medical leave after your release from the hospital."

"That isn't necessary, sir."

"Sorry, Miss Murphy, but I concur with the doctor's orders."

Considering the IV in her hand and the concerned looks on the faces of all present, she relented.

"Right, well, we should be getting to it so you can get back on the mend," Crabtree suggested.

"I'd like a word with Miss Murphy, sir?"

"Take all the time you need, Mr. O'Hara."

As the door closed behind Crabtree, Bannerman, and Barbara, Jack approached Terrie. She turned toward him to appraise his expression—one of benevolent concern for a friend. He cupped her face in his palm, using his thumb to caress her temple.

"What are you doing?"

"Shut up," he whispered, smiling openly. "That's an order."

Her bank of energy spent, Terrie's eyelids collapsed under their own weight, surrendering to this insufferable man for the first time since they'd met. Her voice trailed off, making a final request. "Sing to me."

"All right." Continuing his ministrations, he sang to her. "I am a sailor. You're my first mate."

SIXTY TWO

Portsmouth, New Hampshire
Tuesday, August 6, 2013
06:12 hours

"Get up, sleepyhead. You'll be late for work!" yelled Jack through the closed door.

Terrie rolled a pair of bloodshot eyes at the clock and noticed she wasn't in her bedroom. "Give me a minute," she called out. Rising from her sofa, she dragged herself across the room to answer the door. She unlocked the deadbolt and moved into the kitchen to make breakfast.

Letting himself in, Jack eyed Terrie marching toward the counter like she was the living dead. "Still hunched over, I see. Your back okay?"

"No worse than it's been for the past few weeks," she muttered over her shoulder. "Thanks for asking. You want tea with a bagel and cream cheese?"

"Are you kidding? You still have to get ready for work, you know."

"Don't worry."

"I do. Where the hell were you last night? You didn't get back until after midnight."

"What are you, my father? I took the red-eye from Delaware Sunday night. Called Bannerman and told her I wouldn't be coming in until Tuesday morning."

"Why the hell not?"

"You are my father, aren't you?" she teased.

"You forget we had a date last night? What happened?"

"I'm sorry, Jack. You were preempted."

"By whom?"

"R. J. Clendaniel. I received a call from him Sunday morning. He wanted to meet with me yesterday."

"Concerning?"

"When they officially opened the condo, he was there to hand the propietor the keys. Someone was in the audience to see him."

"Who?"

"Would you believe Dr. Aponte?"

"That's amazing."

"She handed over his book and gave him a personal apology. She also relayed the entire story of how we chased down his book and what we did to get her to do the right thing. He offered me dinner and a conversation as a thank you."

A tinge of jealousy swept through him. "You? Not us?"

"Jack, someone else met him at the condo's grand opening. Someone he told me about when I first met him. It was his daughter. He wanted to share with me how that meeting went and what it meant to him to have his daughter back in his life. He did say he'd like to do a pizza thing with the two of us later, but this tale was something he wanted to share with me alone."

"Okay, I get it. This is a rapport deal, right?"

"You're getting good at this relationship thing, aren't you?"

"We'll work on that tonight, starting with dinner," he said with a smirk. "Meanwhile, can I get those to go?"

The toaster popped out its first bagel. She slathered the cream cheese on it quickly and poured some tea in a disposable cup with a lid. "Here you go. Let them know I'll be there."

Jack and Bannerman were listening to Taro describe the previous night's ballgame, when Terrie entered the conference room. "Good morning, everyone," she announced.

They echoed her cheerful good morning in unison. Bannerman added, "We missed you, Terrie. How are you feeling?"

"Much better now, thank you," Terrie responded. Looking around, she noticed Theo was missing. "Taro, where's your partner in crime?"

"He's still mourning Boston's loss to Houston last night," he joked.

"He's in another high-level meeting with the captain and the commander," responded Bannerman. "They've been having a lot of those the past few days."

Terrie's interest was piqued, concerned over the fate of her running partner's career.

"Theo's been looking kind of down lately, and I don't think it has anything to do with baseball," Jack offered.

"We'll find out soon enough," Bannerman said as the door swung open. She stood up and announced, "Captain on deck." Everyone got to their feet as Derrick, Crabtree, and Theo came through the threshold.

"As you were," Derrick said. Everyone took their seats. "I have some news, but before I disclose it, Lieutenant Theodore has something he'd like to share with you. Lieutenant?"

Theo faced his colleagues with an uncharacteristic awkwardness. "I consider everyone in this room my friend. And as such, I'm ashamed to say I've kept something from nearly all of you. I did so because I didn't want you to think less of me." His glance fell on Terrie. She nodded her encouragement. "While returning from a classified assignment three years ago, I had an accident that resulted in the loss of my left foot."

The gasps filled the room, but Terrie remained strong for him so he could finish what he had to say.

"This should have ended my Navy career, but Captain Derrick pushed to keep me in the service. And with the assistance of the person I thought least likely to help me, I became the first amputee to successfully complete the new PRT requirements to remain in the Navy." All of his teammates stood and applauded. "Terrie, I have no words meaningful enough to thank you for what you did for me."

Everyone turned their surrpised glances to Terrie who responded smoothly, "You're still in uniform, Theo. That's thanks enough."

Filling the silence that followed, the captain addressed them with her news. "Now that Mr. Theodore shared his story and his precedent-setting achievement, I have the pleasure to announce that he will be reassigned to the Pentagon as Navy liaison to the secretary of defense. His new assignment is to develop a physical readiness program model for all services, specifically designed for military amputees who wish to remain on active duty."

"There go your Green Monster tickets," Taro teased.

"Don't worry, Taro. I have the captain's assurance that I'll be sitting on the Monster when they appear in this year's fall classic."

"Keep dreamin'."

"Ahem!" Crabtree huffed, reminding everyone who still had the floor.

"Sorry, ma'am," whispered Taro.

The captain resumed unabated. "Now, what I'm about to share with you is classified." Her preface removed any residual levity. "For reasons known only to the administration, the DOJ has dismissed the case against the Reston Caliphate. Within twenty-four hours of the charges being dropped, they disappeared."

"But what about the evidence, Captain?" asked Crabtree.

"We had an airtight case against them, didn't we?" added Jack.

"That's not for us to decide," Derrick cautioned. "In our line of work we are sometimes compromised by the fact that we don't know the grand scheme of those appointed over us, and we'll leave it at that."

"Understood, Captain," Crabtree replied on behalf of the team.

"You've all performed exemplary service to your country, and I couldn't be more proud. If there's nothing else?" The signal given, the team stood up to allow the captain to depart.

Crabtree looked at his team with the pride of a father. "Ladies and gentlemen, while the outcome wasn't what we'd hoped, allow me to echo the captain's sentiments. This team performed with a diligence, professionalism, and synergy unmatched by any team I've been associated with. I'm proud of you all." Crabtree turned to his second. "Commander Bannerman, we have a fallen team member and another scheduled to depart as we welcome the new senior chief. Please organize the appropriate hail and farewell event."

"Aye aye, sir."

As Crabtree departed, the team filed out of the room behind him—except for Terrie, who took her mug over for a refill. Jack stopped in the doorway and looked back at her. "You coming or what?"

"I'll be right there," she replied, staring down at her morning summary.

"See you in Ops." Jack disappeared down the hallway.

Terrie glanced over the first two lines of her summary.

1) Friday, August 2, 2013: An ammunition dump in Homs, Syria, explodes killing 40.
2) Saturday, August 3, 2013: Insurgent activity across Iraq kills 80.

She contemplated a possible connection between the two incidents as she closed the folder and headed to Ops. Signing in, she heard the banter between her team members already underway but with a greater sense of camaraderie in light of recent events.

Responding to Taro's question, Theo replied, "With this latest design, the wearer no longer has to change prosthetics for certain tasks."

"You can even swim with that?" Jack asked.

"Sure can."

Bannerman looked at Theo's prosthesis. "That's comfortable to wear every day?"

"At first it wasn't, but it's no big deal now."

Ignoring her teammates, Terrie assumed her station and got to work on her latest intel reports. The Ops Center was quiet for the next hour, until Jack whispered a question to Terrie. "What did you do during your medical leave?"

"I didn't have the chance to tell you," she answered. "My aunt secured Dagney's book, the one Philip and company weren't able to lay their hands on."

"Really?"

"Yup. I spent this past week reading it. The chapter on Tunney was very interesting."

"Well, are you going to share or not?"

"His listed accomplishments should've been legendary, but our ship's captain preferred to exist under the radar. Tunney operated closer to President Jefferson's privateer commission to enforce the 1807 Embargo. Under that commission, Tunney engaged any ships he considered the enemy. When the War of 1812 broke out, Madison issued a new privateer commission which restricted their targeting to just British ships. Tunney never accepted it, preferring to operate outside the government's control. From his earliest actions during the Barbary Wars, his engagements demonstrated a preference to obliterate his enemies rather than capture 'prizes.'

During the Second Sumatran Expedition of 1838, he mercilessly retaliated for what Sumatra did to Captain Charles Endicott and his vessel *Friendship* seven years earlier. When Tunney discovered a Moorish privateer off the coast of South Carolina suspected of sinking the USS *Grampus* in 1843, he dispatched it without clemency. The book also listed the Battle of San Gabriel in 1847 as Tunney's final victory at sea."

"Did he really die in 1850?"

"Allegedly," she replied, but that was all she was able to get out.

Theo had cut her off. "Terrie, look, it's him!"

"Who?"

Several media chyrons reported the following breaking news:

> A car bomb explosion kills 18 in Damascus, Syria, today. Defense department officials are investigating if there's a possible link to the series of car bombs reported in Baghdad earlier this morning that killed 25 people. Several high-value Islamic State operatives are suspected to be among the dead, including the reputed leader of the Muslim Illuminati, Kedar Ra'id al Husam al Din.

Jack uttered in Terrie's ear, "Karma's a bitch."

Terrie's expression never wavered as she pulled up her keyboard and got to work. "When his remains are positively identified at the Dover mortuary, I'll agree with that sentiment."

"He was the man who murdered your sister, wasn't he?"

"The video clip showing the bloodstained floor behind Ra'id as he killed the adherant was convincing, but it's not proof he butchered Margaret. I need proof, not supposition." Terrie almost allowed her anger to get the better of her.

"I know you'll find them, Terrie. Whoever and wherever they are," Jack said to calm her down. He watched her nod and smirk before they both got busy with their repective tasks. After a few minutes, he looked Terrie's way. She was staring, but not at her monitor. "Margaret's on your mind again, isn't she?"

Surprised, she turned her head to look at Jack and responded, "No."

"What then?"

"The government classification system. It's been around since the country's founding and for quite some time in its current form."

"What's your point?"

"The Neptune Project wasn't officially classified until Tunney was presumed dead in 1850. Remember the cover letters and memos we found in the classified section of the Newport Library?"

"Yeah, what about 'em?"

"One of Tunney's letters stated the *Trident* needed a crew of seven to keep her operating."

"Bottom line it for me. What are you driving at?"

"I don't believe in ghosts, Jack," she replied with a coolness that was unnerving. "No phantoms could be operating her all these years and if she's been seen as late as 2009, then who's piloting her?"

Jack got a chill down his spine.

SIXTY THREE

Sunday, November 8, 2009

The USS *New York* proceeded at one quarter speed on a heading that would take her out to sea and a week's worth of trials. The previous week, she came within sight of ground zero so she could fire her 21-gun salute to the memory of those taken from us on that horrific day just over eight years earlier.

"Engine room, this is the captain."

"Engine room, aye."

"Prepare to take the engines ahead full as soon as we clear the surface traffic."

"Aye aye, sir."

The *New York* took her time weaving through the smaller vessels that dotted the harbor between the Verrazano Bridge and the lower bay. The captain was just about to order full speed ahead when a voice rose above the din of bridge clatter.

"Captain?"

"What is it, Ensign?"

"Sir, white squall detected portside aft."

The captain used his binoculars to observe the phenomenon for himself. A disappointed smirk graced his face, reflecting the lack of concern he felt as he allowed the binoculars to drift back down to his chest.

"Doesn't look like there's any danger to the ship, Ensign. Carry on."

"Aye aye, sir."

The young ensign took one last look at the atmospheric phenomenon through his binoculars before he lowered them. Scanning the entire port side of the ship, the ensign reported, "All clear, sir."

"Very good," said the captain. "Engine room, this is the captain. Increase speed ahead full."

"Ahead full, aye, sir."

As the *New York* bounded out to sea at full speed, a shiny, crimson specter from some distant past appeared. The skin of its hull gleamed in the sunlight. Its dark maroon shape slowly materialized into an ancient tall ship with dual masts and jack staff.

She turned slightly to a 45-degree angle as a puff of white smoke emerged from her side. One of her 32-pounders sent up a traditional salute. Just as quickly, the masts and jack staff did something completely unexpected—they retracted toward the deck before the ship dissolved into the mist from whence it came…at astonishing speed.